A MOTHER'S PROMISE

RACHEL WESSON

Ebook ISBN: 978-1-80508-125-8
Paperback ISBN: 978-1-80508-126-5

Cover design: Debbie Clement
Cover images: Shutterstock, Arcangel

Published by Storm Publishing.
For further information, visit:
www.stormpublishing.co

ALSO BY RACHEL WESSON

The Resistance Sisters

Darkness Falls

Light Rises

Hearts at War (WWII)

When's Mummy Coming?

A Mother's Promise

WWII Irish Standalone

Stolen from Her Mother

Orphans of Hope House

Home for Unloved Orphans (Orphans of Hope House 1)

Baby on the Doorstep (Orphans of Hope House 2)

Women and War

Gracie Under Fire

Penny's Secret Mission

Molly's Flight

Hearts on the Rails

Orphan Train Escape

Orphan Train Trials

Orphan Train Christmas

Orphan Train Tragedy

Orphan Train Strike

Orphan Train Disaster

Trail of Hearts – Oregon Trail Series

Oregon Bound (Book 1)

Oregon Dreams (Book 2)

Oregon Destiny (Book 3)

Oregon Discovery (Book 4)

Oregon Disaster (Book 5)

12 Days of Christmas Coauthored Series

The Maid (Book 8)

Clover Springs Mail Order Brides

Katie (Book 1)

Mary (Book 2)

Sorcha (Book 3)

Emer (Book 4)

Laura (Book 5)

Ellen (Book 6)

Thanksgiving in Clover Springs (Book 7)

Christmas in Clover Springs (Book 8)

Erin (Book 9)

Eleanor (Book 10)

Cathy (Book 11)

Mrs. Grey (Book 12)

Clover Springs East

To all those everyday heroes whose actions save a life. Thank you.

ONE

JULY 1939

Trudi Beck shivered, despite the sunshine, as she walked past a long queue of Jews outside a travel agency, seeing the desperation written all over their faces. Although the Nazis encouraged emigration, the reality was that leaving Germany was becoming increasingly difficult. It required not only money but someone in the country you wished to emigrate to, to vouch for you. Money was something she didn't have. She'd spent every penny and more to get her fifteen-year-old stepson Heinz released from Dachau, and then onto the *Kindertransport* to Britain.

She clenched her hands and walked faster, determined not to think about the boys and her baby, Liesel. Every night she fell asleep dreaming of her baby girl. Would she even remember her?

She walked through the tree-lined district to the seven-bedroom property Ari had first taken her to, to meet his family, as a young bride. The visit was as clear in her mind as if it had happened yesterday. Chana, her husband's elder sister, had been cold and distant then—and ever since. She made it clear she thought Ari had lost his mind and that Trudi must have seduced him, forcing him to marry her. Ari had insisted he loved Trudi but his protestations fell on deaf ears. They had visited only on family occasions, for Heinz's and Tomas's sakes: birthdays and the special holidays.

She hadn't seen the Arkins since Rosh Hashanah in 1937. Trudi squeezed her eyes tight; she wasn't going to show any weakness. Not in front of the woman who hadn't even replied to Trudi's letter about Ari's death in Dachau.

What was she doing here? Trudi pushed those thoughts out of her head and rang the bell. To her surprise, a maid answered the door and asked her to wait in the hall while she announced her. She hadn't expected her sister-in-law to still have servants. Jews couldn't employ Aryan servants anymore, so Chana must have replaced her original staff. Somehow, too, the Arkins had kept their beautiful home when many had been forced to give them up.

Trudi's heels clicked on the parquet floor as she stepped into the property, standing to one side as per the maid's instructions. Trudi glanced around; everything looked the same as it had when she'd last visited. The mahogany table glistened, thanks to the beeswax rubbed into the grain. She looked up at the large mirror above it, which only served to highlight her shabby appearance in this luxurious setting. She pinched her cheeks in a bid not to look so pale against the backdrop of ruby-red silk wallpaper. Above the tick of the grandfather clock in the hallway, the faint sounds of a waltz filtered in from a gramophone playing in the living room.

Trudi took a step forward to glance inside the library. This had always been her favourite room, not just because of the Steinway. The bookshelves were stocked floor to ceiling with books on just about any subject you could think of. The covers were a mix of different colours and textures. The books weren't there for decoration; both Leopold and Chana were well read, as evidenced by the fact that the book spines were worn in places. She scanned several shelves but there were no gaps.

Either Leopold, Chana's husband, hadn't owned any banned books, or he'd had sufficient resources available to replace them. She suspected the latter.

She could picture Ari, standing by the books, his hand hovering, deciding which title to choose. Such happy memories of her husband should have given her comfort, but it was like a bittersweet taste on the tongue. Remembering him only cracked open the closed-off vault of pain in her heart.

Hearing murmured voices, she slipped back to her position at the front door and waited, glancing around again at the hallway. Hitler and his thugs didn't seem to have had any effect on the Arkins' lifestyle, although she'd heard Leopold had taken early retirement. She'd assumed he had been forced to do so, but maybe it was out of choice. There were enough valuable paintings on the hall walls to finance the rescue of several Jewish families. The fragrance of the fresh flowers in the vase on the table fought with the smell of beeswax polish. However, it wasn't sufficient to mask the tantalizing smell of roast chicken coming from the kitchen. Trudi's stomach growled. She hadn't eaten since lunchtime yesterday. It had been her own choice, though. She'd given her food to her neighbour to feed her little girls. It wasn't the children's fault their Jewish father was paid a pittance as a forced labourer in a weapons factory.

The maid returned, interrupting her thoughts, and asked Trudi to follow her to the living room. She didn't offer to take her coat, nor did she suggest she take a seat, but left her standing.

Trudi glanced around the gleaming room. There wasn't even a dust mote to be seen, although the sun shone through the large windows. Her sister-in-law always kept a well-maintained household and obviously the Nazis weren't allowed to interfere with that. Trudi edged closer to the white couch, tempted to sit down. She was tired.

Trudi straightened as Chana walked in. She looked the

same apart from dark circles under her eyes. Her face was made up, Trudi noticed: a little too much rouge on her cheeks, her hair blown dry in her Clara Bow hairstyle, and the green silk dress she wore swished as she walked. As usual Chana wore a size too small to look slimmer, though it had the opposite effect. No sign of any shortage of food here. Trudi told herself to stop being mean. Diamonds glistened in Chana's ears, at her wrist and on her fingers, and an enormous emerald sat at her neck.

'I don't believe it. The nerve of you, just turning up here. What do you want?'

Trudi swallowed, forcing down an angry retort. She was here for the children, not herself. 'I came because the children asked me to.'

Chana paled, taking a seat and then asking, 'The children? What's wrong? Heinz came to say goodbye, said you were insisting on sending them to Britain.'

Trudi bristled at the implication she'd sent the children away for any reason other than their safety. 'Heinz had to get out of Germany. He was a marked man after his time in Dachau.' She stopped herself from mentioning that he'd been arrested only for being a brave child who'd stopped a Nazi thug beating up a woman.

Chana sniffed. Did she blame Trudi for Heinz's incarceration too?

Trudi modified her tone. 'The children made it to Britain safely, Chana. They are living in a place called Abbeydale, Surrey. That's part of the reason I'm here. I thought you might like to write to them.' Trudi held out a note with the address, but when Chana didn't lift a hand to take it from her, she slapped it down on the table.

'You will address me as Frau Arkin.' Chana stood. 'Part of the reason? If you are expecting money, you won't get a penny from me. You may have cast a spell over my brother but I'm a better judge of character.'

Trudi breathed deeply to steady herself. This woman could sell one painting, or the heavy emerald gold necklace she wore, on the black market and it would raise sufficient funds for Trudi to flee Germany, to Sweden or Switzerland. But she wasn't here to beg.

'I don't want anything from you, Frau Arkin,' Trudi said, trying to keep her voice calm and level. 'The boys and Liesel are healthy and happy, and safe. But they asked me to look after you. You're their aunt.'

Chana's gaze razed her from head to toe. 'You? How can *you* look after *me*?'

Trudi ignored her rudeness, handing Chana a picture of Heinz and Tomas with their parents, Ari and his first wife. 'I thought you might like this. I found it when I was packing up some items in the apartment.' Trudi placed another envelope on the coffee table. 'These are pictures of Ari, his first wedding and, well, other family occasions.'

Chana turned her face away but not before Trudi spotted a tear falling. Whatever this woman did or said, she had loved Ari very much—and vice versa.

She moved closer, modifying her tone. 'Chana, whether you like it or not, we're family. I know your husband served his country and had a prominent position as a well-respected lawyer.' Chana didn't move. 'You seem to be protected, for the moment, at least. Your husband must have powerful friends.'

Chana was so still, for a moment Trudi had an insane thought she should check the woman was breathing. Maybe she was wrong to try to warn her. She should leave. But then her eyes caught Ari's in the picture of her husband that took pride of place on Chana's mantelpiece. Ari would want her to at least try.

'Chana, it's obvious the SA stormtroopers haven't called to strip your home bare. Not yet.'

Chana let out a tiny moan.

Trudi rushed on. 'Don't hide your head in the sand. You can't rely on the fact that Leopold won the Iron Cross for protection. I believe the Nazis will come for you both at some point.' Trudi watched the woman's face closely, seeing her eyes dart around the room, her hand moving to clutch the emerald at her neck. So she wasn't as ignorant of the Nazis as she pretended. 'I was hoping you would consider emigrating.'

Just as she finished speaking, Chana's husband marched into the room, his shoes making a thundering noise on the wooden floors. He hadn't aged badly in the years since she'd seen him, perhaps a little balder and greyer, his lips still pursed in their usual expression of disapproval. Had the man ever smiled? His glowering expression made her focus, however: he'd been listening—and had heard enough.

'Leave my country? How dare you come here making such suggestions! I am a proud German citizen and intend on living out my days in the city of my birth. My family moved here in the eighteenth century.' He threw his chest out, his back as straight as an *oberst* on a parade ground.

'Leopold...'—at the frown on his face, Trudi corrected herself quickly—'Herr Arkin, I know all about your service, your commitment to law and order. But the Nazis don't believe in rules. What happened to Ari and other good men like him is proof of that.' Her words stalled at his pinched expression, matched by the coldness in his eyes.

'What happened to Ari was unfortunate.' Leopold strode over to his wife's side, but didn't take a seat. 'He gave up the chance to leave when asked about his Iron Cross.'

'He wasn't going to leave his son behind with the thugs.' Trudi stopped herself. Arguing with this man wasn't going to achieve anything. 'Please reconsider your position.'

She might as well have suggested he grow wings and fly for his reaction.

'And you, Fräulein, are you going to run away?'

She gasped at the insult of his use of the title 'fräulein'. She might not have his education or privilege but she was a married woman, not an unmarried mother, as it suggested. 'I don't have the same resources you do.'

It was the wrong thing to say, and he gloated. 'So you did come here begging.' He turned to call out to the maid. 'Berta, please show our visitor out. She's leaving. Good day to you.' Leopold clicked his heels before marching back out of the room.

Despite the presence of the maid, Trudi wasn't finished. 'Please, Chana, make him change his mind. The children need their family.'

Chana paled, her gaze flickering to the picture of Leopold dressed in his full uniform with the Iron Cross prominently displayed. 'You heard my husband, please leave.' She glanced at the envelope on the table, her stance softening slightly. 'Thank you for the photographs. That was a kind thought. You didn't have to bring them.' Her voice faltered as she whispered, 'I miss Ari.'

Trudi took a step closer but it was a mistake.

Chana froze her to the spot with a look. Her tone when she spoke was that of a mistress addressing a servant. 'I appreciate your gesture. Here, take this.' She opened her purse and handed twenty-five marks to Trudi. 'Heinz said you had to buy his way out of Dachau.'

Trudi wished she had the nerve to tell this haughty woman exactly what Heinz's release had cost her, but she would only believe it justified her low opinion. Despite her urgent need for funds, her pride took over. 'I don't want your money. Goodbye, Chana.'

Wishing she had thrown the old wedding photographs on the fire, she walked out of the house, head high, and didn't even shudder when the door slammed behind her.

But nothing could stop the tears flowing down her face.

TWO

Trudi didn't notice anything about her journey back to her own home. Reaching the apartment, she pushed the door open, assailed as always by the pain of memories. The cuckoo clock with its cracked face, its hands forever stuck at twenty past one, a silent reminder of the visit from the SA to their home on *Kristallnacht*—the Night of Broken Glass—the night everything changed.

She closed the windows, wishing she could block out the sounds of the parties coming from the apartments across the street. Her new neighbours good German citizens rewarded for their loyalty to the party with recently vacated Jewish-owned apartments. In her mind, they didn't come close to the lovely men and women like Mr Geller who'd previously lived there. Her hand flew to her throat. Why did she have to think about the kindly old man now? A veteran of the last war, invalided in the fight for his country, yet that hadn't mattered when the SA came that night. They'd beaten him to death and laughed while they did it.

She blinked back tears. The silence of her home echoed around her, reminding her of everything she had lost. Not her possessions—she didn't care about them. Ari, the boys and her baby. She picked up Liesel's blanket, telling herself she could still smell the scent of her child. Holding it close, she couldn't help but compare her surroundings to those of Chana.

She stifled a sob thinking of her husband. Ari, devastated at the loss of his livelihood, his identity and his wife, had turned to her for comfort. She had loved him, for his kindness and gentle heart. Had he loved her? Or had she been just a replacement mother to his boys? If he'd really cared for her, wouldn't he have listened to her pleas to emigrate?

Picking at threads in the blanket, she moved to the window. Maybe the sunshine would lighten her mood, help allay the blackness threatening to take over her. A distant train whistled as if taunting her, reminding her they could have escaped. Together. As a family.

Instead, she was all alone in Berlin, and that was Ari's fault.

She'd wanted to leave when they got married but Ari worried about finding employment abroad. When the Nazis stopped him working as a doctor, he'd started studying English and secured a job at the Jewish hospital. Meanwhile, the walls had been stripped of paintings—some sold to keep the family in food, some to generate the funds needed to emigrate. Ari had sold off a lot of items through a gentile friend. She shuddered, thinking of Herr Berchtold.

Not that they had time to plan their escape: *Kristallnacht* had seen to that. What remaining valuables she couldn't hide had been taken by the stormtroopers who'd arrested Ari and Heinz that horrible night.

If it hadn't been for her friend Ada Bernstein and her strength over those following weeks, Trudi didn't know where she'd have ended up. Ada, the woman she'd once thought looked down on her, had proved to be a true friend and hadn't acted out of a sense of duty following Heinz's actions. In return for punching a stormtrooper who'd struck Frau Bernstein,

Heinz had been arrested. He and Ari had shared the same fate as Ada's husband and sons: arrest and imprisonment in Dachau.

Trudi swayed a little as she remembered. Both families had suffered terrible loss but at least Rachel—the girl Heinz adored —and Ruth, the youngest Bernstein, had travelled on the same train as Heinz, Tomas and Liesel, and were safe together in England.

Her sweet baby. With a moan, Trudi picked up the most recent photograph of her baby. Her finger traced the image of Liesel sitting on a blanket, a huge smile on her face as she stared up at her half-brother, Tomas. The children looked happy, and she was glad of that. *Does she even miss me?*

She sank down into a chair, trying to push all the horrible memories from her mind. Like Ada, she was a widow, a letter arriving shortly after Ari had been moved to Dachau informing her of her husband's death from a heart attack.

Heinz had confirmed later that was just another lie.

After the children left, Ada had kept fighting, consumed by the need to secure the release of her sons, Izsak and Gavriel, from Dachau. Trudi's friend, Olga Langen, had helped to raise the money for bribes, teaching Trudi how to sell clothes, blankets, pots and pans on the black market. It was quite amazing what people would buy.

Trudi smiled at the thought of her friends and the happiness they had found together, even at this time: Olga and Gavriel had fallen madly in love, with Gavriel electing to stay in Berlin helping Olga in the resistance. Izsak had fled to Palestine.

She dropped the blanket and forced herself to get up and tidy the apartment. But despite getting busy, washing the few dishes, and sweeping the floor, she couldn't stop the thoughts tripping through her head. Was it only nine months since *Kristallnacht*? In that time, she'd become a widow, a mother without a child and, thanks to the Nazis, much more. If anyone had told her parents that their daughter would become an expert in black-market dealing they'd have been horrified. When they'd died she'd been devastated—now she wondered if they'd been lucky not to live to see just how awful the Nazis were. Every week she heard of Jews committing suicide. Some saw it as desperation, others as the last form of resistance open to them. She'd be lying if she said she hadn't considered it, in her darkest moments.

But she couldn't give in to those feelings. She had made a promise to herself that she would survive this horror. She was a mother, and her children might not be in Germany but they still needed her. Didn't they?

THREE

AUGUST 1939

Heart hammering, Trudi's eyes snapped open, her body rigid with fear. It was only a dream. A nightmare. She wasn't back in that office with Herr Berchtold, but here in her apartment. She forced her breathing to quieten despite how the darkness of her bedroom seemed to close in on her.

It had been pointless going to bed so early in the evening, trying to catch up on sleep. She pushed the covers back from the bed, walking over to the window and moving the heavy blackout curtains, risking a look outside. The sun had only just dipped below the horizon, the Berlin sky transformed into an ever-changing canvas, the vibrant hues of orange and pink mixing with the deepening shade of purple casting a warm glow over the buildings around her. It looked so pretty, you would never know that evil was taking over her city, block by block, person by person.

She leaned her face against the cold glass, wishing there was someone she could talk to, to help ease her worries—not just for herself, but for her baby, Tomas and Heinz. If war broke out, as everyone believed it would, would they be safe? How would the people of England react to German children, even if they were on the run for their lives? Would they be treated with kindness or suspicion?

What was she doing? She had to get some rest or she would be sewing crooked seams tomorrow. She had to keep going, one foot in front of the other. She wasn't giving up. Not now, not ever. The war might not even happen. Her stomach rumbled, sending her to the kitchen in search of something to ease the hunger pangs. She opened a couple of cupboards, the bare shelves taunting her. All she had was a small can of beans, some wilted cabbage and a tiny onion. That was her dinner for tomorrow. She glanced at the remains of a small loaf of bread. No, that was breakfast. She couldn't work on an empty stomach: she had to be able to concentrate. She couldn't afford to lose her job.

She boiled some water, adding some mint leaves from the small window box. Maybe it would help her sleep, and the warm water might convince her stomach it was full. She sat in the kitchen listening to the noises of the late evening before her eyelids starting closing. Maybe now she would sleep. She rinsed her cup at the sink before heading back into her bedroom.

She got back into bed, plumping her pillow and praying she would sleep without traveling back in time in her dream. To the day she'd tried to save Ari, Heinz and the Bernstein men. She picked up the last letter Sally Matthews had sent her.

Dear Trudi,
Thank you for your letter and for allowing me to address you by name. It feels like we are now friends.
Liesel is growing every day, she is such a happy little girl. Always smiling. She cut her first tooth...

The papers fell to one side but Trudi let them fall. She knew every word by heart. She breathed slowly and steadily, waiting for her heart rate to go back to its normal, steady rhythm. Her eyes closed.

. . .

Trudi dressed carefully in a lavender hued dress; the fitted waist and flared, A-line skirt falling just below her knee was flattering while conservative. She smoothed on her last pair of stockings before putting on a pair of modest heels. She glanced at her reflection, pinching her cheeks a little to try to give them some colour. Swallowing hard, she tried to get rid of her dry mouth. Her stomach churned with tension. She added a small pillbox hat and her fur jacket to complete her look.

The bedroom door opened and Ada came in.

'How do I look?'

'Exquisite.' Ada's eyes ran over her, from the top of her head to her heels and back up, meeting Trudi's eyes via the mirror. 'Are you sure you know what you are doing?'

'Ari said if we ever got into trouble to go to his friend.'

'How well do you know this man?'

Trudi shrugged, trying to appear noncommittal. She had only met the man once, but it was enough. Shuddering, she remembered his lizard-like eyes that never seemed to reach her face.

Ada wrung her hands. 'Trudi, I don't think you should go. I've a bad feeling about this.'

Trudi whirled around to face the other woman. 'What choice do I have? You said yourself we don't have enough money to pay the bribes we need to release Ari, your husband or the boys. Leopold refused to help, and I don't know anyone else with money anymore.'

Ada gripped Trudi's hands in hers. 'If I could go in your place, I would. I owe your family so much already. Heinz wouldn't be there if...' Ada couldn't continue as the tears overwhelmed her.

Trudi gave her a quick hug, not wanting to crease her dress. She turned back to look at her reflection. 'Will you look after

Tomas and Liesel if I don't come...?' Trudi couldn't force the words past the lump in her throat. She glanced at Ada in the mirror and saw that she had paled. They both knew what was at stake. Nobody would help Ada find Trudi if she failed to come home. The police wouldn't investigate; they would stand back and look the other way, just as they had done on *Kristallnacht*.

Ada moved towards her. 'No, you can't do it. We'll find another way. We can ask Chana. She's Heinz's aunt. She'll help.'

Trudi shook her head sadly. 'We both know she won't go against her husband. Leopold still believes in the law.' She adjusted her hat on her head. 'Ari trusts this man, said he was one of his closest friends growing up. It will be fine.'

Trudi hoped she sounded more confident than she felt.

Trudi couldn't remember the walk to Herr Berchtold's office. Shivering despite not being cold, she walked up the steps to his office, her heart pounding in her chest as she ignored the red and black flags decorating the building. *Please let this be the right thing to do.* She tried to remember the stories Ari had told her of how his mother had always given him extra lunch for his friend, Martin Berchtold. During the depression years, some families would have starved if not for the generosity of their neighbours. Ari's mother had fed Martin as often as she could afford to.

She walked up to the desk. 'My name is Frau Trudi Beck. May I speak to Herr Berchtold please?'

'Have you an appointment?'

'No but I think he will see me.' Trudi crossed her fingers.

Ari hadn't said anything about his friend being a Nazi. She looked up, right into the eyes of the portrait of Hitler on the wall opposite. Was that there because it was the done thing, or was this man a...

The shrill ring of the phone made Trudi jump. The secretary said something before replacing the receiver. 'You can go in now.'

Trudi stood, resisting the urge to smooth her dress, glad she had worn gloves. She walked to the door of his office, hesitated a fraction of a second before knocking.

'Come.'

Gathering every ounce of acting ability she had, she forced herself to smile as she walked in.

Herr Berchtold didn't stand but remained seated behind a huge wooden desk. She hid a shudder as she took in the uniform he wore. Despite it being well tailored, hinting at his success and power, it didn't quite fit him. His belly protruded over the belt as if he had cinched it too tightly.

She walked over to his desk and held out her hand. He ignored her, a sly grin on his face.

'Take a seat, Frau Dr Beck.'

Despite the slight, that was a good sign, wasn't it? His calling her by her proper title, one not used by any Nazi since they'd come to power.

'Thank you for making time to see me, Herr Berchtold. My husband, that is Ari, told me come to you should I have need of...' Her voice trailed off at his expression of distaste. His cold eyes stared at her as if he had no memory of who Ari was. Even as the thought struck her, she realized it was ridiculous. He had called her by her proper name.

Tension filled the silence as he leaned back in his chair, a predatory look in his eyes.

'Excuse me, Herr Berchtold, but if I could be frank—? Ari told me to come to you if I needed help.' She glanced around, despite the office being empty save for the two of them, before lowering her voice. 'He told me he gave you various paintings, gold and some...'

The man slammed his fist on the desk, making her jump out

of her seat. 'What lies are you telling me, woman? You have a nerve coming into this office, throwing around these accusations. Your husband gave me nothing.'

Despite herself, her eyes moved to a painting—a favourite of Ari's—sitting in pride of place above this man's head. 'I'm desperate, Herr Berchtold. In addition to Ari, they took my stepson and some of his friends too. Heinz is only just fifteen years old. He tried to defend...'

'I've heard enough. Leave before I have you arrested too.'

Trudi couldn't leave: this was her last chance to help Heinz. She stood up, but instead of moving toward the door, moved closer to the desk. 'Please. I don't have any money to pay a... contribution to the cause.'

He pushed his chair back, stood and walked around to her side of the desk. She turned to face him. Leaning in toward her, his finger trailed down the side of her cheek. 'You know what you ask? It wouldn't be good for my career for me to be seen helping a Jew.'

She stayed silent, willing herself not to shrink from his touch. She saw the predatory smile give way to lust as he licked his lips. Despite herself, she took a step back but the desk blocked her escape. He moved in, closing the gap. A breath of wind wouldn't have been able to cut between them.

Trudi closed her eyes, expecting a caress—not the slap that came, so hard she fell across the desk behind her.

Still, he moved closer. 'You expect to come in here making advances to me?'

She whimpered, wanting to find an escape, but there wasn't any. She felt a gentle touch on her hair.

'Such beautiful golden hair, like a true Aryan. You must have been adopted at birth. Your Jewish swine parents stole you from a true German family.'

She closed her mind to his voice and his touch, focusing on the picture of her family, all of them happy together.

. . .

Afterward, he barely looked at her. 'Your husband and his son will be released, but if I ever set eyes on either of you again... you will regret it. Tidy yourself up and get out.'

Too shocked to do anything but stuff her stockings in her pocket and grab up her shoes and coat, Trudi would have run from him if she'd been able. Instead, she forced one foot in front of the other. Holding her head high, she opened the door of his office and strode past his secretary without a glance in her direction, before walking out of the office block's front door and down the steps. She'd have fallen but for her grip on the handrail.

She got to a side street before her composure faltered and she fell to her knees, her head in her hands. She didn't know how long she stayed there before she could summon the strength to gather herself together and return home.

Once inside, Trudi went straight to the bathroom, drawing a bath despite the frigid water.

A while later, Ada knocked on the bathroom door. 'Trudi, you've been back over an hour. The children are getting anxious. Can you let me in?'

Trudi pulled her battered body from the water, throwing a towel around herself before she opened the door.

Ada took one look at her face and pulled her into a hug. 'Oh, Trudi, this is what I feared. You poor, dear girl.'

Shivering, Trudi forced the words out. 'He said he'd do his best for the boys.'

Trudi woke with a cry, drenched in a sweat, the bedclothes tangled around her legs. She couldn't go back to sleep now.

Every time she closed her eyes, she was back in that c.
itchy feel of the wool from his uniform against her bare skii

He'd lied. Had he known? Ari was already dead by the tim.
he'd humiliated her.

But then, senses alert, she bolted upright in bed. Was it just
the nightmare that had woken her? She listened.

Someone was out there. She threw the covers back and
jumped out of bed. She wasn't going to be found lying in bed,
like a victim.

FOUR

In the corridor she heard it again: a light knocking on the front door of her apartment. She knew that signal. She pulled her dressing gown tightly around her before opening the door, admitting a man with a small bag.

Gavriel's disguise would have made it difficult for his own mother to recognize him. The old man's thick glasses he wore, almost square, magnified his eyes until they filled his face, framed by tufts of grey hair. His tall frame was stooped: he still hadn't fully recovered from the brutal beatings he'd endured at Dachau. No longer skeletal thanks to more food, the muscles that rippled beneath his thin skin were those of a much younger boy. His coat, thin and worn, patched in places, smelt of tobacco with a faint hint of soap. His limp, which he played up when walking in public to avoid questions about why he wasn't in uniform, was recovering slowly. Only time would tell if he would fully recover. If he lived long enough.

Despite what he'd been through, he retained his gentle touch as he greeted her with a hug.

'Gavriel, thank God. You look worn out. You are working too hard.'

'Not hard enough, Trudi. It helps to be exhausted when night comes, then the sleep...' He shrugged. He didn't have to finish the sentence: they all knew the nightmares the dark brought.

She looked into his eyes and shivered despite herself. What was wrong now? 'Gavriel, what is it? Your mother?'

He sank into a chair and put his head in his hands, not making a sound, though Trudi could see how distressed he was from the way his shoulders were shaking.

'What is it? Tell me please.' She leaned in closer, to listen to his story.

He held her hand as he told her of the horrors of the trip he and Olga had undertaken, escorting some Jews out of Berlin to some contacts in Aachen. From there they could cross to Switzerland. How close they had come to discovery. 'I told Mutti that Izsak was safe but I honestly do not know. The man who helped him...' His eyes filled with the pain of the memories, his face ashen as his mouth opened but he failed to find the words to continue.

She rose and got him a glass of water from the sink, giving them both a precious few seconds to regain their composure.

'There's a traitor in our ranks, Trudi. They got Herr Stein. By the time we discovered him, he could barely speak.'

Trudi wanted to block out his next words, to cover her ears with her hands. Herr Stein, the teacher who'd advocated for Heinz and the other children to learn English. He could have emigrated some years back but stayed to help the resistance efforts. He took advantage of his status as a protected Jew—his marriage to a gentile offering some buffer against the new regime. But Frau Stein had died some days after an encounter with the authorities in the form of a 'friendly' visit from the SS.

'They murdered his wife, Trudi, just as surely as if they had hanged her from a lamppost. They told Stein that one of our own had led them directly to him.' Gavriel's voice hitched on the last word as he raised his stricken face to look directly at Trudi. 'Could that be true?'

What could she say? Nobody knew how anyone would react in times like these.

His composure broke completely as he sobbed like a small child. She drew him closer, as she used to with Tomas when he was upset, patting his back, trying to soothe his troubles. But it was as useless as trying to stop a tidal wave with a bucket.

Finally, tears spent, Gavriel stood. 'I must go. I can't stay here. If what Stein says is true, and why would a dying man lie, I could compromise you.'

Trudi laughed, a harsh sound to her own ears. 'Being Jewish, I'm compromised already.'

He leaned in and kissed her cheek. 'You are a tower of strength, Trudi Beck. Look after Mutti, please. And... Olga. She won't listen to me.' He picked up his small bag and turned to leave.

'Gavriel, wait. Please. You need some sleep, a bath and some clean clothes. You know appearances are everything. Some of Ari's clothes are still in the closest. Or maybe you will find something in Heinz's wardrobe. Go have a bath and get some sleep. Please. I'd like some company in the house: the empty rooms...' She stopped speaking, knowing he'd find it harder to refuse if he thought she really needed his help.

Indecision played across his face; he was no doubt tempted by the thought of a proper bed with clean sheets. 'A bath would be good. I stink.'

She nodded. 'Yes, you do. Where did you sleep last night? In a ditch?' She walked to the press where she kept the spare towels. Taking one out, she handed it to him. 'Go on. Olga brought soap the last time she visited. It's on the shelf.'

'I will smell like a girl.'

'Better that than the alternative.' She threw the towel at him and they both laughed. It was nice to have these moments of normality in the crazy world they lived in.

Trudi busied herself making some soup. *Gruel* would be a better word for the thin watery concoction, she realized, but at least there were some beans and some vegetables in it. Her wages as a seamstress didn't stretch far. She cut the sawmill bread. The women who'd given the war loaves this nickname were right: there was more sawdust than flour in the dough.

A sudden knock at the front door made her jump again. She turned her heard toward the bathroom, but Gavriel mustn't have heard anything.

Heart beating fast, she moved to the door. This was silly, the Gestapo didn't knock and wait. They just broke in.

Opening the door, she was relieved to see Olga Langen. Her friend greeted her with a kiss and a bag of groceries.

'I thought I'd never get here. I thought I was being followed but it was some stupid man who wanted to take me to dinner. I swear I thought he was Gestapo.' Olga looked at Trudi. 'You were in bed? This early?'

Self-consciously, Trudi glanced down at her robe. 'I'm not sleeping well and thought I'd get an early night...' She wasn't going to admit to being so lonely and hungry that sleep seemed like a good escape. She changed the subject, smiling at her friend. 'I wasn't expecting you back so soon after your trip. You look good.'

Olga was the picture of the perfect German maiden. With her blonde hair braided and worn on the top of her head, she was tall and slim and attracted several offers of dinner a week. Her azure-blue eyes were framed by the most beautiful eyelashes. Her skin was so soft and pale, the thought of anything or, more specifically, Gestapo torture, marring the surface made Trudi's flesh crawl.

She hugged her closer, letting the scent of Olga's light, clean, fresh perfume wash over her.

'Olga, you shouldn't be taking such risks coming here at this time of the evening. The curfew...'

Olga waved off her protests. 'Some hostess you are—you haven't even offered me a cup of water, never mind a coffee.'

Trudi smiled. It was pointless telling her friend to take care. They'd met when Tomas had kicked a ball too far in the park, hitting Olga in the face. Trudi could still see the fear on Tomas's face as the German lady came over to them.

Trudi had never prayed so hard, terrified she would call the police, but instead Olga had smiled, returned the ball and given the children some chocolate. Olga didn't care they were Jewish. She'd become a firm friend since.

Olga had been with the German resistance since Hitler had first come to power. A committed social democrat and catholic, she was determined to undermine the Nazi regime by any means possible.

'Come in and sit down.' Trudi led the way into the small kitchen, gesturing at the table. Olga took off her coat before taking a seat. 'You will never guess who is here.'

Olga screamed with pleasure before Trudi could shush her. 'Gavriel? But where?'

'He's having a bath. Believe me, he needed it. He's been in there so long, you better check he hasn't drowned.'

Olga kissed Trudi on the cheek before turning in the direction of the bathroom.

FIVE

Trudi went into her own bedroom and dressed quickly, before returning to the kitchen to unpack the grocery bag.

Olga returned, her face wreathed in a big smile despite her dress being soaked. 'He's woken up a bit now. He's getting dressed and coming out for dinner.'

Trudi wanted to ask her if Gavriel had told her about Herr Stein, but she didn't want to ruin the younger girl's happiness either.

'Thank you for all of this,' Trudi said, beginning to separate the groceries into piles to give to Ada and other friends. So many families had lost their young folk to emigration—the rich were the only ones who could take their entire family—leaving older people, the sick and the poor to survive as best they could.

Olga put her hand into her bra and withdrew what looked like fifty or sixty marks. She put it on the table.

Trudi shook her head. 'Olga, that's too much.'

'Just last weekend you were telling me about more of your neighbours losing their jobs and being sent to do forced labour.' Olga pushed the money towards her. 'I know you've been feeding your neighbours' children, buying medical supplies and whatever else you can find. It's a small token.'

Trudi took the money gratefully. There were so many in need, barely existing on the pitiful wages they earned doing slave labour in the munition factories. She was lucky: her employer at the dress shop hadn't sacked her. Herr Schneider was a card-carrying party member and committed Nazi, but his profit margins meant more to him.

Trudi was good for business. She was luckier than Ada, Gavriel's mother, not having to deal with the noise or dirt from the machinery used in munition factories, nor the constant abuse from the factory overseers. Herr and Frau Schneider, despite being Nazi party members, didn't care for politics as much as they did for lining their pockets, and her work rate was much cheaper than employing an Aryan of similar skill level.

'Oliver Twist would have turned his nose up at the soup I was making.' Trudi scraped the potatoes clean before chopping them into small chunks and adding them to the beans and cabbage. She cut some meat into very thin strips and began frying it in a small pan, with the onions. 'Now I can prepare a proper meal for all of us.' She added the meat and onions to the pot.

Olga opened a bottle of wine she took from the bag. 'It's not a good vintage but who cares.' She took some glasses down from the shelf and poured. 'I can't believe he's here. I was so worried. I heard some rumours.'

Trudi busied herself cutting a small amount of cheese into tiny cubes.

'You know?' Olga asked.

Trudi nodded. 'Gavriel told me about Samuel Stein. Do you know who the traitor is?'

Olga's pretty face twisted in rage. 'No, but I wish I did. I would skin them alive. Myself. Of all the people to get caught, poor Sam. He was a good man.'

'Heinz was annoyed when Herr Stein told him to learn English,' Trudi said, shaking her head at the memory.

Olga held her gaze. 'Have you heard from him? Has he written?'

Trudi shook her head slightly. Despite everything, Heinz was still angry. At her for stealing his father's affections and replacing his dead mother, at the Nazis, and at the world.

'Sally Matthews, the English lady looking after Liesel and Tomas, wrote again. She sent a picture. Here, have a look.' Trudi took the photo out of her pocket and handed it to her friend.

'Hasn't she grown bigger? And look at Tomas, he seems so proud of her.'

'She doesn't say much about Heinz, but he isn't living with them. Maybe she didn't have room for him in her house? Poor Tomas must be distraught. He adores Heinz, you know...'

Trudi picked up a knife, chopping the vegetables roughly. What trouble had Heinz got into now? He wasn't a child, but maybe that made it more difficult for him.

Olga put a hand on her arm. 'Have a drink and let's give a toast to Sam and to English ladies who look after our children.'

They exchanged a sad smile before Olga handed her a glass and they both toasted the man they'd admired.

'What a lucky man I am with such a feast and two beautiful women to share it with me.' Gavriel walked into the kitchen, looking better for his bath.

Trudi's breath caught as she recognized Heinz's good suit, the last one Ari had bought him. It was swimming on Gavriel, much too large for his skeletal frame.

She steadied herself and focused on thinking practically, saying to Gavriel, 'After dinner, I will take in the trousers for you. You can't wear them like that. But first, let's eat or this will go cold.' She gestured to them both to take a seat before she served the meal.

They ate in silence, with Gavriel having second helpings.

After he was finished, Trudi dished up a small bowl of sliced apple with a hint of cream. 'Imagine it's the strudel your mama used to make.'

This made them both laugh, as Ada's strudel was legendary —though the days of making the rich, butter-heavy dish were long gone.

Gavriel almost licked the bowl clean. 'How is Mutti?'

Trudi couldn't resist. She mimicked Ada's voice. 'Gavriel, the young pup, still refuses to leave.' Gavriel and Olga burst out laughing, so Trudi stood up and continued in Ada's voice, using some of her friend's mannerisms. 'He thinks he's a cat with nine lives. I swear he won't listen to me or to that nice young friend of yours, Olga. For a gentile, she is a good girl. Not that I'm giving permission for a match. My boys must settle down with young Jewish ladies from good families.'

Trudi continued: 'That Olga, she's another one who believes she's immortal. The risks our young people take, it's enough to turn our hair grey. If it weren't that already.' Trudi ran a hand through her hair but then stopped play-acting. It wasn't fair to make fun of her friend, even if she was joking. And Ada's hair wasn't grey. It was white.

Her tone more serious, she said, 'Your mama is being very brave. She worries about you constantly and prays you will follow Izsak to Palestine.' Trudi moved the empty dishes to the sink. She didn't have any tea or coffee to offer them. She leant against the counter and added, 'Your mother has a point, Gavriel. It is becoming much too dangerous for you to stay in Berlin. You know those who were released from Dachau or other concentration camps are marked men.'

'I can't leave Mama behind.' Gavriel's stubborn expression reminded Trudi of Tomas when they used to try to get him to eat his greens.

'You can and you should. I'll keep an eye on Ada and she on me. You have a much better chance as a young man alone without worrying about your mother.' She held her hand up as he opened his mouth. 'You can't say anything to persuade me otherwise. Or your mother, if she were here. She wants you to live. That's all she wants. You owe it to her to at least try.'

Olga stood up and went behind Gavriel, wrapping her arms around his shoulders. 'I want you to go too. This is the best chance we have had in a long time. Please, Gav.'

Gavriel turned to look at her. 'Will you come?'

Olga released him. 'You know I can't leave. Not yet.'

'Then I won't go.'

Trudi glanced at her friends. She knew they needed time alone. 'Well, I'm off to bed. I'll leave you two to talk. Olga, you are welcome to stay too. I have to be up early. Herr Schneider has enough work for ten people to do tomorrow, let alone three seamstresses.'

Olga gave her a hug. 'He's lucky to have someone with your dressmaking skills working there.'

'Ha! Tell him that. He thinks I'm the lucky one because he hasn't fired me. Not that I'm allowed to see the clients. God forbid a dirty Jew like me sullies an Aryan woman.' Too late, Trudi realized what she'd said. It was an awful reminder that Gavriel could be murdered for flirting with Olga, never mind being in a relationship with her. 'Oh my goodness, what a silly woman I am. I need to go to bed.'

The next morning, there was no sign that Olga and Gavriel were up yet.

Rather than risk waking them, Trudi slipped out of the house, taking an apple with her to eat on the way.

The sun was shining and people were smiling at one

another. Life went on, even though horrific things were going on behind closed doors. The people of Berlin didn't care. So long as they were safe, they turned a blind eye to neighbours going missing.

SIX

LATE AUGUST 1939

Two weeks later, heart hammering as loudly as the frantic knocking on her door, Trudi opened it to find Olga on her doorstep, in floods of tears.

'Olga, come inside! What is it? What's wrong?'

'They have Gavriel. He's at the hospital. He was hit by a truck last night but the doctor recognized him and admitted him to the Jewish hospital.'

Chills ran down her spine at Olga's tone. 'He's dead?'

'No. Not yet, at least.' Olga's voice broke. She put a hand up to her mouth.

Trudi rushed to take her in her arms. She held her friend until her tears were spent. 'I'll make you a hot drink.' Trudi moved to the hob to boil the water, making the *ersatz* coffee, taking her time to allow Olga to recover her composure.

'Someone tipped off the Gestapo—they arrived at the hospital. They've moved him to the locked ward. They want him to get better so they can torture him to reveal information, and then he can die.'

Trudi handed Olga the coffee but the girl's hands were

shaking too much to hold it, and she set it on the table in front of her.

Taking Olga's hands in hers, Trudi said, 'He needs to disappear. We'll have to fake his death. Your contacts can get both of you out of Berlin, can't they?' Trudi didn't know any of Olga's contacts, but they seemed to be able to do things other people couldn't.

Olga shook her head. 'I can't go. Too many people depend on me. It's getting worse and...' She broke down again.

'You've done enough. You're living on borrowed time, you know that. The Nazis aren't stupid, they know you are involved in something. Your family hasn't exactly hidden their beliefs.' Olga's father, a newspaper owner, had been one of the first victims of the regime, arrested back in 1934 for speaking out against Hitler and his treatment of the Jews, as well as the laws he'd broken. He'd been arrested and died of a heart attack in prison. That was the official version. 'You and Gavriel need to get out of Germany. You can help from the outside.'

Olga didn't look convinced but at least she didn't argue.

'I can take over some of your work.'

Olga shook her head. 'You have a baby and the boys to consider. If the Gestapo caught you...' The rest of that sentence didn't need verbalizing. They both knew the stories of torture, and worse, victims could expect from them.

Trudi stood up, pacing back and forth across the small kitchen, wringing her hands. 'My family is safe. Gavriel helped protect Heinz. I won't turn my back on him, not now. I've a friend—he's not Jewish, but a doctor who worked with Ari. He might help. It can't be anyone from the hospital—that's too risky.'

Olga listened but couldn't smother her yawn. Trudi took the empty cups over to the sink. 'Go to bed. Sleep here. Go on, it's too late for you to go home. In the morning, on my way to work, I'll try to visit the doctor.'

. . .

Trudi woke early, dressing quietly so as not to disturb Olga, and left the apartment. Taking the tram, she headed for Dr Rust's home hoping to catch him before he started his clinic.

'Frau Dr Beck, how lovely to see you. You're out early. Please come in.'

Trudi smiled as the young man with wavy chestnut brown hair, hazel eyes and a clean-shaven face opened the door and gestured her inside. The fact he'd addressed her using Ari's real title reassured her. But then she remembered the last time she'd thought that. It had gone badly then. A chill ran down her spine as her hands shook. No, this was different, for one the man in front of her didn't wear the hated uniform, and there were no black and red flags hanging from every window. The obligatory portrait of the Führer aside, the office looked just like Ari's had done.

She followed him through the reception area into his office.

'How are things with you? Would you like a drink? I have a few minutes before my clinic starts.' Dr Rust ran his hand through his hair, his surprise vying with curiosity at her presence evident from the expression in his eyes. 'Please have a seat.'

She took a seat in a chair in front of the desk while he walked behind it and took his chair. She was thankful the reception room was empty. It wouldn't do for anyone to overhear this conversation.

'Dr Rust, forgive me for taking advantage of your friendship with my husband. I need your help.'

Dr Rust kept silent but at least he didn't look away.

She ploughed ahead. 'I have a friend—he tried to save Ari, and definitely saved Heinz when they were imprisoned in Dachau.'

'This friend was in Dachau?' Dr Rust's friendly expression was replaced by a closed, hesitant one.

'Yes, he was totally innocent of any crime, apart from the fact he's Jewish.'

'I see. Is he still an inmate?'

At Trudi's look, the doctor flushed. They both knew people rarely survived imprisonment in Dachau.

'My friend and his brother were released in June.' Trudi didn't go into the details of how Olga and her friends had secured their release. She sure wasn't going to explain her part in Heinz's rescue. Nobody needed to know.

She kept to the story she had made up on her way over there. That Gavriel had been too ill to leave Berlin, with his brother. 'He was unable to emigrate to Palestine due to ill health but he recovered and he... he remained in Berlin.'

'A foolish choice.'

Trudi bit her lip. It was pointless explaining Gavriel's sense of duty to his community, his mother.

'The other day, he was hit by a truck on the street. He's not badly hurt—a broken arm, some bruises and a mild concussion. They sent him to the Jewish hospital.' She decided not to mention the Gestapo's interest in Gavriel. 'We need to get him out of Germany. I was hoping you might help us rescue him.'

Dr Rust glanced at the wall clock and stood up, putting distance between them. 'What you're suggesting is illegal. I can't imagine why you came here.'

'You're a doctor, you save lives. Ari liked you, trusted you.' Trudi stood up too and moved closer. 'Please help us. I thought if you gave him something, to make him appear dead or maybe diseased—you know what they are like about diseases. Then we would tell them he died and...'

He refused to meet her gaze, looking everywhere but at her. He crossed his arms, his voice taking on a belligerent tone.

'Why can't the doctors at the hospital help you? They're Jewish, after all.'

'If they could help, I wouldn't be here. They don't have any real drugs at the hospital, they barely have aspirin. It's a hospital in name only.'

He shook his head but she sensed that wasn't news to him. Trudi kept her gaze locked on his until he finally looked at her. He was the first to look away, his face flushing with embarrassment. 'I'm sorry but I can't help. You should go now.'

'Why? Ari told me how he helped you to pass your medical exams. He never asked you for anything.'

The man shook his head as he pointed his finger at her. 'I tried to help your husband. I told him over and over that he should emigrate. To the USA or Britain, but he was a stubborn J—'

Trudi put her hand to her mouth in horror. '*Jew?* So that's why you won't help. You're just the same as they are.'

She picked up her bag to go but he quickly moved in front of her to block her way.

'Please understand. I have a family, a reputation. I won't tell anyone you asked. I won't report you.'

'That's kind of you.' Trudi turned on her heel marched to the door. Just as she opened it, she turned back. 'I hope your children are proud of you.'

He turned scarlet at her words but they seemed to hit the mark. He took a step closer, his voice dropping to a whisper. 'Frau Beck, Trudi—wait, please.' He took the key to his medical cabinet out of his pocket, opened it, selected a packet of something and handed it to her. 'This will give him diarrhoea and nasty stomach cramps, plus a fever. It will be enough to fool anyone who isn't a doctor. The second dose will make it look like he died: his pulse will fall dramatically as his heart rate slows. Leave at least two hours between the two doses. Do not give him a third. Be careful with the measurement. It may buy him some time for you to... to...' He put the powder on the desk as if by leaving it there, he offloaded all responsibility.

She saw his hands were shaking. Catching her looking at them, he shoved his hands in his trouser pockets. 'I'm not a brave man, Frau Beck.'

'Thank you.' She took the packet and put it in her pocket.

Before she closed the door behind her, she heard him call: 'Please don't come back here.'

Trudi rushed home and peeked in to find Olga still asleep. The poor woman was exhausted. Trudi watched her sleep for a few seconds, noting the darkened circles around her eyes. Then she called her name softly.

'Olga, it's time to get up. I'll make you breakfast.'

Thanks to Olga's generosity, they had an omelette made from fresh eggs and some herbs Trudi grew in her window box. She also made some mint tea, preferring it to the acorn-based coffee substitute.

Olga looked across the table at her friend, yawning. 'Sorry I slept so late.'

'You needed to rest. I went to see my... contact.' Whatever illusions she'd entertained, Dr Rust was clearly no friend. Trudi pulled out the packet he had given her and placed it on the table in front of Olga. 'He said this would make Gavriel very sick, that the doctors would know what it was. I don't know what's in it.' Trudi glanced at the medicine in her hand. Could she trust the doctor? What if she was the one to kill Gavriel?

Olga seemed to sense her distress as she closed her hand over Trudi's. 'I'll give it to Doctor Young, he'll know if we should use it. Thank you, Trudi.' Olga stood up and kissed her on the cheek, before picking up her handbag and coat. 'I'll go there now.'

Trudi knew she had to convince this brave woman it was

time to leave. They were taking too many chances. There was Herr Stein's death a few days previously and now Gavriel's accident...

'Olga, get out of Germany and take Gavriel with you. Tell him I'll look after his mother.' She put one hand on Olga's shoulder, using the other to push the girl's chin up so she could look her in the eye. 'You have to leave. Before it's too late. I don't have any other contacts I can use. Next time... there can't be a next time.'

Olga lowered her eyes, her body folding in on itself as she accepted defeat. 'Trudi, there are so many who need help. Children, old people, thousands...'

'You can't help them all. You've done your part. Now go and live your life. Gavriel and you, married with children, that's the best revenge you can take on the Nazis. For your father, Herr Stein and me.'

'Will you tell Ada he's in the hospital?'

Trudi shook her head. She'd thought about it, but it would do Ada no good to know Gavriel was in trouble. Let her believe her son was free. Hopefully, he would be soon.

'I'll tell her he left and couldn't come to say goodbye. She'll understand.'

Olga put her arms around Trudi. 'I hope we meet again someday. I'll never forget you. I'll ask some friends to keep sending you some packages.'

Trudi allowed herself a quick hug before pushing her friend away. 'Go. You must get to Gavriel before the Gestapo come back for him. Live long and be happy. Tell him... give him...'

'I will.'

Trudi grabbed her coat and left for work. She couldn't bear to wait for Olga to gather her things together. It just prolonged the agony of parting. What would she do without this wonderful young woman? It wasn't just the food parcels and the money she gave her, but her company. She was a light in the world of darkness Trudi now inhabited.

Two weeks passed with no word. Trudi went to work and returned home as normal, trying to convince herself no news was good news. When war was declared, she almost gave in to the urge to end it all. Liesel, Tomas and Heinz were now living in a country at war with Germany. Would they be vilified for being the enemy? Would the woman, Sally Matthews, give them back to the authorities or would she look after them, protect them. Keep them safe? How would she know if they were alive or dead when all communication had been stopped? There would be no more letters or photographs now.

As she lay in bed that night she clenched her teeth, trying to keep her emotions from bubbling over. A hard knot expanded in her stomach as she held in the scream of frustration and pain.

Hitler would invade Britain and arrest all those who opposed him. Chills ran down her spine, her heart giving her palpitations. The Nazis would capture her children. She closed her eyes, letting images of Liesel with her golden hair flow through her mind. She could see Tomas, playing with Brown Bear, the bear Ari had given him that he'd taken on the *Kindertransport*. He'd clutch the bear whenever he was scared. Would he do that when the bombers came? And Heinz, he was older. He wouldn't show fear, at least not outwardly, but he would be scared too. Any adult who didn't tremor with fear when they heard the air sirens, spotted the planes making their way across the sky, wondering was today the day the bombs would come whistling down on top of them. She shook her head and asked herself, *what are you doing? You can't give up hope now. You're letting them win.*

· · ·

Trudi woke the next morning to find a postcard pushed through her letter box.

Hands shaking, she turned the card over.

'The mountain air is great for our health. The perfect place for our honeymoon. Wish you were here. Love O.'

She let the tears stream down her face. Olga and Gavriel were in France. They'd got out. The medicine Dr Rust had given her must have worked. If only she'd been able to convince Ari to escape too. She'd still have her family, her baby. Instead, she was all alone, apart from Ada.

Ada? What would she think? She grabbed her bag and headed out the door, this time to go and visit Gavriel's mother to tell her the good news.

SEVEN
APRIL 1940

Trudi shifted in her seat, trying to ease the kink in her back caused from being hunched over her machine, her hands expertly guiding silky material through the needle's rhythmic dance.

The Nazis crowed about victory, how they were going to grind their enemies into the ground. Was it unpatriotic of her to wish, to pray, Germany lost the war? She loved her country, or at least she had until Hitler got in. How many would die before the war ended? There were plenty of invalids from the last war, those missing a leg, an arm, half their face. War was ugly but if the Allies won, wouldn't life go back to normal for the Jews? She'd get her children home. Wouldn't she?

She pushed all thoughts aside: she had to concentrate on the task at hand. She couldn't afford to lose this job even with the regular small gifts/packages of food someone left on her doorstep. Being unemployed was bad enough, being unemployed and Jewish was a disaster.

Despite being exhausted and hungry, Trudi took pride in her work, preferring to concentrate on the beauty of the dress she was creating rather than thinking of the woman who'd wear it. Only those in favour with the Nazis got to go to places befitting this gorgeous creation. A sliver of sunlight streamed through the small window behind her, illuminating the delicate stitches she so carefully crafted.

Once again, she sent up a prayer of thanks to her grandmother who'd insisted she learn how to sew and had encouraged her talent for dressmaking. She worked from the basement, but it was well lit and kept extremely clean; more because her employers were worried about fire risks than her health or those of her colleagues.

Her employers kept her out of sight. The customers might love her work, but they wouldn't wear clothes stitched by a Jew. Herr Schneider was a creep, but his wife kept him in line. At least most of the time. His eyes undressed her every chance he got, but he was the same with all the female staff. Standing too close, putting his hands on her shoulders, his fingers accidentally brushing her chest, but he was too scared of his wife to do much else. In other times, she'd quit and get a new job but for now she just had to grin and bear it. Frau Schneider was the jealous type and did her best to keep her husband as far from the models and seamstresses as possible.

The Schneiders' store's basement was a hive of activity, with other seamstresses absorbed in their own work. Trudi loved working with the daintier fabrics, the silks and satins. Both were notoriously slippery to work with, with silk prone to fraying, while satin could pucker or snag. Not that Frau Schneider ever blamed the fabrics or the machines if something went wrong—it was always the fault of the seamstress.

Helga swore softly under her breath as her sewing machine jammed. 'Not again,' she whispered, glancing around furtively to see if anyone had noticed.

Trudi glanced up and, seeing the blood drain from the woman's face, she carefully finished the seam she was working on—she couldn't afford to stop mid seam—and moved the delicate garment to one side to go to Helga's workstation.

But before Trudi could move, Frau Schneider appeared, her brow furrowed with displeasure. 'Helga, what is wrong now? Frau Brown is due in for a fitting in two hours. That dress should have been finished by now.'

'Sorry, Frau Schneider, I'm doing my best but the machine, it...' Helga's voice fell away as the frown on Frau Schneider's face deepened. Then the boss screamed, 'Is that blood? You're bleeding, all over the dress. Get up. NOW!'

Helga jumped to her feet but almost instantly slumped to the side. Trudi moved fast, grabbing the woman before she fell over. She helped Helga to her own seat. 'Put your head down, that's it. Between your knees.'

As she spoke, Trudi expertly examined Helga's hand. She'd caught the needle in her finger; she didn't normally make such silly mistakes.

The other seamstresses crowded around but nobody offered to help.

'Hand me some of that cotton—that one.' Trudi pointed at a scrap of leftover white cotton.

All eyes moved to Frau Schneider, who shouted, 'Give her what she needs! You want that blood all over my dresses?'

Serena, who at fifteen was the youngest staff member, a runner and treated as a general dogsbody, handed it to Trudi. 'Need any help? Mutti was a nurse, she showed...'

'Stop gossiping. I need this dress finished. Frau Brown won't wait.' Frau Schneider fanned herself with a paper pattern. 'Oh, my... what does Herr Schneider expect from me? I have imbeciles working for me...'

Trudi ignored the onslaught of abuse, gave Serena a grateful glance, and spoke softly to Helga. 'How do you feel? Better? Want some water?'

Helga nodded.

'Serena, can you get Helga a glass of water, please.'

Serena scurried off and returned in a few seconds with a glass of tepid water. 'It's not cold, sorry. I didn't want to go upstairs—he's there.'

Trudi met the younger girl's eyes. They both knew who she meant. Herr Schneider wouldn't let any opportunity go by without putting his hand on a worker if she was alone. Sometimes he touched them even when his wife was in the same room but her attention was focused on something else.

'Sip it carefully. You were lucky. What were you thinking? You could have sewn right through your finger.'

Helga whispered, her eyes shining with unshed tears. 'Got a letter this morning. From the hospital. My baby daughter... she died. Pneumonia. They said.'

It was the most Trudi had ever heard Helga say. She gripped the woman's arm in a gesture of sympathy before standing up. 'Frau Schneider, I can finish the dress for Frau Brown. Helga needs a few minutes.' The poor woman needed medical attention, but that would never happen.

Frau Schneider's lip curled. 'But the blood?'

Trudi picked up the garment. There was a tiny speck on the seam. 'I can hide it, don't worry.'

'She will be here in two hours. You can't finish it that fast. Helga is my best worker.'

Trudi kept her face straight: that was the first time the boss had acknowledged Helga's skills. Frau Schneider didn't praise anyone. But Trudi didn't argue, there was no point, however much she wanted to shout at the woman that accidents happened when overworked, exhausted women worked in basements.

'Let me try. We are wasting time.' Trudi looked at the floor, unsure how her last remark would be taken but she hadn't given up completely. She may have to live in a regime that benefited, even encouraged, bullies of every type, but that didn't mean she had to comply. Not all the time.

Frau Schneider huffed loudly. 'If you don't finish it in time, you will both get docked a day's pay.'

None of the other seamstresses protested this injustice. They didn't care what Frau Schneider did so long as it wasn't aimed at them. Only Serena glared at the boss but quickly looked away when Frau Schneider glanced her way.

Trudi hid a smile. The young girl had more backbone than all the other women in the room put together. But that wouldn't help her or Helga.

'Serena, could you help Helga to the bathroom to get cleaned up? Then her machine needle needs to be replaced and re-threaded. I'll work on my own machine: I know it best.'

Frau Schneider stepped forward as if to countermand Trudi's instructions, so she quickly continued: 'Otherwise there is a risk blood will mess up other fabrics.'

Frau jumped back as if she could catch something. 'Go, go—you heard the woman. Get cleaned up and then back to work. Serena, this place is a disgrace. Tidy up those sewing patterns and tape measures and for goodness' sake sweep up this floor. All those fabric fragments are a fire waiting to happen.'

'Yes, Frau Schneider.' Serena's tone was servile but the light in her eyes was anything but.

Frau Schneider folded her arms over her matronly figure and glared at Trudi, who ignored her, refusing to let the woman get under her skin. Running her hands gently over the delicate fabric, she expertly fed it under the needle as she finished the piece. Helga was an excellent seamstress; it was easy to replicate her efforts.

Trudi worked quickly but carefully, not wanting any more accidents. Frau Schneider grew bored realizing Trudi wasn't paying her the slightest attention. She turned on her heel and flounced off.

Trudi worked steadily, ignoring the call for lunch until the dress was finished, or as much as could be completed prior to the final fitting. She turned her machine off and leaned back in her chair, exhausted but exhilarated.

Frau Schneider returned. 'It's nice you have time to rest. If only we all had that luxury.'

Trudi ignored her. She pointed to the dress. 'It's ready. Would you like me to carry it upstairs?'

'You?' Frau Schneider's eyes bulged. 'You can't be seen upstairs. What would our clients say? Marta, you take it up to Fräulein Sewell. She is attending to Frau Brown today.'

Trudi bit her lip to stop her protest. How could anyone know she was Jewish, unless Frau Schneider insisted she produce her identity papers with its ugly 'J' and her new middle name of 'Sara'? It was not worth arguing her case, despite how much she wanted to see if the dress looked as good on as it felt under her fingers.

Marta moved to take the gown.

'Change your gloves. There have been far too many accidents with this dress already. My heart can't take anymore.' Frau Schneider watched Marta like a hawk until she had left the work room, then she turned back to Trudi. 'You may take ten minutes to eat a sandwich, then finish your own work. That dress must be completed before you leave this evening. Countess Von Pabst will be in first thing tomorrow morning. I won't tolerate any more mishaps.'

Trudi kept her gaze on the floor, not wanting her boss to see she recognized the client's name. She could picture the blonde, beautiful woman who'd been one of Ari's patients. Did the woman know her doctor was dead? Did she care?

The bell for finishing time went but Trudi remained at her machine, her fingers moving expertly over the fabric. Thankfully, she had finished the more intricate parts and was now on the home stretch. She could sew a seam in her sleep if she had to.

Helga didn't leave when the others did. She tidied up her station and waited for Trudi to finish. Only then did she speak to her. 'Thank you, Frau Beck. You didn't have to get involved in my troubles.'

'Helga, please call me Trudi, and you would have done the same for me.'

Helga hesitated before whispering, 'I'm not sure I would have. I never thought you... I mean, someone like you... would be so kind.'

'What do you mean "someone like me"?' Trudi whispered through her clenched teeth.

'A Jew. I never knew one before and the newspapers...' Helga's words died at the look Trudi gave her. 'I'm sorry, I'm making this worse. My head isn't thinking straight. I just wanted to say thank you, and I'm sorry I haven't been very friendly toward you.'

Trudi stamped down her urge to argue that Jews and gentiles were all just people, some good, some bad and most a mixture of the two. This woman was hurting, and it had nothing to do with her injury.

'I'm very sorry about your daughter. I didn't know she was ill.'

Helga glanced around, even though they were alone, before whispering, 'Annika wasn't. She was healthy but was born with a twisted leg, two years ago. She couldn't walk but she was a happy baby, you know?' Helga glanced at her.

Trudi nodded but stayed silent, sensing there was more.

'The officers, they arrived one day and said she had to go to a home for cripples. They wouldn't let her stay with me. Annika screamed and screamed but nobody would listen to either of us. I thought Herr Schneider might be able to help. He has lots of friends, Nazi friends. He said he would if I... I was nice to him. He said they were looking after Annika, giving her the best of care. But then I got this letter.'

Confused, Trudi said, 'But you said it was pneumonia.'

Anguish filled Helga's eyes, her voice trembling as she responded. 'There is a lot of pneumonia around Berlin, Frau Beck—especially if the child has a disability.'

The air escaped Trudi's lungs as if she had been punched; she stared at the other woman in disbelief. She could feel the weight of Helga's grief and couldn't help but think of her own baby. Thank God she was safe in England.

She'd heard the rumours about Hitler and his henchmen killing off disabled children and adults, but she thought that's what they were, just rumours. Surely this woman couldn't think that the regime had murdered her child? Yet this same regime locked up and murdered innocent men like Ari just because they were Jewish...

'Annika was my everything. Her father... he left when she was born so it was just the two of us.' Helga gathered her things to her chest before turning back to Trudi. 'Thank you again for your kindness. I wish I had been kinder to you. I'm not a brave woman, I would never have stood up to Frau Schneider like you did. I'm grateful and I'm sorry.'

The next morning, Helga's machine stood idle. A few days later, Frau Schneider announced that Helga wouldn't return to work at the Schneiders' store, her body having turned up on the banks of the River Spree.

EIGHT

JUNE 1940

Trudi dragged her tired body home, her feet feeling like leaden weights with each step. The news from Dunkirk was disastrous —the British army had been forced to retreat in a desperate attempt to save their lives. But even worse was the grim realization that soon Hitler's stormtroopers would be marching into Paris, crushing the city beneath an iron jackboot. Despair and fear clawed at Trudi's heart.

The linden trees' sweet blossoms offered no comfort to her troubled mind. Once again she wondered if she had made a mistake in sending the children away. What if the Nazis continued their advance and invaded England? Their safety would be compromised.

Her steps slowed, and she glanced around before she took a seat on a bench. Ignoring the 'Forbidden to Jews' sign, she took the boss's discarded copy of the *Völkischer Beobachter* from her purse. Her eyes scanned the news. Everyone knew its content was controlled by Goebbels, but surely some of it was true.

Nothing she read made her feel better.

She should go home. But then her knuckles whitened with

rage as she clutched the paper between her fingers, trembling in despair. She didn't have a home, not anymore. The Nazis had forced her out of the apartment where her beloved child was born, demanding she leave within a half-hour. They'd refused to let her take anything of value, not even basic kitchen items. Desperately, she'd crammed Sally's letters into her bag along with some treasured family pictures and a few sets of clothing. It was all they would allow her to keep.

'Consider yourself lucky. You can still live in Berlin,' the Nazi officer had sneered as he handed her the address of her new home: a tiny apartment in a Jewish house on Potsdamer Strass, a thirty-minute walk away.

'You look troubled, Fräulein. You should feel joyous.' A uniformed man suddenly loomed over Trudi, his eyes widening as she struggled to react. 'France has been defeated and England is sure to follow. Victory will be ours.'

A million possibilities attacked her thoughts as she sat there rooted to the seat, unable to respond, feeling the soldier's gaze penetrating ever deeper into her mind. His frown deepened as he waited for a response that never came.

She thought of Liesel. She'd never see her again. Her eyes filled with tears, and one rolled down her cheek.

The man looked flustered as he fished a handkerchief from his pocket. 'Please don't cry. I can't bear to see a beautiful woman upset.'

She didn't want to touch his hand, but she couldn't refuse the hanky. 'Thank you. I'm sorry. My brother was injured, and I don't know if he will live. Mama said I should be happy to let him die for the Fatherland but... forgive me, I'm being silly.'

'Not at all. Your mama is right, but women have a soft heart. I'm sure he will be fine. We have the best doctors.' He gestured toward the seat. 'May I?'

Trudi wanted to say no, but he didn't wait for a reply.

'I love it here, don't you?' He stared toward the Victory Column. 'The play of the sun on the light yellow flowers contrasts with the green leaves. Nature is so beautiful.'

'You sound like an artist, not a soldier.' Trudi could have bitten her own tongue.

He smiled. 'A lover, not a fighter, you mean?' When she flushed, he hastily continued. 'I apologize. That was uncouth of me. I miss my wife and our children.'

Trudi glanced at her wrist, forgetting the Nazi officer had stolen her watch. 'I'm sorry, but I must get home to Mutti. She doesn't like to be alone for long.' She rose unsteadily to her feet, her muscles trembling in dread.

The man stood and clicked his heels. 'Have a lovely evening and I hope you get good news about your brother.'

Trudi nodded before walking away. Only when she had put some distance between them did she drop his handkerchief in a bin.

Trudi had just reached her apartment building when she froze, not wanting to believe her eyes. An older boy, about twelve or thirteen, loomed over a small, frail child, fist clenched around a raised stick.

Trudi ran towards them, shouting, 'Stop that! Go pick on someone your own size.'

'He's no better than a rat,' the bully responded, as he hit the boy.

'Stop it or—'

The bully turned on her, his gaze sizing her up. 'Or what, lady? You can't do anything to me and you know it.' The boy, his hands tightening on the stick he had used on the child, moved closer. His breath stank but it was the cold, callous expression in his eyes which rendered her unable to move.

'What's going on here?' A policeman was coming down the road towards them, his frown telling Trudi he wasn't impressed.

'I want this boy arrested.' Trudi pointed to the bully with her rolled-up newspaper before she bent to the silent victim crouching on the ground, his eyes wide with terror. 'Let me check your nose. Is it broken?'

'He's only a Jew!' the bully taunted.

Trudi watched the policeman's frown disappear. He said something to the bully, who ran off down the street.

Trudi watched, aghast, and wanted to protest but she felt the fight go out of her. She knew it was pointless.

'As you're female, I understand your concern for a child, but the boy is right. That'—the policeman pointed at the injured child who shrank back into the pavement –'has no place in Berlin.'

Shaking, Trudi tried to stand up, and the policeman held out his hand for her to grip, causing her to release the newspaper. He grabbed it before it could blow down the street. 'Our Führer showed them, didn't he? I wish I could have been there and seen the faces when he marched through Paris. Buckingham Palace will be next.' The sound of whistles blaring from the next street interrupted them. 'Sounds like real trouble! *Heil Hitler!*' The man saluted her before turning on his heel and racing down the street.

Trudi kneeled down on the dirty, gravelly ground and gathered the child to her, his body freezing at her touch. Despite the warm sunny day, the boy's skin was like ice—cold, clammy and tense under her arms. She could feel the sharp edges of his ribcage against her soft forearm.

'Don't worry, I'm not going to hurt you. We need to get you to the hospital. Where is your mother? Where do you live?'

The boy struggled to get his words out, his lips and chin bruised and covered with blood. He pointed a shaking finger to the same apartment building Trudi lived in. Before she could ask anything else, they both heard a scream and a woman came running toward them, dropping a shopping bag.

'Aron... Aron, what happened? Dear God, why are you outside? What did you do to my child?' The woman glared at Trudi through her tears, as she grabbed the boy from her.

'Nothing. I'm sorry I didn't stop the boy from hitting him in time.'

The boy released his hold on his mother. 'Mutti, the lady saved me. The policeman... he...'

The mother paled, swaying on her feet. 'The police—?'

'—have left. Please don't worry.' Trudi picked up the woman's shopping bag. There was very little in it but she knew from experience that the rations available to the Jews, low as they were, were pointless given most of the food available in the shops had disappeared by the time they were allowed to enter. The war had caused shortages—not that the Schneiders and other wealthy Germans appeared to be going hungry.

'I left Aron with his little brother. I had to go out to get food, but I told him not to leave the apartment. It was too dangerous. I told you, didn't I?' the hysterical woman screamed.

Trudi took her arm. 'My name is Trudi Beck. My husband was a doctor, he was murdered at Dachau. We should get your son checked at the hospital. Do you want me to take him or stay with your baby?'

'You're Jewish?' The woman's disbelief was clear from her tone.

Trudi nodded. 'Why don't we go into the apartment?' Trudi didn't want to risk standing outside on the street. The policeman could return and, given his horrible comments, she didn't think he would be pleased to have mistaken her for being a gentile. 'If you don't want to take Aron to the hospital, at least we can bath his face and see what the damage is.'

The woman nodded, picking Aron up and carrying him inside. Trudi followed with the woman's shopping, but not before she put the newspaper in the bin. Her children *were* safer in Britain. Hitler hadn't got there yet, and hopefully he never would.

She followed the woman up the stairs and through the open door to an apartment similar to the one Trudi now occupied, but judging by two closed doors leading off the kitchen-come-sitting room, this one had two bedrooms. Despite the damp, dated décor with peeling wallpaper, it was obvious the woman had attempted to turn it into a home for her family. The kitchen table was covered with a yellowing lace tablecloth, a glass with some street flowers in its centre. Black mould covered the high, impossible-to-reach corners of the room, and no amount of cleaning would remove the years of traffic marks on the wooden floor, but the rest of the place was spotless. A wedding photograph and another one of two children took pride of place on the windowsill.

A little boy, about three years old, was fast asleep on the sofa, a small tatty blanket covering him. The kitchen table was set for four people.

'Your husband?'

'He's working.' The woman boiled up some water and poured it into a bowl, before testing the heat on her bare elbow. She got a flannel and gently cleaned Aron's face. He didn't make a sound, but his tears flowed freely. 'Your nose is not broken, just bruised. It will be sore, but you will live.' The mother kissed her son's head before drawing him into a hug, her fear-stricken eyes meeting Trudi's. 'What sort of world do we live in when the police watch while a child is beaten?'

Trudi stayed silent, wondering what she could do to help the little family, as the mother's tears mixed with those of her son. Maybe she could bring up one of the window boxes of the two she had managed to save from her old home? That way at least the mother would have some fresh herbs to flavour the water they were probably drinking to stave off the worst of the hunger pangs.

'I never introduced myself. I'm Frau Weiss. My other son's name is Peter. Would you like a cup of something, Frau Beck?' the woman asked.

'Trudi, please. No, but a glass of water would be nice, thank you.'

The woman filled a glass and indicated to Trudi to take a seat.

'My husband, he is a mechanic. He works in one of their factories making guns.' The woman shrugged. 'He has no choice but to help the war effort. He is a good man, he worked in a bank before... But his hours are long. Do you have children?'

'Yes, but they don't live here. I sent them on the *Kinder-transport*.'

The mother nodded. 'You are a brave woman. I couldn't give up my children to strangers. We are a family. You know?'

Though it hadn't been an accusation, the woman's words still hurt. Trudi stood up, finished the water and placed the empty glass in the sink. 'I should go home now. But if you need someone to watch your children and I'm not at work, I'd be happy to help. They're beautiful.'

Aron gave her a small smile as he went to sit beside his little brother.

Frau Weiss walked her to the door. 'Thank you for your help today. I can't bear to think what would have happened if you hadn't come home when you did.'

Trudi shuddered seeing the bully all over again, the cold-ness in his eyes. She could imagine how far he'd have gone. But it was pointless saying anything: Aron's mother was frightened enough.

She wearily took the stairs down to her apartment, shutting

the door softly behind her. Then she let the tears fall. What sort of world indeed? Trudi pushed through her bedroom door and climbed into her bed, cuddling an old blanket belonging to Liesel.

She missed her with all her heart, but thank God she wasn't living here in Germany.

NINE

Rachel Bernstein hummed along to the Christmas carols as the nurses sang 'Silent Night'. Some volunteers from the local villages around the Chertsey hospital had brought in small Christmas trees and had arranged to distribute gifts to every patient, many of whom had not only been injured in the London bombings but also lost their homes and belongings.

She glanced at Belle, her friend and colleague, singing along even though she was completely out of tune. The patients didn't care. They were grateful to be alive and out of London, where the Blitz was still raging out of control.

'Wish someone would sing to the Jerries, don't you, Sister?' Bert, an old man with hands like an octopus and a manner to match, addressed all the nurses as 'Sister', regardless of whether they were a matron or a volunteer like Rachel. She smiled, hoping he wasn't off on one of his rants. The man was known to be difficult, but he'd fought in the Great War and lost a son to this one. He had a broken leg and a nasty cut just over his eye— he was lucky not to have lost his sight. He grew belligerent. 'Cat got your tongue, girl?'

Rachel was about to answer, even though every time she

spoke, he accused her of being a Jerry spy, when Belle stepped
in. 'Bert, 'ave you nothing better to do tonight than to give the
nurses an 'ard time?'

Rachel relaxed as Belle fussed around the old man, tidying
his pillows regardless of his protests he was fine. Belle winked at
Rachel before she turned back to Bert. 'Did you get your bed
bath today?'

'Go on with you, Sister. I got a bath last Saturday. Don't
need another. Not from the likes of you. Why aren't you
nursing down the docks in London? That's where you're from. I
know that accent.' Bert's voice grew posher the longer he spoke.

'That's right, ducks. I'm from the East End and us girls are
taught to look after ourselves. So you keep your mouth shut and
your 'ands to yourself or you'll have me to deal with. You
listenin'?'

Rachel put her hand over her mouth to smother her giggles
at Bert's indignant look and scurried off in the direction of some
of the sicker patients. She didn't run for fear of incurring the
wrath of a senior nurse but walked quickly and quietly from
bed to bed, refilling water bottles and removing rubbish. The
paper used to gift-wrap the presents would be reused.

She glanced at the young man in the bed by the door. He
looked like he was asleep; his face didn't bear a mark of the
injuries that had landed him in hospital His body was almost
fully covered in bandages thanks to injuries received from
falling debris. Another of Hitler's victims. He was a similar age
to her: not old enough to wear a uniform, he'd been on fire
watch duty when the bombers came. He stayed by his post and
this was his reward.

He raised a bandaged hand slightly. She moved closer to his
head, bending down and trying to work out what he was saying.

'Water. Nice song.'

She helped him drink, holding the cup close to his lips. He
lay back exhausted after only a couple of sips. The morphine

made him drowsy but thirsty. She knew he was lonely too, wanting to chat with the nurses. Even though they were busy, all of them tried to give him a few minutes. He didn't have any family nearby to come visit.

'Can you sit, Nurse, please?' His large blue eyes begged her to say yes. 'Do you have time?'

She glanced around to check where Sister Godbold was. She objected to nursing aides sitting with patients but thankfully just now she was occupied at the far end of the ward. Rachel sat at the edge of the seat.

'Why aren't you singing?' he asked.

'I don't know all the words.'

His eyes widened as he picked up her accent. 'Where are you from?'

'I'm a German Jew. I came here in 1939 and haven't learned the Christmas songs yet. Which one is your favourite?'

'"Away in a Manger". The matron in the home used to teach it to us kids. She was nice.' His voice was hoarse, probably from a combination of inhaling dust and debris from the collapse.

'Shush, don't try and speak too much. You'll tire yourself out and you need to rest.'

A tear rolled out of one eye, down his cheek. He tried to brush it away, but his bandaged hands couldn't get near his face. 'I'm useless, aren't I? Lying here like a big lump. Not able to do anything for myself.'

'Chris Dolan, stop that. You were a hero. If not for you, those children you saved wouldn't have Christmas to look forward to.' She lowered her voice. 'You are so brave. The doctors are wonderful, and they will do everything they can to get you up and walking out of here as soon as possible.'

He rolled his eyes in disbelief.

'They can, but you must believe it too. Don't give up.'

'Can I take you dancing when I do get out?'

She laughed at his cheeky request but rather than tell him he was too young for her, she decided to flirt a little. It might lift his spirits. 'Maybe. We'll see.'

'That's a nice way of saying no. Do you have a fella?'

She didn't understand that word. 'A fella?'

'A young man? A boyfriend?'

Rachel flushed. She stood. 'I'd best get back to work.'

'So that's a yes. Is he away fighting?'

She closed her eyes momentarily, seeing Harry as she had seen him last: being taken at gunpoint from Sally's house by the Home Guard.

'He's overseas.' She couldn't tell him Harry, who had changed his name from Heinz, was in an internment camp on the Isle of Man. 'I have to go or I'll be in trouble. I'll come back to check on you in a while.'

'He's lucky.'

At his tone, her heart melted. She quickly looked around to check there were no nurses nearby before leaning in and giving him a kiss on the forehead. 'Any girl would be thrilled to have you as her young man.'

Looking up, she caught Sister Godbold staring at her. She lifted his water bottle and moved off in the direction of the sluice room. There was always work to do in there.

Later that evening, Rachel watched as the nurses distributed presents to the men on the ward.

Matron beckoned her forward, her eyes twinkling. 'I think young Chris may prefer if you were to give him this.' She handed Rachel a small, wrapped package.

'Thank you, Matron.'

'Well, go on, give it to him.'

Rachel walked over to Chris's bedside. He was awake, his face etched with pain.

'Happy Christmas.'

His eyes widened. 'Is it for me?'

'Yes, silly. Want me to unwrap it for you?'

Chris blinked away the tears as he choked the words out. 'Thank you.'

She unwrapped the parcel to reveal a lovely, knitted scarf in the softest of wool. 'This will keep you warm when we are able to get you outside into the fresh air.'

'It's lovely, thank you.' Tears spilled down his cheeks. 'It's the nicest thing I ever got.'

Rachel swallowed the lump in her throat. Belle had told her about the children's homes in the East End, how the staff did their best but often the little ones didn't have much. She wondered what had happened to Chris's family to have him end up in one of those homes. Her thoughts went to her parents. She knew her dad was gone now but where was her mother? Was she still safe?

TEN

Trudi walked with Ada Bernstein to the local store to do their food shopping. Would there be anything left on the shelves? It was after four and rumours flew about food being in short supply for everyone, not just the Jews.

Trudi did her best to hide her anxiety, although her chest felt like there was a weight pressing against it, her breathing ragged and shallow. The sounds of the city were muffled, as if coming from a distance, and drowned out by the pounding of her heart. Despite the busy street, it felt like they were being singled out, watched in case they put a foot wrong. As it turned out, it was a wasted trip as the store had nothing left. The shelves had been stripped as bare as a wheat field after a locust attack.

They turned back the way they had come.

Ada's voice trembled with emotion as another Berliner gave them a sneering look. 'I feel like a cow wearing a brand.'

Trudi glanced at the *Judenstern*, or Jewish star, on her friend's coat. The yellow star, outlined in black with the word *Jude* embroidered in the centre, had been introduced in September at a cost of 10 pfennigs each. If any Jew was

caught not wearing the star, they were arrested. It wasn't sufficient to just wear it, the star had to be securely fastened in a
place of prominence and couldn't be covered with a shopping
bag.

'It's to keep track of us, Ada. Makes us easy to spot in the
street so they can see we are obeying their rules.' Trudi glanced
at a tram making its way towards them. She glanced around
before dropping her voice to a whisper. 'Some people don't
wear them. They depend on not looking "Jewish" and risk it.'

Ada shook her head, staring around her as if wondering who
might have heard Trudi. 'You must be careful. We can't afford
to stand out. You heard the elders: they said if we kept our
heads down and out of trouble, we'll be fine.'

'You don't believe that do you?' Disbelief made Trudi's
voice louder. How could anyone believe such nonsense when
they'd just learned that over 10,000 Berlin Jews had been
deported? The constant feeling of dread, that something awful
was going to happen, and soon, was wearing her down and
making her irritable.

Ada gestured at her to shut up as people turned to stare, due
to her shouting. They walked in silence down a few streets
before Ada said quietly, 'Yes, and you should too. Why didn't
you take the job they offered you?'

Trudi stared at the older woman. Was she really that naïve?
The Reich Association of Jews in Germany had been set up by
the Nazis and rumour had it that it worked closely with the
Gestapo. She didn't want to be near those hoodlums.

Would it be better not to know what was ahead of them, to
live in a pretend world where everything would work out fine?
Where she would get to live with her children once more. A
world where Gavriel, Izsak and the girls could return to live
with Ada. No, she couldn't believe in such a make-believe place,
could she? Not after what had happened to Ari, Herr Stein...
her treatment at the hands of Herr Berchtold.

She deliberately shut off those memories. Nothing would be served by going over them.

'I won't work for the Nazis. How can you even ask me that? After what they did to your boys? They separated us from our children—Rachel, Ruth, my little Liesel, the boys... They murdered my husband.'

Ada took her hand and gave it a squeeze. 'Working with the Jewish organization would have benefits. If, as you say, they will be working with the Nazis, then they will have some power.' Ada continued to look around her, as if expecting to be lynched any second.

'What type of power?' Trudi couldn't help but ask. Was there something she had missed?

Ada gave her a look as if to say *don't be stupid*. 'The Nazis will have to have names for their lists. How did they know who to deport in that transport? The Jewish council must have provided them, don't you think?'

Trudi stopped walking, turning to stare at her friend in amazement. 'So you don't believe those deported were criminals, and the rest of us are going to be left to live in Berlin?'

Ada held her gaze for a few seconds before dropping her eyes to the ground. 'I don't know what to believe anymore. Himmler won't allow anyone to emigrate now. Why does he want to keep us here? Not all of us are young enough to work, not on the reduced rations they give us. But what's the alternative, Trudi? What are they planning? Where are they taking those people?'

Trudi took her friend's arm. She could feel the older woman shaking with fear. That was the worst of it, not knowing what was ahead of them. Things had been worsening for the last eight years. Yet most sensed the worst had yet to come. There were rumours of mass starvations and executions in Poland and other places.

'They aren't going to murder Germans. The others were

enemies of our country.' Ada nodded as she grasped at straws. Trudi didn't make any attempt to correct her.

Those recently deported hadn't been foreigners but German born and bred Jews.

'I must call at the Jewish hospital.' Trudi tried to change the subject. 'I told them I'd volunteer this afternoon. Are you coming?'

Ada shook her head. 'Tomorrow maybe. I can't face all those people today. Maybe they have the right idea.'

'The patients?'

'The ones who successfully kill themselves. People like Heinz and Tomas's grandparents. At least they get to die in their own homes at their own hand. That is a choice the Nazis haven't taken from us. You said yourself the rate of suicides is rocketing.'

'It is, but that's not the answer, Ada Bernstein.' Trudi's eyes flashed fire as she looked at her friend. 'You have two girls who need you to live and be their mother. Your boys will need you too. To find them wives and look after their babies. Don't you dare think of anything else, you hear me?'

Ada didn't appear to be listening. Trudi took her friend's shoulders in her hands and shook them. 'Listen to me! I promised Rachel and Ruth to look out for you. You made the same promise to Heinz and Tomas. We're going to live and see our children when all this is over. Do you understand?'

'Stop it, you're hurting me.'

Trudi loosened her grasp but didn't let go entirely. To her surprise the normally non-demonstrative Ada pulled Trudi into a hug. 'I won't do anything stupid, but you have to say the same. Sometimes you frighten me, Trudi. You are too brave.' Ada gave her one last look before turning off down her street toward her home.

As Trudi walked to her own home, she didn't feel brave. She wore the star, worked long hours at her job—although she was thankful she didn't work in a munitions factory like Ada. The stories she'd heard of the brutal conditions made her wonder if the people who turned up every day were the brave ones. She wished she could bury her despair and live in hope that a miracle would happen and save herself and Ada from the fate of their husbands and thousands of others.

She was so caught up in her thoughts, she didn't see the person she bumped into until it was too late. She jumped back, apologizing profusely. A mistake like that was enough to get her arrested, or worse.

The woman put a hand on her arm. 'It was my fault, I wasn't looking where I was going. I'm so sorry. I didn't hurt you, did I?' She grabbed Trudi's hand, slipping something into her pocket as she did so. 'I hope you will forgive us,' she whispered, 'for everything.'

Then she walked away without giving Trudi a chance to recover her wits. When she'd stopped shaking enough to check her pocket, she found an apple and a small bar of chocolate. She couldn't remember the last time she'd tasted chocolate. Her eyes filled with tears as she stared down the street, but the stranger had disappeared, swallowed up by the hordes of ordinary Berliners going about their business.

Maybe miracles did happen after all.

ELEVEN

NOVEMBER 1941

Shivering, her breath making a cloud of vapour, Trudi pulled her thin coat tighter around her body as she made her way home from work, trying to pretend she was wearing her old fur coat. Only her imagination wasn't that good. The bitter wind sliced through her, flecks of snow landed on her eyelashes, her cheeks stung.

It had been a more trying day than usual with Frau Schneider berating her for not completing a dress. It wasn't her fault the woman had taken the customer's measurements incorrectly. She'd thought her boss would make her stay late but thankfully the woman had an invitation to a party and had locked up the store on time.

It was Wednesday, a day when she usually went to her neighbour's home for tea. Frau Krause occupied the apartment on the ground floor of a building on her route home. The Krause family had been Ari's patients in the late 1920s, when he was still a recognized doctor. Ari's usual clients were rich, but he ran a clinic to help working-class families when inflation meant doctor services were outside their reach. Frau Krause remembered that—one of the very few who did. Every

Wednesday for the past six months, she'd been standing at her door waiting to greet Trudi and usher her inside. There she had a hot meal waiting for her, the only time Trudi ever felt full. She'd grown used to seeing a friendly face. But she wondered if she would be there today: the last two weeks, Frau Krause hadn't been waiting for her. Had she moved? Herr Krause was in the army now. Maybe his wife had moved in with her daughter.

Labourers and office workers filed through the streets beside Trudi, their faces covered in scarves, some wearing gloves, others digging their hands deep in their pockets, as they trudged through the wintry weather. She saw more than one person wearing the Jewish star but nobody acknowledged one another, for fear it would draw attention from the Aryans around them. People shuffled along, not engaging anyone in eye contact, frightened of attracting trouble.

A gust of wind sent the pages of a newspaper swirling around her feet but she didn't make any attempt to pick it up. Everyone knew they couldn't trust what was written in the press these days. The *mundfunk*, as the Jewish rumour mill was called, was full of stories of defeat in Russia. The Russians were winning, the German army suffering from a combination of brutal weather combined with larger numbers of Russians. A glimmer of sympathy flitted into her mind for the German men on the Eastern Front—not all of them were Nazis. Many were simply the right age—those between eighteen and forty-five—for conscription, and you couldn't say no to serving. Not if you wanted to live.

Her stomach rumbled so loudly, she looked around in embarrassment in case someone heard. Being Jewish, she was only allowed to shop between certain hours, and Frau Schneider had refused to let her finish early. The half-rations she was allowed wouldn't keep a child alive, never mind a full-grown adult.

She brushed a tear from her eye. It was pointless thinking of how difficult life was. It could be worse. She was still alive, wasn't she?

As she turned the corner, she couldn't help hoping Frau Krause would be waiting outside her apartment. To her joy and amazement, she saw her there, bundled up in a wool coat, scarf wrapped around her ears.

'Frau Dr Beck, I was hoping I hadn't missed you. You're frozen. Come inside and warm up. I have soup on the stove. Come on.' The woman took Trudi's arm and lead her into the apartment building, and into her small home.

'*Danke.*' Trudi took off her coat, shaking off the worst of the snow before she entered the apartment. The heat made her fingers and toes sting but she didn't care.

Frau Krause indicated the table and dished out chicken soup with potatoes and other vegetables.

Trudi sniffed appreciatively, the smell making her stomach grumble loudly once more. 'Excuse me,' she apologized.

Frau Krause waved off her apologies. 'I'm sorry I haven't seen you for the last two weeks. My husband, he came back from the Front. On leave.' The woman's hands shook. Trudi glanced at them, causing her neighbour to clasp them together, her cheeks flushing slightly.

'Frau Krause, did you tell your husband about my coming here? He wasn't happy, was he? I should go.' She went to stand up. 'I'm so grateful for what you have already done for me. I must leave if my being here causes you trouble...'

Trudi hadn't met Herr Krause but his wife had always said he only joined the army because he had to and that he didn't believe in the Nazi doctrines. But maybe she'd been mistaken, or lying?

Frau Krause's eyes filled up and she reached across the table for Trudi's hand. 'No, sit down please. It is not you. It is us. I can't believe we, the German people, have come to this. How can we stand back and let your people be treated in such a shameful way?'

'We are Germans too.' Trudi immediately regretted the reprimand as her host's face flushed.

'I'm sorry,' Frau Krause said. 'Yes, of course, but you know what I mean. Dr Beck, he saved my daughter's life. She wouldn't be living in Hamburg now with her family if it wasn't for his skill. He never took a penny, either. He knew we had no money. Herr Krause was out of work at the time but your husband, he... oh, how ashamed I am.'

Concerned her distress was worsening, Trudi pushed the soup bowl aside and clasped the woman's hand in hers. 'You have been so brave. So helpful. And I know you have fed me with your own rations. But it isn't just that. You have spoken to me like a real person, not treated me like vermin. I will always remember that.' Trudi hesitated. 'Herr Krause, he found out I was coming here?'

Frau Krause nodded. It seemed to take forever for her to lift her eyes to meet Trudi's. 'He said he'd report me to the Gestapo if you kept coming here. I tried to reason with him, but... he's changed. Since they sent him to Russia, he isn't the man I married. We never had much but he was always affectionate, gentle and kind. Now there is a shell. He may look like my husband but my Wilbur is dead. After the things he saw, the things they made him do...' Frau Krause pulled her hands away from her face. 'He had nightmares you see, and he said some things. I asked him what they meant. I wish I hadn't.' The woman moaned and buried her head in her hands. 'I didn't want to know. Now I have nightmares too.'

Heart racing, Trudi whispered, 'What did he tell you?'

Frau Krause looked up, her eyes wide in her pale face. She shook her head, her fingers trembling at her lips. 'I can't.'

Trudi remained silent as the woman sobbed. Then she asked, 'Is it about murdering Jews?'

Frau Krause's eyes widened. 'You know?'

'A little.' Trudi hadn't wanted to believe the rumours circulating around Berlin.

After Helga had told her about her daughter's death and then Helga's suicide, Trudi had found herself listening more to the stories. If the Nazis could murder a disabled child, she believed they were capable of anything. She'd heard stories of mass shootings of men, women and children in the Polish countryside. Some of the Polish slave workers at the factory where Ada worked had whispered about them. Ada and other women told her every day—Jews disappeared from the factory floor. They knew the ones who had been deported, and nobody heard from them again. 'I'd like to hear what you can tell me. So I can prepare myself. You understand?'

Frau Krause stood up, her distress turning to anger, her finger pointing at Trudi. 'Why didn't you go with your children? Leave when you had a chance?' Just as quickly, the anger dissipated. 'Forgive me, I've no right taking my frustration out on you.' The woman's eyes widened as if she just thought of something. 'I have some money—not much, but maybe you could leave now?' Frau Krause moved to the sideboard, and stood on her tiptoes. Reaching up, she searched around before locating a wooden box. With a grunt of satisfaction she blew some dust from it and laid it on the table. Opening it, she pulled out a thin gold wedding ring. 'This was my mother's. Always too small for me and my girls. You take it and sell it. It won't bring much. Use the money and find a way to escape. You have to run, Trudi. Get away before...' The woman sank back into her chair as if her legs gave way.

Trudi fought back the nausea building in her stomach and wished she hadn't swallowed so much of the delicious soup.

If she could have left, she'd have gone long ago, but they had left it too late. She'd obeyed her husband, listened to him when he said the German people, lovers of Goethe and Beethoven, would soon recognize Hitler for what he was. A bully, a racist and an imposter. He wasn't even German.

Trudi had read *Mein Kampf*—well, parts of it, but enough to know how Hitler truly felt about the Jews.

'Thank you, but I can't take your money. You might have need of it yourself. Nobody knows how much longer the war will last.' Before Frau Krause could interrupt she went on, 'Emigration is now illegal for the Jews, Frau Krause. Anyway, there is nowhere for us to go. Nobody wants us.' Trudi flicked a hand over her eyes. She wasn't going to cry.

'You can't just wait until they come for you. Wilbur, he said Goebbels has promised to make Berlin Jew-free for Hitler. He is going to send everyone away.'

Trudi couldn't look at the other woman but stared at the table instead. It was old, worn with scratches and a few scorch marks. A family table once occupied by parents and children. She fought the urge to slam her fist onto it, to get rid of the anger and frustration bubbling inside her. Why couldn't people like Herr Krause fight back? If all the soldiers turned on Goebbels and the others in power, nobody would have to leave.

Frau Krause came to stand next to Trudi. 'You are welcome to come here as much as you want. I can cook your dinner every day. It's the least I can do. You look so thin. I don't have much but...'

'You realize what could happen to you if we are denounced? It is illegal to help the Jews.'

Frau Krause's shoulders straightened. 'I obey only one set of rules. Those laid down by God. This is my way to pay back your husband for what he did for my family. God will look after us.'

Trudi couldn't share her friend's belief. If God existed, why did places like Dachau? How could men shoot down civilians, little children, just because they belonged to a different race or religion? But Frau Krause obviously believed what she was saying.

'Please say yes, please come to dinner.'

Trudi smiled, reaching for the older woman's hand. 'I'm grateful to you for what you have done for me. But I don't want to put you in danger, or cause problems between a husband and wife.' She didn't want to put into words her fears that Herr Krause may have asked his neighbours to spy on his wife to ensure she obeyed his instructions not to help Trudi. Even now, someone may have tipped off the Gestapo. She needed to leave. 'I must go. I don't want to get home too late.'

Frau Krause didn't argue. Instead, she wrapped up some bread and two slices of cheese with an apple. 'Take these with you. For your lunch tomorrow.'

Trudi leaned forward and kissed the woman on the cheek. 'Thank you. Goodbye, Frau Krause.'

'You won't come back, will you?'

Trudi shook her head, not trusting her voice.

Frau Krause opened her mouth as if to argue but then her shoulders slumped as she acknowledged defeat. She hugged her. 'God go with you.'

Trudi wrapped her scarf around her face, closing her coat tight, the food bundled to her chest. It seemed colder than ever outside, but her mind was elsewhere.

Herr Krause could have already alerted the Gestapo. Trudi stumbled as the thought hit her. What information had Frau Krause given her husband? Trudi bit her lip, trying to stem the wave of panic.

She hesitated. What should she do? Risk going home?

She told herself to pull herself together. If Herr Krause had reported her, he knew where she lived. The Gestapo would have already picked her up.

TWELVE

Harry Beck rubbed his sleeve across his forehead, the sweat dripping into his eyes despite the bitter winds coming in across the Atlantic. It wasn't the manual work he hated most but the sheer boredom of digging trenches or constructing Nissan huts. Despite what the officer had said to him back in the classroom on the Isle of Man, his knowledge of German and his physical fitness wasn't enough to secure a fighting position against the Germans. He hit the sand hard with his shovel. He'd been more than clear about his wish to join the troops fighting overseas, but every written request had resulted in a letter of rejection.

The Pioneer Corps was the only branch of the British Army open to people like him and his friends—so called 'enemy aliens' as they'd been born in Germany or Italy. The government didn't believe he and others like him were desperate to overturn the Nazis, to rescue their families and recover property. So, despite swearing allegiance to the king and donning British uniform, being a part of the Pioneer Corps essentially meant they were an unarmed manual labour force to be used at the discretion of those in charge.

He rested his foot on the tool, staring across the grey,

choppy ocean, the waves crashing on the shore below. He wasn't going to get to Germany using a shovel. The salty air hit the back of his throat, making his eyes water.

It had been three years since he'd been arrested and thrown into Dachau.

His eyes closed, remembering his father's strong arms wrapped around him and the scratch of bristles against his cheek. His hands trembled as they gripped the handle of the shovel, his knuckles burning white with rage at the thought of the scarred face that had launched the attack that robbed him of his father. But for Gavriel, Heinz would have died trying to kill Scarface, the nickname he had given to Friedrich Schwarz when he didn't know the murderer's name.

Where were Gavriel and Izsak now?

Harry thought of his stepmother Trudi, the woman who had coerced him into coming to England. How dare she use Tomas to make him leave, to run away like a coward? How much longer before the British would give him a gun and let him join the fight? He'd show her and the rest of them.

'Are we working you too hard?'

Harry swallowed a groan at being caught resting by Sergeant Tanner. How could he have not sensed the six-foot-one tall wall of muscle coming toward him?

'No, sir,' Harry responded, having learned the hard way that his sergeant was even less enamoured with his role. Sergeant Tanner's closely cropped salt and pepper hair didn't cover the fading scar cut across his forehead: a souvenir from a close encounter with a German bullet at Dunkirk. Harry wondered if the sergeant had always looked so stern: had he adopted this look following his posting to train the new arrivals to the Pioneer Corps? As the man constantly reminded them, he'd much rather be back in Europe in the thick of battle.

'Sergeant, have you heard anything about my transfer?' Harry resumed digging as he waited for the answer.

'I got the same news as you got. Nothing.' Sergeant Tanner's piercing blue eyes looked out to sea before mumbling, 'I think they've forgotten us. Too busy with entertaining the town. All these blasted concerts seem to be priority.'

Harry hid his smile from the sergeant. Despite his protestations, the whole Corp knew Tanner had auditioned for a role in Prince Charming in the latest show being put on by the boys, but had been turned down. The corps didn't need amateurs, not when it had a list of who's who from the Berlin or Viennese orchestras. Sergeant Strietzel, a survivor of Buchenwald, was a hard task master, conducting the orchestra. Classical concerts and plays were as much a feature of life in Ilfracombe as digging trenches and army manoeuvres on the beach. Coco the clown entertained the troops and villagers alike. The money they raised for charity helped the local villagers to see their intentions and accept them for what they were: victims of the Nazis who wanted vengeance.

Harry hesitated but decided he had to ask. 'Sergeant, I heard rumours it would be two years before I can transfer out of the Pioneers and into a fighting role. Is that true?'

Sergeant Tanner stood straighter and, one hand brushing some sand from his khaki-coloured jacket, snapped, 'You should know better than to listen to noise. Just keep your head down, work on your English and leave the rest to me.'

Harry tried his best to obey but patience wasn't his virtue. He hadn't survived Dachau, escaped Germany, and lived through being interned on the Isle of Man to be stuck on a beach carrying a stick pretending it was a rifle.

He picked up the pace of digging. At least he'd stay fit, and there could be worse places to be. Here in Devon, the food was plentiful, the people friendly and even Tanner, for all his bluster, had a good heart.

. . .

Harry pushed aside the canvas opening, the odour of sweaty uniforms and feet competing with the smoke from the fire outside.

'Harry, did you see a Swiss guy asking questions?' Taub Heller, speaking in English, looked up from his camp bed as Harry strolled in. Despite Taub's casual tone, his alert brown eyes focused on Harry's, making him nervous. Having lived in Britain longer and being the eldest of their group, Taub had adopted the role of elder brother.

'Swiss?' Harry took off his jacket and hung it from the hook.

Taub stood up, stretching, before he fixed the top sheet of his bed. 'Name of Hartmann. He dresses as a private but... I don't know, he seems more senior than that. Something off about him. He kept asking about why I want to fight and whether I'd consider volunteering for special duties.'

Harry nodded to Noah, who'd glanced over the top of the book he was reading to say hello. Noah's eyesight was bad enough without him straining to read in the poor light from the oil lamp, but nothing would convince him to put his family chumash aside. Noah had told them how his father had gone over those particular texts from the Torah providing his commentary and where applicable, translations. Noah had traced his father's handwriting when telling Harry the story. It was obvious the bond between Noah and his father was like that of Harry and his dad.

Harry took a seat on his own bed, taking off his muddy boots and placing them on the wooden locker at the end of his camp bed. 'What sort of special duties?'

Before Taub could answer, Leo Kohn butted in, speaking German as he always did when the four of them were together. 'He wants us to build Nissan huts in Scotland. We've become the experts.' Leo laughed at his own joke but fell silent when the others didn't join in, his smile turning into a scowl. The smallest of the four, Leo exercised every chance he got, giving him a compact, muscular build. Leo's anger at what had happened in Germany and here in the UK was barely concealed on a good day. He was quick to anger but had proved himself a good ally, especially in a fight. He had a mean right hook.

Taub shot him a look: he'd told them before to use English if they wanted to be accepted in the army, before turning back to face Harry.

'He didn't specify but said it had something to do with going undercover. Like a spy or something. You interested?'

Harry swallowed the excitement in his stomach. Maybe this Hartmann guy was a way out—but what if he *was* recruiting for special forces? They'd heard rumours of French-speaking men being sent behind enemy lines in France. Were they going to do the same in Germany? Sweat trickled down his back as his mind flashed back to Dachau and the sights he'd seen. He didn't want to be a spy, he wanted revenge. To kill those who had targeted his family. Who had murdered his father.

He shook his head. 'No, it's not for me. I want to get there with the rest of the army. Not go ahead with special forces.'

'Why? You said you were in a hurry to get back to Berlin. Turned chicken, have we?' Leo walked over, his arms mimicking the motion of a chicken's wings.

'Shut up.' Harry clenched his knuckles as he tidied away his area, ignoring the urge to knock Leo out. Sergeant Tanner was notorious for inspections and he wanted a pass to attend a music festival at the weekend.

Looking concerned, Taub moved to his side. 'Harry, he's teasing. I thought you wanted to get back at them. It's all you talked about when you first got here. Now you have a chance and you say no. Why aren't you interested?'

Harry glared at Taub. Why couldn't he understand? It wasn't as if he didn't know. Taub had held him when Harry woke screaming from nightmares about his time in Dachau.

He'd never told the others half of what he told Taub. 'I have my reasons.' His tone said to leave him alone.

Leo lay down on his bed. 'You going to talk to Hartmann, Taub?'

'Me? Not a chance. I'm holding out for the RAF.'

Leo threw his pillow at Taub. 'You got straw for brains? They are never going to let one of us into the RAF. That group is for pure British, not some German Jews trying to pretend to be something they aren't.'

'Shut up, Leo.' Taub squared up to the other boy, despite knowing Leo could easily take him in a physical fight. 'We're as good as them. I learned to fly in Germany and finished my lessons here. I've had more hours in the sky than many of the RAF pilots, and it's not like they don't need me. I've taken the king's shilling and pleaded allegiance just like the rest of you. What else do they need from me?'

'British blood?' Leo poked his tongue out to show he was joking, but it wasn't funny. Being young and eager to fight, it was difficult to understand why they had to beg to get into a combat unit to prove their loyalty to the British.

Harry felt a thousand years older than these boys, although he was the youngest. Neither had been picked up on *Kristallnacht* and sent to the concentration camps. Taub, the son of a wealthy banker who'd been a pilot in the first war, had been in a plane almost before he could walk. His family had moved first to France in 1936 and then to England in 1939. Unlike Harry's dad, Taub senior had been prepared for the Nazis. He had moved his money abroad and sold off his assets at a decent price. Taub attended private school while learning to fly, assuming he'd join the RAF. Instead, he'd been picked up as a class-C enemy intern and shipped off to the Isle of Man, just like the rest of them.

'What about you, Leo?' Harry asked. 'Are you going to speak to Hartmann?'

Leo nodded. 'I already did. I said I wanted in. I don't care what he wants me to do, it has to be better than digging ditches. I'm sick of the sand and the seagulls.' Leo flexed his muscles. 'Hartman was impressed by my brawn.'

Taub rolled his eyes. 'He didn't pick you for your brains, anyway.'

For all his bluster, Harry knew what bothered Leo the most. They'd rubbed each other up the wrong way when they first met, despite being both from Berlin. Their accents were as different as their home lives. Leo assumed Harry was stuck-up due to his father having been a doctor. Leo's father lost his legs in the last war and his mother supported their family as a seam-stress. Leo had left school to work whatever jobs he could get to help. Their family—poor even before the restrictions against the Jews had made life difficult—had only had enough money to save one child. They picked their son, so he'd carry on the family name. Leo worried about his parents but particularly his twin sister, Esther. He hadn't heard a word from them since the war had broken out.

Noah put his Torah to one side. He was the quietest of their bunch and the only religious one. 'I signed up too.'

Surprised, Harry could only stare but Leo jumped off his bed. 'What? You can't be a special agent; they'd spot you a mile off. You're as Austrian as they come.'

Noah pushed his glasses further up his nose. They didn't fit properly—not since someone had hit him in the face while he was wearing them. 'I want to do something. To stop them killing more innocents. The man, he thinks there might be a job where I don't have to kill.'

Harry swallowed. Noah's misplaced guilt was evident from his attempt to keep kosher here, in Devon, mainly by eating only vegetables and fruit. Every second of his spare time consumed with his religious studies. The boy prayed more than any rabbi Harry had known. The day his family died, he'd snuck out to a friend's to play football. His love of the game was the only reason he'd survived the attack on his family; his father shot for resisting arrest, his mother and sisters shot for trying to help him. The friend's father had got Noah a place on a *Kindertransport*.

Leo opened his mouth but a look from Taub shut it again. Taub was protective of Noah, said he reminded him of a stray puppy nobody wanted.

'You'd be an asset, Noah. Don't let anyone tell you different.' Taub gave Leo another pointed look.

Leo flushed. 'Did you tell him about all the prizes you won for maths, and the fact you're a chess genius?'

Noah blushed. Harry doubted he'd sold his talents to the Swiss man but Sergeant Tanner would put in a good word. He was always saying Noah didn't belong in the army but in a school or library.

Taub whistled. 'Watch it, here comes Tanner.'

The lads jumped to action, Noah shoving the Torah under his pillow with one hand, the other straightening out his top sheet. Leo grabbed his boots to set them in a straight line while Taub and Harry folded up the spare chairs and stowed them in their proper place. With seconds to spare, their tent was ready for Tanner's inspection.

'At ease, lads. Any issues?' Tanner glanced in Taub's direction but nobody spoke as the sergeant performed the most cursory of inspections. 'Evening passes all around. Think we earned ourselves a pint or two.'

They saluted. 'Thank you, Sergeant.'

Later that evening, Harry lay in his cot ignoring the slightly damp feel of the blankets. He took out his writing paper, wondering what Rachel was doing. He closed his eyes, seeing her beautiful face, the big brown eyes and shy smile. Her curly hair tied up in a bun but with tendrils escaping to frame her—

A pillow hit him.

'Hey, lover boy, ask your girl if she has any friends, will you? She'd be doing them a favour introducing them to two fine specimens like us.' Leo had his arm around Taub's neck, the two of them smiling in a goofy way at Harry.

'Go get your own girls and leave me be.' Harry blew them a kiss before he turned back to his letter.

Dear Rachel,

Thanks for your last letter. Tell Tomas to concentrate in school and learn English properly. Liesel sounds as if she's happy. Has Sally recovered a little bit over her loss? She puts on a good face in her letters to me but I know how much she loved her husband. I'm so relieved you and the others aren't in the path of the bombs. The news from London, Coventry and other big cities isn't good. Every time we think the Luftwaffe have run out of planes, they come back again and again. I wish I could tell Goering he's wasting his time. The British aren't going to back down. Imagine him listening to a Jew.

How are things in Abbeydale? Sally mentioned you were having a difficult time with certain personalities in the village. Ignore them. They don't know you like I do. You're brave and fearless. Show them how strong you are.

I'm glad you enjoy your job but do you have to tell me all about the male patients and how you keep their spirits up? Couldn't you transfer to a female ward or a children's one? You'd be much better suited to work with children.

I have to keep this short but I will write again soon.

Take care,

He bit on his pen, wondering if he should sign off 'love Harry' or not. She never used the 'love' word in her letters, and sometimes he still wondered how she thought of him. But she'd kissed him that last day in front of the soldiers. A lover's kiss, not a kiss one would give to a friend.

THIRTEEN

DECEMBER 1941

The basement hummed with activity. The Christmas season had started and demand for dresses was at its height.

'Frau Beck, did you not hear me? I need you upstairs now. There is an emergency with a client.'

Trudi jumped. She had been thinking of Liesel, wondering if the family who was looking after her celebrated Christmas. Was Christmas as big an event in Britain as it was in Germany? Despite the war, people were still putting up Christmas trees, buying presents and throwing parties.

Trudi glanced around, but yes, Frau Schneider was talking to her. 'Me? Upstairs. With clients?' She sounded stupid, repeating everything, but this had never happened before. The Schneiders were always careful to hide her presence.

'Take off that overall and put this one on, quickly now. The client is waiting.'

Trudi did as she was told, shrugging off her overalls with the hated star and putting on the fresh ones. If only it were so easy to shed all the indignities they had been forced to suffer, such as being forbidden to leave their districts, be out after the 8 p.m.

evening curfew and... Oh, what was the use of thinking of all the horrid things happening? She couldn't change any of it.

She followed her boss out of the room and up into the store. The difference in surroundings was like night and day. No expense had been spared decorating the store, with the silk-covered walls with handpicked paintings and mirrors hanging on every wall. Everything was designed to showcase the collection of clothes in the best possible light.

Frau Schneider had good taste. Rumour had it she'd trained in Paris at the house of Chanel or someone similar, but the woman never spoke of it. It would be unpatriotic to acknowledge Paris was the centre of fashion.

'Countess Von Pabst has an issue with the dress and she needs it fixed for this evening. Come.'

Heart racing, Trudi rubbed her clammy hands in her overalls. Would the countess recognize her?

She held her breath when Frau Schneider pulled open the door to the dressing room. It was impossible to meet this woman and then forget her. Not because of her classically beautiful face—there were plenty of good-looking women in Berlin—but because no matter how much the lady smiled, sadness played in the shadows of her eyes.

The woman pretended she didn't know her, or perhaps she genuinely didn't remember, and began showing her the issue with the dress.

'See how it sits, the bulge right here? Can you fix it? I can't be seen at the ball wearing something that makes me look like an elephant.'

'You are very beautiful, Countess. Nobody will be looking at your dress.' Frau Schneider nearly fell over her own tongue.

The countess sent a glacial look at Frau Schneider. 'That's ridiculous. The dress must be perfect. Leave us.'

'But...'

'I said leave.'

Trudi kept her expression neutral as Frau Schneider withdrew, a stony look on her face.

Trudi fixed the dress as the woman regarded her critically. 'Have we met before?'

'I don't believe so, ma'am. May I please remove the dress so I can fix it?'

The woman stood like a statue as Trudi removed the dress, trying but failing to stop her hands from shaking.

'I don't bite. Well, only those who fawn over me.' The countess giggled but Trudi couldn't join her. Not when her stomach was churning. Trudi identified the issue quickly and was able to fix it. The countess continued to study her. 'I think I know where I recognize you from.'

Trudi kept her eyes on the dress seam. *Please don't remember, please.*

'Yes, that's it. You modelled a collection I saw. That must be it.'

Trudi was saved from replying by finishing the garment. She held it out to the countess to try on.

'Perfect. Now I will make a splash at this ball, although to be fair it won't be hard. All those dear darling Nazis in their dirndl outfits. I thought Eva would have more backbone but even she isn't wearing much make-up these days. What does a man, even our Führer, know about making women look good?'

Trudi didn't know what to do; she couldn't voice her agreement. Those remarks were tantamount to treason and even just being a witness to such comments would be an issue if anyone were to overhear.

Frau Schneider reappeared just in time. 'You look incredible, Countess. The colour really suits your eyes.' She glared at Trudi before dismissing her. 'Go back downstairs. Now.'

'Wait, please.' The countess pushed two marks into her hand. 'Thank you for helping me.'

'Pleasure, ma'am.' Trudi gathered her sewing kit and walked as fast as she dared out of the shop and back down the stairs.

It was worse than Trudi had expected. She thought Frau Schneider would just take the money from her, but instead she fired her on the spot. 'I can't risk the wives coming in asking for you. Go now before I call the Gestapo myself.'

Trudi didn't need to be told twice. She picked up her bag and coat and left.

What was she going to do for money now? She'd have to go back to the Reich Association of Jews in Germany and ask for a job.

As she walked out of the store, she heard someone call out, 'Miss—please stop. I wish to speak to you. Miss...?' Trudi couldn't afford to ignore the call: there weren't any other young women on the street—only children and a couple of old men and a few housewives lugging shopping baskets. If the person calling got any louder or attracted the wrong attention, Trudi's days were numbered.

Turning, she groaned softly to herself as she recognized the countess coming towards her.

'I've remembered where I met you. At Dr Ari Beck's gathering. It must have been 1934 or thereabouts. Don't look so scared, I won't tell anyone. You were the nanny, weren't you?'

It was pointless denying it. Trudi nodded, not trusting her ability to speak.

'What's your name?'

'Trudi, Trudi Beck.'

The countess threw her head back as she laughed. 'Ari always had too much charm. So, he married you, then.'

Trudi didn't respond. Was the woman mocking her?

'Come and have a drink with me—?'

Trudi couldn't hide her shock. Was the woman mad, or was

she playing with her like a cat with a mouse? Her eyes darted around the street but there was no sign of men in trench coats waiting to pounce. She shook her head. 'I'm not allowed, ma'am.' Trudi couldn't help but look pointedly at the star on her chest—as if the countess couldn't see the ugly yellow mark for herself.

'My name is Isla, and to heck with the rules.' The countess took the fur coat hanging over her arm and put it around Trudi's shoulders, covering the star in the process. 'Come on, please. I sent my driver to get my husband's favourite cigars from a store a few miles away. He'll collect me in an hour.'

When Trudi still hesitated, the woman whispered, 'Nobody will know. You look as Aryan as I do and they aren't going to ask me for papers.'

This was a woman used to giving orders and having them obeyed. Trudi followed her toward the coffee shop entrance. She couldn't do much else. If Isla was playing with her, a word in the ear of the waiter or café owner was all that would be needed for the police—or worse, Gestapo—to come running.

Trudi's heart stilled as they entered the coffee shop and came face to face with two soldiers, the buttons on their uniform glinting as the light from the overhead lamps hit them. Trudi wished she was wearing gloves so nobody would see her sweat-covered palms.

She followed Isla's lead and didn't acknowledge the men but walked past, head held high. Isla picked a table in the corner, dimly lit compared to the rest of the shop. It was also a little further from the main bar area, but the din of conversation around them would hopefully stop anyone from overhearing whatever it was the countess wished to talk about.

Trudi swallowed, not sure she would be able to find her voice.

A waiter appeared and held the chair for her. She took a seat and waited for him to help Isla do the same.

Isla ordered, for which Trudi was grateful. She couldn't find her voice. Without moving her head, Trudi looked around her, taking in the couples holding hands, all the men in uniform—some women, too. She spotted a family, their son wearing the Hitler Youth uniform, their little girl wearing the cutest red dress. She was angelic-looking with her blonde hair tied up in braids either side of her head.

Trudi closed her eyes briefly, wondering what Liesel looked like now. Had her hair darkened or was it still baby-blonde?

When she reopened her eyes, the child returned her stare, making Trudi uneasy. She looked toward her companion as Isla lit a cigarette. Even that was a dangerous act, considering the Führer's well-published thoughts on women who smoked.

Trudi's gaze took in the Christmas tree, together with packages all tied up with ribbons under it. Ari, unlike several non-religious Jews of their acquaintance, had never put up a tree. Not even when the children were little and begged to be like their friends.

The waiter returned, balancing the tray with one hand as he laid the table in front of them. A cup of real coffee and a pastry soon sat in front of her. She couldn't believe it, and, suddenly, her eyes filled with tears.

'Please don't get upset.' The countess whispered but her voice was kind, not reprimanding.

The waiter came back and hovered. 'Can I get you something else?'

'No, thank you. My friend, she's had bad news from the front. Her fiancé has been injured.'

The waiter stuck his arm out and gave the Hitler salute. 'Thank him for his service. I would be out there too but for my eyesight.' He marched off.

The occupants of the closest table also saluted before gathering up their things and leaving. Was it her tears that had made them uncomfortable, or did they sense she was lying?

Trudi leaned across the table. 'We should leave.'

She watched a smile playing on the countess's lips.

'Why? Because of that idiot?' Isla indicated Trudi should drink up.

Trudi took a sip of the scalding coffee, savouring the scent and taste. It had been years since she'd had the real thing.

'I take it Frau Schneider gave you your cards.'

Trudi looked up. 'Yes. She threatened to call the Gestapo.'

Isla winced, her face losing all colour. 'I'm sorry, I didn't mean to cause any issues.'

At the concern in her voice, Trudi found herself telling the countess all about the Schneiders. About him pushing himself on her at every opportunity and his wife being equally cruel.

'I'll deal with them, don't you worry. I've no time for bullies.'

The countess smiled. 'Now, is there anything I can do to help you? I know money is always helpful, but I don't carry much cash.' She routed in her handbag before producing about twenty marks, which she passed discreetly to Trudi. Then she glanced at her arm before taking off her gold bracelet. 'Here, take this. I have plenty more at home. You should be able to get a good price on the black market.'

The black market? She hadn't been since Olga had left. She couldn't risk trying anything illegal. Not now, wearing the star. Had this woman been living under a rock for the last seven years? Even Germans got in trouble for using black market traders: getting caught warranted at least a spell in prison.

She shook her head. 'Thank you for the money, but I can't take your bracelet. It's too risky.'

Trudi felt bad at the disappointed look on the woman's face, but she was telling the truth and they both knew it.

'Forgive me. My husband tells me I'm too impetuous.' Isla put the bracelet back on before she took a bite of her pastry, delicately patting her lips with her serviette before lifting her coffee cup. 'Tell me, how is Ari and those lovely boys of his?'

Startled by the sudden change in conversation, Trudi blurted out, 'He's dead. Murdered in Dachau.'

The countess paled, her hands shaking as she returned her cup to its saucer, coffee spilling down the sides. 'I'm so sorry, I hadn't heard. I didn't know.'

Trudi couldn't think how she would know. This woman might as well have lived on the moon. Still she felt guilty at causing the genuine distress on the woman's face. 'His sons escaped—Heinz and Tomas. They are in Britain with our little girl.'

The countess took her hand. 'A baby girl. You are so blessed. I mean, I would give anything for a child. That's what Ari tried to help me with. It worked too. I got pregnant, just the once, but my baby didn't survive the birth. I almost didn't either. I'm lucky Wilhelm loves me. If his friends had their way, he'd trade me for a better functioning model.'

Trudi couldn't help herself; she took the woman's hand in hers and squeezed, hearing the years of hurt in her voice.

The countess sniffed before wiping away a single tear. 'How selfish, here I am blubbing about my troubles when you... you are fighting for survival.'

'We all have our problems, Countess.' Trudi hesitated. 'My children, they are safe. They are living with a lovely lady who used to send me letters. At least until the war started.'

The countess looked at her. 'Isla, please. I wish there was something I could do for you, Trudi. I mean properly.'

Trudi checked to see if anyone was listening before she whispered, 'You've treated me like a human being. That's enough. Thank you. But I'd better leave now, before your driver comes back or someone else sees us.' Trudi downed the rest of her coffee, not caring if it wasn't mannerly. She didn't know when she'd experience that luxury again. 'Goodbye, Isla. Be careful.'

'You too. I feel there is something very special about you, Trudi.' Isla grabbed her hand. 'Are you still living at the same address?'

Trudi shook her head. 'No, I moved to a smaller apartment when...' She couldn't stop her voice trembling as she thought of the children. She could feel Liesel against her chest, smell her lovely baby smell... She pulled herself together seeing the concern on Isla's face, straightening her back. 'They made me move.'

'Can I call on you?'

Trudi's eyes glistened; she couldn't let this woman come to her apartment. 'It's not safe. You could be followed.' Never mind the fact that someone as well-dressed as the countess would stick out like a sore thumb where Trudi now lived.

Isla wasn't to be put off, though. She scribbled something on a napkin as Trudi stood up, before folding it and pressing it into Trudi's hand. 'Please trust me. I'm a friend.'

On impulse Trudi bent down and kissed the woman's cheek. '*Danke.*'

Isla stood up and escorted her out of the café. Only when they were safely outside and had no witnesses did Trudi go to take off the coat.

'Take it, Trudi. If nothing else, it will keep you warm. But you can sell it.'

'Your driver?'

'He barely looks at me and if he notices anything, I'll say I left it at Schneiders'. Go now and take that worried look off your face. Nobody will stop a beautiful woman wearing a gorgeous fur coat. Act as if you are the most important person in Berlin. Acting the part is half of the battle.'

Reluctantly, Trudi handed the coat back to the countess, shaking her head sadly.

The countess nodded as if she understood.

By law, the star had to be displayed on her coat and nobody would believe a Jew would have a fur coat these days. All luxury items like that had already been stolen. She thought of the wardrobes of clothes she'd been forced to leave in her old apartment when it had been seized by the Nazis.

'Trudi, please let me call on you. I think I may be able to help you a little. You have my number. Call me.' The countess turned on her heel and walked off.

Trudi watched her go, noting the admiring glances cast her way. It took a few moments to remember she was standing in the middle of the street branded with the star. She turned and walked as quickly as she could toward her home.

She resisted the temptation to run, but only barely.

FOURTEEN

As Trudi lay in bed that night, she went over and over the conversation with the countess. Could she help? In what way? Was she to be trusted? She was married to a high-ranking *Wehrmacht* soldier, a nice, pleasant man from what she remembered of his behaviour at Ari's get-togethers—but still a soldier. Why would Isla want to get involved with helping a Jew?

After tossing and turning for hours, she gave up on any thought of sleep. She got up, dressed and boiled some water to make a mint drink. She had no *ersatz* coffee. She sipped the drink, moving to the window to watch the scene below. A light frosting of snow covered everything from the rooftops to the streets below, making everything look serene and peaceful. How easy it was to pretend Berlin was a beautiful place, and not one where people were torn from their homes and sent who knew where.

She saw two girls run outside, their faces lit up with excitement as they tried to gather enough snow to form snowballs. Little children just like Liesel and Helga's Annika. Except they weren't like those girls, were they? The children on the street below were allowed to stay with their families, to live. There was no sign of Aron or his little brother. Frau Weiss had been too scared to let the children out of the apartment ever since the day Aron was attacked. Trudi left small gifts at the door: a couple of apples one day, a new blanket the next, but Frau Weiss, although appreciative of the gestures, never invited her into the apartment. She seemed to believe the less she interacted with the outside world, the safer it would be.

Trudi turned away from the scene and her painful thoughts. It was time to go out.

The icy December air bit into her exposed skin, and she pulled her coat tighter, wishing she had a pair of gloves to wear. Her fingertips were turning red from the cold.

The street seemed eerily quiet, with only the distant hum of traffic from the few cars on the road. Trudi approached the telephone, holding the 10 pfennig piece in her hand as if it would burn her. She glanced around but nobody seemed to be paying her any attention. She stepped up to the phone and, despite her shaking fingers, dialled the number.

It rang a couple of times, but just as she was about to hang up a woman answered. Trudi froze, unable to speak. It was now or never.

'Hello, hello?'

Tempted to return the handset to the cradle, Trudi argued with herself. *You need a job, she offered to help.*

'Could I speak to the countess, please?'

'Who's calling?'

Trudi's mouth went completely dry, her throat constricting and reducing her ability to breath. Her heart raced.

'Hello, can you hear me? The static on the line is bad,' the woman said.

'Trudi Beck. Frau Dr Beck.'

'One minute, please, Frau Beck.'

Trudi counted the seconds as her eyes took in her surroundings, paying careful attention to anyone who seemed to be looking her way. Would the maid know she was Jewish from her name? Were they spying on her? *Don't be ridiculous. You are making a phone call, not staging a protest.*

'Frau Beck, how lovely to hear from you again. Did you find my glove? Did I leave it at the dressmaker yesterday?'

Glove? What glove? Then Trudi realized Isla was making up an excuse for them to meet.

'Yes. I was wondering if you would like me to drop it off,' Trudi answered, willing her to say no.

'How kind of you to offer but I am going to the cake store near the coffee shop. You know the one. My husband is back home later this week, and he loves their chocolate torte. Shall I meet you there? Say, in an hour?'

'Yes. Thank you.'

Trudi held the phone in her hand after the countess had said goodbye and hung up. She needed to get a grip on herself: her hands were shaking, and if she stood looking at the phone much longer, someone was bound to notice.

She replaced the handset and turned on her heel, walking smartly down the road as if she had somewhere to be. She did, but not for another hour. How would she pass the time? She couldn't go into a park and sit on a bench. That was forbidden. As was taking the tram or any other form of public transport.

Despite having to walk, Trudi arrived too early for the meeting. She kept walking, not going into any of the stores for fear of being ridiculed. She avoided the Schneiders' store too, in case Frau Schneider made good her threat to call the Gestapo. Not that she really believed the woman would do it, as it would mean her having to explain why she had employed Jews and gentiles on the same premises in the first place.

She spotted Isla walking toward the coffee shop, her outfit as elegant as always. A beautiful fur coat and hat protected her from the weather but not the admiring glances of both men and women on the street. It wasn't just the countess's good looks, it was her regal bearing that drew attention. She walked around as if she owned everything she touched.

She gave Trudi a warm smile and a hug, her eyes checking Trudi's coat discreetly, her smile growing wider as she noticed the absence of the star. 'I see you're learning already,' Isla whispered into her ear, before leading her back into the coffee shop, where they secured the same table and waiter.

He nodded in recognition but didn't make any enquiries, perhaps afraid he would set Trudi's tears off again.

Trudi's mouth watered as the rich aroma of real coffee and buttery pastries wafted through the air as Isla ordered. Trudi dropped her voice to a whisper: 'Before yesterday I can't remember the last time I had a cake, and now I'm having them two days in a row.'

Isla glanced around, before whispering back, 'Sometimes being married to a general comes in handy.'

A chill washed over Trudi, her appetite disappearing. Isla's husband was a general and she was sitting there next to her. Her eyes darted left and right under her eyelashes, seeking out a possible escape.

'I've frightened you. Don't be scared. My husband believes as I do.' Isla passed over the bag she had been carrying. 'I've packed together some clothes and a few other bits and pieces. There is some cash in the pocket of the jacket. I thought you might be able to use it for food.'

'Thank you, you're being very kind.'

'It's easy to be kind when you have lots of everything. Money, jewels, clothes...' Trudi imagined that Isla's next word would have been 'freedom'.

She stopped speaking to allow the waiter to place steaming cups of coffee before them.

'My apologies, we have run short on pastries. The soldiers, they are hungry.' The waiter waved in the general direction of a group of uniformed *Wehrmacht* soldiers, their laughter a sharp contrast to the tense atmosphere.

Isla dismissed the waiter with a graceful nod, her eyes sparkling with determination as they returned to their conversation. 'I have a friend who owns a small dressmaking saloon, a tenth the size of the Schneiders'.'

Trudi's hopes flared, but fell just as quickly as the countess continued speaking: 'She can't afford to hire you full time but will give you as much work as she can. She doesn't want you to work from her store but will bring you the materials. I think this would be safer for both of you. It would cut down on the amount of time you spend out wearing that hideous star.'

Trudi couldn't help but glance around to make sure nobody had heard Isla's comment, but everyone was engaged in their own conversations.

'Renata has her own secrets—she is a companion to a rich and well-connected *gentleman*.' The emphasis on the word got Trudi's attention as the countess leaned in closer. 'He's married, and a member of Hitler's inner circle.'

Trudi could have sworn her heart stopped. The coffee she had just sipped went down the wrong way. She tried not to cough and draw attention to their table but failed dismally.

One of the soldiers ran over as she choked, clapping her on the back while another fetched a cup of water. She would have raced from the coffee shop but for Isla's restraining hand on her knee under the table. Trudi fought to restore her composure.

Isla beamed at the soldier and said, 'Why, thank you, gentlemen. We are so lucky to have such handsome heroes in our midst. I shall be sure to tell my husband, General Von Pabst, of your honourable actions.'

The men clicked their heels and bowed before returning to their seats.

Isla leaned forward and dropped her voice. 'I'm so sorry. Wilhelm always tells me off for putting my foot in my mouth.

Renata has her reasons for acting as she does. She won't breathe a word about you and expects the same loyalty in return. Her maid, Ursula, an orphan she adopted, will drop off the dresses that need alterations and what not, and will pick up the work you have finished. There is no need for either of you to meet in person. I will give you—' Despite the look on Trudi's face, she continued: 'I insist on giving you the difference to make up a full wage.'

Trudi tried to calm her stomach, discreetly wiping her hands on the side of her skirt. 'You seem to have thought of everything.'

Isla shrugged her shoulders. 'I lead a very boring life. Getting one over on these horrid little men is exciting.'

Trudi opened her mouth but shut it again. Was Isla being facetious or was she serious? It may seem like a game to her, but this was very serious. Her life, *both* their lives, might be at risk. If they were discovered, Trudi would be on a train to Poland and Isla... what would they do to her, or even her husband? Was a *Wehrmacht* general untouchable?

'Write your address here for me.' Isla held out a notebook and a beautiful silver pen with a gold nib.

Trudi wrote out her new address, her mind racing over the plans they had made. She'd need a new sewing machine.

'Isla, I don't have a sewing machine. Not anymore.'

Isla shrugged. 'I'll buy one and deliver it later. Now, let's drink up and leave before those heroes of yours decide it's time to come over and join us.'

Trudi didn't need encouraging. She was all too eager to leave, having glanced at the soldiers and found one staring right back at her. Could he tell she was breaking the law? She felt like her guilt was written all over her face, and wished she had half the bravado Isla seemed to possess.

· · ·

Later that same day, a black car drove up to Trudi's apartment block. Looking out the window, Trudi imagined every occupant in the building holding their breath until a chauffeur exited the car.

Trudi recognized him as the Von Pabst driver. He unlocked the trunk and withdrew a large box, which he carried up to Trudi's front door. She opened it to stop him having to place the box on the ground.

'Delivery for Trudi Beck. Where shall I put it? Here on the table?'

'Thank you. Yes, please.'

The chauffeur placed the box carefully on the table. 'Got a second smaller box for you.' He turned and walked back outside to the car. She wondered if she should tip him for delivering the boxes. What was the etiquette? She didn't want to offend anyone.

When he returned, he put a smaller box on the table. 'The countess said to tell you to put the items in the icebox as soon as you can.'

Trudi nodded. She took a couple of coins from her purse. 'Please don't be offended but I would like to buy you a beer. For helping me.'

The man stood to attention, ignoring her outstretched hand. 'I've worked for the countess's family since she was a little girl. Her father and I served together in the last war. She has a kind heart. Don't take advantage.' He gave her a half-bow and left, closing—not banging—the door behind him.

Trudi felt her cheeks flush but she couldn't let his rudeness overshadow her excitement. The smaller box of food was a luxury for which she was thankful, but the sewing machine was a real gift. She could do work for other people as well as this lady, Renata. She could save up some money to pay bribes in case someone she knew was arrested. She might even risk buying some food on the black market. Eggs and other luxuries that were impossible for a Jew to find in the ordinary stores. The possibilities were endless. She lovingly unpacked the machine; it wasn't new, but had been well maintained. Isla had also provided a packet of spare needles and threads in an array of colours. Trudi knew she was a lucky woman to have such a good friend.

FIFTEEN

LATE DECEMBER 1942

Trudi checked the hated star was on full display on the coarse fabric her coat. Normally she didn't bother, but only Jews walked near the *Judenhaus* and she didn't want any policeman arresting her for covering up the star.

The biting wind nipped at her cheeks, the damp chill making her bones feel cold. Was she mad to be walking outside in these temperatures? But it was Hanukkah, and she wanted to do something to celebrate the holiday—even if it was forbidden. When Ari was alive, they had made a point of celebrating the special holidays.

She folded her arms across her chest, pressing the small gift she had for Ada into her coat. Her footsteps seemed to echo down the empty street—the combination of bad weather, fear and it being close to curfew keeping people indoors.

In answer to her knock, Ada's grey face peeped around the door. 'Oh, Trudi! You gave me a fright. I thought it was... someone else.'

'The Gestapo won't knock so quietly,' Trudi teased, as she kissed her friend on the cheek, stepping into the apartment and closing the door behind her. She wrinkled her nose as the odour of boiling cabbage hit her nostrils, but her friend's pale face concerned her more. 'I didn't mean to intrude, but it's Hanukkah and I wanted to give you something. I should have called around before but it's been a very busy week and I figured you would be working and...' Trudi fell silent, her eyes drawn to a piece of paper on the table.

Ever the hostess, Ada pointed at a seat. 'Sit down. I have some soup and a little bread. It's not fresh, but...'

'I ate, thank you, but you go ahead.' Trudi tried to hold Ava's gaze but her friend wouldn't meet her eyes. 'What's wrong? You look very pale.'

Ada sagged and would have fallen but for Trudi taking her arm and helping her onto the scruffy sofa. 'Sit down and tell me what's wrong. Are you sick?'

Ada shook her head, and she pointed at the letter. Trudi picked it up and read it, nausea settling in her stomach. It was a notice from the Gestapo instructing Ada to go to the collection centre, and explaining what to bring with her.

Trudi scanned the list of clothing, her eyes filling with tears. She blinked furiously. Crying wouldn't solve anything.

'I guess I should have expected it, so many other people have already gone. Half this house is empty.' Ada sniffed, her voice shaking as much as her hands. 'Why am I shocked? It was only a matter of time.'

Trudi took a seat beside Ada. 'It's natural to be upset. But you aren't going.'

Ada turned on Trudi. 'Have you lost your mind? I can't ignore the demand.'

'Yes, you can. You know I have a friend... she used to give me food until I stopped going to see her after she told me what her husband had seen, maybe done. He was fighting on the Eastern Front...'

Ada's hands shook, despite her clasping them together on her knee. Trudi leaned closer and took Ada's hands in hers. Ada looked up, her gaze locking with Trudi's, fear and tears mixing for dominance.

'Her husband returned and told her some stories. It seems that...' And Trudi told Ada about what Frau Krause had told her that last time she'd seen her.

Ada pulled away, paling as she leaned forward, her hands reaching up as if she wanted to cover her ears.

Trudi hesitated, but she knew her friend wouldn't act unless she knew the truth. 'What we hear... the rumours, they could be true.'

Ada's mouth fell open.

'The mass shootings, the starvation camps, all of it. You can't just walk to the collection point and get on one of those trains. You need to come and stay with me.'

'With you?'

'Yes. You must disappear.'

Ada blinked rapidly. 'Disappear? How? They've branded us like cattle making us wear that yellow star. The people I used to consider friends don't see me anymore. They either turn their face when we meet in the street, or worse. I have nowhere to go, Trudi. If I go to your house, I put you at risk too.'

'You don't have a choice. I insist.' Trudi stood up, her legs stiff from sitting in the cold, damp room. 'I want you to gather as many warm clothes as you can find.'

'That won't be hard. We had to surrender all our winter clothing, blankets and fur coats back in January. I didn't manage to hide anything.' Ada's voice was heavy with resignation; all the fight that had helped her to save her sons had long disappeared, broken under the relentless cruelty of the regime.

Trudi said nothing. The sanctions against the Jews worsened daily.

Ada reached out, her cold fingertips brushing against Trudi's arm. 'I'm sorry. I didn't mean to lash out at you. I'm scared, Trudi. You're so brave, you walk the streets like a gentile, yet I scurry back here every evening from that awful job. I can't do it. I'm terrified.' Ada hesitated before adding, in a trembling voice: 'Thank you, but I'll just take my chances.'

Trudi stared at her friend as tears ran unchecked down Ada's face. Her work in the munitions factory meant she was subjected to vile abuse and degradations daily. The woman who'd once shown her how to hide valuables from the Nazis seemed to have lost all faith in herself.

Trudi couldn't let her just give in. 'No. Rachel and Ruth need their mother. Gavriel and Izsak would expect you to be strong. You must fight back, for your children's sake, if not your own.'

Ada didn't look convinced.

'If you insist on answering the summons from the Gestapo, I will too.' Trudi sat back down on the sofa, curling her hands under her legs to get warm. The small room was freezing, it was almost warmer out in the snow. She watched emotions cross her friend's face: fear, sorrow, self-pity... but, finally, anger.

'Why are you putting your life in my hands? I'm not responsible for your choices, it's not like we are family.'

Trudi just stared. She couldn't look Rachel and Ruth in the face if she survived the war, and had to tell them their mother hadn't even tried to save herself.

Minutes slipped by. Trudi couldn't help but glance at the wooden clock hanging on the wall. It would be curfew soon. She couldn't stay much longer.

'Trudi,' Ada pleaded. 'I know you mean well but I'm not young like you. It won't work—how will we eat? Our rations aren't enough to keep one person alive, let alone two.'

'We stick together. We made that promise to the children, remember?'

Ada threw her hands in the air, muttering a word Trudi never thought she'd hear the other woman use. 'Trudi Beck, you are as stubborn as they come. I'll do it. But remember I tried to make you change your mind.'

Trudi reached over and hugged her friend. 'Only one bag, so make everything you take count. Now, let's get packing.'

Once the decision had been made, Ada burst into action. She didn't have much, but she put her treasured photographs of her husband and children in the bag first. Then she added some clothes and a couple of trinkets she'd held on to.

Trudi held the bag while Ada locked the door behind them and then, together, they walked out of the building. They didn't see anyone; the weather had turned dismal. Trudi checked continuously behind them but there was no sign of anyone following. She took a circuitous route to her apartment.

'Wait here.' She left Ada at the corner, making her own way to the apartment to check the coast was clear. There was nobody about. For once, things appeared to be going in their favour. She beckoned Ada to follow her inside. 'Welcome to your new home. You can have my bedroom. The sheets are clean.'

Trudi gave Ada privacy to unpack her few belongings in the bedroom while she went to the kitchen to prepare a meal. Thanks to the regular packages arriving at her home, she had some eggs and made a small cheese omelette for them to share.

Ada came out of the bedroom. 'What is that heavenly smell? It's not cabbage.'

They both smiled at Ada's attempt at a joke. Trudi moved her sewing machine to one side. 'Sorry the space is a bit tight. Sit down and make yourself at home.'

Ada's eyes swam with tears as Trudi placed the plate of food in front of her before pouring them two glasses of water.

'Cheers.' She tapped Ada's glass with her own, trying to suck her friend from her despair. Then she took the Hanukkah gift from her pocket and gave it to Ada.

'Open it. You can have it for dessert.'

Ada's hands shook as she opened the little parcel. 'Chocolate! But, how? Where?'

Trudi hadn't told Ada about Isla—not because she didn't trust her friend but because the less anyone knew about Isla's actions, the better. 'A friend gave it to me, along with the eggs. Now eat, before your food gets cold.'

Ada took a bite of the omelette, an expression of bliss on her face. 'It tastes divine. I didn't know you could cook so well.'

'Hunger is a good sauce,' Trudi joked.

They finished the meal in silence, then Trudi allowed her guest to wash up. Ada insisted, and it was nice to have someone else clear the table.

Afterward they sat on the ugly sofa, the springs of which hurt if you sat down too long.

'Thank you, Trudi.'

'You would do the same for me. My neighbours are good people, especially Frau Weiss and her beautiful little boys upstairs. But you need to be careful, Ada. You can't be seen in public so don't go outside or open the door. Stay in the bedroom if anyone comes visiting.'

Ada's face whitened. 'You have visitors.'

'Ursula, a young orphan, comes twice a week with deliveries for me. She takes the work I have finished and gives me whatever alterations are needed. She has yet to speak more than two words to me apart from the instructions our employer sends. She could be dangerous.'

Ada nodded, playing with her hands in her lap, not looking at Trudi.

'I get parcels, too, from a friend. She is a good woman. The eggs we shared tonight came from her. She will do what she can to help, but she must be discreet.'

'Why?'

Trudi felt awful but she couldn't tell Ada about the countess.

The silence lingered as Ada's question went unanswered. 'You don't trust me. And you're right. When the children were younger, all I did all day was gossip. What a waste of a life I lived.'

Trudi put her finger under Ada's chin, forcing her to look at her. 'The less you know the safer you are. We could both be picked up. Living here isn't secure, Ada, but it is safer than you obeying that summons and getting on those trains. They have my name and address, and a time will come when my deportation papers arrive too.'

'You don't know that.'

'Yes, I do. We've all heard Goebbels and his promise that Berlin will be *Judenrein*—free from all Jews. It's only a matter of time before they come for me.' The atmosphere grew heavier. 'Ada, all we can do is pray that by the time they come, I—no, we —will have a better plan of escape. For now, we are just buying some time. Let's not think about Hitler or the Gestapo. What do you think our children are doing right now?' Trudi curled up on the sofa beside her friend. 'I see Tomas trying to be the big man and not a little boy. Ruth is probably treating Liesel like a little doll and Rachel... oh, what a fine young woman she is turning into. Aren't we lucky they found homes close to one another, and those English women looking after them sound so nice.'

Trudi kept up the commentary, allowing Ada time to compose herself. If she helped her friend be brave and face up to the perilous situation they were in, it would help her too. Wouldn't it?

SIXTEEN

Ada jumped at every little noise at first but when it was clear the Gestapo hadn't followed her, she began to relax. She wasn't as good a seamstress as Trudi, but she helped her tack seams and sew buttonholes. They stretched Trudi's rations but would have starved without the regular food parcels Isla sent to them.

'This dress would suit you, Trudi. I can just see you dancing on the arm of a handsome young man.' Ada held the dress Trudi had just finished up against her. 'The colours suit you, although you need a little rouge on your cheeks, and some lipstick wouldn't hurt, either.'

'Wait here and I'll just grab my cosmetics. They're in the closet between my jewels and my fur coats.'

The women laughed.

Trudi was grateful for Ada's friendship. The apartment was small, but having company made such a difference. Ada had insisted they share the bedroom soon after she moved in, as the sofa was uncomfortable to sit on, never mind sleep on. Trudi was still lonely, especially for her children.

'Have you thought about it?' Ada asked.

'What?'

'Meeting a man, maybe getting married again?' Ada put the dress back on the hanger before drawing a protective covering over it.

Trudi sat down. 'You mean if we live?'

Ada tutted; they had agreed not to talk about anything but good things. 'I mean after the war ends. You were very young when you married. We... I mean, I thought Ari was rather old for you.'

Ada looked so uncomfortable, Trudi couldn't take offence. 'You mean you don't believe I took advantage of him and all his money?' Trudi mimicked Chana's voice.

'Don't mind that woman. She had too much to say for herself. You were good for Ari—you helped him get over the loss of his wife, you looked after his children, but...' Ada picked up Liesel's blanket and put it down again.

'But?'

The tension mounted as silence lingered, Trudi keeping her eyes on Ada's face.

The poor woman flushed, her eyes lingering everywhere but on Trudi. 'You aren't making this easy... I just never thought you were really in love. Were you?'

'Of course I was.' Trudi bit her lip, trying to dismiss the conflicting feelings she had about Ari. On one hand, he had been a kind and considerate man, a good husband and father. But on the other hand, she couldn't help but feel some anger and frustration towards him for taking the decisions he had without consulting her. She had rarely found the courage to stand up to him, or even voice her opinions—not that he'd listened. Now that he was gone, regret filled her heart—why hadn't she been more assertive? Was it because he was older, better educated, a man?

Ada's whisper broke into her thoughts. 'But did he make your heart beat so fast you couldn't breathe? My Sol, he did that.' Ada's wistful expression as she shared her intimate feelings twisted the guilt in Trudi's stomach, adding to her discomfort. A picture of Herr Bernstein entered her mind. It was difficult to imagine him generating such passion, but she wouldn't hurt Ada's feelings by admitting that. If her friend was discussing the love of her life, she didn't have to dwell on Ari.

'Sol? I didn't know that was Herr Bernstein's name.'

'It wasn't.' Ada blushed but she held Trudi's gaze, a touch of defiance in her eyes. 'My husband's name was Moses. I fell in love with Sol but my parents, they didn't agree to the match. They said he wouldn't ever amount to anything. He was only a watch repairer, not even that but an apprentice. To his uncle, who would pass the business to his own son. But, Trudi, he was so much more than that. He was so talented, he could repair anything. He made things too, with gold and silver.'

Intrigued, Trudi leaned in. 'What happened? Did he marry someone else?'

'He left for America after I refused to elope. I was terrified of my parents and what they would say. Moses, he was a colleague of my father's, a nice man and he had plenty of money, prestige, standing.' Ada curled the blanket between her fingers. 'As if that mattered. I was so young and foolish.'

'Stop being so hard on yourself. I know what it is like to have no money and limited options. When my parents died, I had few choices but to come and work for the Becks as their nanny.'

Ada patted Trudi's hand. 'You were what those children needed. Frau Beck was so ill.'

Trudi shook her head. 'Let's not talk about that. Tell me more about Sol.'

'He came back once to Germany, to Berlin, in early 1936. He was married and had children over in America. He married a jeweller's daughter, expanded their business and opened stores all over New York and other places. He visited his uncle and the rest of his family, but he also came to see me. Moses was at work and the children at school—well, apart from Ruthie, but she was too young to say anything. He said he would help us escape. He'd pay for us to go to America.' A tear ran down Ada's cheek. 'He said he still loved me and forgave me for marrying Moses Bernstein.'

Eager to know more, Trudi asked, 'What did you say? Were you tempted?'

'To run away? Yes, several times, but only in my dreams. I was a wife and a mother. I couldn't just pick up my skirts and run, no matter how tempting. I think age only made him more handsome.' Ada put her hands over her mouth.

'What's wrong?'

'You must think I'm a foolish old woman who cheated on her husband.'

'Ada, you are only forty, that's not old. And no, I don't think you were foolish. Dreams aren't cheating. You didn't leave. Did you tell Herr Bernstein? I mean, about the offer to get you to America?'

As Ada nodded, a look of such anger crossed her face. 'He wouldn't listen. He never did. Izsak and Gavriel tried to tell him we needed to get out of Germany. But when all those horrible anti-Jewish signs were removed for the Olympics—you remember when the police stopped harassing the Jews and everyone thought it was going to be okay? Well, Moses took that as proof he was right and we were wrong. I argued with him, Rachel too, but he was deaf to our pleas. Of course, when he found out Sol had visited and what he offered... I don't think he would have taken Sol's money even if Hitler himself had held a gun to his head. He was very jealous.' Ada's eyes dropped to the floor. 'I shouldn't speak ill of the dead.'

Trudi drew her friend into a hug. 'People don't become flawless because they are dead. I'm sorry, Ada.'

Ada wiped the tears from her eyes, pushing Trudi away gently. 'Don't be sorry for me. I was happy. Moses was kind in his own way, and he gave me four wonderful children. The boys and my girls.' Ada stayed silent with her thoughts for a few minutes.

Trudi sat still, thinking about what her friend had told her.

When Ada gripped her hand, it startled her. 'If you get a chance at real love, Trudi, grab it with both hands and don't let go. You promise?'

Trudi nodded.

Ada frowned and took her hands, clasping them tightly. 'No, I mean it.'

'I promise.' It seemed like it meant a lot to Ada for her to agree—but who was she likely to meet? She barely left the apartment and when she did, she only saw Isla.

SEVENTEEN

DECEMBER 1941

'Beck, Kohn, Binder, Heller—fall in.'

Harry exchanged glances with his friends, but they looked as bewildered as he was. They stepped forward with the other men who'd been called forward.

'You boys wanted action. Your prayers have been answered,' Tanner said, holding papers in his hand.

'We're going to get a slice of the Nazis!' Taub poked Harry in the arm. 'Can't wait to visit the Berlin Zoo. Mutti used to take us there every spring when we were kids.'

Harry's heart raced as he focused eagerly on Tanner. The army had declared that they would join an elite fighting force. 'We're going into battle? Finally?' His voice brimmed with anticipation, and his whole body throbbed with the thrill of adventure.

'Not quite, Beck.' Sergeant Tanner refused to meet his gaze, his tone not quite managing to hide his frustration. 'We're being sent to London. The local forces need help to clear out the rubble from the bombings. You'll have Nazis overhead but I'm glad to say not on the ground.' His words trailed off, letting reality settle around them like a thick fog.

Groans arose to this news. Harry stayed silent, clenching his fists. How much longer would it be before they could see action?

Tanner coughed, effectively silencing the murmurs of dissent. 'Lads, I know how bad you want to get into the war, but orders are orders. Get moving.'

Harry bit back his reply. They all knew the damage the Blitz had caused and, once again, the bombers were back in a bid to destroy London. Maybe this was a way of showing they were prepared to do almost anything to prove their loyalty. Picking up the king's shilling and swearing allegiance to the crown wasn't enough.

Later, when they were packing, Leo picked a fight with Noah over his chumash. 'Give it here—you must have read it cover to cover already.'

'You'll ruin it. Give it back. Stop it.' Noah's voice trembled. Taub and Harry exchanged a look. Harry wondered if he should intervene or let Noah stand up for himself for once. Tensions had been rising between the non-religious Leo, who blamed God for what was happening to the Jews and Noah, who'd turned to his religion for comfort. The combination of bad weather, lack of information about when they might be moving to a more active role in the fight against Hitler, being stuck in a canvas tent or out digging trenches leading to nowhere had put everyone in a bad mood.

But Harry was shocked to see Noah now lash out, his left hook connecting with Leo's cheek, as he shouted, 'You shouldn't touch it. Your hands are filthy. It's all I have left of them.'

Leo bit his lip, shaking his head a little as he seemed to realize what he'd done. He bent down and, picking the book off the floor, rubbed it with his uniform jacket before handing it back. 'Sorry, Noah. I shouldn't have teased you. It's not damaged, is it?'

Noah shook his head, obviously not trusting his ability to speak.

Before Harry could move, Taub, playing peacemaker as usual, stepped towards them. 'Come on, you two. The bus isn't going to wait for us. London, here we come.'

Taub jollied them along and soon their meagre belongings were packed and the tent dismantled.

The journey took just under seven hours. For the first couple they sang songs, and traded jokes and insults to pass the time. Harry stared out the window, wondering if this was a test. Would the army consider transferring them to active duties if they worked hard? Or would they be sent back to Devon digging ditches, or other so called 'essential' work?

As the bus slowly cruised into London, an eerie silence befell the group. Everywhere they looked they saw destruction —some places were nothing more than piles of rubble, as if a giant had scooped up buildings in one hand and pulverized them in the other. Other sights were even worse: dwellings cut in two, as if someone had taken a butcher's knife and viciously hacked them apart. What had happened to the families who had once lived there.

Harry had never explored London: the *Kindertransport* train had dropped them at Liverpool Station, and from there he had taken the underground to Waterloo and from there a train to Chertsey. His stomach clenched: *what if the raids reached Abbeydale?* The sandbags he had filled and the protections he'd put on the windows many moons ago would be totally inadequate in the wake of this level of destruction.

The bus stopped outside a community centre, their new home for the foreseeable future. They made their way inside, passing crowds of civilians covered in dust, some sporting black eyes, others cuts and bruises; mothers sitting on the floor surrounded by their children. Harry glanced over at Taub, seeing a reflection of his anger on his friend's face.

'Innocents. Women and children. This is not war.'

Harry agreed, but he wasn't surprised. He had survived Dachau, seen the worst of what the Nazis could do.

He threw his bag down with the others'. 'Where do you want us, Sergeant?'

'You should get something to eat and drink first.'

Harry shook his head. 'I want to get started now. These people need our help.'

The other boys nodded in agreement and fell in behind Harry, who caught the quick glance of approval the sergeant threw in his direction.

The air raid sirens rang every night, as Harry and his friends cleared the rubble from the bombs. No shelters for them. They were there to rescue civilians from bombed-out buildings. The carnage took some getting used to, even to those like Harry who'd survived Dachau and other concentration camps.

Their friendship strengthened over the endless days and nights. They worked, slept a little, ate less and then went back to work again.

'Look at that. The whole house has come down. No way anyone survived that.' Taub rubbed his eyes as if to dislodge some grit, but Harry knew his friend was struggling.

The moonlight glinted off something in the garden.

'Taub, look, the Anderson is intact.' Leo pointed to the half-buried corrugated iron structure. Some wooden beams and other rubble from the house had fallen blocking the exit.

'Maybe the family got to it in time.' Leo set off at a run with Harry, Taub and Noah following behind.

'We're coming! Stay where you are! We will get you out in an hour or minute.' Noah was still working on his English and regularly got his words backward. Usually Harry laughed, but not tonight: his mind was focused solely on how they could clear a route to the shelter.

Harry lifted a wooden beam that was three feet wide and half a dozen feet long. 'Leo, grab the end of it.' Leo took up one end and Harry took the other. They heaved it over and dropped it where Noah pointed, next to a pile of rubble. They repeated the process, dividing their workload so they could move twice as fast. Working as a team, they cleared a path to the Anderson shelter with Noah getting to the door first.

He wrenched it open, and Harry peered over his shoulder. By the light of his torch beam, he could see the children lying asleep in their makeshift beds, their mother holding her baby in her arms. Why didn't they move? Had the blast hurt their ears? Turned them deaf? Then the horror gradually sank in, despite Harry not wanting to believe his eyes. He watched Noah shake each child, heard him praying, 'Wake up, little ones. It's safe now. You can... wake up. Dear God, please...' Noah moved from one child to the next, before letting out a string of curses all aimed at the *Luftwaffe* above them.

Harry couldn't move. Noah never cursed.

Taub called to them, 'What's taking so long? Bring them out.'

Harry rubbed his face in his sleeve before turning to Taub, tears marking a trail down his filthy face. 'They're gone. We were too late.'

Their nails were torn, their fingers and hands in ribbons from tearing through the bricks and rubble to get to the shelter. But despite their best efforts, all the inhabitants were dead.

Noah went back and forth, taking care to carry each child as if it were injured not dead. Harry stepped forward to help but Noah stopped him. 'Let me, please.'

Harry didn't argue, sensing this was something Noah had to do. He watched as his friend laid the children out at the side of the road. Leo and Taub carried the young mother, still clasping her baby to her breast, and laid her beside her other children. They covered their bodies with a blanket, awaiting the ambulance crews who'd collect them.

Leo took cigarettes out of his pocket but before he could light up, Harry grabbed his arm. 'The gas mains could be cracked. You risk blowing us all up.'

'Don't we deserve that?'

Shocked, Harry waited for an explanation.

'It was Germans who did this, maybe friends of ours from school.'

Taub spat on the ground. 'We have no friends in the *Luftwaffe* or any other German service. Remember that.'

Harry watched Noah, wondering how his faith would survive after this. Noah took a moment, muttering a prayer under his breath.

The ambulance driver pulled up and started to remove the bodies.

'*Nein, moment bitte.*' Taub protested in German. '*Lass ihn das Gebet beenden.*' He seemed to have lost the ability to speak English as he asked the Englishman to wait for Noah to finish the prayer.

The ambulance driver, startled at the foreign language, took a step toward Noah, his hands turned into fists.

'Please wait.' Harry spoke as he stepped between the driver and Noah. 'We're part of the Pioneer Corps on clean-up duty. He was the first on the scene. It's important to him.'

The ambulance driver shrugged his shoulders and turned to go back to the vehicle but not before the moonlight picked up the glistening tears running down his face.

The man wasn't indifferent but trying to hide his grief. Harry pretended not to have noticed. Then a loud shout caught his attention.

An older woman appeared from a house, which looked undamaged, further up the street. She carried a large handbag and was making her way towards Noah, a furious expression on her face. 'Praying! That's rich when it's your lot that are bombing us to bits! You should all be locked up, preferably on a ship that's torpedoed.'

Harry gasped at the reference to the SS *Arandora Star*, the ship he and his friend, Joseph, had narrowly avoided travelling on that had sunk off the coast of Ireland.

Noah took a step back from the ranting woman, her hair grey—with age or dust, it was impossible to say. He stood motionless as she lifted her handbag and belted him with it.

Harry moved slowly, wanting to protect Noah while not adding to the older woman's distress. Dust and debris had covered their British uniforms. 'Please stop. Yes, we're Germans, but we're part of the British army. The Nazis killed his family for being Jewish. He's... we are all Jewish refugees and hate Hitler as much as you do.'

The woman's face caved as she realized what Harry was saying. Next, she was hugging Noah, begging forgiveness.

Noah stayed standing, his hands by his side, as she wrapped her arms about him, saying in Yiddish how sorry she was. Noah's eyes filled with tears as he replied in Yiddish, over and over how sorry he was too. 'They killed my family too. Papa, Mutti and my sisters. All dead. Like these children. *Mein Gott.*' Noah's voice trembled as his body shook.

The ambulance man, with help from Leo and Taub, loaded the bodies into the back. Once the ambulance had left, there was nothing for the men to do. They'd been working straight through the last eighteen hours. Taub gathered some of their tools, it was time to get back to base—but first they had to get the woman to safety.

'I'll take care of these; you see to the woman,' he said to Harry. 'Your English is better than Noah's or Leo's.' Taub ran a hand through his hair. 'I thought it might get easier, you know. After all the sights we've seen. But it only gets worse.'

Harry knew what he meant but there wasn't anything he could say to make his friend feel better. He moved forward, seeing Noah swaying slightly, not making any effort to rub the tears from his face. He was going into shock. 'Leo, look after him before he falls over.'

Then he turned to the lady. 'Let me escort you to the town shelter. There are some ladies there who will give you a hot drink. It's too dangerous for you to go back into your house and turn on the gas. A spark could be dangerous.' The woman hesitated so Harry added, 'Maybe you can find some of your friends.'

The woman linked arms with Harry, still muttering about her murdered friends. She clutched her handbag with her spare hand. When he looked up, Taub was walking in the direction of the bus stop, in a world of his own. It was unusual for him not to look out for his friends, but on seeing Taub's shoulders shake, Harry guessed he didn't want the others to see him losing control.

Harry took a deep breath before he caught Leo's gaze. 'I'll take her down there and stay with her until someone she knows turns up. You head back and tell the sergeant where I am.'

Noah still hadn't moved. Leo put his arm around Noah's shoulders and led him in the direction of the bus stop. Buses still ran despite the damage inflicted. Another sign the British would never give up.

Harry led the woman down the street, while his friends took a bus back to their barracks.

'Please tell your friend, I am so sorry. It's just that Beatrice and her young family were good friends of mine. They didn't deserve that. She'd been down the country, you know, when the war first started but missed her little house. The tidiest house on the street it was, despite her having four children and the baby.' The woman angrily brushed the tears from her eyes. 'What did those poor children do to anyone, would you tell me?'

Harry let her rant. It was better than her going into shock. He found the shelter and passed the old woman into the hands of the female volunteers. He needed to get back to his bed, his whole body aching from eighteen hours of digging and fighting fires.

He couldn't find a bus. It took forever to walk back to their barracks but when he got there, he wished he hadn't.

Sergeant Tanner waited for him, his face devoid of colour. 'Where the heck have you been?'

'Sorry, sir, but I had to escort a civilian to the shelter. Her friends were killed and she wasn't in... I told Binder and Heller to tell you.'

'Binder, Heller and Kohn are dead.'

Harry staggered back against the wall. 'Dead, sir?'

'A bomb hit the bus they were on. Another lad was with them but I don't know his name or his unit.' The gruffness of his tone suggested the sergeant wasn't immune to the death of his men.

Harry closed his eyes, seeing Noah standing over the children, praying, and Taub and Leo carrying the mother out of the debris. *Why?*

'They'll be buried tomorrow, in East Ham Jewish Cemetery. The local rabbi has agreed to conduct the service. You and I will attend and then we are off to another assignment. You best get some rest.'

'Yes, sir.' Harry muttered the required response and headed to his bed, his mind working overtime. If he hadn't gone with the lady he would have died on the bus too. He hadn't fought this hard to die without avenging what had happened to his father, his family and his friends. He would get overseas if it was the last thing he did.

Now he owed it to Noah and the others too.

After the funeral, Harry approached his sergeant. 'Please, sir, help me get transferred to active service. I want, I *need* to strike back at the Nazis.' Harry ran a hand through his hair: even speaking about his friends was difficult. 'Taub mentioned a private, a man by the name of Hartmann, some time back. He was looking for men. I told Taub I wasn't interested in a suicide mission. I was a fool. Staying here in the Pioneer Corps didn't keep my friends safe, did it?'

Sergeant Tanner studied him for a few minutes, the silence between them growing tenser with every second. 'I've heard of Hartman. He's looking for German speakers. I don't know what the job involves but I can guess. Are you certain this is what you want?'

'Yes sir, thank you, sir.' He was going to make someone pay for this; not just for the children and their mother but his friends. He'd get payback for them and their families. For Noah's sister.

He'd get to Berlin, find Leo's twin sister and tell her what a hero her brother was.

EIGHTEEN

JANUARY 1942

Trudi opened the apartment door expecting to see Ursula, the orphan who worked for Renata at the door. Her heart pounded when she saw who it was.

'Isla. Come in, please.' She held the door open, looking around to check nobody was watching.

Isla gave her a quick hug before moving inside to the living room. Trudi moved the dress she had been working on, glancing at the bedroom door to check it was closed. She hadn't told Isla about Ada living with her.

'I can't stay. There's been trouble.'

'You?'

'No, I'm safe for now, at least. Wilhelm has been posted to France and has ordered me to go with him. It's for my own good. He believes I'm overtired and it's true, Trudi. I'm not sleeping. I feel guilty about not doing more to help and at the same time, I'm looking over my shoulder in case someone is following me. When I do sleep, I have nightmares about being caught. I'm sorry, but we shouldn't be gone for longer than a couple of weeks. I wanted to say goodbye for now and to give you some money. I'm sorry it's not more but the news was unexpected.'

Trudi wanted to interrupt, to tell her friend to slow down and take a breath. She had never seen Isla ruffled before.

'That's not the only reason I'm here. You know Chana and Leopold Arkin? Her husband, he was awarded the Iron Cross.'

'Of course, Chana is my sister-in-law. Leopold got the Iron Cross for bravery in France during the last war. Leopold's so proud of that medal. We used to make fun of him—Ari teased him he would rub a hole in the metal polishing it so much. But now it's his protection.' Her voice trailed off as the woman's expression grew more serious.

'Not anymore. There was trouble earlier today. He's in a bad way, likely to die.'

Shocked, it took Trudi a few seconds to find her voice. 'What?' Trudi modified her tone—she didn't want Ada to rush out of the bedroom. 'But I heard they had a powerful protector, a member of the Nazi party who moved into their house but allowed them to stay in the old maid's apartment... Where is he?'

'They did, but General Astel died at the Russian front. The Gestapo didn't waste any time kicking the Arkins out of their lovely home. Frankly, it's amazing they were allowed to stay in it so long, but then Astel was said to have Hitler's ear. A neighbour took him to the Jewish hospital. I only happened to hear by chance from my contacts.'

Trudi knew her friend was involved in some sort of resistance but had never asked any questions. She held her breath as Isla continued. 'His wife is distraught. She doesn't seem to have any family or close friends.' The countess rapped her fingers on the table. 'If I had any guts, I would have gone and taken her into my home, the poor woman. But my husband, his position, I just...'

'I understand. Thank you for letting me know. I'll go to her. I thought the Iron Cross would save him.'

But Isla continued speaking as if Trudi hadn't said anything. She was really rattled. 'I can't take you there, either. Our driver was replaced, and I don't trust the new one not to say anything. I told him I was collecting a dress from a seamstress. I can tell him it wasn't ready.'

'I have a dress ready to go back to Renata. I could wrap that up for you.'

'I'll carry it on the hanger. That should put his suspicions to rest. I wish I could stay but I must get back. Be careful, Trudi—things are getting worse.' Isla hugged her, her voice choking. 'I don't know when I will see you again. Be careful.'

Trudi didn't escort her friend out but stayed standing at the table until she heard the car drive away.

The door to the bedroom opened and Ada took her by the arm and forced her into a seat. 'You look like you saw a ghost. What is it? I couldn't hear everything but I know something bad happened.'

'I must go to the Jewish hospital. Chana is there. Her husband was injured. Badly.' Trudi put her hand to her mouth before looking Ada in the eye. 'I thought he was untouchable.'

Ada shook her head. 'Nobody is. Not while that man is in power. What will you do?'

'I have to bring them to live here if Leopold is well enough to leave the hospital. There is nowhere else.'

Ada paled, her voice shaking. 'Of course. They are family. I will leave.'

'What? No. This is your home. We will share. It's going to be a squeeze, but we will have to make it work.'

How would they do that when Isla was leaving? It was her money and food parcels that had stretched the pittance she earned working for Renata and the rations. With another two mouths to feed... But what was the alternative? She couldn't turn her back on Ari's family.

Trudi dreaded what she would find when she got to the hospital. She greeted a few of the staff and some of the patients as she searched for Chana and Leopold.

She found Chana sitting by herself, oblivious to what was going on around her. A doctor pulled Trudi aside. 'Her husband died. Kicked to death in front of her. She's deeply shocked. They took her home too, so she's got nowhere to go.'

'Yes, she does. She can come home with me.' Trudi smiled her thanks to the doctor before sitting down beside Chana.

The woman didn't look up, but stayed staring at her wedding band that she was twisting around her finger.

'I'm so sorry about your husband.'

'Herr Astel promised to look after us. He said we were safe. Leopold saved his life in the last war. It was his way of paying him back. They said...' Chana couldn't get any more words out.

Trudi held her hand, trying to think of something to say—but what? She pictured Ari. She knew her husband had suffered a similar fate, but at least she hadn't had to watch. Poor Chana: despite her aloofness and attitude, she'd loved Leopold. Trudi could see the former lawyer, sitting back in his chair as if it were a throne, smoking a cigar. He'd believed in justice, in the law. He was German first, not Jewish. A true believer in the German people, convinced they would see Hitler and his gang for what they were.

'Chana, come on. We need to get home by curfew.'

'I don't have a home. That's why they killed Leopold. They came today to tell us we had to move. Leopold argued. He showed them the letter from Herr Astel, his commander in the last war and a fellow lawyer, which gave us his protection. They grabbed it and tore it to pieces, laughing. They were laughing even as they kicked him. I begged him to just walk away but he kept insisting the law was on his side. What law?' Chana muttered to herself, repeating the same story.

Trudi pulled her to her feet. They couldn't stay at the hospital. Even now, Chana's name was probably on some list. Her husband wasn't just her hero, but her protector. Thanks to his efforts, Chana hadn't had to work in the factories or do any form of slave labour.

'Chana, we must go now. Put my coat around your shoulders. That's right. Now follow me.'

'But Leopold... I have to arrange his funeral.'

There'd be no funeral, but Trudi didn't want to break that news now. 'We'll talk about that when we get home.'

She ushered the protesting woman out of the door of the hospital and down the street, in the direction of her small apartment. They couldn't risk taking public transport so would have to walk.

The only sound was the click of their heels on the pavement and Chana's occasional sob. Trudi glanced around furtively, hoping nobody would stop them and ask for papers. Or worse, grab them and throw them into the back of a truck.

It took two hours to get home, and by that time they were both exhausted. Chana glanced around the apartment Trudi lived in, a pinched expression on her face. 'It's so small.'

Ada walked out of the bedroom at that moment, her face ashen. She gave Trudi a questioning look and Trudi shook her head. Ada moved closer. 'Chana, I'm so sorry for your loss.'

Chana burst into tears and while Ada consoled her, Trudi made them a hot drink of boiled water flavoured with some ersatz coffee. She handed a cup to Chana. 'Makes it easier to keep warm. You can share the bedroom with Ada, and I'll sleep here on the couch. You shouldn't go outside, not until we sort out the proper papers.'

What was she talking about? She couldn't afford to register Chana at her address any more than she could register Ada—it would be like putting out a red flag for the Gestapo.

How was she going to manage without Isla's help?

She'd worry about that in the morning. For now, she had to see to her guests.

Chana wrapped both hands around her cup, seeking warmth from the hot liquid. 'I've lost everything. Not just my husband, but my home, my clothes. All of it gone.'

Trudi knew now wasn't the time to say she knew—she had lost everything too. 'You are welcome to live here, Chana, at least for the moment.'

Chana didn't register her comments. Trudi led her to the bedroom and left her to sleep.

For the first couple of days, Chana didn't leave the bedroom. Trudi guessed it was shock and, despite feeling guilty, she was grateful.

The apartment had been cosy with just her and Ada sharing, their warm friendship helping them to negotiate the small space. But Chana was very different from Ada. She criticized everything, from the food Ada prepared to the fact she had to disappear when Ursula came to drop off and collect the dresses for Renata.

'Chana, please. We can't afford for Ursula or anyone else to know there is more than one person living here. You must stay out of sight.'

'I have a headache. You make so much noise with that machine and Ada... She snores so loudly it's a wonder they don't believe you have a full garrison of soldiers living here.'

Ada flushed but remained quiet, having learned that was the best way to deal with Chana's outbursts.

'I have to sew, or we don't eat. Now, please lower your voice and go back into the bedroom. She will be here any minute.'

Chana rolled her eyes but retreated. Ada went to follow but turned to whisper to Trudi, 'Why don't you ask Ursula if Renata has any more finishing work you could help with. I'm good at the buttonholes and half decent with the seams, now that you have taught me so well.'

Trudi rubbed her arm in thanks. She was very fond of Ada. She smiled, thinking it was funny how she had felt intimidated by her when they'd first met, all those years ago. 'I'll ask.'

She watched as Ada retreated to the bedroom and closed the door softly behind her. Trudi sat at the table waiting for Ursula. She was late. She stood up and went to the window to check outside, but there was no sign. She paced up and down the kitchen floor—what if something had happened? Maybe now that Isla was gone Renata didn't want to use her anymore. Back and forth she went, watching the seconds pass on the clock—until the knock almost made her jump out of her skin.

She rushed to open the door. 'You're late. I was worried.'

'Why?' Ursula looked at her curiously.

Trudi got a grip of herself. 'I thought you might have had an accident or something.'

The girl shrugged. 'No, I was just chatting to a soldier. He was handsome and said I was pretty. He's taking me to the cinema later.'

Sweat trickled down Trudi's back but her voice remained calm. 'How wonderful. Enjoy it. Did Renata say when she wants these back?'

'Tuesday.'

'Does she have any more work for me? I could do with some extra money. For food and that,' Trudi babbled.

'I'll ask her. Are these to go back?' The girl picked up the bundle just as Chana, in the next room, coughed. 'What was that?' She looked at the bedroom door suspiciously.

'My neighbours upstairs. Their little one has a bad chest infection. The walls are so thin, you'd think they were made of paper. You should get going so you can get ready for your date.'

That was enough to distract the young girl. She smiled and headed out the door, leaving Trudi to lean against it once it had closed, thinking her legs wouldn't support her.

NINETEEN

MARCH 1942

Trudi walked along the street, keeping her eyes down. She couldn't let the people around her read her thoughts, and she wasn't a good enough actress to hide her anger. They were starving. One Jewish ration card didn't provide enough food for three people, and she had no money to buy extra food on the black market. She could understand why there were so many suicides in the Jewish community: between the rumours about increased transports and the lack of food, it wasn't easy to keep on living, fighting for survival. Goebbels wasn't happy though: he was pushing for a Jew-free Berlin. What would that mean for her, Ada, Chana and the rest of her friends?

'Trudi! Did you not hear me calling you?'

Trudi whirled around. She couldn't believe her eyes. 'Isla! You're back. You look fantastic.'

She wasn't just flattering her friend, as Isla looked amazing. Her skin was glowing with health, she was a good weight especially compared to the skinny Berliners, and her eyes were shining.

'Come with me. I'm so happy I caught up with you. I didn't want to call to your home.' She walked alongside Trudi, linking arms and whispering, 'You're not wearing your star. Have you got false papers?'

Trudi shook her head, not trusting her voice to behave. After doing her shopping, she'd ditched the star so she could walk unmolested through the Tiergarten. The flowers weren't in blossom but it was still a lovely walk and it gave her some space away from Chana and Ada's constant bickering.

'We need to fix that as soon as possible. I admire your courage, but this is foolish. There are too many checks these days.'

Trudi shrugged. 'I had to come out and buy food. We... I mean I get hungry.'

She hoped her friend hadn't notice the slip but Isla grasped her arm: 'You took Chana to your house? I know I asked you to help her but what were you thinking? How are you surviving? No wonder you look so thin. I know food has been in short supply here in Berlin, but you are positively skeletal.'

Trudi didn't confirm or deny what Isla said. It was difficult for everyone to get food in Berlin, not just the Jews. She'd heard housewives complaining, joking in whispers that the army must be marching on an empty stomach. You never knew who was watching and waiting to report the slightest breach of the rules. The Gestapo paid informants to tell on their neighbours for all sorts of crimes, even petty ones such as not returning the Hitler salute.

'I want you to meet some people. You'll like them. They are good friends of mine. Come on. I've left the driver and car at home.'

Isla pulled her toward a tram and together they got on. A man stood and let them sit down. Trudi's heart hammered but there was no point in giving in to fear now. If anyone got on and checked papers, she'd pretend she was robbed. She inched away from Isla hoping that if they were stopped, she'd be able to pretend she didn't know her. But Isla must have read her thoughts as she linked arms with her once more, talking loudly about France and how fabulous it was to watch the wonderful German soldiers keep the French in line. By doing so, the people around them knew Isla must be well connected; her clothes and bearing would have already told them she was wealthy. Ordinary people didn't travel to Paris.

The crowd around them nodded in agreement. Trudi thought she would be sick, but Isla seemed totally unflappable.

They changed trams and got off in the Wilmersdorf district, walking down the tree-lined, upmarket residential avenue with the beautiful late nineteeth-century apartment buildings. It was like she had gone back in time, to the days when Ari and his wife had entertained, and she'd worked as their nanny.

Trudi assumed that Isla's friends lived in one of the residential buildings, and couldn't believe it when Isla took her arm and pulled her inside the Swedish Church.

'God bless me for all the lies I told. France was amazing, the buildings in Paris are so beautiful, as are the French stores. But it was sickening to see our soldiers parade around as if they owned the place. You should see the Parisian women, Trudi— they made me proud. Most of them anyway.' Isla's lips curled in distaste for a second before she brightened again. 'They dress in their best, always wearing a hat as if to prove their country is occupied but they are not beaten. This despite their wooden-soled shoes making a shocking racket walking down the street. I wanted to shout bravo so many times. Instead, I had to fawn over Wilhelm's colleagues. Oh, the number of Nazis who kissed my hand—there isn't enough soap in the whole of Europe to get it clean.'

Trudi gave a small smile at this; she didn't know if Isla knew just how hard it was to find soap in Berlin these days—almost as difficult as finding food—but she let her friend talk.

Isla wittered on as they walked around the church, and Trudi wondered what they were doing there. Then Isla led her to a side entrance. 'Don't be afraid. We are with friends,' Isla said, as Trudi removed her hat and followed her through the door and up some stairs to a back office.

Isla knocked softly and then entered a large room, full of natural light from its tall, narrow windows, the upper walls painted in a light, neutral beige colour with wood panelling adorning the lower parts, combining to provide a sense of warmth.

Trudi saw a desk that held a typewriter, paper and ink-well, with several pens scattered across it. Behind the desk she spotted a simple framed religious picture. She noted the absence of the obligatory Hitler picture and Nazi flags.

A middle-aged man sitting on a comfortable-looking chair stood up in greeting.

'Pastor Forell, I'm back, and I brought a friend. Trudi, this is Pastor Birger Forell.' She turned to smile at a couple seated on a small couch at the side of the room. 'And Eric Perwe and his lovely wife, Martha. They are heavily involved in the resistance.'

Pastor Forell, a warm welcoming expression on his face, his eyes full of empathy, stepped out from behind the desk. 'Isla! Don't tell the world.' He gave Trudi a gentle smile before saying, 'We merely help those who need assistance, as should every Christian. Welcome.'

Trudi stood, her hands gripping the side of her hat. Did this man know she was Jewish? Why had Isla brought her? Her eyes darted around the rest of the room, taking in the bookshelf with the religious texts, reference books and hymnals. To her right stood a large round table. A faded wool rug covered most of the wooden floor.

Someone came in the door behind her, causing her to jump. She turned to see a wide smile on the woman's face, her eyes full of laughter and joy. Trudi inhaled. She couldn't remember seeing someone look this happy in a very long time.

'Sister Vide. How are you? I brought you a present.' Isla fished in her bag and handed over a small package.

Sister Vide clapped her hands like a child. 'Pralines! Isla, you're the best.' She hugged Isla. 'Have one, please.' She held out the bag to Trudi, who couldn't resist. She popped the praline into her mouth and almost groaned aloud as it dissolved on her tongue, it was so good.

Isla set her bag on the round wooden table. 'I have some stockings for you, Martha. Cigarettes and cigars for you, Eric, to distribute as you see fit.'

'And for me?'

Trudi gasped as a tall, dark-haired man slipped inside the room and swept Isla off her feet in a hug.

'Jakob, put me down. You're making me dizzy.' Isla laughed as she protested.

As he set Isla down Trudi locked eyes with the stranger—and instantly felt like she'd known him all her life. But as soon as the thought came to her she told herself it was silly.

Isla caught the look. 'Jakob, meet my friend, Trudi. She's amazing, a true hero. The risks she runs every day to look after her friends, and yet she manages to maintain a completely unflustered appearance.'

Trudi blushed at the introduction, knowing it for a lie. She'd been terrified on the journey there. She looked at Jakob, taking in his strong jawline, high cheekbones, youthful skin, guessing he must be in his twenties. His eyes held a determined and intense expression that hinted at a maturity older than his natural years.

Jakob took her hand and she gasped softly as electricity seemed to flow between them. Her pulse raced as their eyes locked once more. He'd felt the same connection, she knew it. She'd never had this reaction to any man before.

'Jakob, Trudi needs papers. She's taking too much of a risk not wearing the star with her identification papers in her bag. Can you sort them out?'

Jakob's eyes widened. 'You're Jewish?'

'Yes. You?'

'My father is... was. My mother is a Christian.'

Despite the room being filled with other people, it was as if they were alone. She couldn't tear her gaze away from him, and it seemed he was similarly affected.

'I'm on my way to collect some other papers. Shall we go now?'

Trudi glanced at Isla for permission. Isla shook her head. 'Wait and have a cup of coffee first—the real stuff. I brought it back from France. I have some news. I want Trudi to get to know Pastor Forell, Eric, Martha and Sister Vide. She will be an asset to our group, and I believe she has some friends who will need our help.'

Everyone but Sister Vide and Martha sat down. Sister Vide put her hand to heart, smiling at them all. 'This is such a treat, I can't remember the last time I tasted real coffee. Martha, can you help me, please?' Sister Vide led the way out of the room; Martha, after a glance at her husband, following behind.

'So how was your time in France? Meet anyone interesting?' The pastor's eyes twinkled.

Isla responded, a furious expression on her face. 'You should see them. All those Nazis and their little pets. They eat and drink so much, it's a wonder they aren't all the size of Goering. And the way they treat the French! The Führer said he wanted the army to be on their best behaviour and the ordinary *Wehrmacht* soldiers seem to be following that order. But the SS...' Isla's lip curled in distaste.

'They've been making their feelings known here, as well.'

Trudi noticed the pastor's casual comment raised the tension in the room.

'What do you mean?' Isla reached out her hand and put it on his arm. 'Are you in danger? They can't touch you, though. You're protected with your Swedish passport.'

Jakob answered. 'That's all that has saved him. If he were a German, he'd have been shipped off long ago.'

'I believe I will be recalled soon. Our friends are putting pressure on the Swedish authorities over my continued outspoken resistance.' He shrugged. 'They don't like what I say about them.'

'You do more than speak. Trudi, this man, these people, have been helping Jews and other people persecuted by the Nazis. They have arranged safe houses, false papers, food parcels and even escape routes.'

Pastor Forell gripped Isla's hand. 'Without the help of you and your kind, Isla, we wouldn't have been able to achieve half of what we have done. Which isn't enough. Not when people are being transported in freight cars to the East.'

Martha and Sister Vide reappeared, the latter carrying a tray heaped with china cups. Martha held the coffeepot, her eyes going straight to her husband, her face lit up with a special glow. The rich aroma of real coffee distracted Trudi, making her mouth water.

There was silence while Martha poured for everyone and then the conversation started again in earnest.

'I'm glad you are back, Isla—the food situation has deteriorated. If you were to believe the gossip, it would appear there isn't any hens, sheep or cows left in Germany, at least not in Berlin. We are hard pressed to feed those we are sheltering, both here and out in the community. Martha, Sister Vide and many of the women have been supplementing our stores with food grown in window boxes or in the garden. The hens lay eggs, but we had to bring them indoors. It used to be that the fox was the enemy but now it's our neighbours. Unless you have a contact with the storekeepers it is impossible to find sufficient food to keep our regular guests, never mind our illegal ones. I don't know what to do.' The pastor wiped a hand across his furrowed brow, the deep black circles under his eyes proof he was losing sleep.

'It isn't just food, but fabric too.' Trudi blushed as everyone turned to look at her. 'I've been working for a friend of Isla's. A while ago, I was sewing new dresses but now most of my work is on alterations, and this lady is, well...' Trudi's face grew hotter: she couldn't talk about a Nazi's mistress in a church. 'She's well connected.'

Isla sipped her coffee, before offering her cigarettes around, saying, 'She shouldn't have any problem laying her hands on anything. The soldiers we met in Paris, some of those who were more outspoken told us this isn't just a problem in Berlin. All over Germany people are struggling, although those with access to farms are doing better.' Isla lit up a cigarette. 'Goering doesn't seem to be on rations. If anything, that man is getting fatter by the day.'

'Isla, don't be uncharitable.' The gentle reproof came from Sister Vide. She caught Trudi looking at her. 'I don't like the man or his politics, but it is not our place to cast judgement.'

Trudi didn't comment but glanced down at her hands. She would quite happily feed Goering and his friends to the lions in Berlin Zoo, but she guessed that might not be an altogether Christian sentiment. Her eyes caught Jakob and from his look, it was as if he could read her thoughts. He gave her a slight nod and a bigger smile.

'The Nazis and their women can afford to eat in restaurants. Those with money will always have access to food.' Isla ground out her cigarette in the ashtray. 'For the rest of Berlin, they are forced to eat from the goulash cannons.'

Pastor Forell frowned, 'My dear Isla, those soup kitchens you dismiss so easily are lifesavers to some. But we are not here to argue. We just have to make what we have stretch further, and find new sources.'

'Try rabbits.' Trudi only realized she had spoken out loud when the room fell silent.

'Rabbits?' Sister Vide prompted.

'Yes. They breed quickly and can be used for their meat and their skin. I believe in some parts of Berlin they are very much in fashion.' Trudi wished she had stayed silent, her cheeks burning.

'That's an excellent suggestion, Trudi. Thank you.' Eric made a note.

The conversation went on for another while until Jakob stood up. 'I have to go. I have a meeting. Are you coming?'

This time Trudi didn't look at Isla but answered, 'Yes.'

They made their way out of the church in silence, walking back down the tree-lined street. Trudi tried to quell the nervous feeling in her stomach and stopped herself from checking whether anyone was staring at them. She felt naked without the star on her coat and being in an unfamiliar place. She glanced up and studied the man beside her. In contrast, he looked as if he had every right to be there.

He caught her looking at him and winked. Leaning in closer, he whispered, 'Being illegal suits you—brings a dash of colour to your cheeks!'

It seemed so natural for him to tease her and take her hand. He limped badly, and she wondered if this was his cover for not being in uniform, given his age. As they walked, he chatted naturally and told her funny stories, making her laugh. She guessed he was just trying to allay her nerves.

He really didn't seem to be worried about the risks they were taking. He may have forged papers but she only had her identity card—marking her out to be a Jew. She was breaking the law by not wearing the star and that was sufficient for a one-way trip to the East.

When they got on the tram, he paid for both their tickets. A woman gave him a funny look, and he complained loudly about the shrapnel in his leg and the difficulties the doctors were having to remove it. Trudi had to put a hand over her mouth to stop a nervous laugh when the same woman almost fell over herself thanking Jakob for his service to the Reich.

They changed trams and ended up in a working-class area of Berlin, the contrast between their current location and that of the Swedish church's evident by the overcrowded apartments lining both sides of the street. There were no trees, only peeling paint and dirty windows. But she noticed some blacked-out graffiti on the walls. She'd heard of people writing '1918' on walls as a reminder of the losses they'd endured in the last war.

Jakob led her into a bookstore and then out the back and down some steps, into what looked like a storage area. The men already there glanced up, their expressions turning from welcoming to wary when they saw Jakob wasn't alone.

'Gentlemen, this is Trudi Beck, a friend of the countess. She vouches for her and so do I.'

'Beck?' A man moved forward, his eyes scrutinizing her making her uncomfortable. She moved closer to Jakob.

She was the first to break the silence. 'Have we met before?'

'Not in person, but we have a mutual friend, Frau Dr Beck.'

Trudi was aware of Jakob tensing as the man used her correct name.

Trudi's blood chilled. *Who was he?* 'You knew my husband?'

'By reputation only. He was a good man. My name is Max Lang.' Trudi would have smiled at how inappropriate his name was. 'Lang' meant 'tall' and the man in front of her was short and stocky, with muscular shoulders—a worker, from the dirt ingrained in his hands and under his nails. She already felt she trusted him though: he looked her straight in the eyes. 'Gavriel sends his regards.'

Trudi put a hand to her chest, relief and curiosity fighting for dominance. 'You've spoken to him? How is he? Did he get out of France? Were you the person who sent me the packages?'

Max threw his hands in the air. 'So many questions! We should lend you out to the Gestapo. The last I heard he was still there but that was a long time ago. Yes, we sent the packages but at someone else's request. And, no, I don't have any more news.'

Trudi took the hint not to ask about Olga. She held out her hand. 'Thank you, Max. Ada, Gavriel's mother, was so worried.'

He shook her hand but didn't comment about Ada. Instead, he turned to Jakob. 'Those papers you wanted are over there. Money too, for the bribe. You need to see your friend tonight, as the shipment is due to leave in two days.'

Jakob nodded.

Max turned to Trudi. 'I have to get back now. It was nice to finally meet you. Gavriel said you were very brave and pretty. It seems he was right on both counts.'

A curly haired man blew smoke from his cigarette out the side of his mouth. 'Ah, she is a beauty, Jakob. I can see why your head was turned.' The man bowed and held out his hand to shake hers. 'Welcome to our little group. We are not all Jews— some of us are *Mischling*, others communists, some homosexual, but all have the same thing in common: a hatred for Hitler and his band of merry men.'

Amused, Trudi watched the man kiss her hand before Jakob pulled her over to the desk where a third man, with a nasty scar on his cheek, had resumed working.

The man stood up and bowed. 'Ernst Davidsohn, pleased to make your acquaintance. Now come and tell me what you think.'

Trudi watched as Ernst studied some authentic identity papers. He examined the stamp on the original photograph, before he picked up his tools: a magnifying glass and a fine Japanese brush. Using some watercolours, he mixed up the exact shade of purple to copy the eagle and swastika. He licked some blank paper, that he had cut from the margins at the side of an old newspaper, and pressed it down on the copy, creating a mirror image of the stamp. She held her breath as he pressed the damp newspaper onto the new photograph in the correct corner. Once dry, he fixed the new photo in place using the old eyelets of the identity papers.

'Nobody could guess that was a forgery. You are so clever.'

He beamed with pride.

They took her photograph, telling her the new papers would be ready in a few days.

Jakob insisted on escorting her home, keeping her amused with stories of his childhood. His eyes crinkled as he spoke about his father taking him for ice cream. 'The best place is on Olivaer Platz. You know it?'

She nodded, wanting him to keep talking. She liked the sound of his voice. All too soon, they were at her door. He refused to come inside her apartment. 'Goodbye, for now.' He hesitated before he added, 'Don't take any more risks. Isla will arrange to get the papers to you.' He took her hand, turning it over, and dropped a feather-light kiss on her wrist. 'I'd like to get to know you better, Frau Dr Beck but... I wouldn't want to disrespect Dr Beck's memory.'

Trudi felt an electric spark as his lips left her skin, and she wanted him to continue. She shook her head. 'Ari died in 1938. He was a good man...' Her words were stopped by a tugging feeling in her stomach, reminding her of how much she had loved Ari; she couldn't forget him so easily. 'But a friend told me I have to start living my life...'

She glanced up, paralyzed as their eyes locked. Again there

was a jolt of electricity from his intense desire that she'd never experienced before. He leaned in, his lips barely brushing against hers. Her heart raced and a warmth spread through her body. The faint scent of cloves hung in the air as he pulled back ever so slightly, leaving her wanting more.

TWENTY

MARCH 1942

'What is the matter with you, Trudi? You jump at every sound.' Chana remonstrated with her as they ate their evening meal.

Trudi tried to keep her composure, knowing Chana would be furious if she learned of Jakob's kiss. Even though Ari was gone, he had still been her husband, and Chana would never forgive her for being unfaithful. Was she wrong for wanting Jakob? She dreamed of him at night, reliving the kiss, wondering... She stood up and fetched a glass of water before retaking her seat.

She picked at her food. They'd agreed to make this meal the largest of the day so that they could sleep better: it was slightly easier to sleep when you weren't starving. Not that the rations were stretching far between the three of them.

Ada did the cooking; Chana would still burn water—if she could be bothered to try.

'Chana, leave her alone. Without her, think of where we would be.' Ada lifted the ladle. 'Have some more, Trudi. You need your strength, for your work.'

Trudi worked on her alterations, thankful that despite not

being able to give her a living wage, Renata's connections meant Trudi was exempt from working as a slave labourer.

The knock she was waiting for eventually came. Was it him? She ran a hand through her hair. Chana paled as Ada hurried to clear the evidence that more than one person was eating.

'Go to the bedroom. Go on, it's okay, I will see to it.' Trudi ushered the two women to the room. She didn't want Chana and Ada to see who it was. If it was Jakob, she mightn't be able to hide her attraction. If it were Isla, and Ada and Chana were captured at a future date, they mustn't be able to describe the countess. Or her, them.

It wasn't that she didn't trust her friends—she did—but the Gestapo had arrested over a thousand people in Berlin in the last couple of months. At least that was the latest rumour being discussed in whispers at the markets.

She waited for the bedroom door to close before she walked to the front door and opened it, but there was nobody there. Pushing down her disappointment, she saw a brown envelope on the floor. Looking around her, she scooped it up and closed the door.

Hands shaking, she opened it. It was her new papers and a note to meet for the best ice cream.

The bedroom door opened and Ada came out. 'Are you all right?'

Trudi quickly tucked the papers into her pocket and turned to her friend. 'It was just a note from a friend to tell me she'd meet me tomorrow. Hopefully she has some food to give us.'

Ada shook her head. 'I know you are up to something and don't want to tell us what it is. But be careful, Trudi. You have children who need you.'

'We both do. Don't worry. I know what I'm doing.'

Trudi hoped she did. Isla had proved to be trustworthy, and

it was obvious Jakob was involved with the same group Gavriel and Olga had been with.

But hadn't there been a traitor back in 1939? What if there still was?

'Trudi?' Ada's whisper broke through her thoughts. 'I just wanted to say thank you. For stopping me going to the collection centre. No matter what happens, you gave me a chance and for that I'm grateful. Don't listen to Chana, she's older and she's scared. Everything about her life before now was rules and regulations. She was married to a lawyer. She finds it harder than we do to be breaking the law.'

Trudi felt a wave of fury rise up in her at the mention of the restrictions, as if reminded of the reality of their lives and how they were treated. 'The law that means we must wear a brand and report for transport somewhere East where nobody hears from you again? We know what they did to Ari and your husband and even the way they treated the boys. We can't just blindly believe whatever the Nazis say, that it is for resettlement. What sort of place is it that they can't send letters from?' Trudi saw her own fears and horror reflected in the face of the other woman.

Ada pulled her into an embrace as the tears flowed down Trudi's face. 'You don't have to be the strong one all the time; let us help you carry this burden, Trudi. We're your friends, your family.'

TWENTY-ONE

Trudi ignored the butterflies in her stomach, her heart racing in competition as she walked to the ice cream store on Olivaer Platz. Would he kiss her again? Did she want him to? As she arrived she searched the crowd, hoping to spot him, but he wasn't there.

Despite the sharp breeze, Trudi's palms sweated as she looked around her, feeling everyone's eyes looking at her although she was dressed in her best clothes. Did they know she was Jewish? Did they care? She glanced at the clock then at her watch and at the clock once more. Her thoughts collided in her brain. Where was he? Had he been picked up? Had he decided not to come?

She squealed as someone grabbed her around the waist, turning to find him grinning at her mischievously, a glint in his eyes before her pulled her close, pressing his lips against her cheek, sending a wave of warmth through her body.

'Sorry, I got caught up. Were you waiting long?'

Trudi tried to be angry. How could he act so casually, as if they were a normal couple not two fugitives? But she couldn't as he gave her a long smouldering look. She should take a cold shower: the feelings this man generated in her body weren't normal. They'd only met once before yet he was treating her as his lover. She should be shocked, angry even—she was a well-brought-up woman—but the pull of attraction between them was too strong for sensible thoughts.

As if reading her mind, he leaned in and kissed her, gently, on the eyelids, the nose and then the lightest of kisses on the mouth before holding out his arm. 'I wish I could take you for ice cream, or better yet go dancing but we have work to do. Let's go.'

Once again, they caught several trams and ended up back at the Swedish Church.

This time Max was in the office, talking to Eric Perwe. There was no sign of the pastor. Trudi caught the tension on the men's faces. 'What is it? What's wrong?'

Max stubbed his cigarette out in the ashtray, the bleak look in his eyes frightening Trudi. 'Pastor Forell was invited to a meeting at Gestapo headquarters. He has yet to return.'

Trudi's legs buckled, and she grabbed for a chair. The Gestapo. The poor man. She had only met him once but she'd never forget the kindness that radiated from him. What would those animals do to him?

Jakob paced back and forth across the room, his agitation causing him to fidget with a loose thread on his sleeve. She wanted to comfort him, but how?

Max intervened. 'Sit down, Jakob. I can't think straight with you marching up and down.'

'The Gestapo will just threaten him and then release him. He'll be back, won't he?' Jakob addressed Max, but it was Eric who answered.

'Yes. Hopefully. But we've heard from headquarters. They want him back in Sweden. Seems they are getting too much heat from the Nazis.'

Jakob sat, his legs splayed, his face contorted in a mixture of frustration and anger. 'So, we've lost him. Who will replace him?'

Eric stood up, walking over to one of the windows. His shoulders slumped as if he carried the weight of the world on them. He stared at the view in silence, and the others exchanged glances before Eric turned to look at them.

'My wife and I have discussed this. She is adamant that we remain here and carry on Pastor Forell's legacy. God help us all,' he said, his voice barely above a whisper.

Jakob jumped up and clapped Eric on the back. 'We'll be fine. Kaufman has a huge network of contacts running from his church. He said...'

Max roared, causing Trudi to jump in surprise. 'I told you to stay away from Franz Kaufman and his group! Don't get me wrong, Franz is a brave man but he believes everyone has a heart. A soul. A conscience. He's the male version of Sister Vide.'

Jakob's face flushed. 'He has the connections we need. Forgers, black marketeers and others. He has a contact who goes around to Jewish houses after they have been sealed and liberates the contents, which he sells down the markets. You have no idea how much demand there is for electrical irons or pots and pans. Even bedding. This guy can sell anything. If you stood too close to him for long enough, he'd sell the suit of clothes from your back.'

Trudi couldn't believe her ears. Was Jakob saying it was right to sell the property of those who were deported?

Jakob's nostrils flared as he stared at Max.

Seeing her face, Jakob continued: 'We all know the Gestapo seals the property when the Jews are rounded up and then, a few days later, they send their goons around. They pocket anything of value before releasing the apartment to a *good* German family.' His tone softened, becoming more persuasive. 'Kaufman's man uses the money he generates to help other

Jews. He buys food for the patients in the Jewish hospital, has been known to provide money for bribes where needed—never mind the funds a network like Kaufman's costs to run.'

Trudi relaxed a little: Jakob was on their side. How could she doubt his integrity? *Because you don't know him.* She pushed aside the voice, which sounded like Chana, inside her head.

'Jakob, I said no.' Max glared at Jakob, his hand clenched. 'It's too dangerous. Kaufmann has cast his net too wide, he tries to help everyone.'

Jakob opened his mouth to respond but Max pressed on. 'How many men have the Confessing Church already lost to the camps? Their services are full of informants. I heard one of their pastors even thanked the Gestapo for being so prompt in attending so his service could start on time.' Max rapped his fingers on the table. 'And Kaufman is Jewish.'

'He converted.' Jakob's retort had less fire than his previous outburst. Was he listening to Max?

'That won't save him. Stay away from him. Or leave us and join him. It's your choice.'

Feeling uncomfortable at being a witness to what should be a private conversation, Trudi stood up. 'Will I go and make us a cup of coffee or something?'

Eric smiled. 'Thank you, Trudi. If you go out that door, turn right, down the stairs, you will come to the kitchen. Don't be surprised to find it occupied but tell whomever it is, I sent you.'

Trudi nodded, leaving the men to their conversation.

She followed Eric's directions at first, but soon a delicious smell led her the rest of the way. Entering the room, she found Sister Vide at the stove, stirring something in a large pot. Two other women were chopping potatoes at the kitchen table. They looked at her fearfully.

'Trudi, how nice to see you again. Have you eaten? Would

you like to try my Borst? Or would you like to try some liver dumplings?'

'Do they taste as good as they smell?' Trudi asked.

'I'm not sure—they are made from oatmeal but don't tell anyone. What did you need?'

'Eric would like a drink for him and two friends. I thought I'd make myself useful and come down to make it. They wanted to talk.'

'You mean Max and Jakob were arguing again?' Sister Vide took a spoonful from the pot to taste. She winced. 'A lot more salt and less cabbage, and it would be perfect.'

Trudi laughed.

'Take a seat beside my helpers, Gila and Hadar. They are staying here for two nights before they will move on. They aren't too fond of Berlin, are you, ladies?'

But the women didn't even look up: they kept their eyes glued to their task. Trudi caught the look of sympathy on Vide's face before she set about making the hot drink.

Trudi carried the tray back up to the office, hoping the tempers had settled and, more importantly, that Pastor Forell had returned.

Jakob walked to the door to take the tray from her, his hands brushing against hers. The look in his eyes made her blush.

Max spoke up: 'Trudi, Isla said you are a gifted seamstress. Did you know I'm a tailor? Although I spend my time fixing sewing machines now more often than doing actual sewing. My factory is now used to make uniforms for the *Wehrmacht*. I need someone to check on the quality of the work. I don't care if the seams are straight or not, but it seems the soldiers get upset when the pockets of their great coats are sewn shut or their lining unravels.' Even as he listed the complaints he was smiling. 'I've had a few too many complaints. I need to restore order. Do you want the job?'

'Me?' Trudi didn't know if Max was serious. She darted a quick look at Jakob to see his reaction but he was staring into his coffee cup, his mind preoccupied.

'You need a job, now you have a new identity. It isn't safe for you to continue working for Isla's friend. Her influence may be waning... it's best we don't rely on her discretion any longer.'

Trudi figured that was one way of saying Renata's lover had traded her in for another woman. She hoped the dress-store owner would be okay. She had been kind to her, in her own way.

Max took a sip of his drink, grimacing at the taste. 'I employ several privileged Jews in my factory. Those who are married to Aryans like myself. I also have some slave labour French and Poles mainly. A mix of men and women. All foisted on me, but at least I can do something to feed them.' He shook his head, a guilty expression in his eyes. 'I have to make them work hard to reach our quotas. I can't afford to antagonize my customer by being late. Miserable creatures, they are like walking skeletons most of them, and not just because we are based in Berlin. Their rations wouldn't keep a bird alive, never mind an adult.'

Eric lit a cigarette before passing it to Max, whose hands were now shaking. He took a deep drag, then, with the cigarette hanging from his lip, took out a picture from his wallet and handed it to Trudi.

'My wife, Christabel. A wonderful woman who refuses to divorce me, despite what those Gestapo animals threaten, and who is aware of all this.' Max waved his arm around the room, taking in the parcels on the table, the paperwork on the desk. 'I refuse to let her near this place or get more involved than she is already. But she is quite gifted at talking storeowners, even market traders, into donations. She would have made a wonderful politician.' He rubbed his eyes with his sleeve.

Trudi glanced at Jakob. Was Max upset over what had happened to Pastor Forell, or was it something else?

'I can't bear to think what the Gestapo would do to her if they caught wind of my activities.' He took a pen out of his pocket and scribbled out a message before standing up. 'I best get going. Eric, let me know as soon as you get word.' He handed Trudi the note. 'That's the address. See you Monday morning.'

TWENTY-TWO

MAY 1942

Trudi woke with a start and listened but all she could hear was her own heart racing. Her stomach clenched, her hands shaking as a feeling of dread overtook her. Was she being paranoid? What if they had picked up Jakob? She swallowed bile at the thought of him being tortured. He worked tirelessly helping anyone who asked.

Jakob had introduced her to members of different resistance networks, including Kaufman, who'd welcomed her into his home with a smile. She'd helped hide several Jewish children in Christian orphanages as well as providing new papers to men and women wanting to avoid the deportations and try their luck living as illegals.

Tires squealed outside. Nobody drove cars at night except the Gestapo. The main door to the apartment building crashed open, her fingers clenched on the sofa cushion, fear stopping her legs from obeying the command to move. Yet if she didn't get up and answer the door and they broke it down, things would be worse for her. And they'd discover Ada and Chana.

Boots stamped past her door and up to the next floor, the men shouting, '*Raus, schnell! Raus!*'

She exhaled in relief, only to be hit by a wave of guilt at the screams coming from her neighbours above. Aron's terrified scream broke her heart. She heard Frau Weiss trying to soothe him as Herr Weiss begged the men to take him and leave his family alone. His pleas went unanswered as someone ordered them to pack a bag and get out.

Trudi closed her eyes, putting her hands over her ears, trying to block out the sounds. Then she pulled together the few pieces of bedding she owned, putting it over her head, wishing she had the feather quilt from her childhood, but that was long gone.

The sounds carried though the otherwise still apartment building—it was as if all the residents held their breath and listened to what was happening in the Weiss apartment.

Trudi gave up pretence of sleep and sat up, teeth chattering. She hoped Frau Weiss had had time dress the children warmly, in the woollen coats she had given the family just yesterday.

The Jews had been required to give all their winter clothes, bedding and coats up to the winter relief for the troops on the Russian Front. That was their price for remaining free in Berlin. Free! Was that what you called this existence? Waiting for the Gestapo to come calling as you slowly starved to death on the limited rations allowed? That was if you were lucky to get to a store that still had food available and would serve you. The things they had taken for granted: radio, telephones, tobacco, eggs, fish and milk, were forbidden.

She pulled a picture from under her pillow of the two boys and her baby. Her finger touched Liesel's face. She would be four soon. Would she recognize her if she ever made it to Britain? Would Liesel know her as her mother?

The truck and cars drove away. Trudi moved silently to the window, watching their rear lights disappear into the distance. From the bedroom she heard Ada stifle a sob, and Chana whispering to her to be quiet. Now the people in the building could breathe once more. They were safe. For a few more hours at least.

She knocked at the bedroom door before walking in.

The two women were clinging to one another. Ada stuttered, her eyes wide, her fingers holding on to the blanket for dear life. 'I thought... I was sure that was it.'

Trudi sat on the bed. 'You're safe. They don't know you live here. If they come, it will be for me. If they do come back, stay in here and be quiet. Then when they are gone, go to Frau Krause, tell her you are a friend of mine. She may help you. But whatever you do, don't come out of the room until I'm gone.'

Ada sobbed as Chana spoke, 'But what if they search?'

'Then they will get all of us. But I've heard once they tick off your name on a list, they don't bother searching. They just seal the door and come back later. That's why you would need to go out as soon as curfew was over and go to Frau Krause.'

Ada clawed at the covers. 'You're scaring me, Trudi. You talk like it is inevitable.'

'That's because it is,' Trudi whispered, not sure the other women heard her.

She went back out to the living area but didn't try to sleep. She had to find a new hiding place for them all. Where could they go? She had her false identity papers but what of Chana and Ada?

She had to do something. Staying there wasn't an option. She closed her eyes, squeezing them together, trying not to cry in the dark.

She left early the next morning, hurrying to the factory, hoping to find Max alone.

She was in luck. She knocked, entered the office and closed the door firmly behind her.

Before Max could even greet her, she burst out. 'Max, I

need your help. Our block was raided by the Gestapo last night.'

Max paled, standing and moving to her side. 'Are you alright? Did they check your papers?'

'No, they didn't knock on my door. They went to a neighbour. Max, they took the man and his wife and, despite their pleas, they terrorized their little boys as well. I heard Aron screaming—he's only a child. Not even seven years old. He has a little brother too.' Max put his arms around her as she gave into the tears. 'How could they take the children? What did we do that was so bad?'

Max patted her arm. 'Shush now.'

Breathing heavily she struggled to get her emotions in check.

He rubbed his chin. 'We need to find you another place to live. You should have moved as soon as you got new papers. I'll speak to Jakob.' He took a step but she put her hand out to stop him.

Trudi had to admit why she'd stayed living in the building even though she now had gentile papers. 'Max, I couldn't move out of my apartment. Chana Arkin is living with me. Ada Bernstein too. I need papers for them.'

Droplets of perspiration trickled down his face, which he attempted to wipe away without much success. 'Impossible. I know Chana, she looks too Jewish. She'll have to hide. Ada Bernstein? Gavriel's mother. I thought she was picked up in December.'

'She got the letter. We ignored it. She's been living with me since. She can't live like a gentile, she's too nervous. She'd be caught as soon as she walked down the street. She hasn't left the house in months.' Trudi wasn't being unkind but truthful.

'Trudi, what you are asking...' He held her gaze but was the first to look away. 'It's difficult. We have so many in need, and finding living space for two women is challenging. It's...'

She stood straighter, raising her chin. 'I don't care what it is, we must help them. Otherwise, I stay where I am and take my chances. I won't give up on them, Max.'

Max stared at her before nodding. 'Gavriel told me how stubborn you are. To look at your pretty blonde hair and blue eyes, nobody would guess you have a steel inner core.'

He picked up the phone and made a call. She didn't understand a word of it, realizing he was talking in some sort of code about packages and couriers.

When he hung up, he looked at her with a mix of sadness and understanding. 'There is space at the church.' She smiled and was about to thank him when he added, 'But only for two, Trudi. You can't live there too.'

Trudi's fear for her life and those of her friends had become a constant companion and most days she was in control of it. But the thought of living without seeing Ada and even Chana everyday was daunting. She'd miss them, especially Ada. But it was more than that. They understood her fears, and without them being around how would she handle the nightmares, the memories of the bad times? Most of all, she'd have nobody to discuss the children with.

She felt Max staring at her, and looked up to see a questioning look in his eyes. 'You could leave. We could pass you through the escape network. To freedom.'

For a moment she felt hope rise in her chest. She could escape, live; maybe even get to England to her children. See Liesel and Tomas again, find out how Heinz was... But then her excitement drained as quickly as it had flared. How could she run when so many were in danger? The network badly needed people like her and Jakob. Those who could pass as Aryan. Without people like Isla, Max, Eric, Sister Vide and all their helpers, without Jakob, how many more would die?

She pushed away thoughts of escape. For now, at least. 'I

have my papers. I'll live as a gentile, hiding in plain sight as they say. That way I can continue to help.'

He reached across the desk to take her hand and squeezed, a gesture of comfort. For a second, he reminded her of Ari. Her husband had cared deeply for his fellow humans too.

'I know the Gestapo visit has you rattled. You have been under a lot of stress lately, for even longer than we thought.' He lowered his voice, glancing around even though they were alone in the office. 'I can't believe you hid two women in that tiny flat and didn't tell anyone.'

She'd got used to living with her friends. She'd miss Ada. She pushed aside her feelings. 'Isla knew. About Chana anyway. She guessed.'

'She's discreet—she didn't say a word to anyone. Believe me, I'd know.' He took two pieces of paper from his drawer and wrote something on them.

'These are work permits. Tell your friends they are to say they are starting new jobs. Only if they are stopped at an inspection. They must wear the star on their coats at least for the first part of the journey. Jakob will escort them from your place to the church.'

She put the papers in her handbag. 'I'll go too.'

'No, Trudi. You can't be seen with them. You are an Aryan now. You will have a new address tomorrow. Pack up what you want to bring with you. Now go home and tell your guests what we have decided.' Trudi turned to leave. 'Oh, and tell them they must be quiet and obey the rules. All our guests help Sister Vide with whatever she needs. The women in the kitchen and the men doing odd jobs. If they don't help, they don't stay.'

Trudi nodded, despite worrying how Chana would react to doing chores. Ada would be fine but the other woman... would just have to get on with it.

TWENTY-THREE

Trudi decided to wait until they'd eaten before she broke the news. She placed her cutlery neatly on her plate. 'Chana, Ada, you have to listen. You aren't safe here anymore. None of us are. I have some friends willing to shelter you.'

Ada paled but Chana turned on her, her expression incredulous. 'Shelter us? How? We've tried contacting gentiles we knew, and nobody will help. You saw them, they are scared of their own shadows.'

Trudi didn't want to remind Chana of the times she'd asked for help. When Ari and Heinz were first arrested. Or when Chana and her husband had treated her so poorly when she'd taken around the photographs. 'Chana, don't be so judgemental. Some have been very helpful, giving me a job not to mention the food packages.' Isla had been very generous not that she could tell Chana about the countess.'

Chana glared at her, a look of disdain on her face. 'So they give you charity. That's an act of courage these days?'

Trudi bit her lip, trying to keep her patience. 'Yes, it is. You know the penalties they could face if the Gestapo discovered the both of you living here when it is only me who is registered.'

'Please can you stop arguing,' Ada said as she stood up, collecting up the dishes and moving them to the sink. 'You're giving me a headache.'

'What's new? You always have an ache or pain somewhere.'

Ada blanched as Chana directed her ire towards her. Trudi put her hand on Chana's arm. 'Chana, leave her alone. She's terrified, just as you are. You just show it in different ways. Now I need you to listen, there isn't much time.' Trudi patted the seat beside her. 'Sit down, Ada.'

'Where is this place?' Ada whispered, as she took the seat. Trudi could see her hands were shaking.

'It's a church.' She had their attention now, their eyes almost out on stalks. 'I know the pastor and he is totally trustworthy. Eric and his wife, Martha, along with Sister Vide, are a lifeline to many Jews. Both those they shelter and those they help out with food, clothes and other things. But if you agree to go to the shelter, you both have to agree to the rules.'

Chana sat straighter, ready to argue as usual. Trudi ignored her; instead, she held Ada's gaze, willing her friend to be brave. She wanted Rachel and Ruth to see their mother again. 'This is a good plan, Ada. We can't live here. Not anymore.'

Ada nodded, biting her lip before asking, 'Are you coming with us, Trudi?'

Trudi shook her head, trying to hold back the tears while remaining calm. 'I've committed to helping in other ways.'

Chana blustered, 'If you aren't going, why should we?'

Despite her reaction, Trudi sensed the fear behind the words. She modulated her tone in response. 'I can pass for a gentile, Chana. It would be more difficult for you and Ada. I am younger and... willing to do whatever it takes to survive.'

Ada blushed but Chana narrowed her eyes, pointing her finger at Trudi's chest. 'You won't bring dishonour to my brother's memory. Remember you are his wife.'

Trudi hadn't told either woman about Jakob and their blossoming romance. She knew that Ada would be pleased for her, after her advice to seize the moment. But Chana—she would judge her and find her lacking again. She tried to hide her feelings, counting to ten backwards before she spoke, her voice as cold as ice. 'I'm his *widow*. I have a duty to stay alive for our children.'

Chana puffed up her chest—if she had been a bird, the feathers would be flying everywhere. But before she could say another word, Ada, the peacemaker as usual, cleared her throat. 'What do we have to agree to, Trudi?'

'We have a plan to get you there safely. I have some work permits for you in case you are stopped. A man will take you to the correct place. He is a friend and you can trust him with your life.'

Ada exhaled loudly, her face pale, but there was a determined set to her jaw. She'd do exactly what she was told to do.

Trudi continued. 'Once at the property, you can't leave. Not ever. For any reason, unless the pastor or one of the staff says so. I know it's a lot to ask but the rate of deportations has increased, and we can't risk you being picked up on the streets. You both know a lot even if you believe otherwise. My friend who delivered the food packages, the lady whose dresses we altered, Ursula her maid. You don't know everything, but enough to fill holes in a Gestapo investigation. You could bring down the entire network.'

'Are you suggesting we would tell the Nazis?' Chana raised her eyebrows as if addressing a child.

Trudi's patience evaporated. 'I doubt you would have a choice. They are experts at getting the information they want.'

At the look of distress on Ada's face, the tears in her eyes, Trudi listened to the regret gnawing at her conscience. These women had been through enough, they had lost their husbands, their homes, their positions in society. At an age when they should have been planning their children's weddings, nurturing grandchildren, they were living, no, *existing* merely, in fear for their lives. And she was making it worse.

She softened her tone. 'Chana, please listen to me. I want us all to live to see the end of the war. I want Heinz, Tomas, and Liesel to get to know their aunt. You are the only family they have left. You owe it to them and to Ari and Leopold to survive.'

Ada reached over and patted Chana's hand before asking Trudi, 'How will we pay for our shelter? I don't have any jewellery left; I've given it all to you.'

'Me, too.' Chana's sniff suggested Trudi had used the funds for her own pleasure, but she dismissed that thought. The woman's fear highlighted the less attractive parts of her personality.

Once again, she sought to reassure them. 'Eric doesn't need payment. He just asks we contribute as we can. You two can help the other women and children living there. You are both pillars of the community; they will look to you for guidance. There may be work you can do. Such as sewing and mending.' Trudi smiled at Ada. Her friend's skills had improved so much in the last few months. 'Those services are still in demand and can be done from home. Sister Vide can act as go-between, so you never have to meet the people you are working for.'

Trudi glanced at Chana. 'We all need to pull our weight. And we can't complain. It will be hard. I'm not going to lie. You will have to share sleeping quarters with strangers.'

Chana wrinkled her nose. 'What shall you be doing?'

Trudi wished she had prepared a better answer. She didn't want them to know the risks she was taking. She'd already helped Jakob move some children to a safer location and gone with him to see his black-market contacts. 'Me? I'll be doing what I do now. Working in the factory. Helping where I can.'

Despite her light tone, both women turned to stare at her.

Ada protested, 'You can't. It's too dangerous.'

'I need to work for money and rations. Otherwise people

living in hiding will starve. I'm not the only one. There are many Jews hiding as gentiles, and some are helping people like Eric.'

Chana crossed her arms, a look of suspicion on her face. 'Why is he helping? He's not Jewish. Do we have to convert to his church?'

This time Trudi had to hide a smile. Chana spoke as if she went to synagogue every week when they could. Like Ari, Chana and Leopold had only turned up at the holidays. They were hardly observant Jews.

'No, you don't need to convert. Eric and his congregation are Christians and they don't believe in murder.' She glanced at the clock: time was ticking fast. 'Are you agreeable to the plan?'

The two women exchanged looks before Ada nodded.

Chana coughed. 'I will think about it.'

Trudi clenched her teeth to keep a rein on her temper. If she shouted at Chana, the woman would become more stubborn. 'We don't have time for that. You need to decide now. There are only two places left and others on the list who could be helped instead.'

Ada stood up, frowning. 'Trudi, you mean there isn't room for you. All that talk about you pretending to be a gentile. There isn't any other option. Oh my God, you are giving up your space to save one of us. I insist you take my place. You are younger and Liesel is a baby. My girls are older.'

Trudi walked over to Ada and gave her a hug in recognition of her generosity of spirit. 'Ada Bernstein, how many times do I have to tell you, I'm an adult and make my own choices.' She smiled to take the sting out of her words. 'Now pack a small bag with some of our food and some of your things. Don't pack everything. You leave tomorrow.'

'So soon?' Chana asked.

Hopefully it wouldn't be too late: the Gestapo could come

back that night. But Trudi simply nodded, not wanting to give voice to her fears.

Where *was* she going to live next?

As the two women went to pack, she stared around the apartment. It wasn't a bit like her old home but it had given her shelter, and she'd miss it.

The next evening, they heard a car stop outside the building. Heart racing, Trudi wanted to glance out the window but restrained herself. Was this part of the plan or had the Gestapo returned?

A loud rapping knock nearly gave her heart failure. She opened the door—and couldn't believe what she saw. She held the door open as Jakob marched in looking every inch the German soldier. Another man, similarly dressed, stood at the door, his gun gleaming in his hand.

'Out now!' Jakob barked. Even though she knew him, he scared her. He was so real.

Trudi opened the bedroom door, beckoning to Chana and Ada to come out. 'He's a friend. Do everything he says,' she whispered, but despite her words, the two ashen-faced women looked terrified.

Trudi helped Ada on with her coat, the woman's hands were shaking so much.

Chana turned her back when she offered to help. Then, picking up her small bag, she marched out of the apartment without a word to Trudi.

Ada gave Trudi a hug but then Jakob shouted, pointing at Trudi: 'You too. Out now.'

Trudi gave him a questioning look, but he ignored her. It was as if they had never shared a kiss or a loving embrace. She struggled, hurt beyond measure. She grabbed her coat, the bag she had packed and with a last look at the home she'd had for the past few years, she followed her friends out to the car outside.

Nobody in their apartment block looked out of a window, never mind offered help. They obviously believed it to be a Gestapo raid.

The car sped off through the streets. The three women, Ada sitting in the middle, clasped hands. Jakob sat in the passenger seat, the other man drove in silence. The car stopped two streets away from the church. Only then did Jakob turn. 'I'll take you ladies to your new home. Trudi, you will stay in the car. He knows where to take you next.' Jakob jerked his head in the direction of the driver, who didn't move a muscle, nor did he speak.

Chana protested, 'You can't...'

'Shut up and do as you are told.' Jakob's barked command reduced Chana to a blubbering mess. She was probably remembering the horrible day her husband was murdered. Trudi glared at Jakob. Surely it wasn't necessary to be so harsh. He didn't look at her.

'Be careful, Trudi. Thank you.' Ada kissed her cheek before pushing Chana out of the door Jakob held open.

Trudi watched as Ada took Chana's arm and Jakob led them down the street.

'He's a little too good at playing the part of a Nazi, isn't he?' The driver's words barely registered as the car moved off to an unknown destination. Trudi couldn't get the sound of Jakob's harsh shout out of her mind. What did she really know about the man who'd captured her heart?

The driver dropped her near Max's factory. 'He handed her a piece of paper. 'This is your new address. Frau Weber is expecting you—she's the *blockführer*. A regular party member, an upstanding Nazi.'

Trudi wasn't sure she appreciated the driver's sense of humour. He handed her an envelope. 'This is for Frau Weber.'

'Thank you.'

'See you around.' He nodded at her as she exited the car before he drove off.

Trudi stared after the car for a couple of seconds, trying to compose herself. She was now Trudi Bausch, the widow of a German soldier who'd fallen in the invasion of France.

She picked up her small case and wearily made her way towards her new home. The building was five stories high, with three apartments on each floor. She found Frau Weber's name and rang the bell.

A small, elderly woman opened the door, one hand to her head as if trying to stop the grey hair escaping from her bun. 'Yes?'

'Good evening, Frau Weber. My name is Trudi Bausch. You're expecting me?'

'Ah, yes, the widow. I'm sorry for your loss. God bless your husband for laying down his life for our beloved Führer. Come along. You'll catch a chill standing out here. Your apartment is on the second floor. It's been vacant for a couple of weeks, so I opened the windows to air it for you.'

Trudi followed the woman up the stairs. The hall was painted in an unfortunate shade of grey that only served to enhance the miserable appearance of her new home.

Frau Weber opened the door to the new apartment and pushed it open, indicating that Trudi was to follow her.

The living area was larger than she expected. Trudi took in the swastika flags on the mantelpiece, the portrait of the Führer hanging over the fire.

The woman nodded towards the picture. 'I thought I'd leave that for you. To give you comfort. I know what it is like to lose someone. My son fell at Stalingrad.'

'I'm sorry,' Trudi mumbled, her fingers itching to throw the painting out the window.

Heavy drapes covered the window; she guessed they had been there for years even before the blackout restrictions had been introduced. The walls, scuffed in places, had been painted yellow, possibly in a bid to add some warmth to the room. A worn brown leather sofa was pushed against one wall, and a small wooden coffee table sat in the centre of the room. To the right of the living room, an open doorway led to a small kitchen area. Frau Weber checked the blackout blind was pulled down over the small window before switching on the light. She pointed out the white stove, wooden countertop and porcelain sink. A few pieces of mismatched crockery were held in the drying rail above the sink. A small kitchen table was pushed against the wall, with two chairs.

'That door leads to the bathroom and this one is the bedroom.' Frau Weber pushed open the door to reveal a sparsely furnished room with a wooden double bed, together with a thin mattress. The sheets looked fresh and clean. There was a small wardrobe, a chair, and a bookcase holding only one book, a copy of *Mein Kampf.*

The parquet floor, aged and scuffed from years of use, was partially covered with what looked like a handmade rug. Frau Weber caught her looking at it. 'My last tenant complained her feet got cold on the wooden floors.'

'That's thoughtful of you, thank you.' Trudi forced herself to be polite, to speak nicely to this lady, when all she wanted was to scream at her to remove the Hitler portrait and his horrible book.

The woman stood there as if waiting for something. Trudi remembered the envelope she'd been given. She handed it over. The woman smiled as she counted the cash. 'Thank you for paying in advance.' She left, closing the door behind her.

· · ·

Trudi didn't know how long she sat on the old sofa, listening to the sounds of the night. She wondered if the whole building was full of pin-wearing party faithful. She wrapped her arms around her body, missing her friends—even Chana's acerbic comments. She wondered how they were faring. Were they as lonely as she was?

But it was ridiculous, sitting around feeling sorry for herself. She got up and unpacked her small suitcase. She hung the few items of clothing in the wardrobe, placed her hairbrush on the bookcase. She threw the copy of *Mein Kampf* on top of the wardrobe, wishing she could do burn it—along with Hitler's picture.

Gathering her precious letters and photographs close to her chest, she marched back to the sitting room. With trembling hands, she unfolded the three letters Sally had been kind enough to send from England. Though the words had been etched into her memory long ago, rereading them brought some small comfort and reduced her loneliness. Closing her eyes, she leaned back against the sofa wondering what her baby was doing. Her mind returned unerringly to her constant worry: did Liesel remember her at all? Did she call Sally 'Mama'?

She must have dropped off as she jumped when someone turned a key in the lock. Frozen to the spot, she watched as the door opened and in walked Jakob. She sagged with relief but immediately sat up straighter. What role was he playing now? Nazi officer, resistance hero or lover?

He had changed into his own clothes, but the hesitant expression on his face made her stomach knot. She wanted to forgive him, but she couldn't forget the terror his actions had caused earlier that day.

As she remained silent, his wariness turned to hurt. 'I just wanted to check on you. I... the way you looked at me earlier. I felt like a heel.' He was trying to apologize.

But it wasn't enough.

'You scared them, Jakob, when you came to the apartment and ordered them outside. Two older women who were already terrified. You didn't have to do that.'

'I did what I thought was right,' he said quietly, his eyes full of regret. 'And we both know it. Do you think anyone would look twice at a Nazi screaming at some Jews?'

'They couldn't have heard you in the car. You went too far.' Her voice wavered with anger and hurt.

He stepped closer to her, an apologetic expression on his face. His fingers grazed hers, but she pulled away, not wanting him to think that he could get away with it so easily. She was determined to make him understand the consequences of his actions.

'If I had used "please" and "thank you", anyone watching would have suspected us.' He moved closer but didn't touch her. He took a seat on the sofa but left some distance between them.

Her voice trembled as she put her fears into words. 'You looked so real. It wasn't just the uniform and the gun but you—your face, your expression.'

The faint sound of rain pattering against the windows was the only sound in the room.

Jakob put his head in his hands for a couple of seconds. When he finally lifted it and looked at her, she was shocked to see the pain in his eyes.

'What is it, Jakob?'

'I found out my aunt, uncle and their family were put on a transport. They left last week. I didn't even know they were in Berlin. I thought they were still at home. But someone told them it would be safer for them to hide in a bigger city. Where nobody knew them. Why would anyone tell them that? Why would they believe it? They didn't last two days.' He was looking at her but not seeing her. 'My cousins were less than a year old. Twins. What sort of person would believe they were taking babies as slave labour.' His breath hitched. 'Here I am saving strangers, but my own family... I couldn't help them. Then tonight, something happened to me when I put on that uniform. I know when I'm pretending to be SS or Gestapo, I have to act like I don't have a heart, that I'm made of stone. But tonight, I was so angry. Not at your friends or you, but this whole mess. I wanted to scream and shout and, God forgive me, I wanted a reason to use that gun. To cause one of them pain.'

'One of who?' she whispered. He couldn't mean Chana and Ada.

'A German. Any German.' He held her gaze. 'They are turning me into a killer. For a second, I was just like one of them.' He put his head in his hands again, his shoulders shaking as he cried silently.

Trudi put her arms around him and pulled him to her. 'You didn't murder anyone. You aren't like them, you save people.' She held him close, her heart breaking for him as he mourned for his family.

His sobs gradually subsided and he pulled away from her. He reached for her hand, his thumb tracing circles on her palm. He looked into her eyes, holding her gaze, 'I'm sorry I let them turn me into something I'm not,' he said, softly.

She put her hand over his and squeezed it gently. 'You've been under so much pressure, always playing the hero. Saving so many people. Max told me about some of the near-misses you've had.' She put her hand on the side of his face. 'You scare me.'

He continued to stare, his expression moving from uncertainty to desire, fear to longing. His skin was softer than she'd expected, his scent hinted at pine soap. His finger stroked her cheek, before brushing over her lips—but he held back. He seemed to be waiting for her to make the next move.

Any doubts about the type of man he was disappeared. Trudi leaned in closer, lifting her face for his kiss. His eyes roamed all over her face before returning to her lips and then he kissed her. Deeply, his hands cradling her face. She responded with a passion she had never felt before. It was as if they were both clinging to each other for dear life and the kiss was a reminder that there was still beauty in this world, despite everything that had happened.

TWENTY-FOUR

JUNE 1942

Trudi couldn't believe the scene playing out before her eyes: buildings covered in black flags, the air heavy with fear and grief, the mourners' faces etched with sorrow. The muffled drums echoed her heartbeat as the coffin, draped with a swastika flag and mounted on a gun carriage, rolled through the streets of Berlin past crowds of silent mourners.

All this for a monster, the funeral of the man who embodied the myth of the Aryan race. He had been taller and blonder than most of the inner Nazi circle, a favourite of Hitler—Himmler's protégé. His name, Reinhard Heydrich, turned the stomachs of most Jewish people and even those who weren't Jewish. His reputation as a cold-blooded killer was well known and she couldn't blame the men who had assassinated him.

Isla had told her that those in the inner circle believed the British government had been behind the killing. But revenge had been taken against the ordinary Czech people. Trudi felt sick at the thought of it. Who could murder the inhabitants of a whole town as a reprisal for the death of one man? Lidice was no more, the men of the town killed, the women and children shipped off to a concentration camp. From what Isla said, it seemed Hitler was determined to send a message. He wouldn't tolerate anyone taking aim at his supporters. At least, this was the public reaction of Hitler; in private, it was rumoured he had raged against Heydrich for travelling without an escort, for taking unnecessary risks and even at the end for refusing proper medical treatment. Hitler had ordered his personal doctor to go to Heydrich's bedside, but the man had still died.

The funeral ceremony blasted out over the speakers, and featured the German state orchestra. She listened as Hitler described Heydrich as one of the best National Socialists, a true defender of the Reich.

Trudi didn't agree with anything Hitler said apart from his description of Heydrich as the man with the iron heart.

As she watched the German people around her, women and some men crying openly, she wondered could they know what the monster in the coffin had done? The crimes he had committed either personally or via his orders? Were their tears real grief for the man, or because it was expected, given the high numbers of SS and Gestapo men present.

Trudi shivered, turning her back on the spectacle. Thank God she wasn't one of those who had to pretend to grieve. She hoped Isla gave the performance of her life: now was not a time for anyone to be questioning the loyalty of *Wehrmacht* generals.

Especially Isla's husband and others who helped the resistance.

As she walked home, through streets thronged with people, she couldn't help but think of all the men who'd died for Germany. Goebbels had ordered the newspapers to print a maximum of ten death notices a day, but it was obvious that hundreds, if not thousands, had already died. Did those families wonder if their husbands', sons', fathers' sacrifices were worth it?

As she walked back to her apartment, she wondered how Chana and Ada were faring in their new home. She wasn't allowed to visit. Eric felt it was too early, that her friends would be unsettled. She missed them, especially Ada.

But then if she was living with her friends, she wouldn't be living with Jakob. She still couldn't believe it, but he had charmed Frau Weber, telling her he was involved in top-secret work for the Reich. He backed up his claim by bringing her little packages of luxuries everyone knew were only available to those connected to someone powerful. Some real coffee, a bottle of perfume, a length of fabric went a long way to convince her he was someone important. She had even started to encourage the relationship between him and Trudi, telling Trudi she could do worse.

Trudi grinned. If only Frau Weber knew just how good Jakob was for her.

'Trudi? Trudi Beck? It is you, isn't it?'

Trudi stilled as she recognized the voice of her former neighbour, a woman who'd gloated when the Nazis had possessed her home. She began to walk more quickly, determined not to speak to her. She wanted to kick herself for being stupid. This woman knew she was Jewish, and would enjoy denouncing her to the nearest policeman.

Trudi darted into a side street, picked up her skirts and ran for her life. She glanced behind her but the woman was still coming, shouting now, 'Stop that Jewish scum!' Some passers-by stopped to stare but nobody joined in the hunt. It was only a matter of time before they met a policeman or worse, a member of the Gestapo.

Heart racing, Trudi headed for the railway station and ducked into the public bathroom. She sat on the toilet with her legs tucked tightly under her, her heart thumping against her chest. How could she have been so stupid? Jakob had warned her never to become complacent.

Time ticked by slowly as she chewed her fingernails,

waiting for the door to open, to hear her neighbour's strident tones.

But nothing happened.

Trudi was too scared to leave so stayed, watching the light at the window turn to shadows. Women came and went, some banging on her door impatiently. Then the door to the bathrooms opened, the wheels of a cleaning trolley scraping against the floor.

Trudi bit her lip, trying to resist the instinct to run. She could hear the cleaning woman's heavy breathing as she ran the water, cleaning the sinks. She caught sight of a dirty mop swishing across the floor. Her eyes were glued to the door handle but it never turned. The cleaner slammed the bathroom door closed.

Trudi leaned her head against the wall of the stall, relief making her sweat. That had been too close. She had no option but to stay where she was. Leaving would mean she would be out after curfew.

After a very long night, Trudi flushed the toilet and walked out into the bathroom. Taking a couple of seconds to smooth her wrinkled clothes, she walked back to the street and headed home.

As she put the key in the lock, the door opened, and Jakob pulled her into the apartment.

'Thank God! I was so worried when you didn't come home last night! What happened... and what is that *smell*?'

She kissed him before pulling off her clothes, desperate for a bath even if the water was freezing. 'I spent the night in a public bathroom. I bumped into a woman who knew me.'

He paled, his eyes widening. 'What did she do?'

'She shouted but I think people were so caught up after the funeral they just wanted to get home. I got lucky.'

He pulled her to him despite her protests that she stank. 'I thought I'd lost you. Don't ever do that to me again.' He buried his face in her hair.

After her bath, Trudi returned to the sitting room where he sat, the picture of Liesel and Tomas in his hands. She usually carried it with her, but must have left it on the table last night.

She restrained the urge to grab back her most precious belonging. 'What are you doing?'

He looked up at her, his face serious. 'Making a promise to these children that I will do whatever it takes to reunite you all after this war.' He stood up, took her hand and pulled her toward the sofa. He gently pushed her to sit down, handing her the photo. 'When you didn't come back last night, I kept staring at their faces. Liesel is how I imagine you looked as a child. I swore if you came home, I would never let you go.'

Tears streamed down her face and he tried to wipe them away, but she pulled away from his touch.

He got down on one knee, making her heart flutter. 'Trudi, will you marry me? When this war is over, let's go to England together and find your children and become a real family.'

She wrapped her hands across her stomach, trying to buy some time to put her thoughts into words that wouldn't hurt him. Her love for him could not ignore the danger they were in, nor the odds against their relationship surviving a cruel world that might take them away from each other in an instant.

'I love you. I do. But this... it's all so sudden.' She stumbled over her words as she saw a range of emotions on his face—surprise, embarrassment, hurt—before she found her voice again. 'I'm still grieving Ari and my lost children, my lost friends.' She swallowed hard, grasping at any logical explanation to explain why she couldn't accept his offer right away. 'What if all this'—she waved her hands in the air—'is making us think we are more in love than we are? Life isn't normal... what if our feelings aren't real?'

His eyes darkened as she looked at him.

She panicked, hating that she was hurting him. She reached out her hands, pulling him to sit beside her on the sofa. She caressed his thumbs with her fingers. 'We are living under the threat of instant death, or worse,' she pleaded. 'I want us to be together forever, Jakob—I want us to last. But out there—beyond these walls—who knows what tomorrow holds? Do you understand?' She glanced at him.

He shook his head slightly and replied, 'Not really. I thought you loved me.'

She grasped his hands tightly between hers and looked into his eyes with desperation. 'I do love you! You know I do, but it's all happened so soon, we mustn't tempt fate—not when we're living on a knife edge.' Pulling him closer, she softened her voice. 'Can you ask me again when the war is over? Until then, let's just live each day like it were our last. Enjoy every moment getting to know one another... please?'

He gathered her into an embrace, their hearts beating in time as he said, softly, 'I don't think I could ever say no to you.'

TWENTY-FIVE

AUGUST 1942

Harry picked up his kit in one hand, and patted his pocket containing his rail pass and a letter instructing him to report to the Hotel Great Central in Marylebone London, with the other.

Sergeant Tanner had been tight-lipped but Harry hoped this was going to be his chance to fight and defeat the Nazis. His heart raced with anticipation, excitement mingling with a little fear of the unknown.

Taub and the others still interrupted his dreams: he kept going back over that night. Sometimes he'd insist they all walk the old woman to the safety of the shelter; other times, he was the one who went to the bus with the others. It was just all so senseless. His friends had escaped almost certain death at the hands of the Nazis, only to die in London. He clenched his fist, determination surging through his veins. He burned with desire to avenge his friends.

As he took the bus through the bombed-out London streets, he could see the lads everywhere he looked. He closed his eyes until he heard the conductor announce his stop.

Out on the street, he stood in front of the massive red-brick

Victorian building for a couple of minutes, watching the people come and go. Some wore military uniforms—to his surprise he saw a few wearing tropical kit or exotic uniforms—but a few wore suits. He spotted more than one man wearing the Pioneer Corps uniform, and headed in their direction, following them into the run-down reception hall to check in at the front desk.

'Take this key and go to your room. When they are ready for you, your name will appear on the noticeboard.'

Before Harry could mutter his thanks, he suddenly spied a face from the past—the friend who'd gone to the Isle of Man with him. 'Joseph!' He grabbed his pal's arm and spun him to look at him. 'I didn't think I'd see you again!'

Joseph grinned as he gave Harry a clap on the back. 'You thought you got rid of me, didn't you? What's this all about? You know anything?'

'Only that I had to report here. You?'

'Same. Been digging ditches and whatnot since I got off the Isle of Man. I thought you volunteered to fight.'

Harry nodded. 'I did, but all I got was a bunch of rejection letters. At least until now. Come on, let's put these bags in our room and see what we can find out.'

They found their allotted rooms. Harry's allotted roommate was happy to swop with Joseph so they could share and catch up on each other's news.

Joseph sat on the bed, making himself comfortable before asking, 'So, how is your girl? Rachel, wasn't it? Have you married her yet?'

Harry felt his face flame so he picked up his case and started unpacking his few bits and pieces. He placed a picture of his siblings on the dresser, followed by a second one of Rachel in her nurse's volunteer uniform. Sally had sent them to him for Christmas.

'She's working as a volunteer in the hospital near Abbey-dale. She still lives with Maggie, the widow who took her and

Ruth in from the *Kindertransport*. She's the housekeeper for the rector. She keeps an eye on my brother, Tomas, for me and my sister, Liesel, I mean Lisa.'

'You should put a ring on Rachel's finger the first chance you get. Not many pretty girls would wait for an ugly old git like yourself. I recommend marriage.' Joseph pulled out a photo of his wife and their son. 'He's only a couple of weeks old in that picture. Coming up for three months now, and such an intelligent child.'

'Must have got that from his mother.' Harry teased his old friend—it was great seeing him. It helped ease the hurt of losing Taub and the others. Just a little.

Every day they rushed down to the noticeboard to see if their names had come up, but nothing.

Just as Harry was losing hope of ever being called, Joseph came running back to the room after lunch one day. 'We're up. Our names are there.'

They both stood and faced each other, for a second letting their nerves get the better of them.

'This is what we wanted, isn't it? What are we standing around here for?' Harry clapped Joseph on the back before they made their way downstairs.

Over the next week they went through a series of interviews and exams.

'Why do you want to join Three Troop, Beck?'

'My father was murdered at Dachau, a concentration camp, for the sole crime of being Jewish. My Jewish friends were killed in December, on their way home from clearing rubble in London. A bomb hit the bus they were on. The woman who took in my brother and sister lost her husband at Dunkirk. It's time I got even with those Nazis.'

'You're German. How do you feel about fighting, even killing, your countrymen?'

'I ceased being German in 1933, sir.'

Joseph and Harry made the cut for the final interviews. Harry marched into the office, where he found a tall Hungarian enlisted man who introduced himself as Sergeant George Lane, and a young-looking British captain called Bryan Hilton-Jones.

'Beck, you have excelled in all the tests and exams we set. Your hatred of Hitler and all he stands for is obvious. Are you ready for advanced training in the use of explosives and weapons?'

For a second Harry wondered if they were having him on. Was he ready? He'd been waiting for this since war was declared.

'I'm ready for anything, sir.'

Both Joseph and Harry found themselves posted to the Pioneer Corps camp in Bradford, where they awaited final vetting by MI5. Soon after their arrival, they were ordered to gather on the main ground.

Harry nudged Joseph as he spotted Bryan Hilton-Jones walking toward them.

'You men are going to be trained as commandos. I'll be your commanding officer.' The man glanced around before adding, 'You can call me Skipper.'

All the men gathered there exchanged glances. Harry wanted to cheer but figured it would be the wrong move. He closed his eyes for a second. *This is it, Papa. I'm on my way to finish the Nazis.*

'Each of you will now cease to exist. You must shed your past, including your names, and come up with a British-sounding name and cover story to go with it. You will also be registered as members of the Church of England congregation. You have fifteen minutes.'

'But, sir...?' one man shouted out.

Harry inhaled, waiting for the outburst for the breach of rank. But none came. Another officer stepped forward.

'On completion of your training, you will be sent overseas into enemy territory. Nobody needs to explain what will happen to you, as German nationals, if you are captured. Never mind the fact that many of you are Jewish. Never mind the fact that many of you have family still living in enemy territory. The name and backstory change is for your protection and that of your kin. You have been given an order, now get to it. Line up.'

The men filed into lines outside the CO's office.

Joseph looked bewildered. 'What are you going to say, Harry? What will your new name be?'

'I'm keeping Harry. That's English enough. I'll go with Barnes. Harry Barnes. My father was a Swiss lecturer and we travelled all over Europe, hence my accent. What about you?'

Joseph's eyes darted left and right, panicking as their position in the line moved closer to the head of the queue.

'Joseph Hillman, but my friends call me Joe. My father was a grocer who moved from Austria to England after falling in love with my English mother.'

Harry nodded. 'I think Mr Hillman would be honoured if he were here today.' Harry ignored the dart of pain as he thought of the older gentleman who'd stopped them being sent on the SS *Arandora Star*, saving their lives as it had sunk taking Mr Hillman with it.

Joseph shook his head. 'I think he would have insisted we got on the boat with him to Canada rather than have us in a commando unit. Can you really believe it, Harry? Last month the only weapon we could hold was a broom or pickaxe. Now we will become explosive experts, and marksmen. They said Lord Mountbatten set up Three troop, and he has the approval of Churchill. Do you think that's true? Do you think we will be able to go and visit our families and walk with our heads high, not have to look over our shoulder to check they aren't going to intern us again?'

Harry didn't have time to answer as he was called in next.

'Name?'

'Harry Barnes, sir.'

'Perfect.' The skipper inscribed the name in Harry's new paybook. He also got an army serial number and a fake parent regiment: the Royal West Kent Regiment. 'Sign there and there. From now on you answer to the name Harry Barnes.'

Harry took the items and saluted—'Yes, sir. Thank you, sir'—before turning on his heel and walking back outside.

He waited for Joseph to finish, his friend's face pale as he exited the office.

'What is it? Are you having second thoughts?'

'I thought I had lost everything when I had to flee Frankfurt. The Nazis took my father, our money, our home. All I had left was my name and my religion, and now they have taken those too.'

Harry understood the sentiment, but for now they had to see the bigger picture. 'You'll get it all back, Joseph. By the time we have whipped the Nazis, you will have all that and more. You will be able to tell your son that you were part of the force that finished Hitler and his henchmen. That is something to be proud of.'

They collected their new caps, uniforms and badges from the regiments they had supposedly joined and made their way back to the barracks. Harry's good mood continued until the next announcement.

'Gather up anything that connects you to your old life. That means pictures, letters, diaries and photographs. I want every-thing put in the brown envelope provided, and then put in this bag here.'

'Where is it going?' one man asked.

'It will be held in a secure location.'

Joseph looked as if he was about to cry as he took the photo of his wife and baby from his pocket.

Harry couldn't comfort him; he wasn't keen on giving up his photos either. Especially the one of Rachel.

'Lads, listen up. We're not going to destroy your stuff, we are sending it to a secure place. Nobody wants any of this mate-rial falling into the hands of the enemy. You've signed up for the duration. You'll get it back once the war is over. You can still write to your loved ones under your old identities. The letters will be sent through a secure system and they can reply to you. But you will not, repeat not, disclose your new name, rank or any other details to the civilians in your life. Do that, and I personally guarantee you will spend the rest of the war serving time in one of His Majesty's prisons.'

Harry put Rachel's photo into the brown envelope, sealing it before handing it to the officer.

Next stop was Aberdovey. As the train pulled into the small, quaint Welsh town, children were playing on the streets, bliss-fully unaware of the war. The scene was such a contrast from the bombed-out buildings of London and the big cities.

The men left the train and marched up the hill to their assembly point. The skipper addressed them, welcoming them to Wales. He had them all fall in and they were told to remove the peaked caps from their adoptive regiments. Each man marched in turn, shook hands with the skipper and accepted the green berets and shoulder flashes for their new unit. Then they were ordered to disperse.

'What do we do now?' Joseph asked Harry, as the men around them disappeared back toward the town.

'You heard the skipper. We have to find our own billets. Come on.' Harry didn't think it would be difficult to find a place to stay. With extra ration cards and an income of about two pounds a week, he felt rich.

They met up with some of the other men and together they found the largest house in the village. The couple who owned it were more than happy to give them rooms.

Harry woke Joseph early the next morning. 'Come on, sleepyhead. We've to assemble outside headquarters in thirty minutes.'

Joseph turned over in the bed. 'Go away, it's still dark out.'

Harry threw a glass of cold water over him. 'We go at dawn. Up and at them.'

Together they ran to the assembly point, where the rest of the squad stood waiting. Captain Hilton-Jones inspected them before giving them their orders: an eight-mile run up and down the surrounding hills before breakfast.

Harry took off after the others, and soon found himself staring at a five-foot fence. He watched in awe as one of the other men vaulted it without seeming to give it a second glance. He wasn't about to fail. He jumped too, and kept on going, despite others around him keeling over. His heart beat through his chest as sweat flowed down his forehead, but the thoughts of Taub and his other friends kept him going.

They would have given their all to be in his shoes, and he wasn't about to let them down.

TWENTY-SIX

SEPTEMBER 1942

When Trudi opened the door of the apartment, Jakob was already home. He put his hands over her eyes as he led her into the sitting room. 'Surprise!'

She opened her eyes to see a sewing basket on the table, along with a sewing machine: a replica of the one she'd had in her last apartment. 'I thought you might miss it. And if you ever need extra money, they go for a fortune on the black market.'

She smiled, running her hand over the machine. 'Where did you get it?'

He remained silent, staring at her with unseeing eyes. 'The Gestapo rounded up another twenty-six families two nights ago,' he finally said, in a low voice. 'We cleared their apartments earlier.'

Trudi recoiled as if she'd been punched in the stomach. The woman who had owned this machine was even now probably being herded onto a train bound for an unknown destination, not knowing if she'd ever see her loved ones again. How old was she? Did she have children, or had she been forced to send them away like Trudi had?

Jakob was watching her expression carefully. 'Don't look at

me like that. You know those people would prefer we take their valuables than let them go to the thugs who forced them out of their homes.'

She wrapped her arms around her chest. 'I can't explain. It just feels wrong for me to benefit.'

'We can sell it if you feel that strongly, but I thought you might use it to take in clothes for the people the church have sheltered. Even with the food shortages, the children are growing. It's not like they can go out and buy new clothes—even if there were any to be had.'

He was right, she was being silly and she'd ruined his surprise. She leaned in and gave him a quick kiss. 'Thank you. Of course I can use it to help. Chana complained to Sister Vide that the outfits some of the children were wearing were indecent, due to them being so short.'

'That woman still thinks we live in a normal world. But enough about her. There's more.' He nodded at the sewing basket.

She picked up the basket, which felt heavier than normal. She glanced at Jakob, who nodded that she should look inside. She put it down again and, lifting the spools of threads, needles and scissors, she uncovered a number of official identity passes. She looked at him, but he kept smiling. She leafed through them; they were from all sorts of individuals: men and women, some with professional occupations, other those of servants.

'Where did they come from? Are they real?'

'Yes, they're real. It's not an offence for you to lose your identify card. People have been leaving them in the church collection box at Kaufman's church. I'll pass them on to our forgers, and they can change out the photos for those of Jews at risk of deportation. They will stand up to even the closest inspection.'

Trudi bit her lip, hesitant to even broach the topic, especially after her reaction to the sewing machine. But although fear turned her mouth dry, she couldn't keep silent any longer. 'Those people are very generous, but'—she watched his eyes turning wary, but she had to voice her fears—'but what about Max? He said you couldn't work with this man Kaufman and continue working with him.'

Jakob's face hardened at the mention of Max. 'Max isn't my father,' he spat out. 'He doesn't get to dictate every aspect of my life.'

Trudi could sense the anger simmering underneath his words.

'But what if something happens to you?' Trudi breathed, tears welling up in her eyes. 'You take too many risks.'

Jakob's expression softened for a moment before turning hard again. 'Our whole life is a risk. Can't you see that? One false move and we are done for. Or we could be hit by an Allied bomb.'

She clenched her teeth together as the memories of the last bombing raid flooded back. They'd been on their way home after delivering food parcels to the homes of those people hiding Jews. They couldn't go to the air raid shelters, as the police liked to frequent these places searching not just for Jews but also for criminals and deserters.

Berlin was like a ghost town in the middle of a raid: there was no traffic allowed on the streets; everyone had, by law, to go to a shelter. But they couldn't risk the police checking their papers or asking them where they had been.

Jakob had pulled her into an abandoned building, one previously hit by a bomb. Every muscle in her body tensed as she remembered the terror; huddling for what seemed like an eternity with the plaster falling around them like heavy snow, suffocating them as it filled their lungs. The sound was deafening, thunderous airplanes above and explosions in their wake that shook the very foundations of the apartment building they were trapped in. Jakob had shielded her from the worst of the destruction, his body curved over hers as he whispered promises of love and security even amidst chaos. He spoke of reuniting with Liesel and Tomas, once the war was over.

She didn't want them to fight, she wanted him to hold her and never let go. She loved him with an intensity that made her heart ache if she thought of the possibility that it could all be lost in a single moment.

The pain in his eyes showed that she had hurt his pride more than anything else. With tears welling up, refocusing on what was important, she softened her tone, moving closer to him. 'I love you so much, please understand I'm not trying to undermine you. I just can't bear the thought of losing you.'

He pushed the hair back from her forehead, laying his lips on her skin. He whispered, 'I feel the same way when you go on a mission. There should be track marks on the floor from where I pace back and forth until you come home to me.' He moved to take her face in his hands, looking into her eyes, seeking reassurance. 'If we are going to have a future together, then this war must end. And for that there is no room for fear when it comes to saving innocent lives. Even if it means putting ourselves at risk. You know this, Trudi... we owe it to them. We owe it to our future selves.' His voice trembled as he struggled to get his emotions under control. 'I want to be able to look your children in the eye and tell them I... no, *we* did everything we could to save our people and defeat the evil that has taken over Germany.'

She lay her head on his shoulder, her tears soaking into his shirt.

He caressed her back as he held her. 'Shush, you are exhausted. Normally it is you giving me the strength to carry on.' He kissed her eyes and the tip of her nose. 'I have never met a braver woman.'

She turned her face so he could kiss her properly, holding him tight.

TWENTY-SEVEN

DECEMBER 1942

Harry sat in the corner of the drafty train carriage, on his way from Wales to Chertsey. The rhythm of the train's wheels on the track lulled some people to sleep but he was too excited. In a few hours he'd see Rachel for the first time since he'd been interned.

He kept his eyes on the window, staring at the countryside as it whizzed past. The carriage was packed, mainly with men in uniform either on their way home for leave like himself, or heading back to their units. The overall atmosphere in the carriage was tense as curious eyes darted towards him, probably wondering why he, a healthy young man, was not in uniform. His well-cut suit, tailored to fit his toned body, might have been a mistake. But he wasn't allowed to wear his uniform off base.

He shifted in his seat, trying not to draw comparisons between the icy stares of his fellow passengers and those dirty looks he'd experienced back in Berlin. Then he'd been a 'dirty' Jew; now, no doubt, he was being judged as a coward.

He held his head high: he had nothing to apologize for.

As the green fields of the countryside grew repetitive, he took one of Rachel's letters from his inside pocket, thankful he'd had time to collect them from the office where all their post was redirected to. He knew the contents by heart having savoured every word, examining them for hints she still felt the same as he did. He took out the new photo she'd enclosed, but that was a mistake as the soldiers around him demanded to see it. He passed it to his neighbour but, to his horror, the man passed it around his mates.

'Good-looking lass. She a nurse?'

Harry nodded, sensing the tension in the carriage rising like a simmering saucepan of water reaching its boiling point.

A gruff voice broke through the murmurs. 'How come she's doing her bit and you're not in uniform?' A burly soldier, his eyes narrowed, his jaw set in determination. 'You look fit enough to serve. What's your excuse?'

Whispers and knowing looks now filled the air, the passengers sensing a fight develop. Some looking excited at a break from the monotony of travelling, the women looking anxious.

Adrenaline surged through Harry, his body ready for a fight but his brain telling him he had to be careful. He couldn't afford to get into an altercation, and risk being arrested and blowing his cover. He wanted to scream at the top of his lungs he was a highly trained commando who could kill this bully with his bare hands, but instead he took a breath and with a calm and steady voice replied, 'I appreciate how it looks but, believe me, I'm doing my bit for the war effort.'

The soldier's eyes flashed with indignation but also a slight confusion. Harry guessed the man sensed something, probably because Harry wasn't showing any fear or aggression but remaining calm and collected. Perhaps he also saw the well-contoured muscles despite the suit.

Harry held his head up as the soldier studied him, looking for any signs of weakness.

'That an accent?' the soldier asked, in a suspicious tone.

'Swiss. My father is a lecturer and I spent a lot of time in Switzerland. At school.' Harry held his gaze.

For several seconds it seemed like everyone held their breath, until the soldier, shoulders sagging with resignation, replied: 'I guess it takes all sorts to win the war.'

The tension in the carriage dissipated. Muttered conversations restarted. Relief flowed through Harry, touched with a little bit of pride. He'd passed the test and hadn't lost his temper. His thoughts flew back to how his fifteen-year-old younger self had dealt with suspicious looks back in Germany.

He stared out the window. The situation had been defused but he couldn't afford to let his guard down. This was only the start. The people of Abbeydale, especially those who he'd grown close to, wouldn't be as easily put off. They knew all he wanted was to go back to Germany and finish off the Nazis. How would they react to him wearing civilian clothes? Not for the first time he thought how much easier it would be if they let them wear either the uniform of the Pioneer Corps or even that of the regiments they were supposed to belong to.

But he understood they couldn't walk down the streets of England wearing their green berets and commando uniforms. A troop of elite German-Jewish soldiers was a secret, and that's what it had to stay.

Harry carried his battered brown case as he walked through the village of Abbeydale, past the red telephone box. In the distance he could see the rectory and just a little bit farther, Sally's home, Rose Cottage. Not that there was any sign of roses now, it being the middle of December. He wondered if Sally had put up a Christmas tree or not.

As he walked, he nodded to a couple of people but didn't stop to say hello. He had no idea if they recognized him as the sullen, frightened, angry, sixteen-year-old who'd come to live there back in 1939.

He walked up the path to the front door, a mix of excitement and anxiety washing over him. It had been over a year since he'd seen his siblings and the others. They'd have questions about his lack of uniform and what he had been up to. He knew Sally would want to know what had stopped him coming back to see them. If she didn't, Rachel certainly would.

He knocked on the door. Tomas opened it. His eyes widened as he recognized his brother and he flung himself at him. Harry caught him easily, a wave of emotion bringing tears to his eyes. Tom was the image of their father, right down to his pointed chin. Harry couldn't stop the last image of his papa filling his mind, quickly followed by that of Schwarz. But he didn't have time to dwell on the feelings as Sally appeared holding a little girl by the hand.

Liesel, or Lisa as she was now called, had her thumb stuck in her mouth, her wide blue eyes staring at him.

He gave Tom another hug before he moved to greet Sally with a kiss on the cheek and then bent down to say hello to his sister. The baby he'd almost left behind in Germany. His guilt choked him as Lisa took her thumb out and gave him a shy smile.

'Hello, Lisa. Can I have a hug?'

Lisa nodded, releasing Sally's hand. He swung her into his arms, marvelling at how much she'd grown. She looked more like Trudi than his father but he saw Papa's kindness in her eyes.

'I've got some presents for you. In my bag. If it's all right with Sally—?' He glanced at her now, seeing the pain of losing Derek on her face, the black circles around her eyes, her thinness. She smiled then and it lit up her face. 'Of course you can. Come on in—this is your home, Harry. Tom, take Harry's luggage up to your room and put it on his bed. Then you can run over to Maggie and tell her the news. It's a wonder she isn't here already—she's been counting down the days since you wrote to say you were coming home.'

Harry wanted to ask if Rachel felt the same, but he was too shy. He took the small bag of gifts from his case before Tom raced with it up the stairs.

'Some things don't change—he still runs everywhere,' he said with a smile as Tom disappeared, and he followed Sally into the sitting room.

He put the bag on the table before handing her his ration cards. 'There's some eggs and butter in the bag. Some sugar too, a couple of jars of jam and a few other bits and pieces.'

Sally opened the bag, her eyes widening at the contents. 'You don't have to spend your money on us. You already send enough.'

'You're raising my siblings. It's the least I can do.' Then the back door banged and then in moments he was enveloped in Maggie's arms.

'It's so good to see you, even if you're the worst letter writer in history. Why aren't you in uniform?' Maggie said, holding him at a distance and scrutinizing his face. 'You haven't been kicked out of the Royal Pioneers, have you? Lost your temper again?'

'Maggie! Stop with all the questions and leave him be. If he was in trouble, he wouldn't be home on leave, would he?' Sally rolled her eyes.

Harry needed to distract Maggie from that subject. He spotted Ruth following behind Maggie, his hopes rising that Rachel wouldn't be far behind... but Ruth was alone.

He picked up a small bar of chocolate from the bag on the table and walked over to her. 'You've grown into a pretty young lady, Ruth.' He bowed and presented her with the bar as she blushed furiously.

'Where's mine?' Tom demanded. Harry distributed the

chocolate, keeping back some which he placed under the Christmas tree in the corner of the room. He'd add the other presents he'd brought home later. He passed several packets of cigarettes to Maggie. 'Don't smoke them all. I got rations, and figured you could swap them for other things you might need.'

He wanted to ask where Rachel was but couldn't bring himself to do so. He frowned, telling himself he was being stupid. *You've been trained to kill a man with your bare hands but you can't ask after a girl?*

Sally made a pot of tea, using fresh leaves in his honour, but he barely tasted it, his eyes flicking to the door hoping it would open and Rachel would appear.

'Rachel's shift will be finished soon. Why don't you walk up to the bus and meet her?' Maggie's innocent expression didn't fool anyone.

Tom and Ruth giggled as Tom made kissing noises.

Sally pushed him out the door. 'Go on now, otherwise they'll tease you to death. Harry, it's so good to have you home. We've all missed you, especially Rachel.'

He smiled and, humming a tune, he walked down the road, trying to pretend his heart wasn't hammering.

Turning the corner, he was just in time to see the bus drive off, leaving a couple of women dressed in nurses' outfits in its wake.

His pulse raced as he recognized her, even though she stood with her back to him, chatting to another woman. Then she turned and their gazes locked. His breath caught in his throat: she was even more beautiful than her photograph. He wanted to push the wispy brown curls back from her face where they had escaped from her hat.

The look of recognition and surprise in her eyes gave way to nervousness as he remained glued to the spot. She took a tentative step forward before he got a hold of himself, strode up to her and, picking her up, swung her around before setting her back on her feet and stealing a quick kiss.

He pulled back and looked at her, seeing her eyes filled with tears. 'Rachel, what is it? What's wrong?'

'I can't believe you are here. Standing in front of me. I've missed you, Heinz, so much.' She reached up and touched his face, whispering, 'I didn't think I'd see you again. I thought they would send you... the stories I've heard, the injuries I've seen. I couldn't bear it.' Her voice shook, her whole body trembling with emotion.

He took off his jacket, wishing it was a coat he could wrap around her, as the one she was wearing looked rather thin. He left his arm on her shoulders and she didn't move away. She cuddled into his side and together they walked back down the road towards the rectory.

Once they were off the main road, he pulled her into an embrace. They stood staring at each other before she stood on tiptoes and kissed him. He pulled her closer as the kiss developed.

He didn't know how long they kissed but a cough from a stranger walking by made them spring apart like guilty children caught with their hand in the sweet jar. Laughing, they walked the rest of the way back, holding hands.

Later that evening, Sally told him to take Rachel into the good front room to talk. They sat beside one another on the sofa, listening to the muffled sound of conversation coming from the back room.

'Heinz, what are you doing in the army?'

He stilled. This was Rachel. He didn't want to lie to her. 'Everything they tell me to do. Digging ditches, building fortifications. That sort of thing.'

She poked him in the arm. 'This is me. Sally and Maggie may believe that but I don't. You've changed.'

'It's been a couple of years, Rachel. You're not the same girl I left behind. You're more beautiful and totally kissable.' He leaned in to kiss her and she allowed him a brief kiss before pulling away, her eyes searching his.

'Tell me. You didn't get these muscles digging ditches. And it's not just the physical changes, it's you. You're more even tempered, more controlled or something. I can't put it into words but you're different.'

He held her hands. 'In a good way?'

She laughed. 'Maybe not that different—you're still fishing for compliments.' The smile slid from her face. 'What are you doing for the army? Is it dangerous? I mean fighting is, but... are you doing something more than that?'

'You've an overactive imagination. Is that what nursing has done to you?'

'There's been stories. About secret agents, even French women, being sent into France undercover. Is that what you are doing? I won't tell anyone, I swear. I just need to know.'

He kissed the tip of her nose.

'Heinz!'

'Rachel, my name is Harry. Heinz is gone. For good.'

'Just answer my question.'

He looked her deep in the eyes. 'I swear I'm not a secret agent. On my life. Now, will you stop talking about the war and kiss me.'

The seven days passed quickly and then Harry was back in Wales in his commando uniform. He boarded a train, this time heading to parachute training in RAF Ringway, Manchester Airport.

The emerald Welsh fields reminded him of the Surrey countryside and filled him with a deep longing for Rachel. He bit his lip, hoping that he would make her proud and prove that he was brave enough to go through with this. But the thought of plummeting to earth from the sky brought on a wave of nausea. His hands began to shake as fear coursed through his veins like ice water. He dug his fingernails into his skin, focusing on the mental picture of her sweet smile, and sat up straighter. He was going to ace the training, the last hurdle before he made good on his promise to help end this war and reunite their families.

TWENTY-EIGHT

27 FEBRUARY 1943

'What's going on?' Max asked, but the SS officer ignored him, ordering all the men present in the factory to get into the truck. 'These men are protected Jews. They are all married to gentiles.'

The SS man sneered, his eyes lit with a fanatical hate. 'That protection has worn out. Now, do you want to walk to the truck or would you like to be carried?'

Max blanched at the threat, his expression changing from bewilderment to resignation. He took off his apron and handed it to Trudi, with the keys.

'Tell the boss, please.'

Trudi nodded, heart hammering at her chest. Her false papers were good but would they stand up to scrutiny from this SS officer?

She didn't have to worry.

'Move. This beautiful *Frau* doesn't want to breathe the same tainted air as you.' The officer saluted Trudi before pushing Max and the others out the door. Some men didn't resist but most protested in some form or another.

Trudi waited for them to leave before rushing into the

office. She phoned Max's wife. When the call was connected she said, 'The package has been collected.' She hung up, knowing Christabel would recognize the code.

The next call she placed was to the countess. If anyone knew where the men were going, she would.

It didn't take long for the wives to gather at the factory, a few crying in anguish but most wearing an expression of defiance. Isla arrived, dressed just like any other German working woman. She motioned to Trudi to come into the office.

'They've been separated from the others and sent to the detention centre on Rosenstrasse. There are wives down there already protesting.'

'Why did they take them? I thought they were protected?'

'Goebbels.' Isla shuddered as she named the man Trudi knew she hated most. 'He's fed up with being a laughing stock. He said the day the bombs hit Berlin they were to call him *Meier*. He also told the Führer that Berlin was *Judenrein*. He's been caught out on both counts and is furious. Someone has to pay.'

Trudi rubbed her palms on her skirt, trying to hide her anxiety. Isla never showed any fear. 'What do you think we should do?'

'Trudi, you can't help these men. But their wives can. Tell them to go to the Rosenstrasse and demand their husbands' release. A peaceful demonstration by real German women might work.'

'I want to support my friends. Max is down there.'

The countess grabbed her arm. 'You can't risk everything. It's not just your safety but that of all of us. Think about it. Where are the Jew catchers likely to be today?'

Trudi gasped—she hadn't thought of that. The Jews working for with the Gestapo were the biggest risk to the people like herself. The SS might be easily fooled, especially if a Jew looked nothing like the grotesque caricatures in *Der Stürmer,* but not a fellow Jew. They could have attended the same school, synagogue or even a celebration such as a wedding or bar mitzvah. The countess was right. She couldn't go.

Isla continued speaking: 'I have to get back to the office. Tell the wives what to do and maybe go home. The SS may come back here to check they haven't missed anyone.' The countess leaned in to kiss Trudi on both cheeks, squeezing her arm in a gesture of support before she left.

Taking a deep breath, Trudi returned to the factory floor where the wives huddled in groups. She gestured for them to come to the side of the room, indicating the remaining workers should get back to work.

Trudi spoke calmly, not believing her voice wasn't shaking with terror. 'I had a phone call. Your men are being held at Rosenstrasse detention centre for processing.' Her words caused a few to gasp, others to burst into noisy tears. She gestured for quiet. 'Some wives are already protesting outside the offices. You may want to join them.' She glanced in the direction of the other workers before whispering: 'Keep it peaceful, don't give the SS an excuse to arrest you.'

One woman asked, 'Are you coming with us?'

Trudi shook her head quickly. 'I have to stay here. The boss won't care that half our workers are missing. They won't lower our targets.'

Her excuse was accepted, although she suspected some of these women knew she was Jewish. She walked out with them, returning to the factory floor via the bathroom. She washed her face with cold water, smoothed her hair and, wiping her hands on her skirt, hoped she was ready to face the other workers.

Instead of the questions she feared, she returned to find a

hot drink waiting for her on her desk. The men continued to work, a few sending her supportive looks. Tears filled her eyes. These Polish and French men were prisoners too. Their gesture of support meant so much.

After work, Trudi headed to the Swedish church to see Sister Vide. If anyone knew how to help, Vide Ohmann would. She appeared to have contacts everywhere.

When Trudi stepped into the reception hall the church owned, she spotted her vivacious friend across the room. Her lovely face was marked with tears, her eyes wide. She locked glances with Trudi and hurried over.

'You've heard?'

'They came for Max today, and all the other protected Jews. I was told they were being held in Rosenstrasse. Some of the wives were protesting.'

'Yes, hundreds are down there. Not just the wives of the men but some sympathetic Germans have joined them. Brave actions—I can't tell you how my heart sings seeing my fellow Berliners take action. Trudi, imagine what could have happened if more people had protested earlier. When Hitler first came to power?'

Trudi didn't think it helped anyone to look back. There was nothing they could do about the past. 'I came to see if there is anything I can do. I thought the news may have made some of your residents nervous.'

'Ah, you mean your friends, Ada and Chana.' Vide gave her a knowing look but her eyes were twinkling. 'I think you might be pleasantly surprised. Come and see.'

Mystified, Trudi followed Vide through the church into the staff accommodation. She couldn't believe her eyes. Ada and Chana stood in the middle of a group of Jewish people, who, judging by their clothes and demeanour had just arrived. The two ladies were beacons of calm as they directed the new arrivals to food and, possibly of equal importance, a place to wash and get clean clothes.

'It seems the needs of others have distracted them from their own fears. Isn't it wonderful?'

Trudi could barely recognize the women. They looked almost like they had in the years before Ari died. Chana was in her element ordering people around; Ada was fussing over the women and children like a mother hen.

Trudi stepped forward, dying to hug her friends, but something caught her eye and she froze.

'We never know what people are capable of.' Vida muttered something else, a prayer of some sort, but Trudi wasn't paying attention.

To her horror, she had recognized one of the men in the group of new arrivals.

Trudi turned her face away before he saw her, whispering, 'Vide, could you take me to Eric, please.'

Vide's eyes widened but she didn't protest. Taking Trudi's arm she led her away from the guests and through the church, to Eric's empty office. Only when they were inside did she demand to know what was wrong.

'Trudi, you're shaking like a leaf. What's wrong?'

'Find Eric and bring him here. It's bad, Vide.'

Alarmed, Vide ran to find Eric. Trudi fell into the chair by his desk. Was this the moment it was all over? If she concentrated hard enough, would she hear the trucks, the stomping hobnailed boots on the pavement? Her hands shook so much, she wrapped them around herself, rocking back and forth, whispering, 'Please God, protect us,' again and again.

It seemed like hours since Vide had left but it was only minutes before she returned, Eric behind her. She couldn't tell who looked more concerned.

'Trudi, are you ill? What can we do?'

'Eric, you have to empty the church. Now. Get everyone out.'

Eric exchanged a glance with Vide who moved to take Trudi's hand, patting her on the back. 'Calm down and start from the beginning. What is it?'

'I recognized one of the men in your queue downstairs. Only he doesn't usually look like he does now. He normally is well dressed, frequents the best restaurants and the operas.'

Her friends' eyes widened, exchanging glances before turning to look at her intently.

'Is he not Jewish?' Vide asked.

'He is, but I was warned by a friend that he was captured and instead of being deported, offered to work for the Gestapo at Iranishce Strasse.'

Eric understood first. He took a seat, wiping a hand across his brow. 'He's a Jew catcher?'

Trudi nodded, incapable of speaking.

Vide was the first to recover. 'Maybe he has changed his ways and wants to run now?'

They both stared at her, Trudi wondering how her friend could still believe the best in people. After everything they had seen and experienced.

Eric stood up. 'We can't take that chance. I'll be back shortly. Try to make sure he doesn't leave. Trudi, you should leave. Just in case.'

Trudi was sick of running. It was bad enough losing Max, but she couldn't lose these people too. She shook her head. 'I want to stay with my friends.'

'Stay in here then. We don't want to spook him. He may not have realized you recognized him.'

Grabbing his coat, Eric walked out of the office. Vide stayed with Trudi, gently rubbing her back.

'Vide, how can you be so calm?'

'I trust God to protect this church and to lead Eric to the right people to help.'

Trudi gaped at her. She didn't believe in God anymore. If he existed, the concentration camps, the Nazis and all of it wouldn't exist. But she didn't want to offend her friend.

'Rest here. Would you like me to bring you anything? We have soup and some bread that isn't too stale.'

'No, thank you. I'll be sick if I try to eat. Don't let me keep you. I won't jump out of the window or anything.'

'Trudi, you've spent months living a lie with false identity papers, moving around Berlin just one step ahead of the Gestapo... the stress has become too much. Anyone would have reacted like you did. Now rest. Trust Eric.'

Trudi closed her eyes but she couldn't stop the thoughts jumbling through her head. Could she survive in a concentration camp? Would she live to the end of the war?

She wanted to hold her baby so much. A tear escaped and she rubbed it away. But then another one followed and she gave up. She sobbed, wondering where Eric had gone and when he'd be back. Would it be before or after the SS?

About an hour later, she heard a noise at the door and almost collapsed as a police constable and his chief walked into the room. She couldn't stop the terrorized gasp she let out. But the smaller of the two men sent her a reassuring smile, which emphasized the wrinkles on his face, and she was relieved to see Eric enter the room with them.

'Pastor Perwe mentioned he has an unwelcome visitor.' The constable took out his notebook, looking to Trudi for details. She wasn't sure what to say, glancing at Eric for inspiration.

'Trudi recognized a criminal who has joined the food queue downstairs. As you know this church opens its doors to all who need help, but we have an obligation to obey the law. So we thought it best to inform the police.'

Panicked, Trudi thought Eric had lost his marbles. He was complaining to the police about a man on the Gestapo's payroll when he had about thirty Jewish people downstairs in the church?

'This man, what did he do?'

Trudi couldn't stop her voice shaking. 'He works as a Jew catcher. For the Gestapo.'

The constable's eyes narrowed. 'Hoffman, take this lady downstairs and have her point out the individual. We'll seize him on the street outside. Don't let him see your face, young lady.'

Terrified, Trudi glanced at Eric but he was smiling too. She didn't understand what was going on. She had no choice but to obey. As she walked downstairs with the constable, he told her not to worry.

'The boss hates the SS and Gestapo. Ill-mannered hooligans with no training. They aren't fit to wipe his boots.'

Trudi stayed silent.

'So, this man, he's a rat. Turns in his own for money, is that right?'

'In this case, yes. Though some do it to protect their families from being deported, their parents or children.'

The policeman rubbed a hand across his chin. 'I suppose we don't know what we'd be prepared to do if someone threatened our own.'

Trudi hoped she'd never betray anyone in order to save her life but she didn't say so. You didn't argue with a policeman, even if he seemed to be on their side.

'Still, we can't have him walking around spreading lies and fantasy. Pastor Perwe runs a good church, Sister Vide is a wonderful person and all the good people who work here, they serve the community. We need places like this.'

Trudi couldn't believe her ears. Here was a policeman telling her he believed in saving the Jews.

When they reached the room next to the one where everyone was eating, the policeman stopped her. 'Give me a description and then go and hide in Sister Vide's room. I will walk him out. Put a candle in the window if he's the right man.'

Trudi went to Vide's room and waited. Soon she saw the Jew catcher being escorted down the path by the constable. Instead of the kindly face he had presented to her, he now looked grim, his eyes hard as he stared at the man walking slightly in front of him. She put the candle in the middle of the windowsill. When the cop saw it, she watched as he gave the Jewish man a clout around the ear.

Vide came in the door behind her. 'Eric asked if you could join him upstairs again.'

Speechless now, Trudi walked up the stairs, back to Eric's office. How could these people act as if nothing had happened? The Jew catcher knew everything and if he escaped or spoke to a policeman working with the Gestapo, the entire operation would be shut down and the people arrested, tortured and transferred to concentration camps, if not shot.

When she got to the office, the scent of tobacco greeted her. She opened the door to find the police chief smoking. He stood up as she entered. Eric quickly introduced them properly.

'Chief Mattick has been a friend for a long time. He protects us as best he can. Never play chess with him, though—he doesn't like to lose.'

The men chortled as Trudi just stood there. This wasn't real, was it? She had never met a policeman who protected Jews. Men like the man who'd stood by when the bully beat up Aron Weiss. Yet, here were two police officers who had not only arrested a man working for the Gestapo but were being treated by Eric as if they were close friends.

Trudi had to be sure. 'The Jewish man... the one he'—she looked at the policeman—'took away...'

Chief Mattick answered her. 'He will be dealt with. We have several crimes we can charge him with. Black-market dealing, lack of proper papers... not to mention the fact he's Jewish. Don't worry, he won't be bothering the church again.'

Trudi couldn't stop herself from asking, 'But the Gestapo—?'

'—won't know about it. Please forget about this unfortunate event. I swore to uphold the law and that's what I do. The real law.' Chief Mattick sat back in his chair, his confidant air telling her he believed every word of what he had said and that there was nothing to worry about.

Trudi saw Eric glance at her, his look telling her to drop it.

Chief Mattick pointed to the seat opposite his. 'Why don't you sit down, Frau Beck, and tell me a bit about yourself? I don't need to see your papers.'

Trudi took a seat and began telling him her story. He handed her his hanky when her voice broke as she told him about sending her baby and the boys to Britain.

'Pity you couldn't go with them, but I'm glad you found this church. It's full of good people. Not all of Berlin or Germany are in favour of Hitler's racial policies. We may have thought he was good for us when he built the autobahn and gave people jobs. He gave them money in their pocket, made them stand proud to be Germans. But now...' The police chief shook his head. 'His actions give most of us sleepless nights. Giving power to thugs like those in the SS. Having Himmler and Goebbels lie to us, tell us all about how they epitomize some superior race— one a chicken farmer, the other a cripple. How will history judge us?' The policeman stared into his drink for a couple of seconds.

Trudi wasn't sure if he thought she would console him, agree with him or tell him he was wrong.

The silence continued until he looked up. 'I suppose you have gentile papers, not that I want to know anything about that. Eric, why don't you give us all a drop more of your whisky and turn on the BBC. We might have something to celebrate.'

Trudi downed the whisky in one gulp, causing her to cough. Thankfully, Eric's wife, Martha, arrived. She gave her husband a peck on the cheek before greeting the others.

'Trudi, how lovely to see you. Nice to see you too, Chief. Forgive me but I need to steal Trudi away for a while. We'll leave you boys to it.'

The police chief stood up, bowed and clicked his heels as Trudi placed her glass on the table and walked out of the office.

'I've never been so glad to see anyone in my life. I don't know if I'm dreaming.'

Martha chuckled. 'Chief Mattick is very real, my dear. Such a wonderful friend to my husband and all in our church. Vide told me about your day, it's been horrible for you. I wanted to see what plans you have for the next few days. I thought you might appreciate a trip to the country.'

'Where?'

'I have some guests I need to collect from a retirement home on the southern outskirts of Berlin. The elderly owner, Frieda, phoned to say she had a visit from the Gestapo. Don't worry, they didn't find anything—the couple were out shopping at the time. But we've used the home before so someone may have recognized them. Or it may have just been a spot check. Frieda told the Gestapo the person who sent them must have been senile—that she would never betray her country like that. She insisted on them sitting down and looking through her photograph album of her husband who died at the front.' Martha laughed. 'I wish I'd been there. Once Frieda starts talking about her dear departed husband, she goes on for hours. I doubt they will bother her again.' Martha looked at Trudi, who was embarrassed to be caught in a yawn. 'Stay here tonight. Ada and

Chana will love catching up with you. Then tomorrow, I'll hav
your papers and tickets.'

'What about the factory?'

'We've discussed that and believe it would be better if you
didn't return. Who knows if one of those arrested today may
talk about their pretty work colleague? It's too risky. We'll send
them a note to say you have been called up.'

Although sad to say goodbye to the factory and the people
who worked there, relief flowed through her. Max had always
done his best for the workers, especially the slave labourers,
trying to exist on pitifully small rations. He'd seen they were
treated humanely in the factory. But the new bosses wouldn't
share his values, and how long would she have lasted before
they spotted she wasn't a Nazi either? She trembled at the
thought of what could have happened if she'd been arrested, her
cover blown. Would she...? She took a deep breath, forcing
those thoughts from her mind, trying to concentrate on what
Martha was saying.

'Now relax and let me tell you what my darling husband
has done now. We were at one of those diplomatic gatherings
we have to attend. So boring. But this one...'

Martha's voice zoned out as Trudi's eyelids grew heavier.
When she woke up later, she found someone had put a blanket
over her and left her alone to sleep. She really should get up and
find her friends, but instead she closed her eyes once more.

TWENTY-NINE

JUNE 1943

Looking back, that first eight-mile hike was the easiest part of their training. But no matter what they were instructed to do, be it forty-mile hikes wearing their full gear or fifty-mile runs up and down Mount Snowdon, their skipper lead the way. Day by day, the men's admiration for their leader increased.

'Tomorrow is the final cut, Harry. What if we don't make it?' Joseph asked, as they went for a walk after dinner.

'Stop thinking like that. We will.'

Harry hoped this was the truth: he couldn't imagine failing now. Not when he was this close.

The test the next day began well. They swam across the harbour in full kit, something they had done several times. Next they had to march up the side of a hill, followed by a race back to headquarters. Harry kept running despite his muscles screaming for respite, his lungs burning as sweat flowed from his forehead as the salty remnants of the sea water burned his lips. He had to succeed.

He saw Joseph ahead of him, but then his pleasure turned to horror as his friend fell.

Harry looked around, the other men pushing past him. Nobody was stopping. He was torn between finishing the race and achieving his place in the skipper's troop and stopping to help Joseph.

He couldn't leave him. He ran over and tried to pull him to his feet.

'No, Harry. Leave me. I can't go any farther. I'm done.'

'Joseph, you can't give up not now. Think of your wife, your child. Think of your mother.' Nothing seemed to reach his friend. 'Think of those Nazis gits you left behind.'

That lit a flare in his eyes, but when he tried to stand, Joseph's leg buckled under him. 'I think my ankle's broken. Go on, Harry. Leave me.'

'Never.' Harry glanced around, spotting a low-level wall. 'Crawl over here to the wall and then you can get on my back. I'm taking you home.'

'Leave me.'

Tony McKenna, nicknamed Mac, another member of the troop stopped, wiping sweat from his forehead. 'Need some help?'

Harry nodded. 'Think his ankle's broken. Can you help get him onto my back and I'll carry him?'

Together they managed to get Joseph onto Harry's back, Tony taking Harry's gun.

The three of them completed the race, albeit coming in last.

Once at headquarters, Harry called out for the medics, thinking he was shouting, but his voice had turned from a roar into a whisper. Tony ran ahead to find help.

'Let me take him.' Sergeant Lane was by his side. 'Harry, let go. I've got him.'

The words found their way into Harry's fuddled brain and he released his hold on Joseph. Once Lane had him, Harry slid to the ground, too exhausted to even attempt to stand when the skipper came over.

The skipper whistled to the other men to gather around. He then held out his hand and helped Harry to stand. 'This man epitomizes what is the meaning of our group. We are commandos. That means no man is left behind. If someone faints or is injured, you pick him up and bring him home. Well done, Barnes. You too, McKenna.' Tony had arrived back carrying a stretcher accompanied by the medics. 'Both of you have earned your spot on my team.' He turned back to the other men. 'You lot will run again tomorrow.'

Harry couldn't believe his ears. He'd done it. He gingerly put one foot in front of the other, ignoring the screams of protest from his exhausted body and went in search of Joseph.

Tony helped him and together they found him, his bound ankle raised, sleeping like a baby. A grey-haired man in a white coat sat by the side of the bed.

'Had to sedate him to reset the ankle. Nasty break.' The doc looked up from his notes and glanced at Tony. 'You don't look too hot yourself. Give me five minutes and I'll examine you.'

Tony shook his head. 'I didn't do anything. You need to check Harry, though. I'll catch up with you later.' Tony almost ran out of the room. Nobody wanted to be injured in case they were left behind when the troop eventually moved out.

The doc raised his eyebrows, waiting for Harry's response.

'I'm fine, doc. Nothing a bath and sleep won't sort out. What's going to happen to Joe? Will he still be able to see active service?'

The doctor didn't meet his eyes but paid close attention to his notes. 'Not my call, young man. I just need to get him better. You should get that bath now, otherwise you will catch a chill.'

Harry glanced at Joseph, unwilling to leave him.

'Go on, son, get some rest. He isn't going anywhere.'

. . .

Harry slept for twelve hours straight. As soon as he got permission, he went to see Joseph.

'Thank you for what you did, but you shouldn't have. You'd have come first or second if you hadn't stopped for me.'

'That doesn't matter. How are you feeling?'

Joseph coloured, focusing on the blanket covering his bed.

'What? You can't be embarrassed because you broke your ankle.'

'No, it's not that. I feel...' Joseph looked down at the bed clothes again, his hands gripping the sheet.

'Joe?'

Joseph held his gaze. 'I'm *relieved*. There, I said it. I want to live, Harry. I want to see my son grow up.'

Harry stayed silent.

'This'—Joseph pointed at his ankle—'I didn't do it on purpose, but it's the end of my commando days. The skipper has already been in to see me. He's arranging for me to be transferred to some hush hush unit where I can use my skills to interrogate captured prisoners of war. Doc says I'll likely limp for the rest of my life but at least I'll live.' Joseph rubbed his eye with his sleeve as his voice hitched.

'Joe, you aren't a coward and I'll lay out anyone who ever says otherwise, including you. Concentrate on getting better and when this is all over, you can introduce me to your son and your wife.'

Joe nodded but Harry wasn't sure if he meant it. His friend couldn't look him in the eye. He wondered, if the situation was reversed, would he have been brave enough to admit the relief being forced out of the commandos would bring? Because now the training was over and the real war started, and if anyone said they weren't a bit scared, they would be lying.

. . .

Mac caught up with Harry early the next day. 'Harry, Skipper wants to see us.'

Harry rolled off the bed gently, trying not to groan. Mac didn't look or act injured, whereas every one of Harry's joints were screaming at him.

'You wanted to see us, sir?' Harry faced the desk where the skipper sat. Sergeant Lane stood to his left. A captain he had never seen before stood to his right.

'At ease, Barnes, McKenna. I believe you've seen Joseph Hillman.'

'Yes, sir.'

Harry held the skipper's gaze as the man spoke. 'He will be an asset to his next command. We have need of German speakers in many different divisions in the forces.'

Harry stayed silent, not sure what to say.

'Congratulations, both of you. You are ready. I've had a request for help from one of my old units. This here is Captain Murphy. He and I have served together. I trust him with my life.'

Harry and Mac exchanged a glance. At their silence, the skipper looked Harry straight in the eye. 'This is what you wanted, what you trained for. Murphy needs help and I've volunteered you. I assume you agree.'

'Yes, sir. Thank you, sir.'

The skipper stood up and came around to stand beside Harry, holding out his hand. 'Make us proud, Barnes.' He shook Mac's hand as well. 'You too, McKenna.' Then he turned to Murphy. 'Don't get too attached—they're only on loan.'

THIRTY

AUGUST 1943

Trudi leaned against the windowsill, her breath fogging the glass as she watched the world outside, straining on tiptoes to see the mountains in the distance. Freedom was so close she could almost taste it. What if she and Jakob made a run for it? But even as she tortured herself with thoughts of freedom, she shrugged the thoughts off. They had people depending on them. Innocents, like the group they had just escorted out of Berlin. They had to go back but, for now, they could enjoy the two days they would stay out of sight, away from the war.

She prayed the group they had just escorted had made their way past the quarry and over the border.

The small cottage nestled in a forest was a refuge from the turmoil consuming the world in 1943. Her fingers tapped against the wood; her nerves rattled. How much longer could they survive living this double life? Berlin grew more dangerous by the day, the bombing raids killing thousands but also destroying homes and, in the process, the hiding places of Jews like herself and Jakob, living as U-boats.

Once again, she wanted to grab Jakob's hand and make a

dash to safety. Leave everything and everyone behind them and live.

But she knew that even if she could do that, he would never go. Not while there was one person left in Berlin who needed his help.

Jakob entered the room with a smile for her, carrying a bundle of firewood in his arms. He carefully placed the logs in the fireplace, building a small pyramid.

'Are you sure it's safe to light a fire? Won't the smoke be seen?'

'Luise told me to do it, as it will help air out the cottage and stop the damp.' He turned back to build up the fire, her eyes watching every move he made. He was thinner than when they'd first met but that wasn't the only change.

He grinned as he looked up and caught her staring. 'Trust her, she knows what she's doing. Hasn't everything she told us proved true so far?'

Trudi nodded. They had followed Frau Meir's instructions to the letter, taking the milk train from Stuttgart as there were fewer patrols. They'd dressed the older boys in Hitler Youth uniforms, telling some nosy passengers the children were training in the hills nearby. Hence, they needed their bicycles. The latter were the payment for the various guides and helpers who would get the group to safety, being more valuable than the Reichsmark these days.

When they got to Singen station, they were met by a lady dressed all in black on a bicycle, just as Frau Meier had said. This lady was all smiles as she greeted them warmly, as if they were old friends, and then led them into the woods where they met some other men. Two men relieved them of the bicycles. One gave Jakob and Trudi the directions for the cottage where they would stay for two nights to rest, assuming all went well. They all knew that meant the escape party, now following another man through the fields to the border by the quarry just beyond, had crossed the border without getting into difficulties: should they have been discovered, the whole area would have been locked down.

Trudi had argued against them staying at the cottage, feeling they would be safer getting back on the train and out of the area. But the men had argued that Singen was too small a station and people might remember they had just arrived in a group. It was better to rest for a couple of days and then take a longer, less direct route back, avoiding the area.

Trudi sighed. This war was giving them strange bedfellows. Luise Meir was the mother of two dead German soldiers, both killed fighting with the SS on the Eastern Front. Was it the guilt from knowing her sons had probably taken part in the organized mass killings of Jews that Frau Krause had talked about? Was that what made the wealthy, elegant and well-connected Frau Meier set up an underground railroad to help Jews escape from Berlin? Isla, Jakob and even Max, who was notoriously suspicious of everyone, trusted the woman.

Wasn't that enough for her too?

'Where did I put the matches?' Jakob stood and glanced around but, seeing the look on her face, he moved to her, enfolding her in his arms and making her feel safe. 'Trudi, relax. We're safe here. Enjoy it. Just for tonight, let's pretend the war doesn't exist. Nothing does, apart from the two of us and this cottage.' He leaned in, his breath tickling her ear before he left a trail of kisses along her neck. She shivered.

'What can I do to make you forget? Just for now?' He kissed the tip of her nose before releasing her. 'I best light the fire before we get too distracted.'

Trudi wished it was that easy, but she found it more difficult to switch off. When she tried to relax her mind was filled with concern for her children in Britain. Were they safe? Would the church where Ada and Chana lived escape from the next bombing raid? How was she still free when people around her disappeared every day?

Jakob tilted her chin up, saying softly, 'Trudi, stop frowning. Tomorrow, we go back to Berlin, to our work there. Tonight... please let us have tonight.'

She pushed aside her guilt for still being alive, for sitting in the apartment and doing nothing the night the Weiss family were taken. She watched as Jakob walked over to the fire and took the matches from the mantelpiece. He struck a match, igniting the logs, filling the room with a warm, orange glow.

The heat from the fire began to spread through the room, chasing away the biting cold that had been their constant companion. As the fire roared, Jakob extended his hand to Trudi. She hesitated for a moment, then placed her palm in his, allowing him to pull her closer.

'May I have this dance?' Jakob whispered tenderly.

Trudi nodded, shivers of excitement flowing through her at his touch. Despite their living together, her body responded intensely to his, yet she still felt shy. The adoring look in his eyes as he gazed at her, his touch, smell and taste, made her feel alive, having been alone for so long.

Jakob wrapped his arm around her waist, drawing her closer as they swayed gently to the soft melody he sang. Trudi laid her head on his shoulder, watching their shadows dancing on the walls as the fire crackled.

Jakob looked deeply into Trudi's eyes, a soft smile gracing his lips. She could see her love reflected in his gaze, and it warmed her heart. This was what Ada had meant when she was talking about Sol.

Jakob leaned down, brushing his lips gently against Trudi's forehead, then her cheeks, and finally, tenderly, he kissed her lips. The kiss was soft and sweet, a promise of the love they shared. As they pulled away, Trudi rested her head on Jakob's chest, listening to the steady rhythm of his heart. They continued to dance, the world outside forgotten, their love a shelter from the storm raging beyond their sanctuary.

Later, as the fire began to dwindle, they settled down on the soft rug in front of the hearth. Wrapped in each other's arms, they exchanged stories and laughter, cherishing the moment of peace amidst the chaos of the world outside.

With Trudi's head on Jakob's shoulder and his arm protectively around her, they stared into the dying embers, a comforting silence enveloping them. They knew the world would continue to change, and they had no way of knowing what the future held.

The next morning, Jakob kissed Trudi. Despite sleeping deeply, when she awoke the worries rushed back in, filling her thoughts. Seeing her expression, he murmured, 'Stop worrying, you will give yourself wrinkles.'

Exasperated, she sat up in the bed. 'Can you be serious for one minute? We have to be more careful. Stella Goldschlag would love to bring down the networks.'

'She's not going to catch us,' Jakob insisted, as his hands caressed her shoulders, kissing her neck.

'You don't know that. Chief Mattick made some enquiries and heard the Jew catchers are boasting they can fill a whole carriage on one of the transports East. This Stella person is the most dangerous of all. They say she is very beautiful, blonde and knows all the main places where the hidden Jews go. The cafés, the markets, even the people forging papers for us are known to her.'

'I'd much rather concentrate on the blonde beauty in front of me.' Jakob waggled his eyebrows, making her laugh despite the seriousness of the conversation. And then his expression changed, and her heart rate increased as his kisses turned more ardent.

For the next hour or so, she forgot all about the threat Stella and her friends posed.

For the journey back to Berlin, Jakob donned dark glasses and held on to Trudi's arm as she guided him onto the train. She wore a black armband for mourning, holding a hanky in her hand to dab her eyes whenever anyone attempted conversation. Not that that happened often. The atmosphere was one of fear, with passengers whispering about the bombing of Austria by the Americans. Wasn't anywhere safe? With each turn of the wheels Berlin grew nearer, as did their return to the reality of life living illegally.

Trudi felt a white-hot rage boiling up in her chest, shaking her to her very core. How had it come to pass that they were living under the rule of such a madman? Everywhere around them, people of their country were being rounded up and disappearing off the face of the Earth. Her fists clenched tightly as she tried to suppress her anger, desperately worried that one wrong word would draw attention from the Gestapo. All around the carriage, frightened eyes darted back and forth, everyone on edge and ready for danger. Luck was with them, though—their false identities kept them safe each time they were inspected, and when Trudi tearfully explained Jakob's story of bravery at the front, his blindness earned him salutes.

THIRTY-ONE

SEPTEMBER 1943

Trudi listened to the wailing air raid siren, her nerves shredded. Where was Jakob? He should have been home hours before.

The air raids were making life difficult for all those living in Berlin, legally or illegally. Some Berliners retained their sense of humour referring to Goering as 'Reichsmarschall Meier.' But the vast majority were living on their wits, night after night in the air raid shelters, clasping their loved ones close, listening to the roar of the approaching bombers, the screech of the falling bomb, holding their breath, hoping to hear the explosion rather than feel the effects of the buildings above them crashing to the ground. Jews and other people living illegally were prevented from going to the air raid shelters due to the continuous *Wehrmacht* patrols.

Trudi paced back and forth. When she heard Frau Weber calling her to go to the shelter, she pretended not to hear, hoping the woman would go down without her. But of course she banged on the door, demanding Trudi accompany her.

She followed the woman down the steps into the basement, which had been furnished with a number of cots, chairs and tables. A couple of her neighbours were playing cards, their children trying to sleep on the cots. She wrinkled her nose at the smell, the lack of soap making it difficult for everyone to keep clean. She ducked instinctively, hearing the whistle of a bomb dropping nearby, coughing as plaster dust showered over them.

'Frau Bausch, sit here, please. Where is your fine young man?' Frau Weber picked up the knitting she always carried with her.

'He's out on official business.'

Trudi was glad of the dim light, as the woman scrutinized her face. She didn't want her to guess she was lying.

'He will be fine. God will look after him. Take that worried look off your face.'

Trudi bit her lip, wanting to ask where God was when the Weiss children had been taken or... But she shut off those thoughts.

The raid wasn't a long one but when she returned to the apartment, Jakob still wasn't there. She spent the night tossing and turning.

Jakob arrived back home at ten the following morning. She almost jumped on him as he came through the door.

'I thought you were dead, when you didn't come home!'

He ran a hand through his hair, his eyes bloodshot with tiredness. 'I couldn't get back. The raid caught us by surprise, and we were ordered into a shelter. Even when the all-clear sounded, they weren't letting anyone out. Said it was best to wait for daybreak.'

He went through to the kitchen and poured a glass of water.

'Will you go to bed? You look exhausted.'

He didn't turn around. 'No, I have to go back out.'

She hated how nervous she felt and knew he didn't need

her nagging. But she had to try to stop him. 'Jakob, the pass inspections are increasing all the time.'

'I know that. My papers are fine.' He continued rummaging through the kitchen cupboards. What was he looking for? She hadn't hidden any food. There hadn't been anything left in the store.

'Jakob, look at me. Why are you taking so many risks? You go out too often.'

Jakob paced back and forth, suppressed energy radiating from him.

'Jakob, listen to me, please. You don't need to take such risks.'

'You think? The whole world has gone nuts. A bomb could drop on us any moment. We could be deported and shot or worse. I can't let that happen.'

'I know, but you need to slow down. Eat something. Try to sleep. Being tired leaves you vulnerable.'

'Don't worry about me. I can look after myself. Besides, Kaufmann is careful.'

This was the same old argument. After Max had been arrested and spent a week in Gestapo custody—until Christabel got him released—he and his wife had gone to her family's home near Frankfurt. They had got permission as their home had been hit in the bombing. But with Max gone, Jakob had become more involved with Kaufmann's resistance group.

'Kaufmann? Don't make me laugh. He's a very brave man but the whole world knows the Confessing Church is involved in helping Jews. Franz welcomes anyone who requests help, including those heavily involved in the black market. I think he must be their best customer for false papers.' Trudi drew a breath—she had to calm down. 'Please, Jakob. Eric has sent Martha and the children back to Sweden. *He* knows the circle is closing, and the Swedish Church is less involved with the resistance than the Confessing Church.'

'Everything we do is dangerous, Trudi. You take risks. You use the black market.'

Trudi glared at him. 'I have no choice. How else can I find tobacco to bribe people with, not to mention food stamps, clothes and food for the groups we've hidden? Children have hollow legs, and we can't expect the gentile families to keep feeding our people. One egg costs more than twenty Reichsmarks, a pound of butter is over a hundred. People don't have that type of money. Most families don't get enough to eat themselves.'

Jakob sat down only to immediately stand up again and resume pacing. 'I'm more careful than you believe, Trudi. I've spoken to Franz but he just won't listen. He thinks everyone is a good as he is. He may be a convert to Christianity, but he seems to believe the Christian message even more than born Christians.'

'That's just it. In the eyes of the Nazis, he's a Jew—as is his family. Does he think he can protect them? He hasn't a chance if his black-market activities are discovered. What he is doing, while Christian, is illegal.'

'Jew, Muslim, Christian or atheist. Doesn't make a difference, does it?' Jakob pounded his fist into his other hand with frustration. 'Decent people don't stand by and allow mass murder to happen. They try to stop it. In whatever way they can.'

Trudi let the tears fall. Maybe seeing her as a woman would help. 'I'm worried about you, Jakob. I don't want you to disappear. I couldn't bear it. You've been with me through every step of this.'

He moved to her side, putting his arms around her. She looked up to meet his eyes. He gently rubbed a finger down her cheek, towards her lips.

'Is this your way of telling me you love me?' he said.

'Of course I do. We live together, for goodness' sake.' He moved closer as she said, 'I don't think I could handle losing you. I've lost so many already—my daughter, the boys, Ada and Chana. Even Isla is keeping her distance these days. I need you, Jakob.' She grabbed him by the lapels of his jacket. 'Please stop doing jobs for Kaufmann.'

'You should be the elder one, for all your nagging.' He kissed her on the forehead. 'I have to go. We'll talk about it later.'

She snapped. 'Later might not come. You just won't listen to me.'

'I have to meet someone. A contact. Don't worry, I'll be back. I'll find something for dinner and we'll talk then.' He pulled her towards him and kissed her so thoroughly she thought for a second he'd changed his mind about going. With a groan, he gently pushed her from him. 'I have to go. We'll finish this later.'

And with that he was gone. She could spend the day waiting in the apartment for him to come back or go over to the church and sort out the packages they were gathering for the host families. Being busy would make the time move faster.

THIRTY-TWO

Late in the afternoon, Trudi stared at the pitiful selection of food on the round table. It wasn't enough to feed ten people, never mind the hundred or so now living illegally, for whom the church took responsibility. Eric was away, working his connections in the country, trying to find more potatoes, vegetables or anything else to feed the people sheltering in the church and those he had placed in different homes.

She glanced up as the office door opened, admitting Chief Mattick.

'How am I going to distribute this among all the families? How do I decide who gets more? The ones with children, or those who are ill and need the calories if they are to survive?' She stopped talking at the look on his face. 'What is it?' A cold grip of fear took hold of her heart. She grabbed the back of a nearby chair for support, her knuckles whitening.

'Trudi, thank God you're here. You can't go back to your place.' His voice was different, hollow and distant within the stillness of the room.

Terror surged through her veins. She hung on to his every

word, expecting the worst yet dreading what might come out of his mouth next.

'Sit down.' He gestured to the chair. The grave expression on his face, the sympathy lurking in his eyes, made her stomach turn over.

She sat, curling her fingers into the palms of her hands, nails breaking the skin. 'Tell me.'

'Jakob is dead. He was caught in a pass inspection in Charlottenburg. You know he went to meet a new contact, someone who might shelter one of the families made homeless in the last air raid.'

Jakob dead. He couldn't be. He was so confident, so full of life, always taking risks. For all their arguments, she had almost believed his insistence they wouldn't catch him.

Trudi stared at Chief Mattick, watching his lips moving, but she didn't hear a word he said.

'Trudi, did you hear me? His new contact—it was a trap led by that woman called Stella.'

Stella? The Jew catcher. The woman she'd warned Jakob about, that night in the cabin. She put her hands to her face, wanting to curl into a ball as the pain exploded in her chest. *Jakob.* She could feel his hands stroking her hair, hear his voice as he sang to her as they danced, smell his warm scent...

She sat up and slammed her fist onto the table in front of her, sending packages flying. 'Haven't I lost enough? Why Jakob? *Why?* The war is turning, you can feel it. Nobody likes Hitler anymore. People are whispering, not even whispering sometimes. They blame him for the food shortages, the bombs, the lack of houses, the... Jakob, he can't be...' Trudi jumped to her feet, pulling on her coat.

'Where are you going?'

'Home. He'll be waiting for me there. It's a mistake. He can't be dead. Not him. He's got into trouble before and always come home.'

Chief Mattick moved to her side, putting his hands on the tops of her arms. 'Believe me. He's dead. Jakob is gone.'

She wanted to scream, and rant and rave and hit him. For a second all she saw was his uniform, his position as a man of authority in Nazi Germany.

'Sit down, Trudi.' He led her to the table and then poured her a drink. 'Drink that. Slowly.'

'How did Stella know to contact Jakob?'

Chief Mattick clenched his fists by his side, his gaze tormented and furious, his jaw set as his voice trembled. 'Details are scarce, but it seems like Kaufmann's whole ring has been blown. He's been arrested, along with about thirty other people, including two police officers.'

Trudi groaned. It was even worse than she'd expected.

'Are you implicated? Eric? This church?'

'No, nothing leads to us apart from Jakob and you. But Jakob is dead and there is nothing to tie him to you. They don't know where he was living, but, just in case, you can't go back there. I will send an officer around in a few days to see what the situation is. But for now, you need to stay somewhere else—and not with Eric.'

Trudi couldn't take everything in yet, somehow, she knew there was more.

She picked up her handbag, thankful she'd tucked her precious letters and photographs into the hidden pocket. 'What aren't you telling me?'

'Do the names Rolf Issaksohn or Fritz Newwick mean anything to you?'

'I don't know the first man, but the second, isn't he a black-market trader? But he goes by Wickman—?'

Chief Mattick rubbed his chin, the way he did when worried.

'What?'

'Wickman, as you call him, and Issaksohn, were also arrested. They have both made a deal with the devil. Seems Stella convinced them of the benefits of working with the Gestapo as Jew catchers. For that they get to walk the streets without the star, with extra ration cards and money in their pockets. Better than deportation. I shouldn't judge them, I guess.'

Trudi wasn't really listening. Jew catchers had been part of the war for so long.

But she couldn't think about that—Jakob was dead.

She felt a wave of pain rising in her chest. 'How did they get Jakob?'

Chief Mattick sat down beside her. 'Why do you want to know?

'Did he kill himself so he couldn't give up information under torture? He always said they wouldn't get him alive.'

'He didn't commit suicide, if that's what you mean. Not exactly, but he had a gun.'

Trudi stared. A gun. She'd never seen him with a weapon.

'Yes, the first person he shot was the man beside Stella. Maybe he aimed for her but missed. The man was a known black-market regular, but he made his money from bribing Jews and then turning them into the Gestapo. No loss there. He fired another few rounds, but the Gestapo returned fire and one shot was fatal.'

She stared at him. There was something he wasn't telling her. She could tell from the way he wasn't meeting her gaze.

Trudi was sick of living with secrets. She wanted the truth. She needed to know, no matter how bad.

'He was shot by a Gestapo agent?'

'Of course.' Chief Mattick stared at his hands. 'Who else?'

'Not a policeman on your payroll?'

He stood up and moved away from her side, going to the other side of Eric's desk, shuffling a few papers around.

She froze, her breath hitched. 'You had him *killed*?' Her disbelief made her shriek.

'Keep your voice down. I made Jakob a promise. If it came to something like this, I wasn't going to let him be taken alive. He deserved that much. I just wish I could have done more.'

Suspicion and grief overwhelmed her. 'Why? You didn't know him. I mean, I never saw him here with you. He didn't mention you.' She stood up, flew across the room and started hitting Mattick. 'You ordered him to be shot. You coward. Were you afraid he'd unmask you? As a traitor to your beloved Hitler or...' Trudi's eyes widened. 'Were you the one who led him to his death. Sent him to meet her?'

He grabbed her hands, restraining her so she couldn't hit him, but he didn't hurt her.

She looked him straight in the eye and the depth of pain she saw chilled her to the bone. She whispered, 'Tell me.'

'Jakob was the son of my best friend, a man who died saving my life in the last war. He was born after the war ended, never got to know his father. I tried to look out for him. Wanted him to leave the country, or at least go somewhere nobody knew him. But not Jakob.' He released Trudi and took a step back, his face lit up with anger. 'Jakob was so stubborn. I warned him, again and again. I wanted him to get out. While he could. He refused to become what he called a sheep. He wanted to fight back.' When Mattick looked up again, his eyes were swimming in tears.

'I'm so sorry. I had no idea. I shouldn't have said anything. I...' Trudi couldn't say another word. She let the tears fall. Another death. And this time she was partly to blame. She let herself drop into a chair.

'It's my fault, not yours. I should have stopped him going. I could have saved him.'

'Nobody could stop him from doing what he wanted, even the woman he loved. Jakob was never going to lie down and accept what was happening.' The police chief stood up, patting down his uniform. 'I must get back to the station. You need new papers. Can you get your hair cut or dyed? Do something so people don't associate you and Jakob? Get me a new photograph.'

Trudi nodded. She knew what to do. She'd done it before. But that was when Max was in Berlin and Jakob was alive. Then she remembered the man who'd welcomed them to his home with a smile.

'What do you think will happen to Kaufmann?'

'He'll be deported. After they torture him. If you know anyone in his circle that hasn't been picked up, tell Eric. They need to be warned.'

'Kaufmann isn't going to betray anyone.'

'Trudi, the man has a wife and daughter to protect. Never underestimate the sadism of the Gestapo.'

THIRTY-THREE

OCTOBER 1943

This was it. His first mission as a commando. Captain Murphy had told them nothing about it as they took the train back to London and from there to the south coast. It was all top secret.

They assembled outside the British Legion hall at a place called Little Hampton and were inspected by Major General Sir Robert Sturges. He was the highest ranking commando officer Harry had ever met. Something big was happening, making his stomach churn with excitement. He was sick of training and desperate for action, afraid the war would be over before he got a chance to get involved. He glanced at Mac to see a similar expression on his face.

'This is a top-secret mission and that means nobody says a word outside this room.' The major general, a small man, looked each of them in the eye. 'You will be dropped by parachute near the target area. Small groups, meaning three to six of you, will work together. You will use infrared cameras to photograph the target. Under no circumstances are you to engage with the enemy. We don't want anyone knowing you are there. When the mission has been completed, you will be picked up by the Royal Navy and returned to Britain. Any questions?'

Harry opened his mouth to ask what would happen if they couldn't get to the ships, but shut it quickly at a glare from Captain Murphy. Seems it had been meant as a rhetorical question.

'Captain Murphy, take your men and give them their orders.'

Captain Murphy saluted and then escorted six of them to another room. 'Harry Barnes, Tony McKenna, meet your team-mates. Andre is the only real French speaker among you, so leave it to him to speak to the locals. Philips, Williams and Hughes.' Harry nodded to each man as Captain Murphy introduced them.

Harry, dressed in camouflage like the others in his team, listened to Captain Murphy's instructions. They would find the target, take some photographs, attach the film to a homing pigeon and get home. What could go wrong?

As they walked, Harry whispered, 'Captain Murphy, what is the target?'

Captain Murphy touched the side of his nose and remained silent. Harry didn't try to ask again.

Just before they walked onto the airstrip, Murphy pulled him and Mac aside. 'If you get caught, remember your training. You're British, not German. But given Hitler's order to shoot all captured commandos, don't give them the chance to get you.'

With those words, he turned on his heel and marched toward the plane. Harry and Mac exchanged a glance before they too trekked toward the aircraft, Harry hoping he remembered everything he'd learned at Ringway.

. . .

The jump went like clockwork and they got to the target without incident, took their photographs and sent them home with the pigeon. He caught Mac's eye and they grinned. This was just what they'd trained for.

They trekked back toward the beach for pick-up by the Navy. Harry still didn't know how that would work—he just had to trust Murphy knew.

As they made their way through the dark fields, he spotted the outline of a couple of cottages in the distance. He'd heard how hard the French had it, under the Nazi jackboot. He figured he wouldn't get much help from the French if he had to make a run for it. They would hear his accent and assume he was a Nazi.

He smelt the salt on the air: they were near the beach. As they moved closer, the dirt under their feet gave way to gravel and sand. He stared out to the horizon but couldn't see a thing due to bad fog. Captain Murphy took a torch from his pocket and flashed the signal.

Harry listened carefully but aside from the sound of the waves, he couldn't hear anything. He didn't look at Mac but kept his gaze on the sea.

Then he heard it. The sound of a small, motorized boat coming their way. Was it one of theirs or a German patrol? Harry couldn't see a thing. He had to trust the others, his team, had to believe they were where they were supposed to be. His lip was sore from biting it but he was terrified he'd make a mistake and let down his team. With the silence of the night, even the slight splashes of the water at their feet as they waded into the sea sounded like a thundering tsunami.

Harry's heart beat so fast it hurt. He squinted into the dark, trying to see how far the boat was from them.

Murphy grabbed his arm as they heard a dog barking. And then all hell broke loose. Enemy flares exploded above them, highlighting their positions. They were sitting ducks. Germans opened fire and threw grenades.

Philips was the first to fall. Someone gave the order to swim to the boat. Harry heard the bullet hit his arm, quickly followed by the feeling that he had been hit by a tank. Captain Murphy slung his rifle over his shoulder and, grabbing Harry, half dragged him to the boat, which was also being fired on. Williams and Hughes managed to swim beside them but Harry saw both of them struggling. Mac went to their aid. Harry tried to move but then the world turned black. Then he lost consciousness.

Harry woke in a hospital bed, his arm strapped to his side. Captain Murphy sat in the chair by the bed, reading some papers. When Harry moved, the captain looked up and smiled.

'About time, lad. Too much longer and they'd have had to surgically remove me from the chair.'

'Where am I?'

'Hospital. The food is almost as bad as that back at barracks, but the staff are prettier.'

A nurse blushed prettily as she walked past just at that moment.

Harry didn't know what to say to the man. 'Thank you.' It didn't seem adequate.

'Couldn't leave you behind on your first mission, could I?' Murphy joked, but his smile didn't reach his eyes. Harry knew he must be devastated at how the mission had failed so badly.

'The others?'

'Three dead, three injured.' The captain grimaced.

'Mac? Tony McKenna, did he make it?'

Captain Murphy nodded. 'Without a scratch. He's trying his luck with some girls down the local.'

Thrilled his friend had survived but feeling awful for the men who had died, Harry had to know. 'What went wrong?'

'What didn't?' Captain Murphy shrugged. 'The fog, the intel, bad timing, the blasted dog. Who knows.'

A doctor, his white coat splashed with some blood, walked up to the bed, accompanied by the same nurse they had seen earlier. The nurse handed notes to the doctor, who glanced at them before examining Harry's wound. He tried not to wince as the doctor's fingers probed the wound.

'You were lucky, the bullet went straight through the flesh. It didn't hit any bone. You should be back in action in a couple of weeks.'

Harry nodded in acknowledgement. He couldn't believe he had survived when his team had suffered such heavy losses. What was it about him? He lived and better men died.

He closed his eyes, seeing Taub's face.

'Best get back to your quarters, Captain. This man will sleep for hours with the medicine we've given him. He'll be back with you soon, so long as infection doesn't set in.'

Harry didn't catch the rest of the conversation.

The next day, the pain in his arm woke him. Harry shifted in the bed, trying to find a more comfortable position. Then he grew conscious of a couple of other patients glaring at him.

'What?'

'Did you warn your lot? Was that why they knew where we were meeting the boat?'

Harry sat up straighter, ignoring the flash of pain travelling down his arm. 'I've no idea what you're talking about.'

'Don't play that game. We were there, got another boat out. I lost my foot; he almost lost his arm. Hughes and Williams were our mates. Trained with them since '39. Now they're gone. All thanks to your friends. You're German, aren't ya? Know that horrible accent anywhere.'

Harry glared at the patient but before he could answer, Murphy, suddenly appearing in the doorway, beat him to it.

'Shut up, Private. You've no idea what you're talking about. I was with Harry every step of the way. And he's Swiss, not German. I won't write you up this time. I'll blame the drugs the docs gave you. But one more word...' Murphy glowered, and eventually the man let his eyes drop.

'Thank you, but I can fight my own battles,' Harry whispered, as Murphy took a seat beside him.

'Never turn away from a friend, Barnes.'

That afternoon, Harry was moved to a private room. He couldn't pretend to be anything but relieved. Despite Murphy standing up for him, he'd felt the hatred emanating from the two other patients. All because he had a different accent.

When would he be accepted as just one of the boys? He wasn't Jewish enough for the Jews, but the Nazis saw him that way. As a commando he still hadn't proved his loyalty, wasn't one of the boys. Not to some anyway.

He lay back on the pillow. He had to count his blessings. He was alive, wasn't he? And the bullet wound meant he'd have plenty of time to write to Rachel. It wasn't as good as being able to see her, but how could he explain his injuries when his family didn't know he'd been overseas? When the war was over, he might be able to talk about these secret missions.

He screwed his eyes shut, trying to push dark thoughts away. How much additional training would he have to undergo to get back to being fit enough to rejoin Three Troop? Would he be allowed, or would the failed mission be held against him?

THIRTY-FOUR

Trudi listened to the whispers around her, the talk about the war going against the Germans. Nobody dared to voice it aloud, but the rumours of losing were increasing. All workers engaged in non-heavy war work were entitled to 2,400 calories per day, but how many found sufficient quantities of food to meet the legal minimums?

She had a job as a cleaner in the Nazi district headquarters. Isla had heard their regular cleaner had a daughter who'd been evacuated to the countryside to avoid the bombs. The mother had wanted to go live with her child and her bosses were happy for her to do so, if she found someone to take her place. Isla persuaded Trudi to do it. Not only did the job pay relatively well, it came with a small apartment underneath the building. Isla paid the cleaner a small salary so she wouldn't come back to Berlin due to lack of funds.

Trudi had a new identity: this time her name was Frau Amann, her husband was fighting with the SS in Russia. This would be sufficient to deter even the most ardent of admirers from harassing Trudi if they caught her alone in the office. In fact, she was doing such a good job, her boss hadn't once enquired as to when the former cleaner was coming back.

When Isla had come up with the scheme, Trudi hadn't cared enough if she was caught or not. All she could think about was Jakob, his death and the row they'd had on that last day.

She bit her lip hard to contain the rage and grief bubbling inside her. Jakob had chosen death over giving up names under torture, a choice she understood in her more rational moments. But he had also condemned her to a future without him. An overwhelming loneliness seeped into every fibre of her being, threatening to pull her under. The pain of losing Ari felt like a pinprick compared to the devastation caused by Jakob's death.

Dizziness hit her: she'd given her breakfast to her lodgers, two Jewish boys who'd escaped from the Jewish hospital and needed it more than she did. Since Jakob had died, it took every ounce of energy she had to put one foot in front of the other.

Liesel was the only reason she kept living. If not for the children, for the hope she still held—had to keep hanging on to—that one day she'd see them again, she'd have given up.

On entering the butcher's shop, the conversation ceased. The women waiting in line had been talking about her; Frau Puglisi's cheeks flushed as Trudi pierced her with a look before sweeping the rest of the shop with a casual glance.

Trudi hesitated, knowing everyone was watching her reaction. She had to do something. 'Have you been gossiping about me again, Frau Puglisi? I heard from another friend you've dared to call me a Jew.'

The woman stepped forward, hands on her hips. 'If the cap fits.'

Trudi let her anger and frustration rise to the top, grabbing the woman by the arm. 'I've had enough of your spiteful remarks. Why don't you come with me now to the Gestapo, and let's see what they think of your accusations?'

The woman blanched, her fear-filled eyes seeking reassurance from her friends. But the other women wouldn't look at them. They found the floor more interesting.

Trudi wasn't finished. 'I want to put an end to this speculation once and for all. Do I look like a picture from *Der Stürmer*? Do I?' Her spittle landed on the other woman's cheek but, frozen from fear, the *Frau* didn't attempt to remove it. 'I asked you a question. Do I look like a Jew?'

The woman shook her head but didn't say a word.

Trudi was almost enjoying herself. 'Come on. The Gestapo can answer that question for you. Do you know the penalty for denouncing a true German, never mind the wife of a serving SS soldier?'

Frau Puglisi let out an anguished moan. Trudi hardened her heart. This woman was believed to have denounced several people, not doing it for money or rations but for the good of the Reich. Her type revolted Trudi, who could almost understand someone giving up a Jew in order to feed their starving children.

'Frau Amann, please calm down. Nobody meant any offence. Frau Puglisi was mistaken and sincerely apologizes. She would like to give you some of her meat ration—a gesture, you understand—for upsetting you.' Herr Vogel mopped the sweat from his face with his blood-stained apron, his heavy breathing audible even from behind the counter.

Trudi glared at the shaking Frau Puglisi, who couldn't look at her and seemed to have decreased in size.

A small, wiry, dark-haired woman with piercing green eyes stepped forward, arms crossed over her chest, and addressed Frau Puglisi. 'Apologize, you stupid woman. We don't need the Gestapo visiting this neighbourhood. I told you she wasn't one of them, but would you listen?'

Trudi didn't know the woman who admonished Frau Puglisi but it was evident she held some power, as Puglisi looked more terrified, if that was possible.

'Frau Amann, I apologize. I was obviously mistaken. Here, take these.' The woman pushed the tickets into Trudi's hands before turning on her heel.

Terrified the woman would go out and pull in the first policeman she found, Trudi reached out and put her hand on the woman's arm. 'Please take these back. I have enough. We all need good food, especially with those horrible English bombers keeping us awake.'

The woman's eyes widened as she stared at Trudi's face, as if trying to work out her motivation.

Herr Vogel banged the countertop with his fist. 'Those bombers killed over six hundred people last week. My uncle, he's with the fire service, he said it was horrific. Bits and pieces of people everywhere.'

The group of women cried out, effectively shutting up Herr Vogel's speech. Trudi was tempted to leave but she needed the meat ration: too many depended on the soup she made from it. She took her place in the queue in front of Frau Puglisi and noticed the wiry woman stepped in behind the woman. Was she seeking to keep Frau Puglisi in the butchers too?

Herr Vogel slipped her a better cut of meat than usual and added a few extra bits of fat. He offered them to her with a whisper of thanks. She guessed he had something going on with the black market. He certainly didn't want any official visits at his shop.

Taking her package she walked from the shop, restraining the urge to run and hide. She had to act normally to allay suspicion.

The hairs on the back of her neck lifted as she walked down the street. Someone was following her. She kept her gaze forwards despite wanting to check. Turning the next street corner, she sped up but the feeling didn't abate. She ducked into a shop, glancing in the mirror above the counter—only to see the wiry woman had followed her.

She met her eyes and the other woman indicated they move outside.

Shaking, clenching her bag in one hand, Trudi walked back into the street. The woman dropped into step beside her.

'You did a wonderful job back there in Vogel's. I wanted to applaud you. That horrible woman, Puglisi, had it coming. Someone should put the world out of its misery and dispose of her.'

Heart hammering, Trudi stopped walking. 'I think you're mistaken, Frau...?'

'My name doesn't matter. You can't come back to this area. That was a close call and you handled it expertly but take it as a warning. You need to change your disguise—for goodness' sake, do something about looking so attractive. You don't need other women's jealousy on top of everything.'

Trudi, lost for words, stood there with her mouth open.

The woman took her arm and pulled her along the street, hissing, 'Act normal. We're friends even if you don't know my name. Be careful, Frau Beck, the enemy doesn't always wear the uniform of the state.'

With a big kiss on Trudi's cheek the woman hugged her and left her standing there as she disappeared into the crowd. She'd called Trudi by her Jewish name, a name she hadn't used outside their resistance circle for months.

Trudi glanced around her, but nobody seemed to be taking any notice. She clutched the bag to her and set off again, this time to the tram stop. She needed to get home and think. Home. Was that woman warning her, that her home had been compromised too?

The twins. They needed a new host family.

Trudi caught the first tram that came along without even checking where it was going. She needed to sit before her legs gave out beneath her. What was she going to do now?

. . .

Trudi lit a cigarette, taking a deep drag. She'd only taken up smoking recently: it calmed her down. Her nails were non-existent, a consequence of her cleaning job and her nerves.

She paced back and forth across Isla's sitting room. They couldn't meet in the Swedish Church anymore. Trudi hadn't seen Ada or Chana in almost a year. Between the bombing raids and people taking more precautions after the fall of Kaufmann's resistance circle, it just wasn't safe.

'Trudi, will you sit down, you're making me dizzy. It's time. You have to go underground now. You can't afford to change papers again. Berlin is too small. We don't know who that woman is—the one who recognized you in the butchers.'

'Isla, we've been over this. There is nowhere for me to go. The bombings have destroyed so many homes, it's difficult for real Berliners to find homes. Those who were open to sheltering Jews are running scared. Did you not hear about the woman who reported herself to the Gestapo for sheltering a mother and daughter?'

'That woman should be hanged. She only did that when their money ran out and they couldn't pay her the extortionate rent she charged. The Gestapo believed her story that she thought they were genuine bombing victims in need of shelter.'

Trudi shrugged. She didn't care what the Gestapo believed or what they did to the German woman. The Jewish women had been sent to the old synagogue, now used as a collection centre for those being sent East.

'You can come and live with me.' Isla suggested this plan almost every time she met Trudi, and each time Trudi declined.

'I won't put you at risk like that.' Trudi guessed Isla's husband wasn't in favour of the plan as Isla never pushed the issue too much.

'I know a woman who will help. She's too scared to hide you in her main house but she has an annex. More like a shed. She used to work for my parents. I'd trust her with my life.'

. . .

Less than two days later, Trudi was living in her new home, again depending for her life on a dressmaker. Her host, Frau Schmitt, owned a tiny dress shop. She had an even smaller house with neither indoor plumbing nor running water. A communist all her life, she hated the Nazis with a passion.

The small annex was made from thick, reinforced wood, and was barely big enough to fit one person. The only source of light was via the gaps in the wooden boards covering a window. The air was stale and musty, the damp getting right into Trudi's bones.

Frozen all the time but for an hour in the evening when Frau Schmitt brought her a hot meal and emptied her chamber pot, Trudi didn't see or speak to anyone. It was too dangerous for Isla to visit: a countess visiting a dress-shop owner who was this poor was too far-fetched for even the most stupid of Nazis. Once a week, the old lady boiled a pot of water and provided Trudi with some old towels so she could wash. There was no soap. Trudi was grateful she didn't have visitors as she was sure she stank.

She had too much time on her hands, her thoughts constantly thinking of Jakob, Isla, Ada and Chana, but most of all of her children. Heinz, Tomas and Liesel.

The days passed by, and she lost track of the time. Frau Schmitt tried her best but sometimes there was nothing to eat but bread made from goodness knows what.

'I think they must have made it during a bombing raid and the plaster dust fell into the dough,' Frau Schmitt whispered one day, as she passed Trudi a plate with two slices of bread.

'Have you heard from Isla?' Trudi asked, and immediately regretted it.

Frau Schmitt's expression said it all. 'Her house was bombed. A direct hit. She wouldn't have felt a thing.'

Trudi hung her head in sorrow. Poor Isla, always so brave and generous. A decent German, but the bombs didn't care. If they did, they would have killed Hitler and his cronies. Somehow, they all managed to survive.

THIRTY-FIVE

Lying on her makeshift bed, Trudi started. What was that noise? Had it been a car? She listened for the usual night sounds, an owl shrieking or birds flocking from one tree to the next, but it was too quiet.

She heard a crash, the splintering of wood as the door to Frau Schmitt's cottage crashed open. Trudi jumped but there was no escape for her: the only door out of her shed was via the house. She held her breath, hearing Frau Schmitt trying to remonstrate with a man shouting at her.

Trudi waited, breathing fast, her pulse thumping in her ears, watching the door to the shed. Everything that had happened since the children went on the *Kindertransport* flashed through her head. What did they know? Had they come for her? Was this it? Her heart raced, she clutched her chest, her eyes never leaving the door. Yet when it burst open, she jumped.

A man, dressed in a long leather coat and hat appeared, his gun aimed at Trudi's chest. 'Out. Get out now, you filthy scum. We've been tracking you for a while. There's nowhere for you to run. Spying for the British doesn't pay well, does it?'

Trudi gaped at him. British? Spy? What was he talking about? 'I'm no spy.'

'Tell that to someone who cares. Come on or I'll shoot you here like the dog you are.'

Trudi walked out through the door, spying Frau Schmitt, her eye blackening, lying on the floor. 'Leave her alone! She's an old woman. Have you no pity?'

The man's companion, dressed in a similar outfit, gave Frau Schmitt a slap. 'She is old enough to know she's a traitor. Get out now.'

The man grabbed hold of Trudi and shoved her through the broken door and down the path, into a car outside.

She didn't recognize the route until they reached the Grosse Hamburger Strasse prison. One man pulled her from the car, the other leading the way inside. Trudi shrugged off her captor's hand, and walked, head high, into the prison. She refused to show any fear, although her legs had turned to jelly. She'd heard enough rumours of how prisoners were treated to have an idea of what lay ahead.

They lead her into a large interrogation room where another man sat at his desk, smoking a cigarette. He eyed her up and down before wrinkling his nose.

'Don't you people ever bathe? You stink.'

Trudi didn't reply. She stared at the floor.

'Name?'

What name should she use? One of her aliases or her real name? Would she fare better as a spy or a Jew? A voice in her head told her to tell the truth. She looked up. 'Trudi Beck.'

He smiled. 'The truth. That's a surprise. This is going to be easy.' He ground out the cigarette, still using a soft, modulated voice.

'So, Frau Beck, wife of the Jewish scum, Ari Beck, we meet

at last.'

She ignored the slur on Ari. What good would it do defending a dead man?

'So, tell me, how much did the British pay you?'

'British? I don't know what you are talking about.'

'Frau Beck, don't make this difficult. My men have ways to make you talk. Why don't you just tell me and then you can have a hot bath. With a lot of soap.'

She turned her face to look into his. 'I've had no dealings with anyone English.'

His lips curled but he still didn't touch her. He reached to some paperwork on his desk. Her heart sank as she recognized the stamps. The letters from the children. She'd kept them hidden in the special pocket she'd sewn into her handbag, but obviously they'd found them.

'Those letters are from my children, who left on the *Kindertransport*. I haven't been in contact with them since the war started. I don't know anything about any spies.'

'But you acknowledge you have been in contact with Britain.'

'Yes, but...'

'So you lied.' The man's eyes narrowed.

'No. I didn't. I mean, yes, I got letters from my—'

'Silence!' He cut her off with a shout.

Trudi couldn't stop the shaking. Despite it being May and the sun shining on the Berlin streets, it was freezing in the office and she was only wearing a thin dress.

'I want all the names and addresses of those who helped you. Now.'

He pointed to a pen and piece of paper but she didn't move. Isla might be dead but was her husband? Chana and Ada were still in hiding at the Swedish church. She couldn't give them Eric's name, or those of Mattick and Hoffman.

'Nobody...' The slap was hard and knocked her over.

'Get up.'

She scrambled to her feet, her hand holding her cheek.

'Take her away. Give her time to think about her actions and for goodness' sake get her a shower. The smell is making me retch.'

Trudi followed one of the men out of the office and down some stairs. Another man followed behind, his rifle pushing her in the middle of her back if she moved too slowly.

She tried to ignore screams coming from other rooms and, even worse, the howls of those who seemed to have lost their minds. She stumbled over a step but her captors didn't wait for her to recover, just continued pushing her down the steps.

They led her into a large room with a shower and bath in the corner. Clicking their fingers, they indicated to one of the women in there to take over.

'Murr wants her cleaned up. Get on it.'

The woman ran her eyes over Trudi. 'Her hair is infested. It will have to go.'

'Do what you have to do.'

To Trudi's horror, her two male captors sat down on two chairs, lit some cigarettes and waited. There would be no privacy.

She held back the tears as the woman cut the dress from her back and sheared her head. The shower water pelted her skin like icy needles. The men jeered and laughed at her vulnerability. Only as the water ran down her face did it mix with her tears.

For a second, spying the scissors in the female guard's pocket, she was tempted to grab them and cut her wrists. A death on her terms was preferable to what they had in mind. But she drummed up Liesel's voice, the image of her face. All thoughts of suicide fled. The regime had torn her from her child, she'd not help them finish the job. While she remained alive, there was still a sliver of hope for her and her daughter to be reunited. She had to hold on to that thought.

THIRTY-SIX

JUNE 1944

After a month assembled in a tent camp near Southampton, Harry was ready for action. Rumours flew around the camp that this was it, the invasion was on.

Finally, they were getting over to France, ready to bring the battle to the Germans and push them all the way back to Germany. Harry couldn't wait for the day he reached Berlin. He'd check on his Aunt Chana and all the cousins and other relations he had, and then he was going to hunt down Schwarz and make him pay for what he had done to Papa.

After dark fell, he followed Murphy into a landing craft capable of carrying eighty men. Without a single light, Harry knew there were hundreds of other similar sized boats in the water around hm. They sailed past the Isle of Wight and over to France. He was wet, cold and excited.

They took turns sitting on the steps to the deck whispering back to the others what they saw—until the Germans opened up their welcoming party. Shells rained down around them, sending plumes of water into the air. The boat slowed and the gang planks were laid down. He ran into the water, wading ashore, eager to be out of the water and onto the

beach. This was full of large steel structures to which the
Germans had attached artillery shells to knock out tanks, but
the Engineer Corps was ahead of them, blowing them to
pieces. Harry spotted some German soldiers who'd surrendered. Mac beckoned to him and together they walked up to
them, Mac asking in German for the path through the
landmines.

Mac led the way, with Captain Murphy following behind,
then Harry and the rest of their group who'd made it ashore
from their boat. They got through without a single casualty.

Their orders were to secure the next village. Harry dived
from house to house as they'd been taught by their instructors.
When shells hit the ground, they sent shrapnel flying, which
was lethal to those in its path. Having seen several dead British
soldiers along their way, Harry was glad they had trained so
hard.

To his surprise, killing German soldiers didn't give him any
satisfaction. It was kill or be killed so he didn't hesitate in
returning fire, but it didn't give him any joy. He had little
interest in the normal German army. It was the SS he wanted,
and he knew Mac felt the same way.

Mac and he worked well together, even capturing a platoon
of Germans when they mimicked an officer, telling them to
surrender. The British troops, who had initially viewed them
with suspicion, saw how they threw themselves into every fight,
and soon they had been accepted into the general crowd of
soldiers.

'Mac, I think we've gone too far south or else Murphy's intel
was wrong.' Desperately, he pulled out his map and scrutinized
it in the moonlight. He couldn't put on the torch for fear of
giving away their position.

Battle lines moved fast. They needed to capture a German

officer; he was the only one who would know the plans of attack. Murphy was depending on them.

He crawled up to where Mac was lying, his binoculars focused on the field ahead. 'Harry, have a look.'

Harry took the binoculars and almost let them fall. If they'd kept going they'd have walked straight into a German squad. They weren't paying much attention to the area around them, which suggested Mac and himself had gone much farther ahead of British lines than he'd thought.

'What do you want to do?' he asked as he counted the ones he could see. Seven, possibly nine men.

'Capture them, what else?'

Harry groaned—he'd been afraid of that. Mac seemed to have nine lives. He was the first to volunteer for any duty, no matter how dangerous.

'We'll wait a couple of hours, surprise them before daybreak. Use the same tactics as last time. Order them to surrender. Hopefully there's an officer there that we can inter-rogate and find out more about where they've sent the SS. I was expecting them to be all around us.'

Harry nodded. He was frustrated too, desperate to get his hands on the die-hard Nazis, not troops who surrendered when they heard an order in German. They lay in wait.

The time passed quickly and finally Mac gave the signal to move out. They crept forward and Mac had just shouted, '*Kommen Sie!*' when they had to duck as incoming mortar fire erupted around them, quickly followed by the rattle of machine-gun fire.

Harry and Mac flung themselves to the ground, trying to take shelter, but the trees were too sparse. *This is it.* It was their own side firing at them.

They crawled back the way they had come, back toward the British lines.

'Get up or I'll happily put a bullet in your skull.' Harry

looked into the eyes of a British soldier he didn't recognize.
'Harry Barnes...'

'Shup it and get up. I heard you shout out in German.
Come on, move.'

Harry saw Mac was getting the same treatment. He got up
slowly, despite the fact he could disarm the soldier and kill him
probably before he knew what had happened. But they were on
the same side.

He put his hands above his head and followed the soldier
accompanying Mac out of the forest. He caught a glimpse of
other British soldiers milling around them but he didn't recognize any of them.

'I need to speak to the officer in charge.' Harry's request was
met by a nudge from the rifle trained on his chest.

'You don't get to order us around, you dirty kraut.'

Harry bristled, and it took every ounce of his self-restraint
not to tackle the man and push him to his knees and make him
beg forgiveness. He glanced at Mac who had earned himself a
nasty black eye, but given the look of the swelling lip of the
guard, it seemed Mac had fought back.

Harry, pretending to trip, fell to the ground to buy some
time. What was going to happen now? Surely they weren't
going to be shot? He'd heard rumours of captured soldiers being
shot, but that was only by the Germans, wasn't it? But these
men obviously thought he and Mac were spies.

Harry tried again. 'Look, we were ordering the Germans to
surrender. Our Captain sent us behind enemy lines.'

'Yeah, and I'm the king of England.'

They were tied to a tree with a guard over them.

'If they blink, shoot them.'

The minutes and hours ticked by. Harry heard sounds of an
argument and then Captain Murphy appeared, walking over to
the where they were tied up.

'Stand down, Private. These are my men.'

'No, Captain. They're German spies—we heard them talking.'

'I gave you an order. Don't make me repeat it. Those two men are two of the best commandos I have had the pleasure to command. They were trying to capture a German officer to take him back behind the lines for interrogation. No doubt they would have succeeded too, but for you and your friends.'

'But... yes, sir.' The private took a step back, shouldering his gun.

Captain Murphy looked at Harry and Mac. 'Release yourselves and follow me now.'

The private's eyes nearly bulged out of his face as Harry and Mac released themselves. The only reason they hadn't done so before was because it would have been suicide with someone training a gun on them.

Harry rubbed his chaffed arms.

'Care to explain how you got so far ahead of the lines?' Captain Murphy interrogated them as he marched them to the officer in charge. 'Guess it was your bright idea, Mac?'

Mac shrugged.

'The major is proper army, not like your skipper. Old school, straight-as-a-die British officer, so make the salutes smart, stand up straight and for God's sake don't backchat him. He won't stop when I say don't shoot.'

They marched after Captain Murphy and into a tent, where a short, choleric-looking man was standing. They saluted him, remaining silent while Captain Murphy introduced them.

'Both Barnes and McKenna are part of my commando team. Their orders were to capture a German officer and bring him back for interrogation.'

'Some commandos! My men caught them.' The major sneered at them. Harry saw the twitch on Mac's face as he struggled to restrain his temper. Harry wanted to tell this man just how easy it would have been for them to kill the soldiers who'd captured him but, mindful of what Murphy had said, he stayed quiet.

The major turned to his own man. 'Bring in that German officer you picked up last week.' Then he turned to Harry and Mac. 'Let's see what you're made of.'

The private returned with a man with his hands bound, the SS markings on his jacket making Harry's blood boil. For a second he wanted to skin the man alive.

Instead he sighed, knowing they wouldn't get anything from the German man, who stood straight, not in the slightest bit cowed by having his hands in restraints.

Murphy indicated to Harry to start the questioning, but the man refused to tell them anything but his rank and serial number. The look he gave Harry when he spoke in German was enough to tell the room what he thought of Harry.

'He's useless. He won't say a word. Give us access to the others you have captured.' Mac spoke up then, with a grunt from Murphy, added, 'Please, sir.'

'You think you can do better?'

'Yes, sir, but not from the SS officers. Give us the privates and other ranks. They'll talk, and without us having to use any of the techniques this... man would use.'

The German officer reddened at the insult, taking a step toward Mac and spitting at them before the private guarding him pulled him back.

'See, sir? He understands every word we say. I imagine he was educated in England. Am I right?'

The German refused to answer.

'Get him out of here,' the major demanded. Then, turning to Murphy, he said, 'Take your men out to where the prisoners are kept. They'd better get me something.'

'Yes, sir.' Captain Murphy saluted and turned on his heel. Harry remembered to salute just in time and followed him. He didn't look to see what Mac did.

They found the prisoners locked in what had once been a barn. They entered, taking out packets of cigarettes and offered them around. At first there were no takers but Harry and Mac continued to speak to them in German, telling them that there were other Allied troops marching into Germany, the war was over, that Himmler was suing for peace. On and on they continued, mixing fact and fiction until finally some of the captives broke, indicating they were ready to speak.

They separated these from the rest of the men, moving them to a room in a requisitioned farmhouse, providing them with a hot meal and a drink. Once they started to speak, they couldn't shut them up. They told them their latest orders, where the major reinforcements were, where the minefields had been laid. Everything but their inside leg measurements.

After they had compiled their reports and presented them to the major with Murphy standing by, the major smiled. 'It's true then. We have some good Germans on our side.'

Mac and Harry exchanged a glance. Neither of them considered themselves German anymore, but they weren't about to ruin the major's good mood.

THIRTY-SEVEN

MAY 1945

Despite Hitler's suicide, the fighting wasn't over. Instead, it increased in intensity. Harry, now a Lieutenant thanks to his field commission, and his unit worked their way across the Rhine, onto German soil, going from house to house, finding brutal opposition every step of the way.

Julian, his foot tapping a hundred to the dozen whispered, 'What they fighting for? Ain't they heard Hitler is kaput?'

Feeling sorry for the blond, blue-eyed, raw recruit on his first mission, Harry gave him a friendly pat on the shoulder. 'I guess they can't give up. If they do, they might have to consider why they followed a madman into all this.'

Julian glanced around at the devastation. Death was everywhere. Swollen animal corpses dotted the fields, polluting the river water. Houses were reduced to piles of rubble. Men died fighting for each inch of ground.

'Lieutenant, look.' Julian pointed at three German soldiers waving a white flag as they made their way down the road. Harry put up his hand to signal to the others to halt. 'Keep your fingers on the trigger, it could be a trap.'

Harry stepped forward.

'The war is over.' The soldier holding the flag said, in faltering English. 'Germany has surrendered. No more fighting.'

Switching to German, Harry questioned the man. His companions nodded as the man told Harry of General Jodl's surrender.'

Harry couldn't believe his ears.

'Is it true, sir? Is it over?' Julian asked, his eyes darting from the Germans to Harry and back again.

'General Jodl, the Chief of Staff of the German Army signed an unconditional surrender yesterday, May 7th. He's ordered all German forces to lay down their weapons.'

Julian let out a whoop of joy. The other soldiers clapped each other's back. 'This is it, we're going home.'

'Nobody's going anywhere. The SS won't just give up. Be on your guard. Now isn't the time to lose your head.'

They marched into the next town to find the white bedsheets hanging from all the windows. Still, Harry exercised caution. He wasn't losing any more people to this war.

Harry, Julian and some other men were sitting on the grass verge enjoying a few minutes of calm awaiting their next orders. A fresh-faced recruit ran up to them. 'Hey, any of you Barnes? Need someone who speaks Polish. Captain Murphy said you might.'

Harry glanced up at the soldier. 'Not well enough to interrogate someone, but a little. They may speak German. Why?'

'We liberated some slave labourers working in some coal mines. They are in bad shape, poor ba—' The soldier caught himself as he seemed to see the stripes on Harry's uniform. 'Sorry, sir.'

Harry still wasn't used to men saluting him. He jumped up. 'Take me to them.'

He followed the young soldier, before coming to a standstill before a group of people. They stood in a half circle, and he couldn't tell if they were male or female at first, as they resembled walking skeletons dressed in rags.

A chill ran down his spine as he thought of what could have reduced these people to their dire state.

Harry's voice quavered as he asked, '*Sprechen Sie Deutsch?*'

One man stepped forward, but Harry was afraid to shake his hand for fear of hurting him.

He blurted out desperately: 'What can we do to help you? Has someone taken your names so you can be registered with the Red Cross? Who would do this to you?'

The Polish man eyed him suspiciously and said, 'You sound native,' before taking a step back.

Harry pushed down the glimmer of shame at what his countrymen had done. *You aren't German, not anymore.* Heart racing, he replied, 'I was born in Berlin, but I'm Jewish.'

The man shook his head sadly. 'This is nothing. You should see what they have done to your people. They burned them. In their millions. Men, women, children. Made no difference.'

Harry couldn't speak.

'Sir? You alright?' Julian stepped forward, breaking into Harry's thoughts. 'What did he say? Need something? Water? Something stronger?'

Harry shook his head, unable to answer the boy who'd quickly become his shadow. He turned back to the Polish man, asking him questions. Translating his words, he gave orders to the other men on how to help.

Then he walked away. 'Julian, tell Captain Murphy I'll be back in a bit. I'm taking ten minutes.'

'Yes, sir.'

Harry found a tree he could hide behind and only then did he cry. For his father, his extended family, Rachel's family and everyone else he'd known in the Jewish community. How many were still alive? What news was waiting for him in Berlin?

. . .

'What happened to you?' Mac found him by the tree a little over an hour later. Harry wiped his face on his sleeve but couldn't find his voice. 'Julian said you looked like someone walked over your grave. Must have been bad for you to react like that. After all we've seen.' Mac kept talking, faster now as Harry struggled to find words. 'Harry, out with it. What is it?'

'I spoke to one of the rescued Polish prisoners. From the coal mine.'

Mac waited.

'Mac, he said our people were burned. All of them.'

Mac stumbled back a step or two, shaking his head in a slow, back-and-forth sweep of denial. 'Shut up.'

'Mac, listen to me. I know you are searching for your family too. But that man, he said he and the other prisoners were lucky not to be Jewish.'

Mac dropped to his knees, putting his hands over his ears. 'God, please let him be wrong.'

But he wasn't. The situation was much worse than they could even imagine.

Later, the room fell silent as Captain Murphy informed the troops of the horrific conditions at Dachau. But this was only the beginning of the nightmare. Reports of unspeakable atrocities, all committed in Hitler's name, soon followed. Auschwitz, Belzec, Belsen were only a few of the camps mentioned; each story more horrendous than the last, with tales of pain and suffering that couldn't be put into words.

After the encounter with the Polish slave labourers and the subsequent briefings, their team pushed on through Germany.

They commandeered the most beautiful house in the small town of Josbach on the outskirts of Frankfurt, amazed it had survived in a town where the centre was a mass of rubble from bombed-out buildings. The beautiful patrician house, nestled in a quaint cobblestone street, had been the home of a high-level Nazi. His wife must have been very house-proud as the window boxes were well maintained and adorned with vibrant flowers. The half-timbered structure had its beams painted in a deep rich dark brown, contrasting with the paler stucco. Even the leaded windows were intact. The interior of the house was even more beautiful, with its shiny parquet floors set in a herringbone pattern. Each room was decorated with the best of materials and, save for a couple of blank patches on the wall, the paint a fresher colour than the rest of the room, appeared to be untouched.

Harry wondered what had happened to the Jewish family who'd once owned this fine house. Unbelievably, Mac had been brought up nearby and was able to tell them the history of each building. He was also able to tell them who was a Nazi from the very start; who had thrown in their lot with Hitler in the early thirties.

Perhaps more importantly, Mac had been able to save a couple of the local men from being lynched. Although German, both teachers had treated him well in school. They hadn't been Nazis and had only taken up arms when they had to in the last days of the war. Seeing Mac with these teachers had made Harry think of Herr Stein, the man who'd told him to learn English. Had he survived?

Dearest Rachel,

I'm back. Arrived in Germany about a week ago. It's such a strange feeling standing on German soil having left so long ago. You should see the house I'm staying in. Mac commandeered it for our unit and the lads are so grateful. I swear the bath is big enough to swim in and the beds are so comfortable...

Harry bit the top of the pen, trying to get his thoughts out of the bedroom and back to the page in front of him. In her letters, Rachel asked him what he had been up to. But how could he put into words the things he'd done in France, Belgium, Holland and Germany? He was a killer now, had fought men face to face as well as from a distance. That changed a man, no matter how much they might hate the enemy. He couldn't tell her what the Polish slave labourer had said, either—his story now confirmed by reports from liberated concentration camps.

It's been a rough few months losing many friends but I'm still in one piece. Mac says hello. He drove all the way to Theresienstadt, that's one of the concentration camps in Czechoslovakia, and saw his parents. Both are still alive, in relatively good health and obviously thrilled to see him. He couldn't bring them back with him as that's not allowed but he's been in touch with some people that can help.

Harry glanced out the window at the blue sky, distracted for a minute by wondering how Mac was getting on. He'd taken leave to get married and introduce his new wife to his family.

He was thrilled for Mac whose father had moved the family to Holland when Hitler came to power, believing it to be safer than Germany. Both Mac's brothers had survived, and a grandmother. All hidden by their brave Dutch neighbours. It was only now the war was finally over that they were realizing just how few had stood up for those in need. Millions were dead or missing.

Harry wondered how many of his family had been saved. He hadn't been part of the force to liberate Belsen but he'd met some of the men involved. The stories they'd told him, the pictures... He put his head in his hands trying to get those images out of his brain.

Had his family ended up in a camp like that? Or had they been lucky and met brave people like the Dutch rescuers Mac had introduced him to? Someone said the worst of the concentration camps were in Poland. How could somewhere be worse than Belsen? His grandparents had family there, his father used to write to cousins, aunts and uncles. His mother too—he remembered some of them who'd travelled to her funeral; only vague memories tied up with gifts of sweets and other treats relatives give to grieving children. He had their names in his head and now the Red Cross had them too. Hopefully he'd hear good news soon.

He went back to the letter, trying to find the best words for what he was trying to say.

Harry posted the letter to Rachel, his heart heavy. He didn't want to hurt her, and he was dying to see her. But he couldn't go home now, even though the war was over. There was still work to be done. A lot of his commando buddies were being transferred to fight the Japanese, but he was hoping to avoid that. He wanted to stay in Germany: he had yet to get to Berlin to check on Aunt Chana and his other relatives, never mind track down Schwarz. And Trudi...? Every so often his mind went back to his stepmother. Had she survived?

He'd hated her for sending them away on the *Kindertransport*. But now, having heard the stories, seen those pictures, he realized she'd saved their lives.

Harry didn't get a chance to enjoy the fine house for long. They were ordered to guard a prisoner camp in the northern edge of the Ruhr, where they held members of the Gestapo, high-ranking Nazis, concentration camp guards who'd been lucky to avoid immediate execution when found in the camps, and other undesirables.

His new job was interviewing these animals to see what they could tell him about the real targets the Allies wanted at the end of a rope. Himmler may have taken the coward's way out, but there were plenty more who had enforced his orders.

Harry readied himself for the next encounter. He usually got what he wanted by offering a hot cup of coffee and some cigarettes. Murphy called it his hidden charm. He winced. He was fed up dealing with prisoners, being no nearer to finding Schwarz, the man he'd come to Germany for.

The heavy wooden door to the office creaked open, and in stepped the next prisoner. He was a poster-boy for Nazi ideals: tall, blond, blue-eyed, with a muscular physique that had clearly not suffered any starvation. But it was his smirk, his disdain, that set Harry's teeth on edge. For a second, he was back in Dachau. Soldiers like the man in front of him, albeit dressed in a different uniform, sneering down at the gathered Jews, waiting to deliver their speeches.

Harry's chest constricted. He wanted to pull open his collar, but he couldn't show any weakness. The soldier took a seat without looking at Harry.

'Stand up! Nobody gave you leave to sit,' Harry barked, yet the man stared straight ahead as if Harry hadn't said a word. Harry clenched his fist under the desk, determined not to let this man see how he'd gotten under his skin.

'On your feet! Give me your name, rank and serial number, now!' Harry's words echoed through the room as he stared down at the man.

The man rose slowly to his feet, snapping his heels together in a mocking gesture. He'd got the upper hand, causing Harry to lose his temper, and they both knew it.

The prisoner shouted out his details, but Harry knew they

weren't true. He stepped out from behind the desk and walked up to the man, locking eyes with him and coldly stating, 'You are in fact SS-Unterscharführer Franz Rauff.'

The prisoner's eyes twitched but his body remained rigid. Harry didn't smoke but knew this man did. Lighting a cigarette, he took a long draw, blowing the smoke directly into the face of the prisoner. 'Want one?' There was no response. 'You may as well come clean. We know you were only an *Unterscharführer*.'

'Your German is native. What are you? A communist? Jew?' The prisoner turned his searing gaze on Harry, a fiery accusation in his voice. 'A deviant!'

Harry tried to contain his rage, knowing that the fury and hatred bubbling up inside him could not be unleashed here. 'I'm Jewish. Born and raised in Berlin, just like you. If our information is correct.'

'A traitor and a rat.'

Harry allowed himself a smirk of satisfaction, though it faded quickly away. 'Is that all you've got? It gets old fast.' He paused for effect before continuing. 'So, what really bothers you? Is it being locked up like an animal in this cage? That you lost the war and I, a lowly Jewish rat, outrank you?'

The man spat, catching Harry unawares, and then hissed, 'I personally burned your family, you...' Whatever he was about to say was cut off by Harry's fist connecting with his mouth. A few of his teeth fell out. The next blow hit his nose, the sickening crunch filling the cell.

The yells from the prisoner brought the other guards running and Harry found himself in Captain Murphy's office.

'You should just let us loose in there, Captain. We'd finish off the lot and save everyone the expense of a trial. Never mind the wait. It will take years to process that lot.'

'Barnes, you're a disgrace to the uniform you wear. Confined to quarters for the foreseeable. Get out.'

'But, sir...!'

'Out!'

Two days later, Harry had begun to calm down and realize the enormity of what he'd done. Officially, they'd been warned not to strike a prisoner, the unwritten rule being that you left no bruises and didn't have an audience.

Captain Murphy knocked and walked into the barracks just as Harry thought he would lose his mind with boredom.

'Talk to me. Tell me why I shouldn't boot you right back to England and put you on trial for abuse.'

Harry did everything he could not to tell him, but Captain Murphy was insistent.

He dragged out the whole story of Harry's past. For the first time, Harry told the story about what really happened to his father.

He stopped and started several times, choking back tears. He stiffened when Captain Murphy put his arm around him, holding him like his papa had. But the dam broke and, shoulders convulsing, he cried like a child. Captain Murphy didn't move or say a word. The tears flowed until there was no more.

Gathering himself, he cleared his throat, easing himself back in the chair, putting distance between him and the captain.

'Sorry.'

'Don't be, Harry. But let the hate go. It will eat you up and spit you out long before you get a chance to kill any man responsible for what happened to you and your da. To your people. Believe me, son, I know what I'm talking about. I've seen it back in Ireland. Hatred lives a long time, still pulling families apart over what side they took in the Irish civil war back in the twenties. Not everyone who wears the German uniform is a Nazi. In your head you know that. Some of the poor unfortunates we arrested are little more than boys.'

'Boys who were indoctrinated into the Nazi ways from birth.'

'*Boys*, son. Not men. Many of those kids just want to go home to their mams. They didn't want to fight. You heard the stories of how the SS units went around hanging anyone who didn't join up from the local tree. It's the SS you want. Those evil lunatics have a lot to answer for.'

Harry couldn't disagree.

'But even when one of them lands in your lap, lad, like that animal whose nose you broke, you shouldn't kill them. Not unless someone's life is in danger. If you kill indiscriminately, you become just as bad as they are.'

'I'm no Nazi!'

'No, but you could turn into a murderer, and then they have won. Harry, you have a life to lead after this is all over. The army isn't for you. For one thing you aren't good at taking orders. You have family to find and lives to rebuild. You don't want to get thrown in prison for murdering a Nazi. They destroyed enough of your life already.'

Harry lifted an eyebrow. 'You mean I should just ignore them?'

'No, you just need to report them. To your superior officers. People like me.' Murphy swiped his hand across the top of Harry's head. Harry ducked but even if he hadn't, Murphy would have only ruffled his hair.

Harry tried to curb the wave of hope climbing in his chest. Murphy wasn't going to send him home. 'What's going to happen to me, sir?'

'You're back on duty effective tomorrow but not at the prisoner of war camp. Some papers have fallen into our lap. Seems a good German was tasked with burning all the party documents, membership cards, that sort of thing. Only he wasn't a Nazi, not now, now ever. So he kept them, thinking we might be interested. Someone must sort through them.'

'That's not what I trained for!' Harry exploded.

Captain Murphy straightened, his lips thinning. 'You weren't trained to beat up unarmed prisoners either.'

The reprimand had the desired effect as Harry immediately realized Murphy was looking out for him, giving him a chance. 'Yes sir. Thank you, sir.'

The silence grew between them. Harry forced himself to ask, 'What will happen about the man. I think I broke his nose.'

'He fell down the stairs. Very unfortunate, but he'll recover.'

Harry watched in silence as this protector, his friend, walked out of the barracks.

In his time off, Harry continued his search for his relatives and friends. Aunt Chana and Frau Bernstein had escaped to Sweden in early 1944. When peace was declared, Ada had decided to go to Palestine but Aunt Chana had returned to Berlin. Nobody had heard of her since. He hoped she wasn't in the Russian zone.

Nobody knew what had happened to Trudi. He pushed aside the feelings of guilt her name brought up. He'd been so hateful, so judgemental. Yet she'd done what she did to save their lives. Had she survived?

His letters enquiring after his relations in Poland came back with the same answer: all killed. Murdered in camps, ghettos, by shooting or gas. Every single person he'd met and those he hadn't were now on the lists of the dead.

THIRTY-EIGHT

SEPTEMBER 1945

Harry jumped to his feet as his captain walked into the barracks. They'd recently been transferred to military intelligence, in Berlin, where their training as commandos and interrogators could be put to more use. Harry was determined to hunt down as many Nazis as he could find in his quest to capture his father's murderer. The new outfit suited him better: the rules and regulations were a lot less formal, but Harry acted out of habit.

'Barnes, what have you done now?'

'Nothing, sir.'

'You going to tell me you got that black eye from walking into a door?'

Harry kept quiet but held the captain's gaze. They both knew the answer, but the captain couldn't do anything unless Harry made a complaint. And he wasn't about to do that. He could live with a black eye. He had spent the last year trying to earn the trust of the men he'd fought besides, and he wasn't about to abuse that now by dishing dirt on the man who attacked him.

The captain gave up trying. 'Major Adams wants to see you

zero nine-hundred hours on Wednesday. Maybe he can get some sense out of you.'

'The major, sir?' Harry couldn't help his voice from slipping a little. What did the major want with him?

'Get your uniform cleaned and those shoes shined. Can't let the major think I don't keep my sergeants in line.'

'Yes, sir. Thank you, sir.'

Harry liked Captain Murphy, not least because the man was a bit of an outsider too. Many in the British Army didn't like taking orders from an Irishman but the man had been a regular soldier since long before the war started, and he cared for his men. Many of them were still alive thanks to the bravery of their captain. In truth he should have been a major or even a general, but maybe there were those further up the chain who didn't like the Irish.

Mac believed it was more like the captain kept blowing any chance of promotion by acting on his own initiative, which made for a great commando but was frowned on by the more traditionally minded in the army.

'Enjoy your next few days off. Go visit your old haunting places in Berlin but be back here ready to see the major on Wednesday with your head screwed on properly.'

'Yes, sir.'

Harry had watched the man's retreating back until he was alone once more. His old haunting places. Where should he go? The Allied bombings had destroyed much of Berlin. Still, there was a chance Papa's home was still standing. Maybe that's where Aunt Chana and any others would be, if they had been spared. Maybe Trudi too.

Harry kicked at a box on the ground. He couldn't hang around the barracks wondering what tomorrow would bring. He had to get out of there.

· · ·

Harry walked the streets, hardly recognizing the area he had grown up in. The remains of the synagogue stood amidst piles of rubble, all that remained of the apartment blocks that used to surround it. Everywhere he looked he saw groups of women, old men and children picking up bricks, working at clearing the streets. Those that did acknowledge him glanced at him warily, but most ignored him.

As he walked past one group, a voice cried out weakly, 'Heinz! *Mein Gott*, is it you? Heinz.'

He turned but didn't recognize the woman calling to him. Her grey hair, eyes that had seen too much horror, and emancipated figure, made her look to be in her late sixties. How did she know him? Was she a patient of his father's?

He glanced around to check there were no other British soldiers nearby before moving closer to her. He didn't want to get either of them into trouble.

'Yes, I am Heinz Beck.'

Tears streamed down her cheeks as she clutched his arm, her fingers moving over the cloth of his uniform. 'Heinz, I don't believe it. How good you look! Healthy. And Tomas? He is here?' She looked confused, swaying slightly.

He reached to steady her before she fell. She misunderstood and threw her arms around him. His nose wrinkled as the stench of starvation hit him: her rank breath, rotten teeth and unwashed body. He fought the urge to free himself; instead, he had to hold her tighter and take a step back or they would have both fallen on the street.

'Tomas is in England with Liesel. I'm very sorry, but who are you?'

The woman recoiled as if he had slapped her. 'Chana. Don't you recognize me?'

Heinz couldn't hide his shock. This ancient crone was his glamorous aunt Chana? But she was only in her forties. Yet this woman...

'I have changed. I know. Not just in appearances. I...' She gave up talking as the effort seemed to cost her too much.

'Aunt Chana! You're alive! I'd given up hope. I tried to find you but there was nothing at your old address. Come, let's find somewhere to sit down and talk.'

'I have to work. It is the only way I can afford food.' Her gaze didn't leave the ground.

'I'll speak to your boss. You sit here.' He led her over to a step and helped her sit down before walking back to the group and speaking to the man in charge. He was reluctant to agree to save Chana's job but three cigarettes soon changed his mind.

Harry walked back to Chana, frowning. Was that all someone's time was worth now?

Heinz took Chana's arm and led them to a small café. He didn't care if anyone saw them together, he wasn't fraternizing with the enemy. Chana was family.

He bought them both a coffee and some pastries. Chana's eyes bulged as she stared at the delicacies laid out on the plate. She reached out, her hands black, her nails ragged and torn and, with a humiliated look, clasped her hands back together, placing them in her lap.

'Aunt Chana, please eat. You look like you haven't had a decent meal in a long time. Would you prefer some soup?'

Chana nodded, but he was left feeling she did so to buy some time to think. He walked back to the counter rather than signalling the waiter.

'Fine-looking Fräulein you found yourself,' a soldier sneered at him from a nearby table. Harry clenched his fists, wanting to punch the stranger in the jaw.

'She's my aunt.'

'Sure, and I'm your uncle. Don't you know the rules? If you're going to break them, at least do it with a pretty one.'

Harry lost all sense of reason and before he knew it, he had his hands wrapped in the soldier's uniform, holding him almost off the ground. 'My aunt deserves respect, not your ridicule. Keep your mouth clean.'

The owner rushed forward. 'We no need trouble here. Please stop, you will bring police and they will shut me down. My family depends on this place.'

His words found their way into Harry's brain and he released the soldier. 'Get out.' The man didn't look back.

Turning to the owner, he asked for a bowl of soup and some bread, in German. The man answered, saying how sorry he was. He had tried to help the Jews and... But Harry wasn't listening. He went back to his aunt. She was crying silently at the table. He saw her shoulders heaving.

'Aunt Chana, please don't cry.'

Chana wiped her eyes once more before murmuring, 'I'm embarrassing you. I should go.' She made to stand up but he persuaded her gently back into the chair.

'Stay, eat. I can't lose you now. I haven't been able to find anyone.' He hesitated and added, 'Not the people I care about.'

She glanced up at him and then at the bowl of soup the owner placed in front of her. The owner also told her to eat. 'Wasting food is a sin, after everything we have been through.'

Chana mumbled her thanks. Harry pretended not to notice how she wolfed down the food. What had she been through, and how had she survived when so few hadn't?

She didn't speak until the soup was finished. 'Tell me about your life, Heinz. You are really a British officer?'

'Hardly. I'm a soldier. I joined up in August 1940, lied about my age. I wanted to fight back. The British needed my language skills so I spent the war interviewing prisoners, getting them to tell us where their camps were, how many of them and things like that.' He couldn't tell her the truth. His unit was still top secret, even now the war was over. 'Some would say I was a traitor. To Germany.'

He couldn't look her in the eyes. He could see his uncle,

how proud he'd been of his Germany. How would Leopold Arkin have felt about Heinz fighting in a British uniform?

'Nonsense.' She held out her hand, placing it over his; he could feel the callouses on her skin. 'They stopped us being Germans a long time ago. We were subhuman to them. Not even people. You did well. Your mother, your father, would have been proud of you. I am.'

He brushed way the tears in his eyes with his free hand. Turning his hand around hers, he gently stroked it, trying not to compare her to Maggie. Maggie was older than Chana, yet looked younger.

He wanted to know everything that had happened to her since he'd left Berlin, but on another level, he didn't want to know. He knew she had suffered, that was obvious. He asked, 'Where do you live?'

'With a friend. We share a room in an apartment with ten others. It's not luxury'—she shrugged her shoulders—'but at least I have a roof over my head.'

He could only imagine how awful it was. He'd heard stories of families making their homes in the rubble. There was such a shortage of housing.

'I have been given leave. Please come back with me to my hotel. We have so much to catch up on.'

Her eyes widened as she shook her head. 'I can't go into a hotel wearing this. I look like a beggar, perhaps worse.'

Harry curbed his impatience. 'I need to know. About our family, our friends, even Trudi. I know you didn't like her, but she is Liesel's mother. Sally, the wonderful woman who gave us a home in Britain, she begged me to find Trudi.'

To his surprise, Chana grabbed both his hands and stared into his eyes, tears flowing down her face. 'I was so wrong about Trudi. The things I said to you about her, may God cut out my tongue. She saved me, Heinz. I owe her my life. I would have been dead if not for her. So many owe her their lives.'

Trudi? She'd saved Chana? But how? He stared at his aunt, waiting for her to elaborate but she was too distraught. Maybe if they were alone, she would open up.

'Can I take you home? You can freshen up and when you feel better, I'd like to know all you can tell me.'

She nodded, her hands clutching his. He helped her, gripping her elbow as she seemed unsteady on her feet. Only then did I realize her shoes were too large for her.

He called a taxi despite her protests and asked the driver to take them to her home.

The block seemed to have been untouched by bombs, unlike the surrounding area. Inside the drab brown building, they climbed the stairs to the third floor. He adjusted his step to match his aunt's slower pace. She took out a key, throwing a look of apology in his direction before opening the door. He followed her inside, his nose wrinkling at the smell of boiling vegetables, human sweat and other scents he didn't wish to identify. The people already in the apartment didn't look up as they walked down the hall.

He stood awkwardly at the door to a tiny room, trying to imagine living in such a small space. Twin beds, on opposite sides of the room, with a small table resting on some books, in the corner. The undersized window looked out on the remains of another apartment building. It should have been demolished but, looking out, Harry could see people moving about in the rubble. Some woman had hung out washing to dry. A couple of children wandered about, one kicking at a pile of rags as if it were a football.

Chana indicated he sit on her bed while she went to the kitchen. She returned with hot drinks. They smelled revolting, reminding him of how far he'd come from Dachau.

She sat on the other bed playing with her fingers until the silence became oppressive.

'If it's too difficult...'

'No, Heinz. I must tell you no matter how hard it is. I owe it to her and the others who helped.' She took a deep breath and began speaking so quietly he had to strain to hear. 'After you children left on the *Kindertransport*, Trudi continued living at the apartment. She came to see me one day to ask if I would like some photos she had found of your dear mama.' Chana raised guilt-filled eyes to his. 'I was so rude. When I think of it...' Chana rubbed her mouth with a hanky, her hands shaking. 'Life became more difficult. People disappeared but we told ourselves it was because they were different. They were foreign Jews, the ones who hadn't been born in Germany. Then it was the religious Jews, the ones who insisted on looking different, those with sidelocks and so on.' Chana took a second. 'How we tried to fool ourselves with our petty excuses for what the Nazis were doing. Goebbels didn't hide the fact he wanted Germany to be free of us, never mind Berlin in particular. We had to wear the star, of course you know that. We couldn't shop for food until certain times, our papers only entitled us to smaller rations and so on.' Chana continued telling him of instances of horror. 'I was so proud back then, of my house, my standing, our family's reputation. I didn't think they would dare to touch us. When they ordered us to leave the house, I thought they were joking. Your uncle, he tried to remonstrate with the officer but he wouldn't listen. He warned Leopold to obey without question. I begged Leopold not to do anything silly but your uncle, he never listened to anyone, you know?'

Harry nodded although he'd never known his uncle that well.

'Leopold was taken to the Jewish hospital, but it was pointless: he died. I sat there, no idea where to go or what to do. I'd always done what Leopold told me to do. Somehow Trudi found out, and she came to find me. She offered to share her apartment with me. Imagine, after me shutting the door in her face.' Chana started crying again.

Harry stood up to look out the window, trying to give her privacy while fighting the urge to escape. He wasn't sure he wanted to hear any more, at least not today.

'So I moved in there. Another lady was living there, a Mrs Bernstein. Nice lady but prone to dramatics, you know?'

He forced himself to keep a straight face. From what he remembered about back then, Rachel's mother was a saint compared to his aunt.

'I thought it was a squash, after what we were used to. How I laugh at that now. Look at how I live.' Chana glanced around as if surprised to find herself in the room. 'Anyway, I digress. We didn't last long in that apartment.'

His aunt was rambling, reliving her terror. He tried to get her back on track.

'Chana, you survived. You were the brave one.'

'I wasn't brave. But Trudi, she was magnificent. She pretended to be a gentile. She looked like one, didn't she?'

He thought of the blonde hair and blue eyes. He had misjudged his stepmother. He knew she'd got him out of Dachau and all three children on the *Kindertransport*—but to save his aunt and Mrs. Bernstein as well...

'Trudi was right. All those who went on those transports, they never returned. Not people my age. Some younger people, they came back. Walking skeletons they are, and their eyes... they are dead inside. Younger than you, yet they seem older, the horrors they have been exposed to have aged them.' His aunt lost focus for a few seconds before she picked up the thread. 'We lived in a church. Trudi didn't live with us. There was only room for two women. She gave up her place so Mrs. Bernstein and I could live.'

'Where is she? I've asked the Red Cross to help find her,

searched the lists that appear, but I can't find any mention of her.'

Chana rocked back and forth, her face deathly pale. 'She's dead. She was caught. We were told she was tortured, they knew she could tell them where other Jews were hiding. They wanted to know who helped her, those brave people who stood up against the regime. She didn't talk. No matter what they did to her.' Chana's voice rose slightly as she relived the horror. 'I should have persuaded her to take my place in the church. I'm older, my husband had died, my children reared. She had a baby.'

'Chana, stop, please. Trudi made her own decisions. Maybe she was sent to a camp. Where was this church? Maybe some of those priests could help me find her?'

Chana shook her head violently. 'She's dead. They shot her on the first of May 1945. It was in the records. I checked when I got back from Sweden. They sent us there in early 1945 to get us away from the Russians.' Chana shuddered. 'I couldn't stay in Sweden after the war, I had to come back to Berlin. To find out if anyone was still alive. Ada gave me Rachel's address in England but I lost it. I didn't know where you lived so I thought, I hoped... I'd find Trudi and she would find you. But she died.'

Harry cursed under his breath. The Nazis had insisted on keeping records of everything, a decision they would probably learn to regret. The evidence these records provided would be used in their trials for war crimes if rumours were to be believed. If the records proved Trudi was dead, she probably was. Still, something made him ask: 'Maybe it was a mistake? Trudi could have been sent to a camp? Maybe she escaped. Did you check with the pastor at the church?'

'Eric, Pastor Perwe, died in 1944. The man who helped us was sent home, back to Sweden. His plane crashed. They said it was an accident but we know he was killed for helping us. They didn't like Jews either—nobody does. The whole world hates us.' Tears rolling down her face, Chana continued to rock back and forth, her hot drink forgotten.

Embarrassed, Harry glanced around. Where were her things? Her clothes and personal belongings? She didn't appear to have anything at all. 'What of the lady who shares this room with you? Is she Jewish?'

'No. Isla was...' His aunt hesitated before she grabbed his hand. 'You have to keep quiet about this.'

Harry nodded, to indulge her more than anything else.

'Isla is or should I say was a countess. Married to a general—General Von Pabst.'

Harry couldn't help himself. 'General Von Pabst who was part of the 1944 plot to kill Hitler?'

Chana nodded. 'Not that we knew it at the time, but the general helped Isla to help us. She and Trudi were great friends. She only survived as her home was hit by a bomb late 1943 and the General put out rumours his wife had been killed. He sent her away to his estate in the country. Maybe she wishes that was true. She has suffered deeply, at the hands of the Russians. You know?'

Harry knew. He blushed, not wanting to hear the details.

'Did they know she's a countess?'

'No. For that they would have killed her, or dragged her off to Russia. It was bad enough they just knew her to be a woman.' Chana's face flushed, her eyes focused on the floor. 'She helped save my life. It was Isla who found out about Trudi. I think that almost finished her off. She has nobody else, so we live together.' Chana wiped the tears from her face, finally looking at him. 'Look at me, I'm a mess. I'm so glad to see you, Heinz. I prayed every night that someone I knew would come back. My friends, my extended family... they are all gone.' The tears flowed again.

He pulled her toward him and held her as she cried. 'What am I to do, Heinz? There is nothing for me here. I'm too old to rebuild my life and who would I build it for, anyway?'

As she cried, he grew angry. Look at how she was living, trying to rebuild a city destroyed through no fault of hers. She was a victim of the Nazis. She should be taken care of, allowed to sleep in a decent bed in a nice area away from all the memories of what she'd been through.

'Aunt Chana, I must get back now, but I will come and see you tomorrow. Here.' He emptied his pockets. 'Take this money and these cigarettes. Buy food or whatever you need. When I come back tomorrow, I will bring you some things. I will help you find a proper home.'

'My home is with you, Tomas and Liesel. You are the only family I have left.'

Tom was in Britain, and Harry had unfinished business in Berlin. He had to find the man who murdered his father or at least get confirmation he was dead.

Chana grasped his arm. 'Take me with you, Heinz. Please.'

He gently removed her hands from his jacket. 'I can't. But I will be back. I don't know how I can help you, Aunt Chana. But you don't need to work on that building site anymore to earn money for food or rent. That much I can promise.'

Harry left his aunt and made his way back to the barracks, walking slowly, deep in thought. Trudi had saved Chana's life, and others if his aunt was to be believed. He kicked out at a stone on the ground. Why had he thought the worst of his stepmother? She'd saved his life and those of his siblings by getting them on the *Kindertransport*. His mind flew back in time to the arguments he'd heard between Trudi and Papa, Trudi begging his father to leave Germany, to send him and Tomas away, to get them papers from the church. His breath hitched as he remembered the last time he'd seen her at the train station. The sneering faces of the uniformed soldiers as they pushed the children onto the trains, making fun of them at every opportunity, the man who'd torn Brown Bear from Tomas's arms.

In the whole sequence of events that flitted through his mind, the clearest image of all was that of his stepmother. Her eyes huge in her pale, tear-stained face as she watched the train depart the station, the train carrying the most precious of all cargo, her children.

And he'd thought she was selfish. What a fool he'd been. An ungrateful, ignorant *fool*.

THIRTY-NINE

'You wanted to see us, sir?' Murphy said, after they had both saluted.

Major Adams returned the salute. 'At ease, gentlemen. In fact, take a seat. I get a crick in my neck looking up at you.'

Murphy and Harry exchanged glances but sat down. Murphy sat on the edge of his, obviously uncomfortable at sitting in the presence of an officer. Harry didn't have the same problem. As Murphy had pointed out, he didn't have the right respect for authority to fit in with a long-term military career.

'Lieutenant Beck, I've been hearing a lot about you.'

Harry held the major's gaze. What had he heard? Had Harry been seen giving food to the local children? It was against all rules but he would have to be heartless not to help those starving. He remained tight-lipped. He didn't know what the major knew and certainly wasn't going to land himself in trouble by admitting any of his so-called crimes.

'You have a personal issue with the Nazis from what I gather, even though you are German.' The major shifted some files on his desk. 'Are you going to say something?'

'I was born in Germany but I don't consider myself to be

German. The Nazis took that right away in 1933. They made me stateless.'

'Ah, yes, you're a Jew.'

Harry didn't comment. He didn't have any religious beliefs: they had died with his papa.

Adams continued to shuffle paperwork as Harry remained silent. He knew it was a tactic used to make people talk but Harry was used to having to keep his opinions to himself. He resisted the urge to tap his foot and sat up straighter. The major wasn't going to intimidate him.

'I've heard good things about you from your superiors.'

At that Harry couldn't stop himself looking surprised. He glanced at Murphy but his captain was staring straight ahead.

'Not just Captain Murphy, although he gave you a glowing report, but others. You have a reputation for getting the job done, you remain calm under pressure and you are remarkably single-minded when it comes to achieving goals.'

Harry allowed himself a small smile.

'You are also undisciplined and inclined to follow your own interpretation of orders.'

The smile slid away to be replaced by his taciturn expression. He knew it bordered on insolence but he couldn't stop himself.

'You have been cautioned more than once for using excessive force against the enemy. There have been a couple of incidents where you have got into a fight over your beliefs—judging by your face, the last one was fairly recently.'

He remained silent, causing Murphy to mumble something. He rebuked Harry with a look and then spoke. 'Sir, if you allow me to explain. I believe Lieutenant Beck was taunted for being German and things got out of hand.'

Harry didn't move a muscle. Major Adams scrutinized him for a couple of seconds but when it became clear he wouldn't speak, he asked him out straight. 'Is that true, Lieutenant?'

'That would be a matter of opinion, sir. That's all I would like to say on the matter.'

Another grumble from Murphy but the major smiled. 'Your reputation for not snitching has also been reported.' Then the smile dropped as Major Adam's hand slammed into his desk. 'Lieutenant Beck, get this straight. We may be Intelligence. Our command structure may be less formal than the usual army. But, *you* will answer my questions. Understand?'

'Yes, sir.' Harry used his more respectful tone. What was he doing there? Was he going to have to listen to a lecture on his good and bad attributes for long? He had better things to be doing with his time.

'Good. I have an opportunity for you. I am not ordering you to take this assignment although I hope you do. But as there are serious risks involved, I want to be clear that this is a volunteer role. Understood.'

Harry inched forward in his seat. Was Major Adams going to let him back into active duty? Translating German documentation into English could never be called interesting.

'Captain Murphy has recommended you for this role. I admit to having some reservations given what we have just discussed, but the captain says you have grown in maturity in recent months. According to him, you are the type of person we need.'

Harry could barely keep his mouth shut. Would the major stop waffling and get to the point? Where was he going to be sent?

'I want to you to assume the identify of a *Wehrmacht* soldier. You will be transferred to a camp in Munich.'

Harry sat back, too stunned to argue.

'You will act as the other SS do, by hiding in plain sight, so to speak. Although presenting as a conscripted private, you are a die-hard Nazi—your parents fed you on a diet of *Mein Kampf* and you gobbled up every word.'

Harry opened his mouth to protest but at a look from Major Adams he shut it again.

'We know there are high-level Nazis, even SS soldiers, who are still in Germany, probably in these camps. You know as well as I do Nazis are escaping all over the place by hiding in plain sight. What better way to hide than in a crowd of Germans? You have a better chance of spotting a Nazi than just about most of us here. You know these people, you lived through the Hitler years. You heard the lies, the propaganda. If you take off the blinkers of hate, you can distinguish between some poor sod shoved into a uniform he despises and one who glorifies in his shiny boots.'

Harry listened, still not quite sure what the major wanted him to do, but the temptation to get his hands on SS men was overwhelming. He might find the animal who'd murdered his papa. He'd recognize him in an instant, even after all these years. His bad teeth might have been fixed but there was nothing that could be done about the scar at the corner of his ear just above his shirt collar. Or the mark on his upper arm, only visible when he had taken off his uniform jacket to stop it getting dirty from the blood spray.

Harry swallowed hard.

'Make no mistake, Beck. You are not being given carte blanche to attack these men. Your job is to befriend them.'

Harry jumped to his feet. 'I can't do that. Make friends with those scumbags.'

'Lieutenant, take control of yourself.' Murphy roared but the major just indicated he take a seat.

'You will befriend them and find out where their leaders are hiding. There are some who believe by putting the Nazis currently in custody on trial, the whole of Germany will suddenly become Nazi-free. That is farcical. We need to root out all the die-hard fans. The ones without whom those idiots Göring and his friends would not have succeeded. The men we are after are intelligent, cunning and desperate. They will stop at nothing to resurrect the Great Reich as they call it. Your job will be to help stop that.'

The major stopped speaking. Harry didn't know what to say. Could he do it? He could pass for a Nazi, that wasn't exactly hard. All he had to do was repeat the abuse he'd received for years but pretend it was aimed at someone else. But could he restrain himself from attacking one of those who had killed his family? His papa? All those poor unfortunates who had been murdered at Auschwitz, Dachau, Treblinka and goodness knew where else?

The major eyed him. 'What do you say? Are you in?'

'How would I report them? Surely that would blow my cover. Also, won't the guards minding the camp immediately suspect me? I don't look like a starving soldier.'

The major ignored his comments.

'You will have a team working with you. Men who are also fluent in German but not necessarily German. I have a couple of English officers in mind who might be perfect.'

'They won't work.'

The major glared at him. 'Pardon?'

Murphy shook his head but Harry wasn't taking more chances than he had to. He modulated his tone to be more persuasive.

'Speaking German isn't enough. You have to think like a German, otherwise they will be rumbled. You said yourself the SS are intelligent. Not all of them, but the ones you are interested in. They will know a German from someone who pretends to be.'

'I don't think I agree.'

Harry forged ahead: 'I don't care whether you agree or not, this is my life on the line. You said it would be my team. I get to pick them.'

The major looked as if he was likely to explode. Briefly

tempted to try another line of persuasion, Harry decided to stay silent. The major was used to people not questioning his orders, but this was a different type of war. There were no rules. The silence built. He felt the major's stare but refused to lock gazes with him. Instead, his eyes wandered over the map hanging above the major's desk, briefly lingering on Britain. What was Rachel doing now? He turned off those thoughts. He had to concentrate, not fall at this late stage.

He looked back at the major, whose jaw was clenched, his eyes glittering with rage. Harry kept his expression neutral. He would not speak first.

Captain Murphy intervened. 'Who have you in mind, Beck?'

'Neuman, Kruger and Udet, Sir.'

The major's face turned to stone. 'The orderlies? Out of the question, Beck. They aren't soldiers.'

'But they were, sir. German ones. All conscripts. I've read their files, spoken with them. Neuman was married to a Jew and didn't divorce her. He was hiding her until he was conscripted into the army. She was denounced while he was in Russia. Kruger is a loyal German but he is an anti-Nazi. He always has been, right from the start.'

The major raised his eyebrows, his lips pressed into a thin line. 'So why is he wearing a uniform?'

'He isn't wearing an officer's uniform. He was part of the punishment brigade, having refused to shoot civilians.'

'And what sort of saint is Udet?' the major asked, sarcastically.

'He's a die-hard Nazi. Some would sell their mother or their wife for the cause. He'd sell his whole family, plus his farm and the clothes off his back.'

Major Adams blinked rapidly. 'Impossible. With those feelings, he would never have got a job here.'

'And yet he is, and he did. He's about as stupid as they come on paper, but he has the cunning of a fox and the bravery of a lion. Which makes him extremely dangerous.'

Harry watched the man's reaction. He was taking a risk but he had to improve the chance of success.

'So why suggest him? Surely he would denounce you as soon as you set foot in a camp.'

'He would. Unless you pay him enough to keep his mouth shut.'

The major stopped in the midst of lighting another cigarette. He shook his head but his eyes never left Harry's. 'A die-hard Nazi who can be bribed. I can't see that working.'

Harry didn't back down. 'You don't know him. I do. He wants to get to South America to join other Nazis who already escaped. He's desperate to get the money together to go. He believes that's where the phoenix will rise from the dead. He's heard a rumour that Hitler himself is in South America.'

'That's nonsense. Hitler is dead, by his own hand.'

'Udet believes that to be Allied propaganda. He despises Göring and the others you have locked up. He would kill any of them with his bare hands for their lack of loyalty to his Führer. As for Himmler trying to negotiate peace? You just need to mention that and watch his blood pressure rise.'

'Why didn't we notice this? Only those who didn't have strong affiliations were supposed to be cleared to work with us.'

'I said he was cunning. He's made himself useful. He knows how to get things, women, you name it. I can list more than a handful of officers who are in his debt. He's blackmailed several and has a large portion of his fare saved.'

'These officers?' The major pierced Harry with a gaze but he held firm.

'They shall remain nameless, for now at least. You won't serve any purpose by arresting them, and it will only push Udet underground. Keep your friends close but your enemies closer, Major.'

The major rolled his eyes as Murphy looked fit to burst.

The major lit another cigarette. 'And he just told you all of this?'

'Of course not. He hates me.'

The major watched him, as if waiting for more. Harry stayed silent, forcing the man to speak. 'He knows you are Jewish?'

'Not sure, sir, but he knows I know him for what he is rather than the image he sold to you.'

The major leaned back in his chair, blowing a stream of smoke in Harry's direction. 'So why are you still alive?'

'He believes I am interested in a piece of his action. I may have given him names of potential customers. Some turned out to be rather profitable.' Harry ignored the dirty look Murphy sent his way. 'Udet knows I have a letter written, to be opened in the event of any suspicious death that may befall me, denouncing him and his schemes. With proof.'

The major whistled as he rested his arms on his desk. Even Murphy looked surprised, and his face usually never showed a reaction to anything.

'I think we underestimated you, Lieutenant.'

'Most people do, Major. But you don't get to survive the Nazis, and internment as a foreign alien with Nazi prisoners of war, and not learn how to survive. If I hadn't, I would be dead.'

Major Adams looked embarrassed. 'I heard about your internment. Bad business, that.'

Harry didn't comment. It was history, he told himself, but it still rankled. If he'd been arrested and imprisoned with other Jews, that might have been understandable. They were Germans or at least in the eyes of the British. But to have been thrown in with known Nazis and shipped off to the Isle of Man, to live on an island with those animals? That was something he would never forgive. Or forget.

'Will these men volunteer to go into a POW camp with you?' Murphy broke the uncomfortable silence.

'Yes, sir. Neuman and Kruger hate the SS, have their own reasons for wanting revenge. They also want to prove they are decent Germans. Udet will jump at the chance to earn enough money to reach his Führer.'

The major steepled his fingers. 'So, assuming we can get agreement for this group to go with you, how do you intend keeping Udet quiet? If our suspicions are correct, and we believe they are, he will meet quite high-ranking SS men in the camps. It would have made our lives much easier if every SS man had been inked.' The major frowned. 'They will have more money to bribe him with, not to mention trigger his loyalties to the party.'

Harry pressed his foot to the ground to stop it shaking. He hadn't figured everything out but he wasn't about to admit that. He hoped his voice sounded more confident than he felt. 'That's a risk I'm prepared to take.'

Captain Murphy spoke up. 'Harry, I'm not standing by to watch you take on a suicide mission. I didn't keep you alive through the war just to see you get your head staved in now.' He seemed to remember where he was as his face turned red. 'My apologies, Major.'

The major didn't take his eyes off Harry. 'This is a rather extraordinary situation. We should all speak our mind, regardless of rank.'

Harry nodded. 'It's alright, Captain Murphy. I'm not stupid and I don't have a death wish.' *Not anymore.* There had been a time when he would have welcomed death. But now he could see a way to complete his mission and then to get back to Rachel and Tom and Liesel. He took a chance. 'I intend to use Udet to get myself accepted, then he will be eliminated.'

The major's eyebrows rose but he stayed silent. Harry took

out his lighter, lit a cigarette and took a deep drag. How much should he tell?

'I can provide proof of his actions against the Führer and the Reich.'

Murphy interjected: 'I thought he was a die-hard Nazi.'

Harry glanced at his long-time mentor and, much as he hated to admit it, his protector.

'He is. He's innocent of betraying Hitler, but do you care? I can manipulate some evidence to make it look like he is betraying Nazis for money. His friends will take care of him for me.'

The major smiled but Captain Murphy just stared at him. 'I never knew you could be so devious.'

'With all due respect, Captain, you don't really know me at all.' Harry turned his attention to the major, not wanting to see Murphy's reaction to his comment. This wasn't the time for friendship. He needed to get into the camps to find Schwarz, and this was his best chance. He pulled on the cigarette again and then, faking confidence, he began.

'There are certain other things I want.'

'Such as?' The major couldn't hide his interest.

'I don't want anyone trying to countermand my decisions. Present company excepted, of course,' Harry added, to soothe the already blistering egos. 'I have an aunt in Berlin. She is struggling and her accommodation makes a mockery of that word. I want to move her to one of the houses we commandeered. She doesn't need the whole house and will be happy to cook and do other chores if necessary. But I want her out of the hovel she calls a home.' Harry allowed those words to sink in. 'These are my terms.'

The major stood, 'Your terms! You are a soldier, young man, and as such under my orders.'

'Yes, sir. I will do my duty. You won't have any reason to

regret it. But as you said yourself, this is a suicide mission. What have you to lose?'

The major sat again, took a deep drag of his cigarette and studied Harry intently.

Harry held his gaze. He knew what he was risking, but this could be the best chance he had of finding Papa's murderer.

FORTY

SEPTEMBER 1945

Rachel walked down the stairs, putting a hand to her mouth to stop another yawn. Between working at the hospital, helping Sally with the children and sleepless nights worrying about her mother, brothers and Harry—mostly Harry—she was shattered. Yet she wasn't doing enough. She had nursing skills now, despite not being fully qualified. With the news reports coming out of Germany and other areas, she was torn between doing more to help her people, and staying here with her family. Waiting for Harry to come home.

'Morning, love. Sit down and have your breakfast. There's a boiled egg and some of my brown bread made just how you like it. Wish there was a way I could put a smile on your face.'

Rachel tried to smile at the older woman. Maggie had loved and cared for her and her sister since they'd first arrived on the *Kindertransport*, and a nicer woman you couldn't meet. She'd put up with a lot, including horrible comments and nasty remarks from neighbours who felt that all Germans should be interned for the duration of the war, even children fleeing for their lives. Rachel knew Maggie paid little heed to the gossip but, still, it must have hurt at times. But she'd never blamed

Ruth or her for anything. In fact, Maggie only worried about them even more.

Rachel knew Maggie was concerned about what would happen with the war being over. Would their mother come back and take over, leaving Maggie alone once again? Well, apart from the reverend, but he was young enough to marry. What would happen to Maggie then? Would she move in with Sally?

They both heard the postman whistling before the letter box rattled as letters fell onto the mat.

Rachel went to stand back up but Maggie shook her head. 'You eat up while I get the letters.'

Maggie walked out to the hall leaving Rachel to start buttering her bread. She spread the butter thinly, grateful again for Maggie's connection with a local farmer. Sally said Farmer Doocey was sweet on Maggie, who retorted the old farmer was trying to gain favour with the rector.

Maggie came back in with a large smile. 'This will cheer you up, love. It's from Harry. I'd know his scrawl anywhere.'

Maggie poured the tea while Rachel ripped the letter open. She started reading but then the words blurred as her eyes filled with tears.

'Rachel, what's wrong?' As Maggie put her hand on her shoulder, Rachel couldn't stop the tears and turned into the older woman's embrace, the letter slipping to the floor. Maggie patted her on the back, muttering, 'There, there. Don't cry.'

She sobbed until her tears were spent. But it wasn't fair leaving Maggie in the dark—she was probably imagining all sorts of scenarios.

'It's Harry. He's not coming home.'

Maggie paled, taking a seat at the table. 'Why?'

'He's volunteered for a dangerous mission which he says may lead him to the man who murdered his father. That's the most important thing. He cares about that more than he does for me. Why?' Rachel's anger bubbled up and, clenching her fists by her side, she marched over to the window staring out at the village, not seeing the rectory garden with the rows of vegetables sprouting thanks to Maggie's green fingers.

In her mind's eye, she saw Harry the last time she'd seen him. She'd gone to London to meet him and wave him off as he marched off to war.

She whirled around and banged her fist on the table. 'He promised, Maggie! He said he'd come back for me. The war is over and he still doesn't care enough to come home.'

Maggie shook her head. 'I know, love, but men are different to women. He loves you, we all know that, but he's got his own war to fight. From what you told me, he feels guilty for his father having been in Dachau. If Harry hadn't been arrested, his father would have been released due to his military record.'

Rachel knew that was true: Harry did blame himself. 'Yes, but not for long. The Nazis would have caught up with him eventually. It's not Harry's fault. He is being stupid.' Rachel hiccupped. 'I'm not wasting any more time waiting for him.' She walked back to the window not wanting to look at Maggie, not wanting to see the hurt on the woman's face. 'I told you Matron asked for volunteers to go to Germany to help.'

Maggie rose and came to her side, turned her around to face her. 'Rachel, don't do anything hasty. The war may be over but there is a lot of anger and danger in those places. You have a chance here. With all your experience you could go to university and become a doctor. Like you said you wanted to.'

'No, Maggie. That was a dream of a stupid young girl. Look at what my people have been through. I have to help.'

Maggie didn't argue but pulled her into a hug and whispered, 'I love you, Rachel. You're the daughter I wish I had. I just want to protect you.'

Rachel returned the embrace. 'I love you too, Maggie, but I have to do this. Please understand. Will you keep Ruth here, with you?'

She wished she could retract that last comment as the hurt flared in Maggie's eyes.

'Ruth's home is here and always will be for as long as she wants it. She may decide to join your mother in Palestine. If she can.'

'That's not likely, is it, Maggie? The British have made their feelings clear.' Rachel hated the bitterness in her tone but she couldn't believe, after the news of the murders of thousands of Jews, that they still were prevented from travelling to Palestine.

'Rachel, life isn't fair but we have to work around things. You are too young to sound so bitter.'

Rachel knew Maggie meant well but she felt stifled. She kissed her friend on the cheek. 'I must go and tell Sally. I will be home later.'

Maggie didn't argue.

Rachel walked across the lane but she couldn't face seeing Tom and Lisa now, or telling Sally that Harry wasn't coming home. She'd let Maggie do it. She kept walking, not caring where she went. Friedrich Schwarz of the SS guard battalion, the man Harry was looking for, was more than likely dead. Couldn't he see it was a waste of time? Time they could be spending together building their lives—to prove to the Nazis and their supporters that they hadn't succeeded in destroying the Jewish nation. Wasn't that the best revenge of all?

FORTY-ONE

NOVEMBER 1946

Harry stilled: he'd heard that voice before. It took every ounce of restraint not to whirl around and face the man he'd been searching for. The hair on the back of his neck stood up. Despite knowing he was safe, no longer a child at the mercy of a powerful bully, fear swept through him, closely followed by white-hot anger.

His knuckles turned white on the pot he was holding.

'You going to serve that?'

Harry glanced up as Kruger indicated the pot in his hands and the queue building at the counter. Harry turned, without looking up, and placed the contents in the tray. He put the empty pot back on the trolley, desperately trying to get back into the character he'd played for the last six months. The die-hard Nazi who was hiding in plain sight, ready for the chance to escape.

One hundred and ninety-three days he'd been stuck in this camp, this version of hell, although it had been over a year since he'd agreed the scheme with the major, ironically starting his imprisonment on the same day the Nazi elite had gone on trial at Nuremberg. He'd wanted to applaud the Allies for seeking justice; instead, he'd had to commiserate about the fate of the captured generals. He'd toasted the bravery of Hitler, Himmler and the others who'd committed suicide rather than fall at the feet of the victors. Not that anyone in this camp recognized the war was over or victory had been lost.

Overcome with nausea, he swallowed hard desperate not to do anything to attract Schwarz's attention. His hands gripped the side of the counter as he struggled to get his feelings under control.

'You got an itch you can't scratch?' Kruger's comment dragged him back to reality.

Despite the vulgar comment, he knew Kruger meant well. He was an intelligent man and had offered Harry his loyalty. He said they needed to watch each other's backs.

'A voice from the past. Wasn't expecting it,' Harry whispered, without moving his lips.

Kruger's eyes widened. 'One of our targets?'

Harry nodded in response as he continued serving the waiting men. His hand shook as Friedrich Schwarz moved down the queue. Would he recognize him? As quickly as that thought crossed his mind, he dismissed it. He didn't look a bit like the fifteen-year-old scared Jewish kid at the mercy of Schwarz and his SS buddies. He doubted the man would have recognized him even if Harry pointed out the fact they'd met before.

As far as Schwarz was concerned, Harry and the other canteen workers were invisible. It was an unwritten rule that the party members got the best jobs. Schwarz probably assumed Kruger and Harry were loyal SS followers.

Out of the corner of his eye, Harry glanced at the man moving closer as the queue progressed, the man he had hated for the last seven years. In his nightmares, 'Scarface' had been taller, stronger, more menacing. This man's small frame contrasted with some of his comrades. His hair was balding, his features more angular. But for the scar marking his hideous face, Harry would have questioned his recognition of that voice.

Harry didn't flinch when Schwarz touched his fingers when taking his plate. He kept his eyes down, not wanting his prey to see his hatred. After nights of dreaming of this moment, of what he would do when he laid eyes on this murdering scoundrel, he was fixed to the spot. He couldn't have moved even if someone pulled a gun on him.

'Keep working, act normal or you're going to look suspicious. You know how paranoid those lot are. Why don't you go back to the kitchen and grab the refills and I'll take over the service?' Kruger clasped Harry's arm, his giant muscled arm guiding him in the direction of the kitchen.

With a push in his back, Harry remembered how to move.

He got to the kitchen, breathing hard, trying to stop his heart from beating so rapidly. He fingered a kitchen knife, tempted to secure it in his uniform. He'd pick his moment and when Schwarz least expected it, he'd attack. He dismissed that idea as soon as it came to him. Schwarz wouldn't allow himself to be alone, the SS tended to move in packs. Safety in numbers and all that.

He spat on the ground, the thoughts of all he had said and done over the last months giving him a bad taste in his mouth. He'd waited so long for this moment and now it was here, he'd froze. He'd volunteered to be imprisoned in this camp for the SS elite and their supporters, surrounding himself with the worst of the dregs of humanity. The Allies had let the forced conscripts go first, those who were barely old enough to vote, then those who had fought for Germany but didn't share the Nazi ideals. Each day, men were pulled from the ranks for so called de-Nazification, with only the worst offenders thrown back into the swill pen he called home.

As the weeks turned into months, he'd had days when he wondered if it had all been worth it. Shouldn't he have taken his discharge papers and run back to England, into Rachel's waiting arms? He'd persuaded himself it was worth it. To take the chance, to find his father's murderer.

Nothing had prepared him for how this moment would feel. It had seemed so simple. Find Schwarz, kill him.

'Need food out here. Starving men to feed.'

Neuman joined them as they were clearing down the tables. 'You get all the cushy jobs. I swear if I have to clean another... what's up with you?' Neuman glanced at Harry before turning to Kruger. 'Trouble from Udet's buddies?'

Kruger shook his head. 'That lowlife scum didn't have any friends. Nobody's been to his grave since he landed in it. Alive.'

Neuman swallowed. He had hated Udet as much as the rest of them had, but when Harry tipped off a *Scharführer* that Udet had taken money from Allied personnel in return for ratting out SS men, the staff sergeant had signed his death warrant. Harry had proof of his accusations—he turned over a significant sum of money he claimed to belong to Udet. The SS had descended like a pack of rabid dogs, eager to dish out some revenge for their humiliating defeat at the hands of the Allies. Udet had been beaten almost, but not quite, to death. Then they unceremoniously buried him alive, without feeling an ounce of regret or remorse. Although Neuman's wife had been brutally murdered and Kruger's punishment squad experience still haunted him, both had a hard time reconciling their part in the events. Harry had seemed to take it in his stride.

Harry glanced up. 'Our target has landed.'

'The man who murdered your father?' Neuman clarified.

Harry glanced around, making sure nobody was listening. He nodded.

'You going to kill him? How?' Neuman paled. Harry watched the sweat bead on the man's lip. His friend was no coward, having hidden his wife for years from the regime, and refusing to divorce her. Why was he upset?

'I stayed in Germany to exact revenge. I have to kill him. What else is there?'

Kruger wiped his hands in a dish cloth. 'You could denounce him to the authorities. Have him tried as a war criminal. It's what the Allies did in Nuremberg. Now that trial is over, the next trials will move faster. They've proved the legal concept.'

Harry paced back and forth, a couple of steps in each direction. 'I can't just sit back. I'm a commando. This is what I trained for.'

'Murder?' Neuman focused on a spot on a table.

'What? You know what those animals did to your wife! To my extended family! To millions of innocents—and you care what happens to Schwarz? He murdered my father with his bare hands.'

Neuman fell silent but Kruger spoke up, his voice strong and steady. 'I don't care about Schwarz or any of the rest of them.'

'What then?'

Kruger caught Harry's gaze. 'I care about you. The world thinks all of us Germans are murdering animals. That we are all Nazis. We need to prove them wrong. We have to show some of us remembered our values, the right to life, the right to love, the right to... be a human being.' Kruger grabbed Harry by the shoulder. He was so surprised he didn't fight him off. 'Do what you want. You always do. But, remember, if you kill him, you aren't any better than he is.' With that, Kruger marched off, hastily wiping the tears from his face.

Stunned, Harry stared after his friend. Feeling Neuman's stare, he glanced at him. 'I guess you feel the same?'

'I'm torn. If he was the man who ripped my beautiful Anna from our home and sent her to the hell at Auschwitz, I'd want to squeeze his dying breath with my bare hands. At least in my dreams I do. But if I cross that line, Harry, what makes me different to men like Schwarz?'

'You killed in the war. For Germany!' Harry spat back. He regretted it immediately at the look on Neuman's face.

'Yes, I did, and I will always regret it. At least if I had been on the other side, I would have been fighting for freedom. I killed people for a regime I despised. Guess that's why I'm in here.'

Neuman's shoulders slumped as he turned to leave.

'Neuman... Klaus! Wait! I'm sorry. You're different. We both are.'

'Are we? You do this and you will be the same as they are. A murderer.'

FORTY-TWO

Harry stood in front of the major, waiting for him to read his report. Relieved to be back in the British offices, away from the SS, he knew it would take time to recover after almost a year undercover as a SS supporter. Had it been worth it? Only time would tell. He'd told Rachel he'd had to stay in Germany to avenge his father, would she think him a coward?

The major looked up a few times but Harry refused to show any emotion, steeling his face into a blank expression. He still wasn't sure he'd done the right thing by not killing Schwarz, or Scarface—as he continued to call the man in his mind.

'This is excellent work, Beck.' The major leaned back in his chair. 'I have to admit this isn't the outcome I expected.'

'Sir?'

'You didn't think I believed you were going into that camp just for our benefit. I sensed this was personal but hoped you would act in accordance with your military training, rather than commit murder.'

Harry didn't blink. He didn't want to admit to anyone just how difficult it had been not to kill Schwarz with his bare hands.

The major looked back to the papers in his hands. 'Ari Beck. He was your brother?'

'Father, sir.'

'You witnessed his murder and are prepared to testify to the same in court?'

It was all in his report. That, and the fact Schwarz had been promoted repeatedly, his cruelty toward prisoners making him a legend with his own men. 'Yes, sir.'

'You know the prosecution will dismiss your claims on several grounds.'

'Sir?'

The major ignored his interruption. 'One, how can you prove you were even in Dachau, let alone escaped. Then there is the matter of it being seven years since you saw Schwarz. And...'

'And?' The pulse at the side of Harry's neck throbbed as he struggled to keep his tone neutral.

'You're Jewish, Beck. You may be acting out of revenge.'

Harry stepped up to the desk and, gripping the wooden edge, leaned across. 'If it was revenge I wanted, I'd have killed that snake myself. Slowly. By the slowest, most painful means possible. Instead, I passed him over to you to allow justice to take place. Are you telling me I made a mistake?'

'At ease, soldier. I'm not the enemy here.'

Captain Murphy moved to put his hand on Harry's shoulder. Harry flinched, causing Murphy's hand to fall by his side. 'Sit down, Lieutenant. You've been under immense stress over the last few months. I can't claim to feel what you are feeling but I want to kick the living daylights out of this bloke and all the others like him. I'm not Jewish, but that doesn't mean I can't be appalled by what the Nazis did. I admire your restraint. I'm not sure I would have shown the same if it were my father.'

'Thank you, sir.'

'You will be called as a witness for the prosecution. Given

the long list of alleged crimes and your fantastic work at finding witnesses, my guess is he will face the death penalty.'

Harry nodded, not trusting himself to speak. He was close to breaking down and desperate to get out of the office and find some space to be alone.

'Take some time, Beck. Get some sleep and decent food. I've arranged for the men that worked with you to be released. They will be offered positions in British Berlin.'

'Thank you, sir.' This was more than he'd expected True, Neuman and Kruger had put their lives on the line, but still. The Allies weren't known for being generous to Germans.

FORTY-THREE

AUGUST 1947

It took six months for Friedrich Schwarz to come to trial, and when he did, Harry secured one of the best seats in the courtroom. He wanted Schwarz to see him, to realize he was the reason he was being held accountable for his crimes.

He glanced repeatedly at the clock, his foot tapping on the floor until the defendant was escorted into the dock. Harry leaned forward in his seat, his eyes not leaving Schwarz's face. He willed the man to look into the room, to see him. He waited as Schwarz, his features a mask of disdain, swore his oath.

The man took his seat and spent a few seconds adjusting his bulky frame, presumably to find a comfortable position. He threw a malevolent glance at the judge, making his feelings for the legality of the court clear. Then with a gloating expression, he sat back in his chair, almost as if he was sitting in his own home and not fighting for his life.

Schwarz stared at his nails as the charges were read out. His face showed no sign of emotion, not when he was accused of killing men with his bare hands, sending women and children to the gas chambers, and other crimes. Not even at the accusation he had shot children in the back—and the resulting gasp of horror in the court—did his facial expression change.

Harry glared at the man, willing him to look up and meet his gaze. He leaned so far forward, he was almost sitting on the man in front of him. Eventually, his perseverance paid off as Schwarz raised his head and looked around the court.

His controlled expression caved as soon as his eyes met Harry's. Harry saw the flash of recognition, followed just as quickly by confusion and fear. He could almost read Schwarz's mind. What was a fellow SS officer doing sitting in the viewing gallery of the court?

Harry allowed himself to smile, the resulting pallor in his adversary's gaze telling him the penny had dropped. Schwarz, seeing Harry wearing the uniform of a British soldier, slumped back in his seat. All signs of defiance disappeared. Now he resembled his real self: a bully who'd used his position of power to cruelly torture and destroy people for no reason other than their race. Beads of sweat broke out on his face, his hanky not efficient enough to remove them completely.

Harry listened to the charges with one ear but he knew them off by heart, having worked closely with the prosecution team. He wasn't called as a witness, the prosecution choosing some more credible witnesses. Men and women who looked like walking skeletons, not a healthy-looking British soldier who may have an axe to grind. Initially resentful, Harry had understood the wisdom of their choice after listening to the grilling the poor witnesses endured by the defence lawyer. Harry tried to believe the man was only doing his job; after all, entitlement to a fair trial was the very corner stone of a democracy, but he had to try hard.

He exchanged a glance with Murphy, who took out a pen and wrote the lawyer's name in his black book. Murphy would see the man was investigated over his behaviour during the war and, if their suspicions proved correct, he might go on to need a lawyer himself.

Each witness gave a compelling account of the trauma they'd experienced. Harry couldn't stop thinking about Trudi and the other members of her network. Had they been subjected to the same, or had they mercifully been shot quickly?

He'd heard of the specific tortures reserved for those who resisted Hitler and his cronies.

The hours passed, then the days. He took the same chair every day. Schwarz refused to look in his direction but Harry didn't care. The legal arguments droned on. Schwarz 's attorney was trying to argue he had only followed orders and therefore wasn't guilty. When that didn't work, the solicitor tried other, equally abhorrent defences.

Growing bored with the legal dramatics, Harry took out Rachel's letters. They'd been waiting for him when he got out of the camp, and he could almost recite them by heart.

A paragraph caught his attention.

Harry, the men who killed my father, your father and all the other members of our families will win if you allow this bitterness in your soul to dictate the rest of your life. By taking a man's life, outside of the battlefield or the legal process, you become the same as the worst of the Nazis. A murderer is a murderer regardless of the number of people he kills. Walk away, Harry, before the evil penetrates your soul and destroys the life you have left to live. If you can't do this for yourself, or for us, do it for your father. Ari Beck was a wonderful, honourable man who went out of his way to help his fellow man regardless of their religion or race. Let that be how he is remembered. Don't let his legacy be that of a murderer's father.

Harry closed his eyes, Rachel's voice echoing in his thoughts as the words swirled around his head. He could see his father as he had been, that last night of freedom. While others had cowered in fear or engaged in orgies of violence, his father and others like him had stood up to be counted. He could see his dad put his hat on his salt and pepper hair, could see the fear and determination fighting in his eyes. His father had walked out that door, no doubt knowing at some level the danger he was walking towards. Yet he hadn't hesitated.

Overcome by a wave of nausea, Harry pushed himself to his feet. Mumbling excuses to those around him, he shouldered his way out of the crowded courtroom, out of the building and into the fresh air of Berlin.

'Beck? Harry? Breathe, that's it. In and out. Slowly. Sit down before you fall down.' Harry felt himself pushed to the steps of the courthouse.

He couldn't think, the voices in his head were all mingling, the faces of those he'd lost, and those he'd lose if he didn't get back to Britain fast. Not just Rachel, but Tom and Liesel. He felt a longing to see his siblings stronger than he could remember.

'Do you need a doctor? Or a decent drink?' Murphy's words finally registered.

Harry glanced up into the concerned face of the man who'd become a friend.

'I'm fine. I just... I think it all came back so fast. Too many memories.'

Murphy scooted down to sit beside him. 'Can't say I blame you. I've seen some stuff in my army career but what those men and women were saying... it beggars belief.' Captain Murphy exhaled sharply. 'Not that I don't believe them, I do, every word. I just look around me at those civilians over there. How could they have allowed this to happen? Harry, when did a whole nation lose its decency, its morality? How can they come back from this?'

Harry glanced at the men and women Murphy had pointed to. They didn't look like a conquering Aryan race, but a bunch of victims of a war brought about by a madman. Who knew what their crimes were? Maybe among the ragged, emancipated bodies were true heroes. Those who hid the Jews and other victims of the Nazis. Offered food, support, papers, turned a blind eye. Who knew by looking at someone what their war had been like?

Harry briefly bowed his head, letting out a deep breath, allowing the clarity he was experiencing for the first time in years to wash over him. Rachel was right. Vigilante justice wasn't the answer. The courts could deal with the monsters who perpetuated the violence. He'd survived. He'd won. The Nazis hadn't destroyed him, although it'd been a close call.

He stood up and, holding out his hand to Murphy, pulled him to his feet. 'You ever have a proper Jewish meal?'

Murphy shook his head.

'Come with me. My aunt and her friends make the best in Berlin.'

'Aren't you going back in to hear the verdict?'

Harry glanced at the courthouse before shaking his head. 'My war's over. Now, are you coming or not?'

Murphy grinned before slapping him on the back and enveloping him in a bear hug. 'Does this mean I get to be best man at the wedding?'

'What wedding?' Harry protested.

'I've seen the goofy look you get when you read those letters from home. You've been well and truly caught, lad Your future has been decided.'

Harry started to protest but stopped and grinned. It had been, and he had no problem with that.

EPILOGUE

SEPTEMBER 1947

Harry got off the train at Chertsey station, walking to the exit to catch the bus to Abbeydale. He hadn't told anyone he was coming home. He wanted to surprise them. He held his hand out to the woman by his side, putting his arm around her skeletal frame, protecting her from a push or shove from a fellow traveller.

'Are you sure you want to do this? You should wait here and I can call a taxi.'

'Stop fussing over me, Heinz. I won't break. This looks like a very pretty place. Does Lie—the children live far from here?'

'The next village. We will need a taxi or the bus, whichever comes first.' He didn't want her to walk too far. He glanced at her. She looked dreadful, so thin, and that racking cough seemed to be worse than it had been when he'd first found her. He wanted to force her to rest, but that wasn't his decision. 'Do you want to freshen up before we go to Sally's house?'

'No. It's been too long already. You remember your promise?'

Harry stared at her, knowing he was being unfair. He wanted her to change her mind. She held his gaze and he was the first to look away. 'Yes, but I still don't agree. She is your daughter, Trudi. After everything you've been through, you deserve to see her grow up.'

She touched his arm. 'We both know that will not happen, whether I stay here or not.'

'But...'

'Enough, Heinz. I want to preserve my energy.'

He bowed to her softly spoken request. A taxi pulled up outside, allowing them to travel in comfort. He saw the look the driver gave Trudi, but thankfully the man didn't ask any questions.

They drove along in silence, Trudi leaning back with her eyes closed. The trip had sapped her strength despite her protestations she was fine. He should have persuaded her to stay longer in the hospital in Berlin, at least until she was stronger. But the clock was ticking.

It had seemed kinder not to tell Sally of their arrival, but now they were closer to the house, he wondered if that had been the right decision. He was about to upset the whole household—especially Liesel and Tomas. How would they react to Trudi, coming back from the dead?

'The cottage up on your left, driver, please.'

The taxi pulled to a stop, and Heinz paid the fare, adding a tip as the driver had jumped out to help Trudi from the car, his face a mask of concern.

Harry looked at the house. It was covered in roses and looking every bit like a country cottage on a postcard. For a couple of seconds, it was almost like he had never left—the horrific things he had seen and done over the last few years, the friends he had seen mown down, the bodies, the devastation of bombed-out cities—all seemed like a bad dream. This house, this village looked untouched. What about those who lived inside?

'Heinz, it is so pretty here. Look at those apple trees! And the size of the garden. How lucky the children are to grow up here.'

Loud voices announced the arrival of the children as Tom and Lisa came tearing down the street.

Tom recognized him first. 'Harry! You're home! Why didn't Mum tell us?' Tom skidded to a halt just short of bowling them over, Harry instinctively putting his hand out to protect Trudi. He felt her shudder, heard the small moan that escaped before she clapped her hand over her mouth. Her eyes, shimmering with unshed tears, were focused on her daughter, who in turn was looking back at them curiously.

Trudi took a step forward just as Lisa turned and ran in at the gate, screaming: 'Mum! Harry's home! Come quick. He's got a lady with him.'

Sally came running, a baby in her arms, followed by a man Harry recognized from Sally's wedding pictures, although Derek looked different now. Time as a prisoner of war would do that.

Sally was beaming, tears in her eyes as she hugged him, the baby between them. 'Harry, how wonderful. You should have told us you were coming. You look fantastic.'

Sally stepped back and her smiling expression fell as her eyes settled on Trudi. She glanced at Harry with a questioning look on her face.

Harry said gently, 'Sally, this is Trudi.'

Sally wasn't fast enough to cover the look of terror that flashed over her face, quickly followed by a glance in Lisa's direction. For her part, Lisa moved to hold Sally's arm.

'This is my mother. Not you,' Lisa said, her tone challenging.

Harry winced and glanced at Trudi. Her face didn't show a visible reaction, but Harry saw her fingers were clenched, showing her white knuckles.

'Liesel, don't be rude,' he said. 'Sally, could we go inside? Trudi has been ill and can't stand for long.'

'Of course, forgive me. My manners are lacking. Lisa, take your sister and put her down for a nap, please. Tom, go and find Maggie and the girls. Derek, could you take Mrs Beck inside, and their bags? We can make the introductions inside. I'll put on a pot of tea or coffee. Why don't I just do both?' Harry knew that Sally's incessant chatter was an attempt to hide her shock. He felt crestfallen. He'd been wrong: he should have written, prepared them in advance.

He gave Trudi his arm, patting her hand in a gesture of comfort before they walked into the house. Trudi's step faltered and, afraid she would fall, he picked her up and carried her over the front step. How light she was.

He pushed open the door to the back room, knowing Trudi would feel more comfortable in a homely environment rather than the formal front room. He wondered how she was feeling, seeing Liesel after so long. She must have dreamed of a different welcome, but they had talked about it, and he knew she was prepared for this too.

Once he settled Trudi on the couch, Sally offered him a blanket to tuck around her legs.

'It's still a bit chilly. Let me go put on the kettle.'

Sally bustled out to the kitchen, leaving Harry and Derek standing, both looking at Trudi, who rested her head back on the couch, eyes closed.

Derek turned to Harry and said, 'Harry, I've heard a lot about you. Thank you for looking after my wife when you lived here.'

'I think it was the other way around, Mr Fletcher. I'm glad you got back. Congratulations on your daughter.'

'Derek, please. I was lucky Sally took me in. My return wasn't my finest moment, as no doubt Tom will have told you.'

Harry didn't know what Derek was talking about but said

nothing. It didn't really matter, given the current situation. He saw the curiosity in Derek's eyes but he couldn't explain until Sally came in and sat down.

'Your friend looks like she spent some time in the same camps I did.'

Trudi's eyelids fluttered open. 'You were a prisoner of war, Mr Fletcher?'

'Derek. Yes, from 1940 until '45. I was lucky. We had a wonderful time compared to other prisoners.'

At the acknowledgement of the suffering of the Jews and other subjects of Nazi hatred, Trudi nodded slightly. 'Being a prisoner is always horrible but you are kind to say so. Thank you for all you have done for me and my—I mean your—family.'

The tray in Sally's hand crashed onto the table, the jolt making the dishes jump and clatter. Just then Maggie came in, huffing and puffing, closely followed by Ruth. There was no sign of Rachel, causing a wave of disappointment in Harry.

'It's true, you're back!' said Maggie. 'Oh, am I glad to see you, although I could also box your ears for you. Why did you stay away so long, you young pup? You had our hearts broken and our hair turned grey.'

'Glad to see you missed me, Maggie.' He picked up the older woman and swung her around, causing her to laugh and protest to be put back down on the ground. He did the same to Ruth but when he reached out for Lisa, she moved to Sally's side, but not before giving him a look of hatred.

Taken aback, he wanted to call her out but Trudi spoke first.

'Mrs Fletcher—Sally, if you allow me... I wish to thank you for what you did for my... the children. They've obviously been well cared for. Tom, do you remember me? You've grown into a fine man. Your father would be very proud.' Trudi's eyes moved on from the blushing Tom to her daughter. 'Liesel...'

'My name is Lisa and this is my mum. You shouldn't be here. Go back to Germany. We don't want you here.'

Before anyone could react, Lisa ran out the back door. Derek moved first but Tom stopped him. 'I'll go. Come on, Ruth. They got adult stuff to sort out.'

Ruth didn't need to be asked twice. Maggie took charge, pushing Sally into a seat and pouring tea for everyone whether they wanted it or not. She added sugar before handing the cup to Trudi. 'There you go, love. That will warm your bones and the sugar will help with the shock. Don't mind the child, she doesn't know what she's saying.'

'You are the kind heart Heinz told me about, Maggie. Forgive me but I can't remember your surname.'

'Maggie is perfect, love. Lisa is a kind-hearted girl but I guess it is a shock.' Maggie hesitated. 'Harry wrote to say you were dead. The letter only came a couple of weeks back.'

Harry glanced at Trudi and saw she was fading fast. He stepped forward, putting his hand on her shoulder as a gesture of support. 'We all believed she was dead. Aunt Chana, Isla and me. Isla couldn't believe her eyes when she was assigned to nurse a patient who'd been in an asylum since the end of the war. The nurses thought Trudi was lying about her being Jewish and having survived months of torture.'

'Seeing my baby'—Trudi glanced at Harry—'and my boys again was what kept me going. In the end my jailor felt sorry for me and entered a false record. The Russians were coming, it was chaotic in the prison. He'd have set me free if I could walk. Instead, he switched me to a different cell. Then the Russians arrived.'

'Lisa, I mean, Liesel, kept you alive.' Sally's voice trembled.

Trudi nodded, putting the cup untouched on the table beside her. She leaned forward. 'I want you to know I haven't come here to claim my daughter... my children. I just wanted to see her and Tom once more. I will leave now. We should have written to you first. Heinz, perhaps you can call a taxi.'

Sally stood, upset. 'No, don't leave. Not yet. You are Lisa's mother, you always have been. I just... I mean, we were...' Sally couldn't continue.

Derek moved to his wife's side, putting his arm around her. 'What my wife is trying to say is that while we love the children, we always knew this was a temporary arrangement. Some day you would return and take them home.'

Trudi lapsed into a coughing fit, and Harry ran for a glass of water, Maggie taking a seat by Trudi's side and rubbing her back.

Harry handed her the drink. It took a few minutes before Trudi could speak.

'I don't have a home. That was lost long ago. I have nowhere to take the children and, even if I did, that is not why I have come. I would like to ask you something. It is a big ask but I hope you will agree.'

Sally and Derek exchanged a look, and Harry saw Sally's knuckles whiten as her grip on her husband tightened.

'I am sick.' Trudi tried to laugh but it triggered another fit of coughing.

'You must rest.'

'No, Maggie, I don't have time to rest. But thank you. I needed to be sure. Heinz told me you were lovely people but I... I had to see for myself. He was correct. You are everything I hoped for, and more. I want you to keep the children. To bring them up as your own. Perhaps when they are older, you could explain to Liesel how she came to live here. With her parents.' Trudi's voice broke. Tears glistened in her eyes as she clasped her hands in her lap.

'But you came back. You must want your child.' Sally broke the silence.

Trudi closed her eyes, one tear escaping to run down her cheek. Sally moved slowly to kneel on the floor by Trudi's legs. 'Please don't cry. We don't want to take your baby.'

'Not take. I give. With my heart. I can die happy.'

Sally gasped and glanced at Harry. He couldn't deny or confirm, barely able to see though his own tears. Sally looked back at Trudi.

'I don't have long left. If I listened to the doctors, I would be dead already. They didn't reckon on my stubbornness. I had to see where my children had gone. I promised myself. It was their image that kept me alive through... everything. Please say you will keep my children. Liesel, my daughter, but also my son, Tom. Despite what he and Heinz feel, I love them as my children too.'

Tears were running down everyone's cheeks at this point. Heinz glanced at Derek who, after wiping his eyes with a large hanky, indicated they take a walk.

Leaving the women behind, Derek led the way out to the back garden. He lit up a cigarette, offering the pack to Harry.

'I'm sorry. I should have written or sent a telegram. But we weren't sure Trudi would survive the trip. She was told not to leave the hospital. When they heard she intended to come here, the doctors were incandescent.'

Derek put his hand on Harry's shoulder. 'Her stubbornness probably kept her alive. It is a shock, but it is right that you came. You did the right thing.' He paused. 'Did you visit the camps?'

Harry shook his head. 'No, I spoke to a lot of survivors but never made that trip. I was in Dachau. That was enough. Trudi was arrested by the Gestapo and tortured for her part in the resistance. She helped save the lives of many Jews. I totally underestimated my stepmother. She is an amazing woman.'

'You aren't too bad yourself from what I've heard. You found the man who murdered your father...'

Harry took a drag on the cigarette, trying to keep his hands from shaking.

'He was condemned to death?'

'Yes. He was hanged last month.' Harry swallowed, before crushing the cigarette butt under his foot.

'Let's get back to the women.' Derek gave him a slap on the back as he winked. 'I know a certain young lady who is dying to see you.'

Harry couldn't wait to see Rachel either, but was Derek right? Did she really want to see him?

Trudi awoke disoriented, her throat dry. She could barely remember Heinz—no, Harry!—carrying her to the bed. As her eyes adjusted to the darkness, she noticed Liesel's shadowy figure perched in the corner of the room.

Trudi grappled with her English. She had to find the right words to use. To convince her child she loved her.

'Please... could I have some water?'

The child slowly lifted a glass toward Trudi, but her hand shook so vigorously that she couldn't take it from her. The water spilled onto the floor.

'Let me.' The child held the glass to her lips.

'Please.' With every fibre of her being, Trudi wanted to grab her daughter and never let go, but she held back, sensing that it was too soon. She heard the clink of the glass on the bedside table.

'Would you like the lamp lit?' Liesel whispered.

'Yes,' Trudi whispered, watching as a warm light filled the room, trying in vain to calm her racing heart.

Liesel's little face was contorted in pain and rage. 'How could you do this? How could you give me away... and, now I'm happy, you come back?'

Trudi's heart beat faster. How much did the child know of what had happened in Europe? How could you tell someone so young of the horrors in the camps? Of the numbers killed?

Over one and half million children. All dead.

'I wanted you to be safe. To live.'

'But why didn't you come with me?' Liesel folded her arms across her chest, her jaw clenched as she almost spat out the words. 'You sent me away. Sally would never leave me. She's a real mother.'

Trudi ignored the darts of pain her child's words inflicted.

'Liesel...' Liesel's eyes burned with anger as Trudi spoke, and she quickly rectified her mistake. 'Lisa, I'm so sorry. I tried my best to escape before the war started. I did everything to stay alive and find you—I love you.'

'But now you're going to leave me again,' Liesel retorted.

Trudi wept as she admitted the truth, 'Yes, I am. But this time is different. I...' How could she tell a child she didn't want to die? Trudi took a deep breath. 'Sally will be your mother, a woman who loves you just as much as I do. She will never abandon you, my sweet girl.'

'But why do you have to die?' Her daughter's lip trembled as she swatted the tears from her eyes.

Trudi's chest seized with a racking cough that refused to relent. Lisa's cry pierced the air as she ran desperately for Sally to help. Trudi pushed the covers back to get out of bed, trying to grab her daughter in an attempt to soothe her fear, but the pain was too much and she crumpled to the floor.

Sally came running into the room. 'Trudi! Harry, hurry!' she shouted frantically as Trudi fought against the over-whelming darkness engulfing her.

Trudi awoke suddenly, a chill running down her spine. She'd dreamt she was back in the asylum in Germany, nobody believing her story. Her forehead was damp with sweat, someone was gently rubbing a cool cloth across her brow. Liesel. Trudi's heart soared.

Her baby was humming a familiar tune. Trudi slowly began

to join the words of the song that brought back such tender memories.

'Tomas used to sing this to me when I was scared or alone. He said you used to comfort me with these same words when I was a baby. He told me what you looked like. But no matter how hard I've tried, I can never get a picture of your face.' Liesel stared into her eyes—and there was a distant spark of recognition that only they could share in that moment.

'Mummy, I mean Sally, told me about how difficult it was for you to make this journey. How heroic and courageous you were and how those cruel men threw you in jail. They didn't even give you a doctor and that's why you're so sick right now.' Liesel stretched out her hand to brush away the hair from Trudi's face. 'You must really love me, don't you?'

'I love you with every ounce of my being. You are my precious child, Lisa.'

Lisa climbed up on the bed, causing a jolt of agony but Trudi didn't care. She held out her arms to hold her child.

Lisa snuggled in close. 'You can call me Liesel and I'll call you Mummy Trudi. When you are a bit better, I will show you your tree. We planted it in the garden. Tom said he was lucky to have three mothers. The one who gave birth to him, you and Sally. I think he was right.'

Trudi blinked back her tears. Liesel leaned in and wiped them away before kissing her on her cheek. 'I love you, Mutti.'

That evening, with Maggie's blessing, Harry headed to the bus stop, patting his pocket to check on the ring he'd brought back from Germany.

The evening sun hung low, casting a warm glow across Abbeydale. He walked down the street, smiling at a few people out and about. They returned his smiles. It appeared Maggie had already told the villagers about the part he played in winning the war.

As he approached the bus stop, his heart raced with anticipation and nerves. Would she forgive him for being away for so long? Did she still love him? What if...?

He stopped in his tracks, his breath catching in his throat as he spotted her. His gaze devoured every inch of her pretty face. She'd cut her long brown hair and it now framed her face, setting off her delicate features. He liked it, especially how the curls seemed to point to her beautiful eyes.

Rachel saw him then and a warm smile lit up her face as she ran toward him.

He swept her off her feet into a deep kiss.

Pulling back, she hit him on the chest, but not hard enough to hurt. 'You should have come home. How long did you intend to keep me waiting?'

'I'm sorry but I'm here now and I won't leave your side again. Not if you don't want me to.' Her eyes widened as he bent down on one knee in the middle of the road. 'Rachel Bernstein, will you marry me?' He held out the ring in his hand.

She squealed, her hands going to her face to rub away the tears. 'Yes, yes! Get up off the road before a car hits you.'

He held her tight, whispering into her ear: 'Rachel, I love you. I've loved you since that first time we met back in school. All these years, there hasn't been anyone else but you.'

She kissed him but he pushed her back gently, cradling her face in his hands, looking deep into her eyes. 'I know I hurt you and I'm truly sorry. I had to see Schwarz punished. I made a promise to Papa and I had to see it through.'

'I know...'

He stopped her with a small kiss. 'Rachel, you saved me. But for you, I think I would have killed Scarface as soon as I met him in that camp. I'll tell you the whole story one day. When I heard his voice, my blood boiled and everything went red. I could have killed him. But I heard your voice in my head. I knew it was wrong and that justice could be served another way. You did that for me.'

He laid his forehead against hers. 'Thank you.'

She reached up and drew him down into a kiss. 'You're home now.'

A LETTER FROM THE AUTHOR

Dear reader, thank you for reading *A Mother's Promise*. I hope you enjoyed finding out what happened to Trudi after sending her children to safety on the *Kindertransport*. Harry's quest for revenge played out slightly differently from what I initially had in mind but, like most of my characters, he had his own ideas of how he wanted his story to unfold.

If you'd like to be one of the first to find out about new releases, please sign to my newsletter!

www.stormpublishing.co/rachel-wesson

If you enjoyed this book and could spare a few moments to leave a review, that would be hugely appreciated. Even a short review can make all the difference in encouraging a reader to discover my book[/s] for the first time. Thank you so much!

This book involved a lot of research into not only what happened to those persecuted by the Nazi regime but also what became of them after the war had ended. It's difficult to imagine now, with the internet and all the social media sites, how challenging it was back then to reunite families. Some people disappeared forever, believed dead when they had in fact survived. During my research, I read time and time again of family members who survived the concentration camps only to live out the rest of their lives believing all their family had perished. Mothers cried for children who were not only living but trying desperately to find them. Can you imagine surviving such horror and then not being able to gather your living relatives together? The infrastructure in Europe was destroyed, and the camps homing the displaced were overwhelmed with survivors left homeless, penniless, and suffering physical and mental trauma. Some were kept apart by the changing international boundaries—after the war, countries were once more divided, and borders set up, preventing the emigration of people, and thus families remained scattered to the wind.

The devastation caused by this murderous regime extended beyond the lives taken, as the Nazis deliberately sought to obliterate entire cultures. Synagogues were razed to the ground, as were Jewish offices, hospitals, homes, etc. Special attention was given to eradicating vital family records: Jewish Bibles were burned, and birth, marriage and death registration records destroyed. Jewish gravestones were repurposed as paving slabs for new roads, obliterating not only the existence of recently deceased individuals who died before the 1930s and 1940s but also erasing the memory of their ancestors.

The Nazis and their disgusting beliefs are, hopefully, a thing of the past. But the destructive waves of their hate are still being felt generations later. At a time when most of the people who lived through WW2 are either of advanced years or dead, those trying to find family members are up against a ticking clock. We are all aware of the advances in genetic science and how much easier it has become to trace your family, going back centuries in some cases. Recently, I watched an episode of a television programme focused on researching lost families. A genealogist explained how, for some families, knowing their DNA doesn't help. No matter how advanced the science becomes, how qualified she and her colleagues are, nothing can fill what she referred to as the 'black hole' caused by the Nazis' destruction. It is, she said, quite impossible for some to trace their Jewish ancestors in Europe, as the necessary records simply do not exist. She said 'her stomach sinks' when she is contacted by someone searching for their family, who were potentially victims of the Nazis, as she knows she may cause the individual more pain. Entire family lineages had been wiped from collective memory. So even from beyond their graves, these evil men and women are still inflicting pain and suffering on their victims and their families.

My research often uncovers incredibly brave, so-called ordinary men and women who didn't turn a blind eye to what the Nazis were doing. These people, in many cases, their names lost to history forever, helped save their neighbours. Some simply turned a blind eye and didn't report those they suspected were Jewish using false papers, or those they suspected were hiding Jewish people. Some hid one person, others hid entire families. Some gave up their rations and their money to help those in hiding. Others placed their identity cards in the church collection box, knowing their papers may help a potential victim escape.

Some people took a more active role. Some fought from the start; others were initial supporters of Hitler's regime but saw the light and rediscovered their humanity. People like Frau Meier, whose two sons died at the Eastern Front. Did they tell their mother of the atrocities committed? I guess nobody will ever know what led her to help save the lives of Jewish people by leading or organizing groups of escapees to Switzerland.

We hear about the heroes who saved thousands of lives like Frank Foley—a British Embassy employee in Berlin who will feature in my next book. He is credited with saving the lives of over 10,000 Jews. Robert Smallbones, another embassy employee based in Frankfurt, may have been responsible for saving around 48,000 lives. I love reading about these amazing men and women who decided to do something when others thought nothing could be done. Some will say, in the case of Smallbones and Foley, it was easier for them to do something given where they worked. But what of Ida and Louise Cook, two ordinary British sisters who directly saved twenty-nine lives and indirectly countless others by their heroic actions? They could have chosen to do nothing. After all, they didn't know the German and Austrian people they saved; they were from another country, another culture, another race and religion. They didn't even speak the same language. You can find out more about these incredible sisters and their friends in my next book, *Sisters in the Shadows*.

Once again, thank you for your interest in my work. I appreciate your support in helping me share these important stories with the world. If you have any questions or comments, please feel free to reach out to me.

Rachel x

www.rachelwesson.com

 twitter.com/wessonwrites

AUTHOR'S NOTE

The story of the German Jewish boys dying when a bomb hit their bus really happened and the victims are buried in East Ham Cemetery.

In the Second World War, all so-called enemy aliens—be they German Jewish refugees or those who had moved here after the First War—were classified according to the 'risk' they posed to Britain's security.

Those who wished to fight the Nazis were at first only allowed to join the Pioneer Corps. They didn't have weapons and were assigned to units doing menial but necessary tasks. The story with Harry and his friends clearing the rubble during the Blitz is based on the true story of four of these young men, although I changed the exact details in the story. They were killed on 29 December 1941 and are buried in the East Ham Jewish Cemetery.

The woman and her children who died in the direct hit is fiction, and there is no record, at least none I'm aware of, of anyone assaulting them like the old woman did—until she realized who they were and what they were doing.

With the approval of Churchill, Three Troop of Ten Inter-allied (IA) Commando was organized by Lord Mountbatten, the Head of the British 'Combined Operations'. It was originally called X Troop but the name was dropped due to being seen as suspicious. George Lane, the son of a Christian father and Jewish mother, spoke Hungarian, German and French, and was the first member of Three Troop to be recruited. He'd initially been recruited by SOE but declined to take part in operations in Hungary due to his fear of the reprisals that would be incurred by Hungarian civilians. He was returned to the Pioneer Corps but used connections in the upper classes to secure a transfer to the commando troops under Lord Lovat. He volunteered to help Hilton-Jones recruit and train the men of Three Troop. Leading by example, he was independent and brave, and thrilled to be fighting as a commando. The stories of Three Troop are laid out in Leah Garret's book *X Troop the Secret Jewish Commandos*.

Mac—Tony McKenna—is very loosely based on the real-life commando Manfred Gans. His book, *Life Gave Me a Chance*, is well worth reading, especially the amazing story of how he borrowed a jeep and drove to Terezin to find his parents. They were alive, and lived out a long life in Palestine. Manfred Gans was promoted from Private to Lieutenant—a very rare battlefield commission. The story of Mac and Harry in the various scenes in this book are fiction.

Pastor Forell saved many lives before he was recalled to Sweden. Eric Perwe and his wife took over. Martha Perwe returned to Sweden with her children in 1943 and Pastor Eric flew out in 1944, but his plane crashed. It is assumed to be an accident not murder, as Chana claimed in the story.

While their scenes are fiction, Chief Mattick and Constable Hoffman were two real-life Berlin policemen who saved many people from the SS and Gestapo. Chief Mattick was killed in a bomb attack when a grenade hit him as he crossed the road.

Other books I relied on heavily are William Shirer's excellent series written after the war about living in Germany as a foreign correspondent. *Stella* by Peter Wyden outlines the life of the infamous Jewish Jew catcher, her reasons for helping the Gestapo, and her impact on the lives of those she knew. She didn't become a 'Jew catcher' until after August 1943, the previous times she revealed names was under torture, but for the sake of the story, I had to use artistic licence.

It is a myth that the Jews walked like lambs to the slaughter. Many fought back in the best ways they knew how: parents, by sending their children to safety, to strangers in a country few had visited; those who went underground in Berlin and other cities, others who lived as gentiles, always peering over their shoulder waiting for the day they were captured. Some fascinating books on this subject include *On the Run in Nazi Germany* by Bert Lewin, *The Last Jews in Berlin* by Leonard Gross and others too numerous to mention.

The story of Frau Luise Meir and the trip to Singen is also true. She did lose two sons at the Russian front and only then saw the light and fought back against the Nazis by saving numerous Jewish lives.

ACKNOWLEDGEMENTS

I struck gold the day I met Vicky Blunden, my extraordinary editor. Thank you for your patience and kindness. Through Vicky, I was introduced to the amazing team at Storm Publishing. Thank you so much for your editing and proofreading skills, the fantastic covers and marketing graphics and everything else that goes on behind the scenes.

As always, I'd like to acknowledge the support I receive from my readers. I'm so grateful for your positive comments on social media, emails and cards. Without you, I wouldn't be able to live my dream life, telling my stories to the world. Thank you.

I'd like to specifically thank three very special mothers: Meisje, whose insight into my characters and the journeys they should take, leaves me breathless; Sherry, your positivity, and light shines through every time we speak, you do a fabulous job with my readers group and I'm grateful for your help with story issues too; and Valerie, what can I say about an eighty-plus-year-old ballerina who inspires me every day? You are more youthful than most people half your age. Thank you.

Pat and Becky, nobody could ask for better friends. Although both of you now live in a different country, you are always right by my side when I need you. Thank you.

And last, but not least, my three incredible children. Adam, Nathan and Megan, you are my world. I love you, and you make me so proud to be your mother.

Printed in Great Britain
by Amazon